JOHN WHITE

QUEST for the KING

THE ARCHIVES OF ANTHROPOS

Cover illustration by
Vic Mitchell

Interior illustrations by
Jack Stockman

InterVarsity Press
Downers Grove, Illinois

InterVarsity Press® is the book-publishing division of InterVarsity Christian Fellowship®, a student movement active on campus at hundreds of universities, colleges and schools of nursing in the United States of America, and a member movement of the International Fellowship of Evangelical Students. For information about local and regional activities, write Public Relations Dept., InterVarsity Christian Fellowship, 6400 Schroeder Rd., P.O. Box 7895, Madison, WI 53707-7895.

Interior illustrations: © 1995 by Jack Stockman
Cover illustration: Vic Mitchell
ISBN 0-87784-592-1

Printed in the United States of America ∞

Library of Congress Cataloging-in-Publication Data

White, John, 1924 Mar. 5-
    Quest for the king/John White; cover illustration by Vic
Mitchell; interior illustrations by Jack Stockman.
      p.   cm.—(The Archives of Anthropos)
    Summary: When they travel to Anthropos to search for their missing
uncle and his bride, the cousins become part of a fierce battle
between Gaal and the evil sorcerer who seeks to destroy him.
    ISBN 0-87784-592-1 (pbk.: alk. paper)
    [1. Fantasy.] I. Stockman, Jack, 1951- ill. II. Title.
III. Series.
PZ7.W5837Qu 1995
[Fic]—dc20
                                         95-10887
                                           CIP
                                         AC

17	16	15	14	13	12	11	10	9	8	7	6	5	4	3	2	1
09	08	07	06	05	04	03	02	01	00	99	98	97	96	95		

To my grandchildren,
Susan, Bethany, Dana, Meghan, Kirsty, John,
Robin, David, Brennan, Catlyn, Conlon

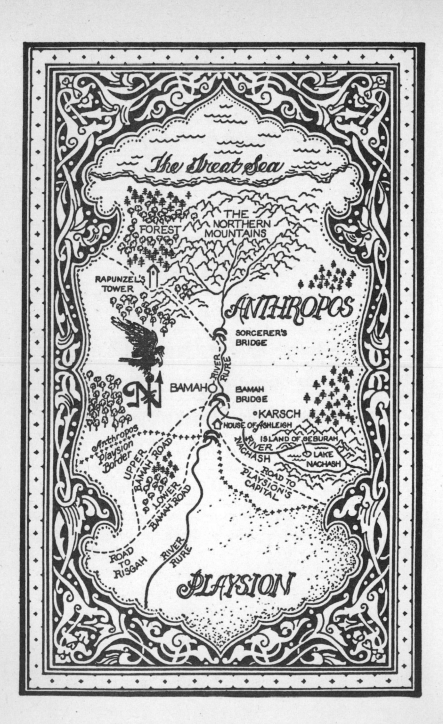

1
The Disappearing Newlyweds

So this was it. *Finis!* The wedding was actually taking place.

It was very unfair. It should never have happened. Think of it—married at the age of fifty-two for the first time to a lady who looked like somebody's grandmother. They said she was only fifty—*only*, if you please!

Mary had needed, and still needed, Uncle John for herself. She lived with him, along with her three cousins, Wesley, Lisa and Kurt. They had their own mother and father—and were with them now on a visit to Singapore—but Mary had no one. Mary had always felt she had an extra claim on Uncle John. She could have managed if she could only have hung on to him. But now this. Mary's thoughts were not the kind you were supposed to have in church, especially in an Anglican church. But then, people shouldn't marry when they're positively ancient. Mary kicked the kneeling stool in front of her.

She sat in the front pew of Saint Andrew's Church on Nathan Road in Kowloon. Mrs. Choi sat next to her, smiling at her from time to time. Mary did not smile back. The vicar was yelling (yelling things you should say, not yell, at weddings). The vicar yelled because typhoon winds howled and screamed round the church and torrential rain beat against the windows. "The worst in seventeen years," a TV commentator had called the typhoon. All ferry services had been discontinued. Before the typhoon everyone had said the wedding was going to be lovely, but no one was saying that any longer. "They should have canceled the whole thing, really they should. This is ridiculous! No wonder there's almost no one here!" Mary heard one man grumble.

For Mary the wedding had been a nightmare from the start. She had never from the first moment understood why her very own Uncle John should get married. Bachelors didn't marry, with or without swords (though why he wore one half-hidden by his morning coat she could never imagine. Was he military?). Certainly bachelors of fifty-two were not supposed to marry. And why did he have to come to Hong Kong of all places to get married? Why couldn't he and this Eleanor person get married in Uncle John's own Winnipeg? As for the typhoon, it was the last straw. She had read about typhoons, and was finding the reality worse than the description.

Each time she had tried to explain to Uncle John about bachelors and marriage, he had laughed and teased her. Sometimes he had looked solemn and said, "But darling, I know I could wait until you're a little older. But that wouldn't be fair to you. I mean, you wouldn't want to marry someone old enough to be your great-grandfather, now would you? You need someone younger."

The one compensation had been that she would go to Hong Kong with him. That, at least, had seemed exciting—in anticipation. Right now it was misery. She had expected the others to be there—her cousins, Wesley, Lisa and Kurt, and her Uncle and Aunt Friesen. Wesley was two years older than Lisa. Kurt was the youngest of the three but still a year older than Mary. She had never met their parents, her uncle and aunt, and had only talked to them occasionally on the telephone. Wesley, Lisa and Kurt had flown to be with their parents for a couple of weeks in Kuala Lumpur. (Their parents belonged to the Canadian Diplomatic Service and kept being moved to "trouble spots" around the globe.)

Even though she was a little jealous of her cousins, they did share the bond of some very wonderful adventures in Anthropos, and they would have been a comfort at the wedding. At least that had been the plan—until the typhoon. Now the Friesens were stuck in Singapore, and she had to go through this business on her own. And, to add to it all, ever since the Eleanor person had arrived in Hong Kong, Uncle John had been acting like a little kid half the time, and rushing round distractedly the other half. He smiled all the time and seemed to find quite ordinary things enchanting. The glow seemed to have to do with the old woman who had turned up—the great Eleanor. Mary felt lost, abandoned.

She admitted, rather grudgingly, that the Eleanor person seemed to be all right. Not a real grandmother—no kids, no grandkids. Old of course, though with a grandmotherly kind of oldness. She was not in any sense *with* it. Neither she nor even Uncle John knew anything about power. Or did they? What was the mysterious aura that rested on both of them? It was very hard to tell. Power was not on them in the way dark power was. It was, Mary decided, somehow different. What's more, they were not the sort of people you could talk to about things like that. They were too respectable, too square. And now it would never be possible to tell Uncle John. Bitterness flooded her mind. It was a long-standing bitterness that had never thoroughly been resolved.

From the age of three she had stayed in Toronto with a mother who was not her real mother, and who had a series of men living with her—"uncles." One of them had done something to Mary that Mary did not like to think about. If anyone knew about it they would hate her, despise her—at least that's how she felt. She groped back in her memory to vague feelings about her real mother. Everything in that area of her memory banks seemed misty, ill-defined. There were horrible bits of memory, which she might have dreamed, or which might be true, though it hardly seemed possible. All she knew was that her mother was dead. If only she could *belong* to real parents, her very own parents. Couldn't Uncle John adopt her? What if she could get the power to *make* him do so!

Had it not been for the typhoon, Uncle John's getting married might have been just about bearable, but the typhoon had turned a bad thing into a major catastrophe. All flights into Hong Kong had been canceled. A complete stranger had to give the Eleanor person away, someone Mary didn't know. In fact Mary didn't know anyone except Uncle John and Mrs. Choi, whom she knew just a little bit. The church was largely empty, and what guests there were seemed old to Mary. "Old and wet," Mary said to herself, shivering a little and sitting a bit closer to Mrs. Choi, wishing the wind would stop howling. Hong Kong was supposed to be hot, wasn't it? It *had* been hot—even muggy—when they arrived, but gradually, as the rain shrieked horizontally across the city, the temperature had fallen.

Her mind went back to Winnipeg and to the fun she enjoyed at the witches' club. Two of the boys told her they went to a large Bible church there. "But they don't have power like we do," they said. Power? Was that what had attracted her? She often wondered. She remembered overhearing a conversation between her Uncle John and a school social worker. Her retentive memory had registered every word.

"In answer to your question—I really don't know. There are the most bizarre rumors circulating in the family about her biological mother. Indeed they are firmly convinced that her great-grandmother put the story out that she herself was a powerful sorceress."

The conversation had continued for some time, but since Mary should not have been listening, and had heard Uncle John beginning to cross the floor just then, she crept around a corner quickly. What was it that had so powerfully drawn her to the coven? Lisa had told her she was "just being mad at Uncle John for getting married." Why had she gone back? It made no sense. She remembered the joy with which she had been reunited with Gaal earlier that year, and the powerful hold the witch had over her on her visit to Anthropos. Yet she also knew she could not have resisted the school club. There was a magnetism about it that had pulled her as though she were a puppet on a string. Then once she had experienced in the real world the physical sensation of power flowing into her own body, she knew where she really belonged.

At last the ceremony in St. Andrew's Church came to an end, and Mary and Mrs. Choi followed the bridal couple as they left. Once in the open, wind and rain whipped and pelted them mercilessly, and the large umbrella the chauffeur held for them turned inside out. The rain lashed Mary and Mrs. Choi pitilessly as they struggled to get into a second white limousine. Soon it began to follow the one with the bridal couple, as it wound down to the exit to Nathan Road.

The air conditioning inside the limousine was turned up fully. It made her shiver and sneeze. Mrs. Choi said, "It was a lovely wedding, and isn't this car beautiful! There's even a bar and a television!"

Both limos nosed their way along Nathan Road, the bridal limousine leading the way, splashing through the water covering the partly flooded roadway. They followed it toward the harbor as far as Harphong Road, where they turned right, working their way beneath the overpass, then via Canton Road and Peking Road to the entrance of the Ramada Renaissance Hotel. Throughout the short journey Mary sat rehearsing in her mind what she had been told to do when they reached the hotel.

"I have to open the limousine door quick. I mustn't wait for the doorman to do it unless he's already there. I have to go to their limousine and say, 'It was simply *wonderful!* You both looked great!' " She sighed. "Then I have to curtsey—and 'not be in their way' or be a nuisance and bother them." Her face clouded. "I wish it didn't have to be like this."

They were pulling up to the doorway, and it was there in the gloomy hotel entranceway that what had seemed like a bad dream turned into a nightmare.

13

Mary hopped out of the limo before the doorman reached it, her eyes on the limousine in front of them. Embarrassed and a little nervous, she hurried to greet Uncle John and his bride, just as she had rehearsed in her mind.

The uniformed chauffeur opened the limousine door, and then simply stared inside the car, his mouth wide open and his eyes dark with bewildered consternation. Mary stood beside him. Nobody was getting out of the limo. What was the chauffeur staring at? Where were the newlyweds? Why weren't they getting out? She pushed in front of him to stare into the car.

Nobody was getting out because there was nobody inside to get out. Uncle John and Mary's new Aunt Eleanor were nowhere to be seen.

"They could not, *could not* . . . there was no way they could have gotten out along the way," the chauffeur, who had turned to the two hotel doormen, protested in English. "No way! No way! We didn't stop or even slow down!" He looked round defiantly as though expecting someone to contradict him. The doormen and a bellboy advanced and then stopped, looking uncertain. Didn't limousines usually have guests inside them?

Mrs. Choi and their own driver joined the little group. Excited chatter in Cantonese began to echo amid the muted sounds of the storm and the blaring of horns and the hollow echo of cars driving in an enclosed space. Everyone around the hotel doorway seemed to be talking at once. Mary tugged at Mrs. Choi's coat several times. "What are they saying, Mrs. Choi?" she asked repeatedly. "Mrs. Choi, please tell me. What's happened to Uncle John? Do they know?"

Mrs. Choi looked very worried. "It makes no sense." She shook her head and turned to address Mary. "I was watching the limousine all the way here. I know they didn't get out. They couldn't have. And their chauffeur said the moment he got inside the car he had locked all the doors from his control panel."

Suddenly, Mary was very frightened. "You mean, you mean . . . But, Mrs. Choi, *they can't just have disappeared* . . ." Her voice trailed into silence as an unhappy thought gripped her. It was a memory of the

way in which she herself had been whisked into the land of Anthropos, into another place and another time, and how many strange adventures had befallen her there over a period of two years in Anthropos time. It was then that she had learned to trust Gaal. But it was one thing to disappear yourself, and quite another to have people disappear on you and leave you all alone in Hong Kong.

And there was something else. She had joined "the other side." Anthropos was the last thing she wanted just then. She remembered now—why had she forgotten?—that Uncle John had said he had one more trip to make to Anthropos. Her shoulders drooped and she began to feel a little dizzy. What good was her power now? Unless—unless she could go after him by using her *real* power. But right then she was too frightened to know what to do. She was not sure whether she wanted to cry or to be sick.

"I think I'm going to be sick," she finally said.

Mrs. Choi took charge briskly. In no time she had Mary back into her hotel room in bed, and was making her hot Chinese tea from the loaded tray each hotel room provided. But Mary did not drink any of the tea. Nor did she want to stay in bed. She really did not know what she wanted to do. She stared at the television, but it had no appeal. She no longer felt sick, and was doing her best not to cry.

Mrs. Choi had picked up the telephone and was talking in Chinese. There were several pauses, then suddenly she switched to English. "My name is Mrs. Choi. I am with Mary in the Ramada Renaissance hotel in Hong Kong. Mr. Friesen? . . . He is not there? . . . Please—who is speaking? . . . Wesley? . . . I think Mary would like to talk to you."

Eagerly, Mary grabbed the phone from Mrs. Choi.

Wesley held the telephone in their hotel room, a bewildered look on his face. "It's Mary—I *think*—an' she won't stop crying. She's sobbing her heart out. Something's happened." He spoke into the telephone again. "Mary—what *is* the matter?"

Lisa whispered to Kurt, "There's a phone in the bathroom. I'll grab that—an' you get the one in your bedroom."

Wesley continued to listen. After a few minutes, he said, "That's better, Mary. Now look, just don't worry, eh? They're sure to turn up. They wouldn't leave you in a hotel room and abandon you. You know Uncle John as well as I do. He wouldn't do that." Then in a startled voice, "What did you say?"

Lisa's voice came through the bathroom phone. "Mary, what makes you think they've gone to Anthropos? Look, do stop crying. I can't make out what you're trying to say. An' please—you mustn't call her 'that old woman.' She's *nice*, Mary."

For a few moments there was confusion, no one having a clear idea of what Mary was saying. Finally both Kurt and Wesley had it straight. Wesley said, "O.K., Mary, I think we have it. You say they disappeared right out of the bridal car, and that it didn't stop anywhere. I guess you're right. They must have gone to Anthropos.

"Now look. Stop worrying. We'll probably be able to fly there first thing tomorrow. Cathay Pacific says we're to be ready to fly. Mebbe there's some way we could get there ourselves—to Anthropos, I mean."

Kurt's voice interrupted him. "Mary, it's no use talking to Mum and Dad. Dad won't let us say anything about Anthropos. He gets mad whenever we do. He says the subject is taboo, an' we mustn't even talk among ourselves about it. We do, of course. But cheer up. We're coming tomorrow!"

They hung up eventually and gathered in the small entrance lounge to the suite. Wesley said, "What can we do?"

"Nothing, as far as I can see," Lisa complained. "I wish she wouldn't cry so much."

"Oh, Lisa—you must admit she doesn't often. An' it must be no fun being all alone in a typhoon," Kurt protested.

"Mrs. Choi's with her."

"O.K., O.K., you two!" interrupted Wesley. "Let's not start quarrelling again. Mebbe there *is* some way we can get to Anthropos. But I can't think of any right now. We'll have to play it by ear."

For a while they sat with worried frowns on their faces. Finally Kurt said, "If they really have gone to Anthropos, mebbe we'll go too."

Wesley shook his head. "How would we get there? In any case, he goes to a different time in Anthropos history than we do."

Lisa said slowly, "Oh, I don't know, Wes. If Gaal arranges the trips I don't see any reason why he can't send us, or him, anywhere he wants to."

Wesley's voice got squeaky, a sign that he was irritated. "Yes, yes, yes! But *how?* When Uncle John went the second time he could *choose* whether to go or not."

Kurt shook his head. "He had no choice the first time. He opened a door—and hey, presto!—there he was in some sort of never-never land. An' even the second time he wouldn't have had a choice if Gaal hadn't provided him with one. All that happened was he realized the opportunity had presented itself."

"O.K., clever sticks! So how do *we* follow him there?"

Kurt shrugged his shoulders. "I don't see how we can unless Gaal gives us the chance. If we're to go, then he will."

"I'd like to get to go," Lisa said, longingly.

Wesley drew in a deep breath. "Well, it's a worry. Dad will go crazy. He'll search Hong Kong by telephone, then start on the various islands. I wouldn't put it past him to go to Macau, or even into mainland China."

Lisa grinned. "Just don't any of us say *Anthropos!*"

Kurt said, "Yes, but Mary will."

"Oh, shucks. You're right. There'll be no stopping her. I can just hear the two of them—Dad and Mary—hard at it right now!"

There was another long pause. Then Kurt said something that proved prophetic. "I have the horrid feeling that something pretty frightful—or mebbe merely frighten*ing*—is going to happen, an' we'll just be whisked into Anthropos whether we like it or not."

2
Torn from Lion Rock

The storm abated during the night, and by morning the Friesens were able to fly to Hong Kong. Aunt Jane Friesen called from the hotel lobby as soon as they arrived.

"Hello! Is that Mary? This is your Aunt Jane—you know—Lisa's mother. We're here in the hotel. Just got in. Darling, we've been so worried about you! How are you, dear?"

"Oh, hi! I'm O.K., thanks."

"Did they come back?"

"You mean Uncle John? No, Aunt Jane."

"Oh, you poor dear! What a nightmare you've had! Never mind, darling, we're here now. We're just going to the restaurant for lunch. Would you like to join us?"

"Aunt Jane, are the kids with you?"

"Yes, darling, we're all here. Cathay Pacific called us from the airport early this morning. It was a rough flight, but we're fine."

Mary heaved a sigh. Her aunt and uncle would not understand, but the kids would. It was a comfort, an enormous comfort, to have someone she knew nearby. "Thank you, Aunt Jane, I'll be right down."

Lunch was a bit of a strain. The Friesens were tall and thin, and Mr. Friesen was "picky"—a stickler for "doing things properly." (Wesley's polite but slightly fussy frown was a reflection of his father's.) Throughout lunch Mr. Friesen never wore any other expression. Mrs. Friesen spent her time smoothing down any ruffled feelings after her husband upset them.

"I still can*not* comprehend what got into them!" he exclaimed. "You just don't turn your nose up at your own wedding reception. What happened at the reception, Mary?"

"I don't know, Uncle Fred. I didn't go. Mrs. Choi put me to bed. I wasn't feeling well."

"You poor darling! I don't blame you a bit." Her aunt, who sat next to Mary, reached over and squeezed her hand.

"It was a totally unacceptable thing for them to do," he continued. "You just don't snub the guests at your wedding reception. And to abandon a child like that, without the slightest warning—" He stopped suddenly and looked hard at Mary. "You're sure they didn't tell you where they were going? You're not trying to keep their secrets for them, are you?"

"Darling, please! Of course she's not!" his wife protested.

Wesley's voice was indignant. "Look, Dad, she was crying her heart out last night! She could hardly talk to me, she was so scared!"

He snorted. "It's utterly, totally . . ."

But at that point the waiter brought their orders on a trolley to the table, and for a few moments the regular conversation gave place to a discussion as to who had ordered what. The children had little interest in eating. The issue of Anthropos drove normal things from their minds entirely. Mary glanced at her cousins gratefully, feeling that the ground under her feet was becoming a little more solid.

Wesley began to relax. "Danger over—I hope," he thought.

Lisa stared at Mary, wondering whether she had anything up her sleeve. In her mind she was saying, "You can never tell with that girl. One minute she's crying, and the next she's into a witch's coven. I don't trust her."

Once their various dishes had been sorted out they addressed themselves to the food. Mr. Friesen said, in a rather genial tone, "You children must not mind our not spending much time with you over the next day or so. We have to trace John and Eleanor, and that may take time. You haven't any suggestions where we start, have you, darling? I'll call all the hotels, of course, and interview the drivers of both vehicles."

"They could be on one of the islands," his wife said. "Chung Chau could be a lovely place for a honeymoon."

Mary said, "You won't find them. They're in Anthropos. I just know. They got *into* the limousine but they didn't get *out*. It'll be a waste of time to search for them—they've gone where we can't get at them."

Wesley drew in his breath sharply. "Here it comes," he thought.

Silence fell on the table as everyone paused in their eating and looked either at Mary or her uncle. The only sound was the hum of conversation from neighboring tables and muted traffic sounds from outside the restaurant windows. Uncle Fred finally broke the silence. "Mary, our children know that they are not to talk about this—this Anthropos. I believe they have gotten over the—hm—well, rather childish ideas they used to have. I'd rather you didn't encourage them. There is no such place as Anthropos."

Though his voice was quiet, there was a hard edge to it that his own children recognized at once. But Mary had never been easily intimidated by grown-ups, and though she was a good deal more polite than when the Friesen children had first known her, she still didn't seem to make a distinction between children and grown-ups.

"Oh, but there is! I've been there, Uncle Fred! I was there with them last time and—"

"There will be no further talk about Anthropos, Mary." Mr. Friesen's face was red, and his voice louder. "I have already arranged to interview both limousine chauffeurs this afternoon. I am not satisfied with their stories. People do not simply disappear." He paused, and

21

when he continued, his voice was gentler. "I'm sorry I asked you whether you were holding something back. I don't believe you are. I realize what a terrible shock this whole thing has been to you, Mary, but there must be no more talk about Anthropos."

"Uncle Fred, I know what I'm talking about. I don't care whether you believe me or not. I—"

"Mary—I warn you—"

Mary rose to her feet, red-faced. "You're not my father!" Her voice was loud and shaky. People from the next two tables turned round to see who was shouting.

Mrs. Friesen, who was seated between them, laid a hand on her husband's arm. "Darling, she's just been through such a lot." Then to Mary, "It's all right dear. He doesn't really mean it."

She placed her other arm around Mary's waist, pulling her close. To the rest she said, "Let's get on with lunch. Mary'll be all right in a minute. She's quite a girl, aren't you, Mary?"

Mary bit her lip, grateful to lean for a moment against Aunt Jane. She was still angry, but the anger began to subside. The comfort of a motherly arm began to melt it. Kurt watched her carefully. As she sank back into her chair he smiled at her across the table. Then, making sure his father was not watching, he gave her the thumbs-up sign. His smile broadened as she smiled feebly back. In Kurt's mind was the memory of their first supper together at Uncle John's, and of the way Mary had stormed out of the dining room at his own insulting remarks. He liked Mary, and he knew that both of them had changed since those earlier, stormier times.

Wesley made an attempt to get the conversation on another track. "Dad, d'you think it would be O.K. for us kids to go to Lion Rock? It used to be one of your favorites."

"What a wonderful idea! That would fit in excellently with our own plans. I'm really sorry I can't come with you—I would love to do so, but for all this business. And your mother, I think, would rather rest. This afternoon I really must call some hotels, for John and Eleanor have to be somewhere."

22

Mrs. Friesen's eyes widened as she glanced at Mary. Rather quickly she said, "Let's talk about Lion Rock. How will you get there, Wesley?"

"Oh, it's easy, Mum. We just go along Peking Road to Nathan Road and get the underground at Tsim Sha Tsui station. You know the one —it's right in front of the Hyatt and directly opposite the Holiday Inn. We change to the train at Kowloon Tong."

"It sounds very complicated to me." Their mother was uncertain.

"Oh, no, Mum, it's not really. We did it several times last time we were here. The Chois—I called them before lunch—live in Shah Tin. So do the Freeman Chans—you remember them?—Freeman and Sook Kit and their two cute kids. Freeman's the architect, and Sook Kit writes."

His father nodded. Now that the conversation was no longer about Anthropos, tension seemed to have drained out of him. "I'm not sure whether we remember them, but you did go to Shah Tin several times. Don't forget that you have to change before getting to Kowloon Tong—"

"I know, Dad!"

"—and do you really know how to get to the beginning of the climb up to Lion Rock? We only went together once. What about the trails? Can you remember them?"

"Oh, they're easy, Dad. You forget that Lisa and I went up them three times. An' it's only a year ago!"

"Don't forget, whenever the path divides keep taking the left fork. Will you see the Choi boys?"

"They're both in Canada, Dad—at university "

"Goodness, how time flies! By the way, make sure you have jackets or heavy sweaters. The wind will be strong, and you'll need something warm once you get there." It seemed to them all that they must have dreamed his sternness.

"Sure, Dad."

An hour later the four children found themselves walking the Hong Kong streets again. For the Friesens the crowded sidewalks represented the excitement of visiting old haunts. In contrast, Mary was seeing Hong Kong streets for the first time. Since her arrival, her contact with the city and its inhabitants had been confined to the view from hotel windows and taxis.

All four children seemed older than they really were, having spent years in Anthropos in dangerous adventures. But the years in that other world of Anthropos passed in moments in our time, so the children were older on the inside than you would think from the outside. As a result, their parents often gave them far more freedom and trust than other children would have received.

It was no longer raining, but the skies were gray and a strong wind was blowing. They found themselves struggling to stay together as they dodged and pushed their way along the crowded sidewalk on Nathan Road. Car engines honked and traffic roared. You could hear snatches of conversation in a dozen languages. Out of the corners of their eyes they caught sight of store windows where haughty clothes props displayed the latest fashions, others where jewelry sparkled dazzlingly under bright lights, and still other little places where money could be changed. Soon they were plunging down a long stairway that opened up to a surprisingly spacious (but horrendously crowded) underground station. They bought plastic multi-journey tickets.

Kurt had decided to take Mary under his wing, and was walking beside her. "You push the plastic ticket into the slot at the turnstile," he told her, "and it pops up again at another opening. It's mostly Hong Kong people rather than ex-pats who use the underground—tourists are often too scared—or too picky. We like it because it gets you where you want to go real fast."

Mary looked a little scared. Toronto had not prepared her for the Hong Kong experience, and Winnipeg, where she had lived with Uncle John, had no underground railway at all. Wesley, Kurt and Lisa were in their element. Here everyone moved to an inner rhythm of rush, rush, rush. Like ants, the hurrying crowds seemed to know exactly where they were going and what they wanted to do. Uniformed school children (many of them younger than any of the children) hurried past them. No one waited for you to make up your mind.

Mary followed Kurt to the turnstile and inserted her ticket. The machine snatched it from her fingers, and flicked it up from another opening. Kurt was waiting beyond the turnstile. "Grab your ticket and come through." Then they hurried forward. "When you leave the system you'll have to go through another turnstile, and the machine will light up and show you how much money you still have in the ticket."

Lisa and Wesley waited for them to catch up, and soon they stood behind a crowd of people that stretched the full length of the platform, four or five deep. And more people were soon crowding behind them.

"All these people will never get in," Mary said.

"You'd be surprised!" Lisa laughed.

When the train arrived they found themselves being pushed forward toward mechanically opening doors, straining past people who were as anxious to get out of the train as the rest were to get in. It seemed to the children that they were almost lifted and carried into the train, where they eventually grabbed steel posts so they could plant their feet and keep their balance. As the train began to move each of them turned to locate the rest. "Did Mary get on?"

"She was with Kurt. Oh, there she is!" Lisa grinned at Wesley.

"Wes says to get off at Jordan, 'cos we can go down to a lower level and get on an empty train there," Lisa called to Mary. "We would normally change at the station after Jordan, but we'll have a seat that way."

The posters that lined the station wall were gliding rapidly backward, and the next moment the tunnel swallowed them. Two stations later they struggled to leave the train against people who were trying to get in. Somehow they managed to alight and to regroup on the platform.

"You *like* this?" Mary was bewildered.

The other three children grinned at her. "It's not always as bad as that," Lisa said. "But even when it's crowded it can be fun."

They descended another stairway to find an almost empty train standing beside the platform. Five minutes later it began to move.

Their destination was Shah Tin, and they eventually arrived there on a regular, above-ground electric train. But the station was inside a large shopping complex—an arrangement that further bewildered Mary. "It's not just arriving in the middle of the shopping center, it's all the people. Is all Hong Kong as crowded as this?"

"Pretty well," Wesley replied. "That's one reason we like to see the other side of Hong Kong—the trails on the mainland, and the smaller islands."

In Shah Tin they parted company with Mary. Mrs. Choi had come to meet her and to take her to the Chans'.

"Mrs. Choi! How nice to see you," Wesley had cried on seeing her. "Dad and Mom want to thank you for looking after Mary last night. It was so kind of you!" For a few moments the Friesen children and Mrs. Choi chatted and exchanged news. But Lisa was staring at Mary.

"You're going to the Chans'?" she asked.

Mary nodded. "Uncle John's computer's there!"

"You don't want to come up to Lion Rock?"

"Not really. I'd rather fiddle with the computer."

Lisa shrugged her shoulders. "It's your decision."

There was an awkward pause. Then Wesley again addressed Mrs. Choi. "Well, it's been lovely to see you. But I guess we'd better move if we're to climb Lion Rock today."

After they parted, Lisa said, "She's up to something. I can feel it in my bones."

"You're too hard on her, Lisa," Kurt protested as they began to make their way to the taxi stand.

"She can be as tough as nails when she wants to be. That's what worries me," Lisa countered fiercely. "One minute she's crying her eyes out, and the next, she's up to one of her schemes."

No one knew why Uncle John had brought his laptop computer from Winnipeg to Hong Kong only to leave it at the Chans'. "It's crazy!" Wesley had pondered at the time. "He'd only just bought it.

He'd hardly used it—hadn't even loaded much software into it. Anyway, you can buy computers much more cheaply in Hong Kong. It's like shipping coals to Newcastle, or wheat to the prairies—it makes no sense!"

They proceeded by taxi to the ascending trail for Lion Rock.

Alighting from a taxi, they crossed the road. On the far side of the road they ascended steep steps in a stone-faced hillside, and in no time found themselves standing and staring at a map behind a glass case.

"I'm sort of scared of what we'll find on the rock," Kurt muttered uneasily.

"Oh, why?" Lisa asked him.

"I dunno. It's a feeling I got."

"It's a feeling you *have*, not that you've got," Lisa admonished in an older-sister tone.

Kurt seemed unruffled. "Sure. But I got it anyway. An' I feel real uneasy, like something's going to happen."

Wesley turned to his brother. "Oh, don't worry, Kurt. It's a pretty easy climb. It's not a bit dangerous if you stick to the trail."

"It's not Lion Rock, Wes. It has to do with Anthropos somehow. Like something wild is going to happen."

"You probably ate something at lunch and feel out of sorts."

Lisa asked, "Can you figure out the map?"

Wesley nodded. "Anyway, I can still remember it. We can't really go wrong if we keep climbing. There's only one summit—Lion Rock. At one point if we take a right fork it would take us to Amah Rock. We'll just keep to the left."

Above them the early October sky grew clearer, and though the wind was fairly strong and gusty, the weather looked as though it was changing for the better. Clouds scurried across the sky, revealing an occasional patch of blue. Soon the noise of the traffic on the tunnel road died down behind them, as their path wound upward among trees and bushes. Before long they began to feel the pull of the ascent in their thigh muscles. From time to time they crossed the same stream on stepping stones, and once they spotted a picnic area on their right. Also on their right, tall bamboo shoots soared to incredible heights. The children passed through a sort of defile, and as they emerged from it, suddenly Amah Rock stood clear and sharp against the cloudy gray of the sky.

"It really does look like a Chinese peasant woman with a child on her back," Kurt gasped, trying to catch his breath.

"But it's more obvious from down below, I think," Wesley panted.

"Andrew Choi once told me that lots of people take this hike," Lisa added. "But we seem to be the only ones here now."

"Dad loves the walks around here. It was listening to him talk that first made me want to try this one." Wesley took a big breath. "But what's the hurry, guys? Let's take it easy. We've a long way to go yet. You'll be surprised at how tired you will get."

They proceeded Indian file, Wesley leading the way, then Kurt, then Lisa. Lisa sighed. "I wish I could have been at the wedding. I bet Aunt Eleanor looked just great!"

Kurt laughed. "You mean they'd dress up? At their age? They're *old*, Lisa."

"Oh, I don't know. Fifty's not that old. She was going to wear white, and I bet she looked pretty. He was to wear a topper and a morning suit. I hope they took photographs." Lisa had a dreamy, faraway look in her eyes. "Y'know, they knew each other when they were kids. I think Uncle John stayed single so long 'cos Eleanor was the only one he ever loved. It's real romantic."

"Romantic?" Wesley turned round grinning, and his plain and freckled face was transformed. His eyes twinkled with mischief. "What's romantic about a man marrying a heavy-equipment operator?"

"What d'you mean?" Kurt asked.

"I mean that Eleanor was once a heavy-equipment operator. She was also a foreman at a construction site in California. She drank like a fish and bossed the men around."

"Oh, don't be silly. She's not a bit like that," Lisa declared scornfully.

"Not now she's not. But she used to be."

"Who said?" Kurt asked.

"Dad told me. He said it was a phase she went through, long ago when she was a lot younger. It had to do with the way her dad treated her when she was younger. He was an alcoholic, apparently."

Lisa sounded angry. "I don't believe it. She's such—such a *neat lady*. I bet he was fooling you. How could she be a construction foreman and a university professor at the same time?"

Wesley grinned again. "I guess the professor bit was later, after she finished her doctorate at UCLA."

They emerged from the trees and were confronted by a wide, cement-lined ditch, about twelve feet across and six or seven feet deep, which crossed their path at right angles. Rushing water coursed along the bottom of it.

They crossed on a bridge and soon were climbing steeply again and breathing hard. The sound of the stream in the steep drop on their right grew steadily more pronounced. Wesley had already removed his sweater, and soon pulled off his sweatshirt. Lisa tied a large handkerchief round her head to catch the perspiration and stop it from getting into her eyes. "I sure envy Mary," she panted, her thoughts back at the wedding. "She got to see it all—but what did you think of lunch?"

"I was a bit scared," Kurt said. "I thought Dad was going to blow his top."

"Mary still hasn't learned," Wesley murmured.

"Oh, come off it, Wes," Kurt protested. "She's far better than she used to be. Don't you remember the night she came to Winnipeg? I felt like murdering her then."

"And don't forget, she'd never met Dad," Lisa added. "We're used to him, but Mary's only had Uncle John—an' those weird men who used to stay at her stepmother's apartment in Toronto."

"But I'm sure she's heading for trouble," John said. "It began when

Uncle John and Aunt Eleanor were writing all those letters to each other. She knew what was going on."

"She's jealous. Of us. She thinks she should have exclusive rights to Uncle John. She ought to grow up," Lisa said. "Anyway, he's our Uncle John more than hers."

"He's hers far more than ours. Don't talk like that, Lisa. You know what a rotten deal she's had." Kurt was indignant. "Uncle John was the first grown-up who was ever decent to her. We may have been the first to know him, but Mum's his cousin, not his sister."

"I know. You're right," Lisa said after a minute or two. "But she was so good after we went to Anthropos. She was—well, she was real nice to live with. But since Eleanor came on the scene she's been getting fat and mean again."

A frown creased Wesley's face. "You know she's started attending a witches' coven."

Kurt assumed a lofty air. "That started when Uncle John told us he was thinking of marrying Eleanor. But it's just kid stuff—isn't it?"

"I wish I could be sure. Uncle John once said something about a curse that comes from the female line in her real family. At least, I think that's the phrase he used. I asked him what it meant, but I think he realized he'd said too much."

"I even thought of telling Uncle John." Lisa paused for a moment. "The trouble is she's such a whiz at school. She gets nothing but A's and A-pluses. And that impresses him."

Kurt sighed. "I know. I wish I had half her brains. She's an absolute whiz at computer studies. The teacher says her programs are 'models of elegance and economy,' whatever *that* means. She's way ahead of anything they teach us at school. And as for hacking . . ."

He didn't have to complete the sentence. Mary had once hacked her way into the University main computer, and left a number of insulting messages about the sloppiness of the computer's security system.

For a time the three children continued to climb in silence, commenting occasionally on the few flowers and blossoms that remained here and there. They had long since left the stream behind, and for a time were unable to see anything of the hill above them, shut in as they were by two walls of bushes and trees.

Kurt felt uneasy. "I wish this feeling would go away," he said. "But it's getting worse. Something's going to happen."

"Something nice?" Lisa asked.

"N-no. Something drastic. It's a scary feeling. It began when we got on the train."

"You said it had to do with Anthropos." Wesley frowned.

"Why should Anthropos be scary?" Lisa asked.

"It's not that Anthropos is scary—though lots of scary things happened when we were last there—the scary part somehow has to do with Lion Rock . . . I don't know what I mean. But I'm scared."

They continued to climb. The air was still, and the only sounds they heard were the sounds of their own footsteps and their own heavy breathing. Eventually they stopped to rest, squatting on the side of the path.

But Wesley, who was anxious to get there, said, "Let's hurry on a bit. We can rest later." They quickened their pace as they resumed their walk, and quite suddenly the sounds of traffic below began again. They rounded the shoulder of the hill and the vegetation dropped away sharply.

"This is the dry side," Wesley said. "The prevailing winds hit the side we've just come up. That's why there's more vegetation there." Ahead of them the Lion Rock itself towered majestically. Kurt had never seen it close up before. "Wow, is that ever something!" he cried. "Though it doesn't look too much like a lion now. But how do we get up? Y'know, I really am scared. It looks horribly open and exposed."

Wesley said, "What's got into you, Kurt? You're not usually like this. Look, the path we follow is easy. It winds behind the rock again. You have to scramble a little bit at the end, but it's kid stuff, really."

Kurt said nothing.

Their trail now ascended more steeply, sometimes with cement steps to help, and at other times not. The terrain was almost bare, but here and there low bushes bloomed with a fiery red blossom.

No one spoke for a moment or two. Lisa gasped, "My muscles—feel—like water. Can't we—go—a bit slower?"

"Sorry," Wesley apologized, slowing his pace. Kurt, secretly glad that he had not needed to complain, made no comment.

At last they reached the foot of the rock and began to scramble up a gully, then behind the rock along a narrow pathway, and finally, at its far end, a place where they could climb up fairly easily. A cement fence, molded so as to look rustic, protected them from the face of the rock, and a notice warned them of danger. Before long they stood at the summit. Wind chilled them, so that they began to pull on their sweaters again.

"Look down there—the airport—and oh, just *look*—there's an aircraft coming in to land—an' it's *below* us!" Lisa cried. For several minutes they looked on the scene beneath them. Wesley and Lisa began to point out the landmarks. Below them crowded apartment buildings jutted vertically like clusters of white and gray dominoes. They could see the main streets and avenues, watch the traffic crawling along them, see the harbor beyond and Hong Kong Island on the far side of the channel. Lisa was fascinated with the planes, especially those taking off. "You hear the roar of the engines several seconds after they actually begin to barrel down the runway," she said excitedly.

"Yes, it takes that long for the sound to reach us," Wesley explained.

"I know that, Wes! I'm not dumb."

She turned, and for some minutes began to look in the opposite direction. Then, with fear in her voice she shouted, "Oh, look!"

The urgency of her tone made the others turn around.

Lisa pointed at a funnel that curled down serpentlike from one of the low-lying clouds. "Surely they don't have twisters here!" she said in amazement.

"Uh-huh. Here we go!" Kurt cried. "This is it. They sure don't have twisters in Hong Kong. There's only one explanation for what's about to happen. This thing's coming for us!"

Suddenly, far more suddenly than it takes me to tell it, the writhing monster swooped at them like something alive.

"Down!" Wesley shrieked. "Lie flat!"

They flung themselves on their faces, and with the roar and thunder of a thousand waterfalls the funnel fell upon them. Horrified, they felt their bodies being sucked from the ground. Light—brilliant, pale blue light—dazzled them. Their breath seemed to be torn from their lungs.

Then came silence.

3
The Keys to Magic

Mary sat before the computer screen at the Chans', writing a program. The Chans were out, and she had told them she would walk back to the Shah Tin Mall and get the train home. She assured them she knew her way. Kurt had often said, "Mary's amazing. Sometimes she goes to pieces completely. But the next minute she seems sort of hard and tough—the toughest person around."

The Chans had seemed uncertain about Mary being alone in Shah Tin, but they could hardly stop her if they were not at home. And if, she thought, *if* the program worked, it would serve Uncle Fred right if it did. 'Cos then she'd have disappeared from Shah Tin to join her Uncle John in Anthropos. And nobody but the other kids would know where she'd gone.

Uncle John. She *had* to win him back, and she would *do* it! He was all she had ever longed for, the father she never had. He was better than all her stepmother's boy-friends put together. She needed more power. Power was real. It tingled deep within her whenever it came on her. She had never experienced anything like it before—and now she had a use for it. Even the witch's power in Anthropos was nothing but the means by which the woman got her to do whatever *she* wanted. But the power she had now received was something she could use for herself. She could manipulate people with it. Control them. She would now be able to make Uncle John love her as he had before. (It did not occur to her to ask whether a love that you controlled was what she was after.)

She checked her computer program carefully, making sure the words and symbols of the ancient spell were properly included. It ought to work. Maybe she was going to be the first person ever to move across space and time using a witchcraft spell programmed into a computer! She drew in a breath and struck the ENTER key.

At first nothing happened. Then the screen went blank and there was total silence. She stared hard at it. Did it—or was she imagining it—no, there was a blue tinge . . . Yes, it was definitely getting larger.

Or was she getting smaller? She glanced down at herself, only to discover that the darkness on the screen was all about her. She could see nothing anywhere except vaguely swirling pale blue mist. She could not even feel the stool under her. Was she floating? When she looked up at the screen, she could no longer see it.

Yes, it was working. She smiled. "Anthropos, here I come! And by my own magic. *I come when I want, not when you fetch me, Gaal!* I'll really surprise Uncle John!"

She began to fall, down, down, down . . .

Mary hit the ground hard, and for a few moments the wind was knocked out of her. When she got her breath back she sat up and muttered, "Well, I did it anyway! I knew I could, an' now I've really done it! That'll teach 'em."

To her surprise, the jeans she had been wearing had been replaced by a long dress of rose-colored silk. It had long, tight sleeves. Her fingers sparkled with jeweled rings, while her feet found themselves inside boots of the softest dark green leather. She stared at herself for the longest time. Then she said, "Wow! I really did it properly!" There was a strong smell of lavender, and she could not tell whether it came from the dress or from herself.

She checked her surroundings cautiously. She was sitting in a forest glade on a summer morning, with diamond dew still sparkling on the grass. The sun was behind her, so that as she moved her head she was aware of pale greens, yellows and an occasional ruby red from the fractured reflection within the dewdrops.

Twenty yards away, near a tall tower of pinkish stone, two men and a young woman sat around a small wooden table. They were too busy talking to have noticed her arrival, and in any case she was mostly concealed from them by a low bush. She crouched behind it, peering at them and straining to hear what they might be saying.

Who were they? Would they know where Uncle John was? It seemed unlikely—but one never could tell. She decided to make no move until she could size them up. She could hear the sound of their voices clearly, and sometimes the actual words when the breeze died down. At one point they dropped their voices, leaning toward one another. One of the men and the woman seemed to be disagreeing with the third, an unusually big man. Then, after a while, they leaned back in their chairs again, smiling at one another.

On the table lay a simple repast of fresh fruits and oat cakes, along with a silver flagon of wine. Mary's mouth watered. She had not eaten since lunch—and that seemed hours ago. A little distance beyond the table a magnificent war horse and two smaller palfreys were munching grass. All were equipped like those horses of bygone days that carried wealthy nobility.

One of the men was obviously very tall, even though he was sitting. He was dressed simply, wearing a sleeveless tunic of purest white with a leather belt. His legs were bare, apart from the crisscrossed leather thongs that held his sandals in place. He might have been any age between twenty and two hundred, yet there was a vitality about him which seemed to dominate the forest glade. A sword lay on the bench beside him. "I guess the biggest horse is for him," Mary thought.

"You could not have chosen a better place, Risano!" the shorter man addressed the giant.

The short man picked up another sword and held it in front of him—a sword with a jeweled hilt and a jeweled scabbard. He examined it carefully and then nodded, as if satisfied. Mary's pulse quickened, wondering if she recognized it, even from twenty yards. Surely it couldn't be! Yet the hilt, to say nothing of the scabbard, looked awfully like it! How the stones sparkled in the sunlight!

A strange nostalgia softened her heart as she remembered how only months before she had carried the sword triumphantly into the kitchen of the house on Grosvenor, and of Wesley's awed whisper, "It's the Sword of Geburah!"

The man who was looking at it was young, perhaps twenty-five. He wore his red velvet cape with a dashing air, and was generally a model of medieval fashion. His hair was long and his beard was neatly trimmed. He wore a blue satin tunic that (she later discovered) matched the deep blue of his eyes. Its wide sleeves were gathered tightly at the wrist, so that the sleeves ballooned elegantly around his lower arms. The light was so clear that she could even see beneath the table that he wore blue pointed shoes of soft leather, and wrinkled plum-colored stockings above them.

"Bit of a popinjay," Mary decided. "I wonder what his name is."

Risano smiled, and his smile embraced both of his companions. "I rejoice that the tower pleases you, my Lord and Lady Nasa of the Chereb, but this place was not my choice. The Emperor ordered me to prepare it for you."

"So that is his name," Mary muttered to herself. "Lord Nasa of the Chereb." The wind had died down, making it easier to listen.

"That was most kind of him," said Lord Nasa. "I take it that the Emperor and the Changer are one and the same?"

"It is as you say. He thought it might be an ideal place for you to celebrate."

When she heard the word *Emperor*, Mary pondered, "I wonder what emperor they are talking about, and where he got the sword from—

if it is *the* sword." Her heart began to beat. The Changer. Uncle John had talked about the Changer. And Gaal had also mentioned the Emperor when she had been here last time. At any rate she knew she must have arrived in Anthropos. But she would have to be careful if these people were Gaal's sort of people. Still, she would have to start by getting to know someone. How else could she link up with the beings she wanted to link up with, the sources of *real* power? And *was* that sword the Sword of Geburah?

She was still wondering how to approach them when the tall man rose to his feet—proving far taller than she had realized. He towered above the seated pair, standing his full ten feet. He smiled at them, and like him, they both rose to their feet, two dwarfs before a giant.

"It is time for me to leave you," Risano said. "But I have a last reminder: you will be guided through the forest as far as the river by a column of smoke and blue fire. Once at the river, it will disappear for a while."

He nodded his head at each of them, saying, "Lord Nasa! Lady Roelane—farewell! It has been good to speak with you!" Then, as the words left his mouth, he disappeared as completely as if he had been transformed into air. No trace of him remained.

"Wow! That's *power!*" a startled Mary breathed to herself. "I'd love to be able to do *that.* Where's he gone, I wonder?"

She continued to stare at Lord Nasa and his lady, uncertain when she should make a move. They were still standing and talking, intent on their conversation. She could see the lady's face, and it was frowning in response to what Lord Nasa was saying.

"She's pretty," Mary said grudgingly, "and *man,* what a dress!"

Lady Roelane's long kirtle was made of green velvet and had long tight sleeves. It fell over white silk slippers and was everywhere crisscrossed with strings of tiny pearls and embroidered with flowers. From her tall, pointed hat a white silk net fell down her back. Her face was flushed, but it cleared as she listened to her husband's words.

After a moment the lady drew in a deep breath and spoke. "Well, my lord, I suppose there is nothing for it but to go and look for her.

But where do we start?" It was a lovely voice, reminding Mary of someone. "Of whom?" she wondered. "Must be someone I like."

Obviously the couple were expecting someone. It made sense, for there were still three horses though the tall man had gone. Whoever they were expecting must have gone for a walk or something. Perhaps she should let them know she was here without delay. Did they live in the tower?

Mary was not one to hesitate. "They look harmless enough." She rose to her feet and began to walk toward them. For a moment or two they did not see her. They were once again talking to each other. But the lady must have caught a glimpse of her out of the corner of her eye, for she suddenly turned toward her.

She gasped, pointed at Mary, and cried, "Why, there she is!"

His lordship turned sharply. "Sooner than we expected!"

Mary advanced steadily. "They're mistaking me for someone else," she thought. "Hi!" she said as she drew near. "I'm sort of lost. Could you help me, please? I came here by magic from another world."

For a moment they stared at her, their faces inscrutable. Then Lord Nasa of Chereb said, "You must be the Lady Mary McNab."

Mary stopped in her tracks. Her heart began to pound, and for a moment her mouth hung open. Clearly, they must be some of Gaal's folk. But there was nothing to be gained by running away, so she might as well brazen it out. She said, "You mean—you were *expecting* me?"

The lady said, "Yes, Risano told us you were already here, and would come to us. He is one of the spirits—the spirits of light. Pray come and sit with us and join us in our repast."

"*Spirits?*" Mary gasped. "He didn't look like a spirit."

Lady Nasa smiled. "No, I suppose not. But that was just the form he adopted so we could see him and talk to him."

Even though she was hungry, Mary ignored the suggestion about eating. She was more concerned about her reason in coming. "My Uncle John is here—I think. I want to find him. That's why I came here. He's—he's very important to me."

The lady and the gentleman exchanged glances. Then his lordship said, "Did you say you came by magic?"

"Yes, I'm getting pretty good at it. I—"

"And how did you learn magic? We understand you are from another world. Do they teach it in your world?"

Mary decided to level with them, though pride rose up in her. "Well not exactly—not in our school, anyway. But there is a witches' club at school, an' I joined it. We learn a lot about how to get what we want in life. I'm a witch. I've managed to apply what I know to computer technology. In fact that's how I got here—via computer." She wanted them both to know that she could stand on her own feet where power was concerned. The girl who had been so frightened at finding herself alone in Hong Kong was for the moment transformed. Mary felt thoroughly in charge of her life again.

The couple stared at her, their faces blank and uncomprehending. Did they not understand her? She had been about to launch on an explanation about what computers were, but something checked her. If these people were Gaal's people, then the less they knew the better. Instead she said, "I really would like to find my Uncle John. His name is John McNab. He's the Sword Bearer and—"

"And this is the sword that must belong to him." Lord Nasa placed the Sword of Geburah into a scabbard attached to his belt.

"My love, the lady is standing," Lady Roelane said. "Come and sit, my dear. There is no need to weary yourself. Let me offer you food. I have fruit juice if you would prefer it to wine."

They sat, and Mary began to eat. "You don't have milk, do you?" she said. The oat cakes made dry eating.

"Indeed we do, my lady!" Lady Roelane laughed. "Fresh and cool and creamy." She excused herself and returned a moment later from the tower bearing a large pewter jug filled with milk.

Mary poured milk into a wine cup and drank deeply. "Boy, that's good!"

"I am the Lady Roelane. And my husband is the Lord Nasa of Chereb. Risano wants us to take you to Bamah. Perhaps you will find your uncle there. I do hope so."

"Bamah?" Mary said in a startled voice. "But Bamah was destroyed, years and years ago. The ruins of the city and the temple all sank under the lake! My cousins told me about it. They were there."

There was a pause, and then Lord Nasa said, "There are prophecies that one day it will be destroyed. But today the city stands."

The thought of a city called Bamah puzzled her. How could it be? Perhaps there was another Bamah now. She frowned, wondering what it all meant. Unless—unless she had arrived here *before* the time when she was here last. And if it was before, how many years before was it? Was it only years? Could it even be centuries? She began to feel dizzy with bewilderment and fear. Perhaps her Uncle John had arrived in a different century—even in what was now the future. If she had come to the wrong century, there would be no Uncle John. And without Uncle John how would she get back? She had no bewitched computer here anyway. Whatever had she been thinking of? How could she have been so stupid? Icy fingers of fear continued to close around her heart.

The Lady Roelane was leaning toward her and staring. "Are you all right?" she asked. "You appear to be unwell, my lady. Can I do anything to help?" Mary was grateful for the respite. She had begun to like Lady Roelane, and wondered whether she had been wise to tell them about the witches' club at her school. But it was too late to change that now.

"It's just my Uncle John—I don't know where he is. Perhaps I've come to the wrong century   ." Her confidence was draining away in rivulets of misgiving. It looked as though she had done something really stupid. But no, that thought was much too scary. She was far from ready to admit to herself that she had made a serious mistake. Where was Uncle John? He just *had* to be here. If only she could find him, all would be well. He need not know how she got to Anthropos, so long as she could find him and get back again. And in any case, the dark powers might be around again. If she could contact them . . .

Lord Nasa of the Chereb spoke. "My lady, to play with magic can be dangerous. In our country we have a legend of a magician's nephew. Its moral is this: a little knowledge can be a dangerous thing, and a little knowledge of magic can be deadly."

Mary felt herself getting angry. "I don't know a *little* about magic, and I don't *play* with it. I know a lot! Enough to travel through time and space, anyway! You need more than a little knowledge to do that." She always felt more confidence, more in control, when she was angry. "I already know computers inside out," she thought. "I even harnessed one for magic! Who is this pompous ass of a lord to lecture me?"

"Listen," she said. "In our world you need power in order to get what you want. You can't trust people—especially grown-ups. You never know who's going to let you down next. I want power—so I can't be hurt. Even Uncle John . . ."

"How do you get power, Lady Mary? In our world people torture animals to obtain it. Is this so in your world? Do you keep them alive as long as you can so they will experience more pain?"

Mary blushed. "How did you know? Anyway, it was only a mangy old cat. Listen, if you want real power you have to overcome your fears and weaknesses. You have to make yourself do things that make other people vomit."

"My darling, she has hardly touched her food. Let her eat. We can talk later. Mary, dear—may I call you Mary?—have some more milk. Eat your oatmeal cakes—and there is an abundance of fruit. We have no servants with us, but we plan to eat well this evening."

Mary drew in a deep breath, again pushing down thoughts about the horrible mistake she might have made Uncle John didn't *have* to be in another century. In any case, she would have to make use of these people. Better to lay her cards firmly on the table. "Look, I know you're Gaal's people—an' I'm not. Not at the moment, anyway. I—I hope we can still be friends. I don't know anyone here "

Lady Roelane laid a hand on Mary's arm. "Of course we can. After all, we are going to be traveling to Bamah together, that is, if you are willing to come."

Mary smiled at her. "Sure, I'll come. D'you think Uncle John will be there?"

"You never know! It is a long time since last we visited Bamah. Anything is possible. Perhaps you will find him there. I do hope so."

In spite of the conversation and of her own part in it, Mary had not stopped eating. The oatmeal cakes were disappearing, as was the milk. She had now begun on the fruit, some of which she could remember from her previous visit. With her mouth full she said, "Do you live here?"

"No, my dear. We have been staying just for a few days."

"So where do you live?" Mary asked.

"We are returning to Anthropos from some of my husband's properties overseas. We traveled several weeks to get here, and now we proceed to Bamah. Risano came only today, and told us about your arrival. He said we were to take you, if you were willing, to Bamah, where we are to be attached to the royal court. We are friends of Queen Suneid."

Mary felt uneasy. It was the second time they had mentioned Risano's knowledge of her coming. "One of the spirits of light" they had called him. Were the others spirits of the darkness? Lisa had described to her the strange practices in the old temple of Bamah, and Uncle John had once said something about them. But if Risano knew, then the Emperor also knew of her coming, and that meant that Gaal knew . .

She spoke her thought aloud. "The Emperor must have known I was coming."

"There is very little the Emperor does not know, Lady Mary. They say he knows all things."

"And Gaal knows too? You know who Gaal *is,* do you?"

Lady Roelane's eyes softened. "I know him very well, and love him dearly."

Mary began to feel embarrassed, and a little ashamed. She remembered very well her own feelings about him. She thought of the dance of the celestial giants (were they the same as the spirits of light?) in the deep heaven on the night of the northern lights, and of the walk with Gaal at sunrise. Her heart began to soften, but she hardened it resolutely. She was on the other side now, and the other side had given her the ability to control people.

Lord Nasa said, "Mary, from what Risano told us, the Emperor has great interest in you. He knows things about you that you do not even know about yourself. And he wishes to rescue you."

Mary stiffened. "What does he know? And what do I need rescuing from?"

"I know not. I only repeat what Risano said. Something about your parents."

"My parents? I—I don't remember either of them. I had a step-mother, but—well, she was O.K., I guess. I wonder what he knows. Anyway, I don't think I need rescuing. I'm not in prison or anything. I do what I like, an' I like using what power I have. It feels great. I wish I'd used it before it was almost too late."

The blue eyes of Lord Nasa twinkled with suppressed merriment. "That is—before you got yourself into difficulties!"

Mary bit her tongue and said nothing, feeling resentful of this lord from the far islands. She turned to Lady Roelane and asked, "When are you going to Bamah?"

"Tomorrow morning, now that you are with us. It will take several days to get there. We begin by following the trail to the Rure River. Even that will take a few days. Have you ridden horseback before? And can you ride side-saddle?"

Mary had once had a lesson in Toronto—but one lesson had been enough. Perhaps it would not be so bad in Anthropos. She looked at the horses again and said, "Side-saddle? Oh, gosh, no! Women wear jeans or jodhpurs in our world. I only tried to ride once, and didn't like it. I'm no good at that sort of thing. I don't know how I'll manage side-saddle."

Lady Roelane nodded. "Do not worry. Nala, the horse you will ride, is very gentle. You may experience a little discomfort at first, but I suspect you will do well."

Mary could eat no more. She resisted the urge to wipe her mouth with the back of her hand (a bad habit she had only fairly recently acquired). In any case, the jeweled rings on the fingers of both hands would not make for a comfortable wipe. The silk dress had also wakened feelings of wanting to be a lady. And since she had discovered a small linen handkerchief tucked into her left sleeve, she withdrew it and dabbed her lips delicately in the way she had seen women do in restaurants.

For some time a question had been haunting her. The pinkish brown stones in the tower reminded her of the stories Uncle John told about his second visit to Anthropos. Was this tower the one he had described?

"Is this Rapunzel's Tower?" she asked.

The lord and lady exchanged glances.

"Rapunzel?" his lordship asked.

"You know—or do you—Rapunzel got shut up in a tower by a— by a witch, an' her lover would say, 'Rapunzel, Rapunzel, let down your long hair.' An' she would let it down, an' then he would climb up it to be with her."

"An interesting story," Lord Nasa murmured, "but what was it that made you think this tower might be it?"

"Well, when Uncle John was in Anthropos once he got into a mess there. There was a girl called Eleanor with him. Shagah the magician had arranged a trap for them, and hair came down when they asked."

"Shagah we know about," Lady Roelane said quietly.

"And the forest isn't enchanted?"

"Not as far as we know."

"An' Shagah's not inside his portrait in the Tower of Geburah?"

"No, dear. He is an evil sorcerer in the service of the spirits of darkness."

Mary was both puzzled and dissatisfied. In spite of the fact that they did not seem to know about Rapunzel, Mary had the growing conviction that it was the tower Uncle John had described. Obviously, Shagah was "now" (whenever "now" was) neither in this tower nor in the

Tower of Geburah. So perhaps, after all, she had arrived before Uncle John did on his visit. It was very confusing, and again she pushed the thought away from her.

"This tower was built by Gaal," Lord Nasa began, but Mary interrupted him.

"If it's the same one that Uncle John talked about, then it wasn't Gaal who built it, but his father."

"That is what Gaal would say. His father, the Emperor, planned it, but Gaal did the actual building. Gaal has a special thing about his father. He is father-oriented, so to speak."

Mary sighed tremulously. Fear filled her. What had she done? However could she find out and be sure about Uncle John? Was he even here?

The rest of the day passed quickly. Lady Roelane showed Mary the horses and introduced her to Nala, the palfrey she was to use. Then came a riding lesson, and though Mary still felt insecure, she did not fall off the gentle horse.

They had their evening meal indoors, for the evening was chilly, and soon after she had eaten Mary decided she was too tired to stay up any longer, so she went to bed in the room Lady Roelane had told her was the room prepared for her. Soon she was asleep and dreaming. But in one of the dreams she heard the voice that she knew was Gaal's, saying, "I am, and I am here. I am, and I am here." Gaal was in the doorway of her room, and walked toward her until he stood at her bedside. It was dark, but light accompanied him wherever he was, for he himself was the source of the light.

For the first time since she came to know him, his face was stern and his eyes deeply grieved. Mary had the feeling that he was reading every secret in her heart, and she did not enjoy the feeling. For what seemed like an age he stood in silence without speaking a word, and the longer he stood, the more frightened she became. She wanted to say, "Aren't you going to speak?" but she was too frightened. She found she could not even open her mouth. When she tried to do so even her throat seemed to close. Finally he spoke. "You did not come here by magic. *I brought you here.* The glass on the computer screen was made from a proseo stone—but that is neither here nor there. I instructed Risano what to do when you arrived. Mary, I have already delivered you once from the power of a witch. Have you forgotten?"

Mary groaned in pain, and her body began to shake. Suddenly, only the light was there, and Gaal himself could not be seen. Then the light gradually faded, until she was once again in darkness. For the rest of the night she remained wide awake, longing for the dawn to come.

4
The
Three
Philosophers

"Where are we?" Kurt whispered. All he could see was the blue mist surrounding them.

In response, Wesley also whispered, "We seem to be on firm ground, but I can barely see as far as my waist, let alone what we're standing on. Whose hand am I holding? Is it yours, Kurt?" Wesley gave the hand a squeeze.

"Yeah."

"So where's Lisa?"

"She's here holding my other hand," Kurt said, but his whispered reply was cut short by Lisa, who giggled nervously and said, "Why are we all whispering?"

Wesley didn't laugh. Bewilderment and anxiety did not affect him in the same way. "I dunno. After that terrible racket the silence seemed almost like church. But I wonder where we are? What's this mist? Uncle John talked about a blue mistiness on both his visits to Anthropos."

"I hope that's where we are," Lisa responded. "It must be somewhere Gaal-ish, anyway."

"Unless we're all dead!" Kurt said in a spectral voice.

Irritated, Wesley detached his hand from his brother's, and almost immediately saw Kurt's disembodied hand groping toward him. "Don't do that, Wes!" Kurt cried, his voice now sounding panicky.

"I think the mist is clearing," Lisa breathed softly.

She was right. They could dimly perceive one another's ghostly outlines. Wesley and Lisa found themselves facing each other, both holding hands with Kurt. Before long they could see one another fairly clearly, and instinctively released their hands. Kurt said, "There's a sort of—I can't see what it is—but it's like a big blue light area ahead there."

The others turned to look. "Is it changing, or am I imagining it?" Lisa asked.

"I think *you're* changing," Wesley said with a thoughtful smile. "Wait a minute, though—no, no I believe you're right!" He sounded excited. "And I sort of feel good about it—not irritated or anything. Anyway, Uncle John experienced something like this more than once. It must be Anthroponian."

"Hush!" Lisa said, half scared.

"Why?"

"I think it's coming nearer."

"So?"

"Oh, don't be so smart. It could be anyone—or any*thing.* "

For a moment or two there was silence as the strange blue area grew in size. Then it resolved itself into the figure of a man emerging from the mist. The area surrounding them immediately grew clear, like they were entering into a large bubble. Inside the bubble everything was clear, but beyond it the mist remained. It was darker blue mist now, for they saw the light was coming from inside the man.

"Gaal!" cried Lisa. All three children flung themselves at him.

"Oh, Gaal!" Wesley said.

"I've missed you!" cried Kurt, half excited, half tearful.

"You still smell like a freshly sharpened pencil!" Lisa murmured, laughing a little.

They sat down—on something that was reasonably soft, though they had no idea what it was. "Where are we?" Kurt asked.

"We are in the zone where time does not exist."

"Like the hole where time ends?" Kurt asked, remembering their first visit to Anthropos.

"The same sort of thing," Gaal replied. "And you see me as you are accustomed to see me. When you next see me we shall all be in time, not in this 'no time' where we are now. You will be quite bewildered by my appearance, and will not recognize me—though Mary will. So do not forget, *we are not in time, but outside it at present.*"

"But why won't we recognize you?" Wesley asked. Gaal smiled but made no reply.

They spent the next few minutes—or what seemed like minutes— telling him what had happened, how they had been stuck in Singapore and unable to attend Uncle John and Aunt Eleanor's wedding, how Mary had been upset over the disappearance of the newlyweds, of their parents' disbelief in Anthropos, and of their worries about Mary and the witches' club. At every item he nodded, smiling, as though he already knew what they were going to say.

"Yes." Gaal had a quiet smile still on his face. "I knew, but I enjoy listening to you tell it. As for Mary, she does not know quite what happened. I arranged for her to be brought into Anthropos, though she still believes she came by her own magic. She will have been in Anthropos several weeks before you will arrive there."

"How? I mean, how could she come by her own magic? And how did you bring her?" Lisa asked.

"She incorporated several spells on a floppy disk. Her idea was to come through your Uncle John's computer. She suspected that he would be back in Anthropos and was determined to follow him if he was, wife or no wife."

"And did she? I mean, has she?" asked Kurt.

"She would have landed in serious difficulties if she had tried."

"I bet she did try!" Wesley said cynically. "That's probably why she wanted so much to go to the Chans' place in Shah Tin. It worked out real well for her!"

"But not exactly as she herself planned," Gaal said, still smiling.

"Why not?"

"I told your Uncle John to send his computer over either to the Chois' or to the Chans'." Wesley's eyes widened, but Gaal continued. "You see, he once had a *proseo comai* stone that he stored in a glass jar in the attic where he kept his computer system."

"I know," Kurt said gloomily. "It disappeared, and he thought one of us might have taken it."

"So now you will be able to tell him what happened! One day Mrs. Janofski put water into the jar and stuck some flowers in it. The stone dissolved."

He paused, and the children stared at him, their mouths open, waiting for him to go on. Gaal looked at each of them in turn and then continued.

"Later the same day Mrs. J. brought some hot water upstairs and washed, among other things, the attic window. She also, rather nervously, washed the screen of the new laptop computer your uncle had bought, but seemed worried with the result. So she took the flowers out of the jar, poured some of the water from it over the washcloth and squeezed it out a couple of times. Then, unaware of the extraordinary power in it, she gave the screen a final wipe, and turned it into a doorway to Anthropos."

Lisa shook her head in wonder but said nothing. Wesley said, "I couldn't figure out *why* Uncle John would bring it to Hong Kong! It has a hard disk, but he'd never bothered to transfer his stuff onto it. I see now . . ." He began to laugh. "Poor Mary! This has been a rough time for her."

"It's time she grew up," Lisa said.

But Kurt said, "Gaal, why have you brought us here?"

Gaal rose to his feet, and the children did the same, hoping that he was not going to leave them, and wondering what would happen next.

"I shall send you on to Anthropos to rescue a young king."

Kurt asked, "What young king?"

But Gaal just went on speaking as though he had not heard him. "Listen carefully. You will arrive in Playsion and will meet three men on horseback. With them will be three saddled horses and two pack mules. They will stop and discuss whether to hire you or not. You are to let them see that you will be willing to be of service to them, but if they ask questions of you on the first day or so, you must tell them you are on the secret business of a Great King, and that he has requested you to be silent."

"Won't they be suspicious?"

"Yes. At first, certainly."

"But they'll hire us?" Wesley's voice had its usual worried note

"They will hire you."

"How can we be sure it's them?"

"They will be the first persons you see after your arrival."

"Where will we be?"

"You will meet them beside a road in the southern forest of Playsion. The road leads from the port city of Risgah in Playsion to Bamah, which is, as you know, the ancient capital of Anthropos. You will be two or three days' journey from the frontier of Anthropos."

"Bamah?" Kurt wondered. "Did they rebuild it?" But before he could ask his question Lisa spoke.

"About the young king. Where will we find him, and what are we to do?"

"You will know all that when the time comes for you to know it. Trust me. I will have my eye on you every moment. Your story begins as you meet the three men."

There was no sound, no sense of rushing through space, nothing to tell them that they were being catapulted into another world. All they were aware of as the mist lifted was a forest of spruce and pine, with a few huge and ancient oak trees. They stood at the side of a dusty, rutted road running through the forest, but at first they saw little of it, for they were looking mainly at Gaal. Curiously, they were wearing the clothing of people associated with the royal court. Lisa wore a long white dress. There were expensive silk shirts on the boys, and silk hose. From the boys' shoulders satin cloaks hung, while Lisa's was pulled around her shoulders.

"Remember, I shall be with you all the way," Gaal said, bidding them farewell.

"Don't go! *Please* don't go!" Kurt cried. But even as his voice rang out, Gaal was no longer with them. He had disappeared, and they were alone. For a moment they were too shocked to speak. Wesley was the first to stir as he moved to the bank at the roadside and sat down. Slowly his brother and sister joined him.

Wesley was talking softly, as though going over a lesson. "Three men on horseback, three more saddled horses and—"

"And two pack mules," Lisa finished.

"Oh, why did he have to go?" Kurt kicked a stone. "I had more I wanted to talk about."

"Why the pack mules?" Wesley frowned.

"Supplies of some sort, I suppose. But why on earth three saddled horses without riders?"

"Spares, perhaps?"

"Doesn't make sense—unless, of course, they're intended for us. But they wouldn't know there were three of us." Wesley frowned.

Kurt continued to kick at stones. "We hardly spent two minutes with him—an' now he's gone."

"He said he'd be with us all the way," Lisa murmured thoughtfully.

"Yes, but what did he mean about Bamah? It's been destroyed. How can we take anyone there?"

"Maybe it has been rebuilt," offered Wesley.

"Or maybe we've arrived in a time before it was destroyed," Lisa suggested.

Kurt glanced at the roadway where Gaal had stood and sighed. His voice was unsteady. "Oh, that's not what I'm concerned about. I just didn't realize until we saw him how much I've missed him. If only *Dad* understood. Ever since we talked about Gaal he's seemed more distant than ever—cold."

The others said nothing. Soon the sound of horses reached their ears, and, as Gaal had predicted, three horsemen came into view round a bend in the road, followed by three saddled horses and two pack mules. Silently they watched the party approach.

The men were dark-skinned, richly dressed, and obviously wealthy. The first two bore themselves with dignity. The third horseman was overweight, and even before the party reached them they could see a worried, uncertain expression on his face. As they drew level with the three children, the men reined their horses and halted.

The man in the lead addressed himself to Wesley. "Is this, young sir, the road that leads to Bamah in Anthropos?"

His face was lean, his nose long and beaked, while thick black eyebrows almost met over dark and burning eyes. As the man stared fiercely at him, Wesley was reminded of a particular schoolteacher he greatly feared.

Kurt spoke before Wesley had time to say anything. "Yes, your lordship, it is!"

Surprised, the man glanced at him, but turned again to Wesley. "And what might the three of you be doing, walking alone along a road through wild country?" Wesley felt he was being accused of something.

Again, before he could say a word, Kurt answered. "That, sir, we are forbidden to tell. We are in the service of a—a *Great King!*"

There was a startled pause. Wesley was angry. "I wish he wouldn't do that," he thought. But what he said, he said in a calm voice. "He means no disrespect, my lord." He added cautiously, "But the fact is that we are sworn to secrecy"

"To secrecy, indeed! Among yourselves, I suppose. What would there be to be secret about?"

Wesley drew in his breath sharply. He thought, "What do we say?

Now the fat's really in the fire. We were supposed to get ourselves hired by these people."

He glanced at the second man and saw that he was smiling. Their eyes crossed, and the second horseman shook his head in obvious amusement. His face was identical in shape to the first man's, yet in some mysterious fashion it conveyed an impression of merriment and warmth. "It's his eyes," Wesley thought to himself. "They're so alive and friendly."

It was true. The man's eyes danced, and his white teeth lit up his dark brown face. "Mebbe there's hope after all," Wesley thought, hoping that no one could hear the beating of his heart.

Without taking his eyes from Wesley, the second man spoke. "Have done, Gerachti!" he cried. "I like them. Especially the young boy. I have a good mind to ask them to ride with us."

"Not by my counsel!" Gerachti turned round fiercely. "My lord, we know nothing about them! Who can say what they are doing here, or what their business is? Secrecy indeed!" He spat on the ground.

The third horseman, whose round face bore a perpetually anxious look, said, "Gerachti, please! Alleophaz is our leader. We swore to abide by his decisions." His voice was high pitched, contrasting strangely with the deep voices of the first two speakers.

The second horseman said, "Thank you, friend Belak! But all I can do is invite them. Who knows how they will respond?" He addressed himself to the children, glancing in turn at all three. "Young lady, young sirs, would you care to ride with us? You are heading in the same direction. As you see, we have horses to spare. Three men we hired to look after the animals have left us, fearing the dangers of our journey. The horses are saddled and equipped, since our helpers deserted us but an hour ago, and our own knowledge of horseman-ship is defective. What say you?"

Lisa had been worried about her silk shoes, realizing they were hard-ly suitable for the terrain. "We shall be grateful, your lordship," she said quickly. "Your offer is unusual, and we must not say why we are here or what we are about. But if your lordship is willing to trust us—"

"My lord, that is exactly my point!" Gerachti interrupted. "The children have honest faces, though they might be skilled in deception. But why are they alone? By their clothing, by their bearing, by—by everything about them—we see they are not peasants. Who knows what trouble will fall on our heads if they should be found in our company?"

Alleophaz addressed the children again. "Gerachti thinks you have run away from your parents—or perhaps from your guardians. He is afraid we might be accused of luring you away, of stealing you for ransom perhaps. Are you in fact escaping from parents or guardians?"

The three children responded at once—all in the same way. "No, my lord." "Certainly not!" "No!"

"Then where *are* your parents or guardians?" Gerachti cried impatiently.

Wesley thought of Hong Kong and of trying to explain. He smiled to himself at the thought and said, "Our parents, not our guardians. And they are a long, long way from here—in fact, it would be impossible to explain where they are."

"But *someone* must be responsible to care for you." Gerachti's fierce eyes glared first at Wesley, then at Kurt. He avoided looking at Lisa altogether, and this annoyed her.

"The person who looks after us is here with us. He's here right now. I know you can't see him—and that is just as well. But he's *here*. And nothing will happen to us that he doesn't want to happen." Lisa was not trying to be impudent, but the thought of Gaal's presence filled her mind.

"Drat her!" Wesley thought. "Why must those kids keep putting his back up?"

Nobody spoke for several seconds. Then Gerachti said, "You are the smoothest and most accomplished liars I have ever met. Either that, or you are mad. And I do not believe you are mad."

"Enough, Gerachti!" Lord Alleophaz said sharply, his eyes flashing. He quickly dismounted, offering his arm to Lisa. "Let me assist you to mount side-saddle." Then to the boys, "If you two will be good enough to mount and follow me, we will lead, and my good friends Gerachti and Belak will bring up the rear, keeping an eye on the pack animals."

Gerachti said nothing, but his face twisted with anger. As he and Belak made their way past the children they heard the squeaky, ineffective voice of Belak. "Believe me, I know how you feel. But you must show him more respect. It makes me very nervous when you—" They could not hear the rest, for they were busy with the saddles, adjusting their stirrups, mounting and settling themselves into their saddles. Soon they were on their way.

Wesley was relieved, and his heart exulted. So far so good! He would have to talk to the other two, but there would be time later for that. It was done in only two or three minutes, in spite of the tactlessness of Kurt and Lisa. Now they were on their way to Bamah—but to do what? To rescue a king? Would he be in Bamah, or someplace else? How would they know where? How would they rescue him once they did know? Would their search begin in Bamah?

They rode two by two, first Alleophaz and Wesley, then Kurt and Lisa, followed by the two pack animals and Gerachti and Belak.

The road slowly descended ahead of them. On their right the forest sloped downward, but it rose on their left up a steep incline. There was little or no undergrowth, and the ground was covered with a thick carpet of moss.

Wesley's thoughts were interrupted as Alleophaz began to speak to him. "You do well to take us on trust. But I'm sure you would like to know who we are and why we are here."

"My lord, your face makes it easy for us to trust you—"

"You mean Gerachti's does not?"

"Well—I didn't mean that exactly, but—"

"I am teasing you. However, I feel I must give an account of our presence and our mission. We are philosophers."

Wesley had only the vaguest notion what philosophers did, but he said nothing.

"We search for truth. I, Lord Alleophaz of Enophen in the land of

Glason, am the leader of a small group of disciples who search for truth—truth about the world, about the universe and about mankind—where we come from and what our destiny is. I am descended from kings, and among our family possessions there is a stone that has existed, or so they say, from before the time when the worlds were created. It is called the Stone of Truth, and legend has it that it will one day reveal to us the key to truth and the key to life."

"What does it look like? I mean, what does the stone look like?"

"It is smooth, gray in color, and weighs several pounds. It is plain, and does not look like any animal or bird or created thing. No hidden lights shine from it. In short, there really is nothing remarkable about it. Yet I have spent many hours staring at it, touching it, wondering about it. Often I concluded the legend must be false, but again and again I would go back to it and stare again, not knowing what drew me.

"About two years ago I did this when I was very tired, weary of the endless arguments of my disciples. We sought vainly for a truth that was unshakable, unanswerable. We sought the basis of *all* truth. Late in the night I sat and stared at the stone, and cried out to the gods, saying, 'If gods there be—come to my aid and give me understanding! Lighten my darkness, I pray!' But there was no answer."

Wesley looked at the lean face, and saw that the man's eyes were focused in the distance and that his face was filled with emotion. After a moment Alleophaz continued.

"I began to get drowsy—indeed, my head began to nod, for it was after midnight. Suddenly, overwhelmed by a weariness I could not control, I fell forward, my arms sliding down either side of the stone. I remember hearing the sound of my forehead striking the rock, and even of saying in astonishment to myself, 'Why—that was my head!' Instantly I was snatched from the room into some place of beauty of a kind I had never even before imagined.

"It was as though I had been translated to the most lovely palace in the world. The palace was utterly real. I was not dreaming, but really was inside a wonderful building. I stood on *gold* pavement, surrounded by pillars of gold—but *clear* gold, gold into whose amber depths my eyes could penetrate, gold that shone gently from its very depths with the light of the sun.

"And before I was aware of anything else in my surroundings I saw a living column of smoke approaching me from a distance. I say *living* smoke because that is how I thought of it, and as it drew nearer, it seemed to glow with inner fires of pale blue. It approached until it hovered a yard or so from me. I began to tremble. Then its form changed, and it became a being in the form of a man, a man from whom the same pale light was shining. I could not bear the power of the shining of his countenance, and fell on my face at his feet, my body shaking uncontrollably."

"I bet that was Gaal!" Wesley cried.

"Gaal? Who is that?"

"He's—I mean we—oh, dear, it's sort of complicated, an' it's part of the secret. But do go on with your story. I'll try to explain later."

Alleophaz looked ahead, drew in a breath, and started again. "When the person spoke, his voice was the sound of an earthquake, and he said, 'I am Truth. I am the key to all understanding. I shall be born as a man-child on your earth in one week's time. When I come, the history of the world will take a new course. I want you to see me there during my childhood. You will learn where I am if you inquire at the royal palace in the ancient and evil city of Bamah in the country of Anthropos.' "

"That's what Gaal called it once—'the ancient and evil city of Bamah.' " There was a frown on Wesley's face. His thoughts were confused. In his mind was, "Ought I to tell him all we know?" But Alleophaz had turned to him with interest, his eyes alight with intelligence.

"Gaal again?"

"Oh—well, like I said before, it's complicated—and Uncle John talks about the pale blue light a lot, too. It must have been the person we call Gaal who was talking to you."

Alleophaz was still watching Wesley keenly. "Then you really know something. Obviously Gaal is a key. How much *do* you know?"

"We—we know quite a bit—but, as I say, it *is* complicated. Obviously I must explain, but later. *Please* go on with the story!"

Alleophaz's face bore a quizzical smile. "That is really all there is to tell . . . oh, except this. The strange being turned and pointed to a painting that hung from one of the wide gold pillars. 'Look at it carefully,' he said, 'before I send you back to where you were.'

"On the picture I saw three children on horseback. Two were boys, one was a girl. They appeared to be following a pillar of smoke— identical with the one that had first approached me. They looked rather like the three of you. 'You will meet them in Playsion, and they will guide and instruct you.' Then immediately, and without any warning, I was back in my ancestral home, my arms embracing the stone and my head resting against it. Strangely, as I raised my head and sat up I saw that the sun had risen. What had seemed to take but a few brief moments had actually used up several hours."

Wesley was frowning. His thoughts had wandered toward the end of the narrative, and he was trying to figure into what epoch they had arrived. He knew that Anthropos time and earth time were totally unrelated. "When was that vision?" he asked.

"It took place nearly two years ago. I decided at once that I must leave for Bamah. But it took a week to make preparations for such a long journey, and we have been traveling since then. The child, if it was born as he said, must be nearly two years old."

For several minutes Wesley had been conscious of the sound of rushing water, which grew constantly louder. The road was still descending, and soon they caught an occasional glimpse through the trees of sunlight on the river below them on their right. Wesley was still thinking about the story.

"Two years! That's an awful lot of traveling! How did you get here?"

"We have had two sea voyages. We were shipwrecked during a storm on a small island in the Pasgal Sea, and it was nearly a year before we were able to take ship for this part of the world. We arrived in Playsion a week ago and purchased these animals along with provisions. There were five of us when we first set out, but two of my disciples returned home after the shipwreck."

"But Gerachti and Belak stayed with you."

"Yes." Alleophaz smiled. "I like Gerachti. He does not accept my views without argument, and can be as stubborn as a mule, but he, too, hungers for truth. It is just that he is hard to convince! He is rather suspicious of my vision as a source of truth."

Very soon they found themselves following the river bank, and as soon as they could they dismounted and led their horses to drink. The river bed was wide, almost two hundred yards across, though the actual channel—or rather channels—through which it flowed might number three or four at any one time. It proceeded in the direction opposite to the one they were pursuing, constantly dividing and uniting among islands of stone and rock. The water was swift, absolutely clear, and pale green in color. Its bed was lined with boulders and small stones, and there were fish to be seen in the five feet or so of deeper water.

Once the horses were watered they resumed their journey, now ascending slowly in the direction of the river's source. And because the river followed many bends, the scenery changed constantly. They could catch glimpses of peaks and distant mountain ranges both behind them and in front of them.

"I wonder what the river is called," Lisa said to Kurt.

"I've no idea. But surely it must become the Rure higher up. Remember the legend of the magician."

The voice of Alleophaz broke in. "It is the Rure. It is joined by a smaller river—the Nachash, its most important tributary—which turns a sharp corner to join it. The river flows from its source in Lake Nachash, which is bordered by a swamp."

Wesley's mind received a jolt. That confirmed what Lisa said about Bamah. He saw that they had arrived "in Uncle John's time." Hence the way the river was flowing. The legend about the sorcerer who built the bridge now made sense. "Well, I never! The sorcerer and the bridge!"

"Then this road really *will* take us to Bamah, and we follow the river—or some river all the way . . ." Kurt turned to interrupt.

"But the Rure is—well, more sedate than this river," his sister said, frowning.

Alleophaz smiled. "True, and I can see you are familiar with the country. As for this river, I imagine that it can be dangerous when it floods. Probably this road gets washed out at times."

All of a sudden Kurt saw with his own eyes the "living column of smoke" on the road ahead of them. It was on the left-hand side of the road, the side of the forested slope. Merging with the trees, pale gray in color, it seemed to Kurt to pulsate with a life all its own.

"Look, Lisa, there it is!"

"There *what* is?"

"The column of smoke that Alleophaz talked about. Look—there—ahead of us on the left!"

"Where? Where? I can't see anything!"

Kurt pointed. "See that tree that leans forward?"

"Yes."

"Well just this side of it—almost right against it."

There was a moment's silence.

"Kurt, I can't see a thing," she said. "You're sure you're not imagining it?"

"You could be looking in the wrong place. Look, it's only ten yards ahead now! See, right there!"

Lisa shook her head, laughing a little. "Kurt, there's nothing! I can't see a thing."

Kurt's face was red. "We're passing it now, it's as clear as day!" he cried in anguish. He turned to his sister, whose face was full of concern.

"Kurt, I'm sorry. I'd see it if I could. But all I see are trees and the slope of a hill."

Kurt looked back. "It's still there." His shoulders drooped. "It's—it's as clear as a bell—glowing with inner fires of pale blue, just as he said. Lisa, I'm not making it up!"

5
Kurt
and the Column
of Smoke

At that point the road swung left to follow the river bank, so that whatever Kurt saw, or thought he had seen, was lost from view. It was a point at which the main channel, which must have been fifteen or twenty feet across, and very deep, flowed with unusual speed. As they looked at the water flanking the road they saw it fast, deep and only a foot below the level of the road. On their left there was a face of rock rising sheer for thirty feet or so. Twenty yards ahead the road ended abruptly. It had been washed out. Two or three hundred yards further ahead they could see where a large tree had fallen out of the bank over the river, and beyond that point the road emerged to rise above the level of the river once again.

Alleophaz reined his horse and dismounted, handing the reins to Wesley.

"Oh, boy, that tears it!" Kurt said.

Alleophaz walked toward the point where the road was washed out

Belak and Gerachti hurried to join him. Lisa, weary and aching after sitting side-saddle, released her left foot from the stirrup, slid down and stood beside her horse, still holding the reins. Kurt longed to join the men, but restrained himself. They watched the three men discussing the situation. Sometimes one or the other would point ahead and they would look at the rock face on the left, or back in the direction from which they had come. Gerachti seemed to point frequently to the river itself, and to the far side of it.

Wesley turned to his brother and sister. "I hope he isn't trying to talk him into crossing it," Wesley said. "That would be absolutely insane. That current would sweep us away in no time—and the horses . . . !"

"I think he is suggesting we use ropes."

"Insanity!"

They were relieved to hear Alleophaz saying as the men returned, "No. Absolutely not. It would be far too dangerous. In any case it is time we stopped to eat. We will all feel better when our stomachs are full."

They opened the leather panniers on the pack animals and, seating themselves in the roadway, began a meal of oat cakes, fruit and sweet wine. They positioned the horses on the side nearest the break. The men began to discuss the situation again. Alleophaz and Gerachti did most of the talking, but after half an hour nothing was resolved.

"Where's Kurt?" Lisa asked Wesley in a low voice.

"Goodness knows. He's not here. Did he eat?"

"I don't know. I think so."

"Where would he go?"

"Just before we got here he thought he saw a column of smoke like the one Alleophaz saw in his vision. I couldn't see anything—an' I think I must have hurt his feelings. Perhaps he's gone for another look."

Alleophaz was still talking. "I think we should go back slowly, looking for some point where we can enter the wood, and circumvent the washed-out area. We may have to dismount and lead the horses."

At that moment Kurt rounded the corner. "You won't need to look," he said. "There's a trail that starts fifteen yards back. I followed it a little way. It's easy enough for the horses."

Kurt seemed elated and very sure of himself. Alleophaz looked at him with interest. "I wonder . . ." he said.

"You wonder what, my lord?" Gerachti responded.

"Well, in Risgah, before we set out for Bamah, they told us our choice for the first twenty leagues lay between the high road and the low. The low, they said, mainly followed the river and was easier and broader. The high road was narrow in places and could be water-logged at this time of the year. They also said there were trails connecting the two, but that you had to know what you were doing to follow them. The forest was full of dangers, they said, and it is very easy to lose yourself in it."

He turned to Kurt. "It puzzles me that I did not see this column you saw as we were passing."

Kurt colored. "I didn't mention the column, because I didn't want you to think I was crazy."

"It is not given to humans to see into the spiritual realms every moment," Alleophaz replied. "But do you know what you are doing?"

"Yes, my lord, I do."

Wesley looked at his brother, amazed. He could see that Kurt was not being brash or cocky. He was both excited and very sure about something. Evidently Alleophaz was satisfied. "Very well, lead us along the trail you found."

In no time they repacked the panniers, mounted, and turned back on their way.

Then, fifteen yards beyond the turn in the road, Kurt directed his horse between a tree and bush, doubling back in the direction of the cliff. For several yards they ascended steeply, and in the end were forced to dismount. The narrow path followed the top of the rock face for several yards so that they looked down at the rushing water below. Then Kurt led them sharply away from the river along a more level area so that they could ride again among the trees.

Alleophaz was immediately behind him and watching him keenly. The trail seemed hardly a trail, but Kurt was looking everywhere about him, not at the trail, but as though he were searching for something. Sometimes he looked back, a puzzled expression on his face. Then he would pause, look forward and, "Ah—there it is!" they would hear him mutter, as he started ahead once more.

"He obviously knows what he is looking for," Alleophaz murmured.

It was very interesting to watch Kurt. Even when the trail was clear and easy to follow, Kurt's eyes were everywhere. Mostly he looked ahead, but sometimes he would stop suddenly, look around, say, "Hm," nod his head, and almost double back, turning around a tree and following an almost invisible trail for a little while. The trail would join a wider one going in the same direction, and for a few minutes it would be plain sailing.

Once he stopped, looking very puzzled. "I think we may have to go back a bit. Just a second, I'll dismount and walk back." Then, after a few yards, he nodded. "No, I was right. We'll just have to go on a bit." Then fifteen yards later—"Oh, there it is! I see it now."

"There *what* is?" Wesley asked wonderingly.

"I think he must mean the column of smoke," Lisa replied.

"No. You could be right, but I don't think so. If you watch him carefully he seems to be examining the larger, older trees, and also the rocks that jut out of the ground all over the place. It's like he's reading clues—but I can't see what it is he's seeing."

After a few moments Lisa said, "Gerachti doesn't seem to share our confidence. I can't tell what he's saying to Belak back there, but he doesn't sound very pleased."

"Gerachti's a pain in the neck!" Wesley was indignant. "I don't like the guy, and I don't see why Alleophaz is so taken with him."

A moment later Gerachti crowded past Wesley and Lisa and made his way to Alleophaz. "My lord," they heard him say, "the child does not have any idea what he is doing! He is following a haphazard series of animal trails, purely according to his own fancies."

"Not at all, Gerachti!" said Alleophaz. "You have been too busy grumbling when you should have been observing. One can learn things from a child, you know. He is actually taking a great deal of care, and knows exactly what he is after. I notice that he focuses most on rocks and older trees. It could be the moss on the trees, but I doubt it because he keeps doubling back."

"Yes, that is just the point. We are probably going in circles."

"Not in the least. On the whole we are following a consistent course. In spite of the dips we are progressively gaining altitude. In spite of the twists and turns our general heading remains the same. It is toward Bamah and may well be by way of the upper road. Have you been keeping your eye on the sun?"

"I know nothing about celestial navigation."

Alleophaz laughed. "Then do not presume to criticize someone who is navigating expertly—though I wish I knew how he did it."

Just then a large rock forced the trail to skirt its sides. Kurt stopped and looked at the rock, smiled broadly, then nodded, and after a moment turned round a large tree and looked back almost in the direction that he had just been pursuing. "Yes, that's it," he breathed. "I think we may have to dismount."

By now Gerachti was back with Belak. They heard him say, "This is the height of absurdity."

As they followed Kurt round the tree, they saw what he was doing. A steeply sloping hill, which for the previous hundred yards had risen precipitously on their right-hand side, was now on their left. An almost invisible trail led upward. The going would be far from easy, partly because of the steepness of the ascent, and partly because of the narrowness of the trail.

"Are there no limits to this folly?" Gerachti demanded, furious.

Alleophaz stopped and turned to face him. "Stop behaving like a child! In Risgah, when I was looking for the three children I saw in my—whatever it was that happened to me—you insisted on hiring the three men. Perhaps it was as well you did, or we may never have met the children. These are the children. And they are guided by the same being who addressed me nearly two years ago. They know more about what we are doing than you or Belak or myself. Get rid of your absurd pride. It will precede a personal catastrophe if you do not."

Gerachti stared back at him, his lips pressed tightly together. Then he turned to Belak and muttered something.

"Please, Gerachti, *please!*" they heard Belak half whisper, half squeal.

For nearly half an hour they labored up the steep incline, and finally emerged onto a knife-edge ridge, just wide enough for them to mount and ride. There was no sense of height. Tall trees rose above their heads from the slopes on either side, giving them a sense of security. The trail led them along a meadow which broadened steadily, and for about three hours they hardly changed direction at all. Then, to their surprise, they saw a roadway curving out of a wood to join the direction in which their trail led. It was about six feet across, muddy, and bore the marks of horses' hooves.

Gerachti seemed pleased. He looked at Kurt. "Congratulations, young sir. You seem to have done better than I thought. Now we shall be able to follow the upper road."

Kurt looked startled. "No—I'm afraid not. We're going to have to descend again."

"Why?"

"Because it's the way we're supposed to go."

There was a long pause. Finally Gerachti said, "Well, it is not the way Belak and I will go. With your permission, my lord, we will take one of the pack horses and meet up with you in Bamah. I am grateful to have come this far with you, but I—"

"But you will proceed alone. Belak and the pack horses will stay with us," Alleophaz said quietly but firmly.

Gerachti's began to tremble, but with rage rather than fear. Then, in a husky voice he said, "Very good, my lord, may it go well with you all." He turned, not in the direction of Anthropos and of Bamah, but of Risgah—the port from which the three men had come. He spurred his horse to a gallop, and they watched him disappear along the road into the wood.

"Shall I continue, my lord?" Kurt asked eventually.

Alleophaz sighed. "Yes, we may as well. Lead on until we come across a spring, and we will stop for a drink."

They soon found one, and rested awhile after they had drunk from it, having first watered the horses and mules. They also splashed water over themselves.

The summer evening light was slowly fading.

"Have you thought how we shall spend the night?" Alleophaz asked. "We do have bedrolls."

"I suspect Gaal has a place for us to sleep—perhaps even a meal," Kurt said. "Maybe we'll find a Gaal tree. Uncle John told us about them. They're absolutely amazing." His eyes were sparkling and there was merriment playing around his mouth. Clearly his mood was buoyant.

Alleophaz said, "I gather from one of Kurt's remarks that you children have experience in caring for horses, as well as in riding them and harnessing."

"Yes, my lord," Wesley said.

"Very sensible. I think all children of your own station in life should be taught things of that sort. Tell me, for one gold Anthropos crown a day for each of you, would you consider taking care of the horses?"

"My lord, you cannot expect children of this sort to act as our servants!" Belak sounded distressed.

"No, I agree. But that is not what I intended. I doubt they have money with them, and they look like children who are accustomed to having plenty!"

"If only he knew!" Wes thought.

"What I am suggesting is that I provide them with a little pocket money, but that I would appreciate it if they would do something you or I do not know how to do. In any case—it is for them to decide."

"It's very generous of you," Wesley said. "We'll be delighted to do whatever we can, won't we, guys?"

The other two nodded. "Sure!" Kurt said.

Suddenly there came the sound of something or someone crashing through the wood toward them from above. Alleophaz leaped to his feet, but relaxed as Gerachti collapsed pale and panting before them.

"Thank the heavens I found you!" he cried. "We are hunted! Armed soldiers patrol the high road, soldiers from Anthropos—and they seek *us.*"

"Us?"

" 'Six humans with six horses and two pack animals' is all they knew. Their magicians have discovered us, and they believe our presence is a threat to the royal house."

"We seem to be getting a warmer welcome than we anticipated," Alleophaz said. "Tell us more. What happened to you?"

"Soon after I left you I saw spears glinting in the distance—a group of marching men. I took my horse into the trees, tied it, and returned to hide near the road. But next I heard the sound of a horse's hooves from the direction of Bamah. Then a lone officer stopped in front of me, dismounted, and sat down on the bank at the far side of the road.

"The platoon on foot stopped in front of the officer.

" 'Seen anything?' he asked them.

" 'No, sir!' the sergeant replied. 'However, we entered Risgah to learn if there was gossip. There was. We learned that three men and three helpers from Risgah are coming, all mounted and with two pack mules. Apparently the party took the lower road.'

" 'So! Excellent! Now we know what to do,' the officer replied. 'Return at once to Risgah, and offer a reward of one hundred gold crowns for the capture of these men. At least one section of the low road, we understand, is washed out and impassable. That means that either they will return to Risgah and follow this road, or else they will perish in the forest. You are to return to Risgah and look out for them. Chain them and manacle them when you find them.

" 'I am told there is only one route in the forest itself that gets you safely to Bamah. We know the exit point and have hidden a patrol there. But no living person knows the path, so we hardly expect them to emerge from it. What with bogs to suffocate men, and cliffs to fall over, and trails that lead you in circles until you die of starvation—

hardly anyone who enters it survives. Your orders are not to enter it *under any circumstances.'*"

Gerachti continued, "My lord, once they left I came back to warn you. There is unearthly power abroad—this is no place for us! Let us abandon this foolish quest and return to Risgah to take ship home!"

"And be arrested in Risgah by this patrol?" responded Alleophaz. "Many people in Risgah know us. We can hardly stay there unnoticed, and we might have to wait weeks for a ship. Remember, Anthropos and Playsion have a military alliance at present. Even if the soldiers fail to spot us, there are many citizens who would turn us in for a reward."

"Then what does my lord propose?"

"I propose, provided our guides are willing to proceed, to do what the being in my vision told me to do."

"But in Bamah we are in even greater danger."

"Possibly. But remember, I bear letters from our own sovereign. Manacles do not attract me, and we may well be arrested, but if so I would prefer to be arrested as close to Bamah as possible. Remember also that trade with our own country, Glason, is of very great advantage to Anthropos. The letters I bear propose an extension of our trade agreements, something, I imagine, that the Anthropos sovereign will leap at. We may find ourselves highly honored guests."

Gerachti sighed. "I hope so. But what of the perils in the forest?"

"So far we have done very well. For the moment I prefer the forest, with all its perils, to marching manacled and in chains along a highway."

Soon they were on their way again. For two hours Kurt led them obliquely downward, still moving in the direction of Bamah, but zigzagging for two hours in the waning light. Suddenly he stopped beside a closely placed group of poplars and spruce trees. "Listen!" he said. "I can hear the river." A smile broke over his face. "We're almost there." And, changing directions a little to the right, he led them past the trees and directly downhill.

Soon they had to dismount. They found themselves descending

into a dell covered with moss and graceful ferns. The trees were more widely spaced. Falling in a series of tiny waterfalls, a stream on their right ran downhill from a spring at the head of the dell, then plunged over a precipice ten yards to their left. The path led them by stepping-stones across the stream, where they saw a small cabin built curiously into the side of the hill. There was a railed balcony in front of it. Through the trees they could just see a glimpse of the river and the low road.

"Pleasant, but quite useless," Gerachti sneered, referring to the hut.

"We have not yet seen the inside," Belak responded brightly.

"What are we supposed to do?" Gerachti asked. "How can we sleep six in a place where there is hardly standing room for three?"

"Real wet blanket, isn't he?" Wesley said to Kurt and Lisa. "Nothing like having a drip with you on a trip through the wilds." Wesley, who hours before had feared to offend Gerachti, now despised him and did not bother to lower his voice. He turned his back on him, as Gerachti glared in his direction, and said, "Philosopher indeed! Well, I suppose even philosophers can be cowards!"

Kurt said, "I'm going to try the door."

He mounted the step on to the platform overlooking the cliff and turned the knob on the door. It opened easily and swung back silently. Kurt gave a yell. "I knew it! I knew it would be like this!" He turned to his brother and sister, a wide grin beneath his dancing eyes. "It's like Chocma's cottage—come and look!"

Alleophaz was already behind him, and the others followed. They encountered the same phenomenon that Uncle John had described in Gaal trees and that the children themselves had found in Chocma's cottage. The *inside* was infinitely larger than the *outside*. Beyond the door they found themselves inside a large and commodious stable, softly illuminated by lanterns hung round the walls. Eight roomy straw-filled stalls awaited the horses and mules. A feeding trough ran the length of the stalls, and a nearby stove bore one great cauldron of hot mash. At the far end stone steps led to an archway, beyond which a lighted hall could be seen.

Gerachti and Belak were still outside. Alleophaz strode to the door. "Bring the horses in here!" he called. "This is the most amazing thing I have ever seen! There is an enormous stable here—stalls and everything. Bring the horses!" He dived back inside.

"He is gone mad," Gerachti said.

"We might as well see what all the excitement is about!" Belak retorted, a look of intense interest on his face. He led his horse toward the door, then stopped and stared. "Gerachti!" he called. "It is true! Bring your horse!" Bewildered, Gerachti did so.

The children also tumbled out. "We'll take them all in," Wesley said. "We can unpack the mules once we get them inside. There's loads of room, and we can also rub them down before we feed them. This stable's like an attached garage—only much larger!" In no time at all they had the saddles and bridles off, and the pack mules unloaded and each animal in its own stall.

They began to rub the horses down. Lisa sighed. "I didn't realize how tired I was till we started on this." For a few more minutes they continued to work without speaking.

Then Wesley said, "D'you remember the scene in *The Sword in the Stone* where Wart has to wash all the dishes in the basement?"

"What about it?" Kurt asked.

"And the one in *Fantasia* where the magician's apprentice tries to work a spell to clean the place, but it goes wrong?"

"Uh-huh!"

"I know what you're going to say," Lisa giggled. "You're going to say, 'Wouldn't it be nice if Gaal did for us what Merlin did for Wart, and pronounced a spell by which the horses were rubbed down by magic.' But Gaal isn't like that."

"But it would be nice, wouldn't it?"

"Oh, sure, but—"

"I don't see why Gaal wouldn't have the horses rubbed down by magic. After all, he could. It would save a lot of energy for us. So why not?" Kurt asked.

"Uncle John is always talking about the difference between magic and the Changer's power," Lisa said. "I think this is probably an example. His power isn't just to make life easy for us."

Wesley was frowning. He said, "This place certainly does make life easy for us. I bet there will be bedrooms—like in the Gaal trees—and a good meal. But I know what you mean, Lisa. It wouldn't seem right for us to have *no* work. In any case, we're being paid a gold crown each, every day, for what we're doing. But I don't see any logical reason why Gaal wouldn't do things like that by magic."

"I'm not sure I can explain it either," Lisa sighed, "but I feel it would be all wrong. One of the ways he uses power is to show his love to us."

"It'd be very loving to do the horses for us!" Kurt grinned mischievously.

"No, it wouldn't. This way we become partners with him in his plan, whatever that plan is. And in any case I think he wants us to treat the horses the same way he treats us, to show them love and kindness. To animals we *are* the Changer."

"Still, it would be nice," Kurt said.

It took them another forty minutes to finish the animals, and another five minutes to ladle the hot mash into the long manger that ran the length of all their stalls. As they were finishing, Alleophaz poked his head through the door that led to the rest of the house.

"It's a bewilderingly large and well-appointed place," he said. "We are being entertained royally. A dining table in the next room is laid for six persons, but so far there's no food on the table. There are also bedrooms—all with soap, water, towels and other provisions for our comfort."

"I think the meal will be there when we're ready," Kurt said. "If you'll let us have a couple of minutes to freshen up, my lord, we'll be as quick as we can."

"Choose whichever room you wish," Alleophaz said. "They are all the same."

All three children hastened to get ready for supper.

6
Mary Hangs On

While helping Lord and Lady Nasa pack their baggage for the journey to Bamah, Mary saw a box with holes in it. "What've you got in that box?" she asked.

"Ah, yes." Lady Roelane looked at it with little interest. "That is the pigeon."

"The pigeon?" Mary asked frowning. "Is it a pet?"

"No, it is a messenger pigeon—to release it, Risano told us, when we are within a day's journey from Bamah. Apparently we could encounter difficulties if we arrive at the palace unannounced."

"Oh? Why?"

"Risano did not say. It probably has something to do with a difference of opinion between the king and queen. The queen knows we are coming—evidently she understands all the ancient prophecies, and our visit this time seems to be included in one of them. Anyway, she wants to be sure that we are *her* guests, and have her royal protection."

"Does the queen believe all those ancient prophecies?"

"Yes, Mary, I believe she does."

But Mary was also thinking of another queen whose acquaintance she had made, Queen Suneidesis. Queen Suneidesis also believed in the histories and prophecies contained in the ancient book. Mary remembered how in the presence of Queen Suneidesis she had decided to forsake her attachment to a terrible witch and to place her trust in Gaal. "I guess this queen must be on Gaal's side also," she mused silently. "I wonder what made me switch from her side to his. I must have been crazy. I must not, must not, must *not* switch again." But there was an uncomfortable feeling inside her that the switch had not been crazy, though her present course was.

The journey to Bamah from Rapunzel's Tower took several days. And for every one of those days they were guided by the strange column of smoke and blue fire. A sense of awe possessed them as it led them through untrodden paths in the forest. "What is this wondrous thing that guides us?" Lord Nasa asked on the first day. "It seems more like a *being* than a *thing!*"

"I feel almost afraid of it!" said the Lady Roelane. "Yet my fear differs from other fear. What if it is a form of a being we ought to worship? Is it a spirit of light, or is it Gaal himself?"

Mary disliked it. "At night when you can see the blue fires inside it, it reminds me of—of someone I once knew."

Sometimes they camped at night, and at other times they slept in Gaal trees—trees whose trunks one can enter, only to find how enormous they are inside. It was Mary's first experience of Gaal trees, and she decided that she did not like them. She slept poorly, wondering whether Gaal would repeat his unpleasant visit. The first three or four days were also painful, for riding side-saddle was not easy. She was still on edge, and her horribly stiff back ached until she became used to the horse's motion.

For long days they followed a winding path southeast through the forest. As they rode, Mary's feelings about her two companions gradually began to change. She had set out from Rapunzel's Tower very determined not to let the two grown-ups affect her. "They're not going to lecture me about witchcraft. I won't take it!" she muttered to herself. "My life is my own, an' I'm gonna do what I like. I'm not in Winnipeg now. Someday they'll realize what I am."

But keeping them at arm's length was not easy, and as day followed day Mary became progressively more friendly. For one thing, the two adults aroused her curiosity by their behavior.

At one point the Lady Roelane had ridden a little ahead of her husband and Mary. Lord Nasa said, "There is something I wish to discuss with the Lady Roelane. Will you excuse me while I join her?"

"You gonna talk about me?" Mary asked.

Lord Nasa grinned happily, though Mary thought his face flushed a little. "We could do so, I imagine! I did not think of that. No, Lady Mary, we have other matters to discuss." He still seemed slightly embarrassed—but somehow Mary knew that he was not embarrassed at the idea of talking about her behind her back. Still, she was annoyed.

"Well, I can't stop you if that's what you want to do. An' I don't intend to spy on you," she replied ungraciously.

His lordship looked keenly at her but said nothing, riding ahead a little to join the Lady Roelane.

After that, Mary watched them closely—not only when they rode ahead, but when the three of them were together again. They seemed to laugh a lot, and were forever grinning at each other, as though they were enjoying secret jokes. "It can't be just about me," Mary pondered, confused. "They seem—well, happy. Like two kids." She thought about the way her stepmother used to behave with her boy-friends. "They must be in love. That's it. Mebbe they haven't been married long enough yet."

On the third day of their journey the Lord Nasa confirmed her suspicions when he said, "You must pardon us if we behave foolishly. We, just like this Uncle John and his bride that you have been telling us about, have not been wed many weeks." Suddenly Mary's patronizing attitude drained away. She no longer felt grown up, but empty, lonely and very left out. "Everybody has someone to belong to," she thought. "Well, I'll *make* Uncle John be a real uncle! Or I'll do something to these two. There must be spells I could use."

Yet she could not really object to the behavior of the young married couple. Most of the time they did not leave her out of their conversations. They would include her, point things out to her, ask her about her life. And sometimes she would catch a glimpse of one or the other of them looking at her with what, she was almost sure, was a look of compassion or affection.

"It's nice that they're in love," she thought. "I hope they stay like that. Why do grown-ups have to fall *out* of love so quickly?" She was still thinking of her stepmother's many affairs.

She almost began to wish she and the newlyweds were on the same side. In fact the more she got to know the Lady Roelane, the more she liked her. Soon they were spending a good deal of time together, so much so that the Lady once said laughingly, "I think I must spend more time talking to my husband, or he might grow jealous of you."

She even found herself softening toward the young man she had once seen as a popinjay. She began to catch his little jokes as he teased the Lady Roelane. Once when she watched him chase Lady Roelane, she found herself saying, "You're funny!" and grinning delightedly as she spoke. She remembered a saying of her stepmother's and repeated it in her mind: "I suppose everyone loves a lover." But since thinking about her stepmother always made her sad, she switched back quickly to thinking of Lord Nasa. "I feel kind of fond of him," she thought. "I wish—oh, phooey—a fat lot of good wishing will do me. *I must get hold of a good book of spells.*"

Mary sighed. She had a feeling that the people she was really beginning to like would never approve of her dark ambitions to control people by magic. "But if I'm to get anywhere, I gotta act. I mustn't start getting soft," she told herself. "No one increases in supernatural power that way. I've got to hang on, I've got to hang on!"

"*Gotta hang on, gotta hang on!*" She began to say the words rhythmically as a sort of inner chant, repeating them endlessly till they drove other thoughts and feelings away. Yet she could never overcome the growing tension inside her. For the longer she was with them, the more she wanted to be close to them, to have them like her. Somehow, and in spite of her plans for Uncle John, she knew it would be wrong to use magic to make these people like her. (It is curious, of course, how the plans you have for people always seem different when you are in their actual presence. You never quite say the things you felt sure you could. Nor do you put into practice the things you were sure you would, once you are facing them.) Therefore she had to work on her feelings extra hard, and would chant her "gotta hang on" chant furiously to herself.

They emerged from the forest on the fourth morning to see a wide river valley at a point where a stone bridge crossed the river. At this point the column silently disappeared.

Without crossing the bridge, they followed a dirt road south for three more days to Bamah. Even Mary missed the blue column once it was gone, for it seemed as though they had lost a member of their small party. Lord Nasa frowned. "It was not just an it. It is like losing a guide."

But the river was to be their guide from this point on. Most days were fine, but there were rainy days, too. On those days they were especially grateful if they were able to sleep in a Gaal tree, though Mary's discomfort at being inside a Gaal tree never lessened. And finally, what she had dreaded happened—inside a Gaal tree.

Whether she was awake or dreaming she was not quite sure. But one night she was aware of *him* standing again beside her bed. This time his eyes were gentle as he looked deep inside her, and his voice was filled with tenderness. "You still belong to me, Mary. I have not let you go, nor will I ever release you to the horrors of darkness. This time I will break the deeper spell by which your mother tried to bind you to her fate. But first you must discover your revulsion of what you are vainly, and in ignorance, trying to choose."

Mary screamed in blind terror, and her own scream woke her from her dream. It was daylight, and morning sunlight streamed through her window. She was perspiring and trembling, and could not shake her memories all that day.

Then came the moment when they were less than a day's journey from the ancient and evil city of Bamah. That morning Lord Nasa opened a door in the pigeon's box and coaxed the bird out. It hopped out of its box and took flight, circling over their heads once and vanishing over the treetops off in the direction of Bamah.

Mary sighed as she saw it go, and sadness stole over her. Her feelings were confused. She had particularly enjoyed the company of her new friends during the previous two days. She found it hard to say which of them she liked better. She felt something akin to adoration for the Lady Roelane, and had told herself, "If only my real mother had been like that!" At the same time Lord Nasa filled her with admiration. "I can't think why I was so down on him at first," she mused. "He reminds me of someone—mebbe Uncle Alan." Uncle Alan had been one of her stepmother's boy-friends. He always smelled of cigars and whiskey, and he scratched her face with his whiskers when he kissed her. Yet she had always been fond of Uncle Alan—the one man who had brought her comfort in the strange life of that Toronto apartment. He had never tried to do the awful things one or two of the others had.

She turned her thoughts ahead to the palace. Her heart beat faster as she thought of the possibility of making contact with powerful sorcerers. What secrets might she learn from them? But—and this was the painful part—what would Lord Nasa and Lady Roelane think?

"It'll never work," she thought. "They'd be sure to find out. Well, I don't care! Let them find out!"

The trouble was that she *did* care and care very much. In spite of all her efforts to stay aloof, she knew she had grown too fond of both of them. So all that day, as sunshine danced on the dappled waters of the Rure and the late summer breezes of Anthropos helped to cool them, she repeated her lines until she was almost hypnotized: *"Gotta hang on, gotta hang on, gotta hang on . . . !"*

They ate lunch beside the river while the horses grazed on the lush grass. The Rure flowed gently south, murmuring softly and musically.

The wind was still, so that there was none of the rushing sound that came when it played its various games, some wild, some more gentle, with the trees. A fly buzzed annoyingly round them, though Mary hardly noticed it. Her anxiety slowly mounted the nearer they got to Bamah.

She frowned, swallowed what she was eating (her manners had improved during the journey) and asked, "Are you sure it will be O.K. at the palace? I mean, it sounds grim if the queen is having rows with the king."

"Let us hope the pigeon does what it is supposed to do," Lord Nasa said thoughtfully. "Anyway, we will find out when we get there."

"What's it all about, anyway?"

"Queen Suneid is Anthroponian—descended from the Regents and is pure-blooded Regenskind. King Tobah Khukah is from Playsion, and Playsion is in rebellion against the High Emperor," Lord Nasa explained. "The king wants to introduce the religious beliefs of Playsion, which the Emperor has warned against. Many people in Anthropos also are following this false religion. But the queen is ardently loyal to the Emperor."

The Lady Roelane cleared her throat. "We do not altogether understand what is going on. Risano explained a little, but there are many gaps in our understanding. One of the problems concerns the queen's prophetic powers."

Mary caught her breath. She did not know why the words *prophetic powers* should affect her so shockingly, but she found it hard to breathe. Her heart began to thump in her chest, yet she managed to say almost calmly, "What do you mean?"

"It would seem that the Emperor communicates with her—"

"Oh, I see. I thought you meant she had some kind of supernatural power. You mean he writes her letters and stuff."

"No, my dear. I suppose you would have to call it—how do you say it?—'supernatural stuff.' No one has ever seen the Emperor. It is as though he talks to her spirit."

Mary felt dizzy. "You mean she has ways of knowing things—things ordinary people don't know?"

Lady Roelane nodded.

Lord Nasa said, "She knows, for instance, that the Emperor is going to bring terrible disasters on Playsion, and on Anthropos too, unless his majesty the king awakens to reality and ceases to worship the dark lords."

Mary was still having difficulty breathing, yet she managed to speak. "The Emperor sounds like a monster!"

"It may sound like that, but I do not think so. He knows the plans the evil powers have for the two countries, and unless they return their loyalty to him their fate at the hands of the dark lords will be far worse," Lord Nasa said.

"How do you know that the evil powers are evil? Why do you two take sides?"

Lady Roelane spoke quietly, and as Mary turned she found herself looking directly into her steady gaze. The older woman was smiling quizzically. "Mary, you have already taken sides. You know yourself the difference between good and evil."

For several minutes nobody spoke. Mary stared blankly at the surface of the flowing water, hardly noticing what she was looking at. Her heart was still pounding, and she was having difficulty with her breathing. She felt sure her face was getting blotchy, as it did when her heart and breathing went "out of whack." Eventually she said, "How much power does the queen have? Is she hot stuff?"

"We do not know her very well. We have yet to spend time with her, you know," Lady Roelane replied.

"But suppose you're walking into a trap. Some of the king's sorcerers might have real power."

Lord Nasa smiled. "Let us say we do not mind an adventure. And— well, we like truth."

Mary would never forget the afternoon ride that followed. Her fear grew greater with every mile. What would happen when they got there? Would the queen see through her? Did she already know about her? If so, what would she do? What could she do if the queen knew her secrets? Would she be able to make contact with the sorcerers?

Or, supposing the king got to them first. Would he put them in jail? She could, of course, explain that she was really on *his* side. But would he believe her? And how could she do it without her new friends finding out? She squirmed inside as she thought of it. "I'm supposed to be able to kick my best friends in the teeth if they stand in the way of my having power," she mused. "That's the way you get power. What's wrong with me?" Frantically she began on her mantra again, *"Gotta hang on, gotta hang on, gotta hang on."* But in her heart of hearts she knew she was continuing to lose ground in her struggle.

Late in the afternoon they emerged from the forest to see the walls of Bamah on the hill above them. The road led up the hill to the city gates, where two other roads converged—one from the south, and another from a bridge over the Rure. They noticed that uniformed officials guarded the far side of the bridge and were conversing with people before allowing them to cross it and approach the city. There was a similar holdup at the point where the road from the south emerged from the forest.

"What is the explanation of this state of affairs, I wonder?" Lord Nasa mused, frowning.

Slowly they followed the road upward, staring at the open city gate. "We enter by those gates, and follow the street facing us to the palace," he added, pointing ahead.

Hardly had the words left his mouth than they heard distant shouting from their right. Seven or eight uniformed horsemen emerged from the forest they had just left. The leading horseman was waving at them, and galloping hard toward them. Lord Nasa drew rein. "Soldiers—probably a patrol. I wonder what they want."

The three remained stationary but turned toward the approaching horsemen. Mary felt the choking sensation in her throat increase. She grew dizzy, and fought for breath. "I hope it's not trouble," she whispered hoarsely.

"We might be required to explain your presence," Lord Nasa replied. "If we tell them you have come from another world and another

time, it may complicate things. Forgive me—but you must henceforth be a niece of mine from overseas—"

Mary kept behind them both, bowing her head so that they would not see the look of alarm she could not keep from her face. The leading horseman soon reached them, and his followers were hard on his heels. The young lieutenant bowed. "My lord, ladies, please pardon our unseemly haste, and our shouting to you. His majesty the king today issued instructions to identify all visitors to Bamah and to inquire about their business here. It would appear that enemies of Anthropos and of his majesty may be on their way to the city. Who are your lordships, and where are you from?"

Lord Nasa laughed merrily. "Enemies indeed! No, lieutenant. We are no enemies of Anthropos. I am the Lord Nasa of Chereb, and this is my new wife, the Lady Roelane."

Though he was still on horseback, the lieutenant took off his hat with a flourish and gave a half bow. "I am honored to meet your lordship. Even here in Anthropos we have heard of your fame and goodness." He bowed also to the Lady Roelane.

"We are just returning from my territories overseas," Lord Nasa continued, "having spent our honeymoon on an island off the north coast. From there we proceeded to an ancient tower in the forest for a few days, where we were joined by my niece from other lands. We are here at the queen's invitation. She requested that we arrive today."

"From the forest tower? Are the legends of the magic there true—and you come at her majesty's invitation?"

"Just so."

"Your lordship will pardon me, but I am afraid it will be necessary for me to accompany you to the city gate, where we will await confirmation of your visit from the palace. I regret this, and assure you that all will be well, but I am under orders to accompany all significant visitors."

Mary's heart sank, but the Lord Nasa smiled easily, saying, "You must certainly do your duty. As for ourselves, we will think of you as our guard of honor."

7

A Growing Madness

As Kurt had predicted, a meal awaited them inside the dining room that lay beyond the stables. On the table were roast beef, roast chicken and fresh fried salmon. There were roast potatoes, boiled potatoes and steamed wild rice, and all the condiments you can imagine. There were hot cooked vegetables, and two or three intriguing salads. Several silver platters were piled high with fruits. A jug of wine had been set beside each plate, and with each jug an intricately carved silver chalice.

But it was an uncomfortable meal, eaten largely in silence, since Gerachti's strange behavior dried conversation like an electric hot plate sizzles a drop of water. He spoke to no one, and took no notice of remarks addressed to him. He was not trying to be rude, but was gripped by paralyzing terror. His eyes were glazed, zombielike, as though he was unaware of his surroundings. His fear had begun as he entered the strange little cabin and found it was no cabin at all.

Belak described it to Wesley. "He just stopped at the entrance, staring. All the color drained from his face, and he looked gray. He was sweating and trembling a little. I had a grim time getting him to come inside, and he has not spoken since."

Kurt had asked for the roast potatoes, which were in front of Gerachti, and asked again when there was no response. "Mr. Gerachti, sir, would you please pass the potatoes?" After receiving no response he repeated, "Mr. Gerachti, sir . . ."

Alleophaz reached for them and passed them to Kurt. Everyone else pretended not to notice, but the tension remained.

Gerachti ate nothing but poured himself chalice after chalice of wine as Alleophaz watched him anxiously. Finally, after the fifth full chalice had been poured, he said, "Gerachti, do you not think you had better get something on your stomach?"

Gerachti began to drink his fifth chalice.

"It's all right, my lord," Wesley said hurriedly. "He won't get drunk. It's Anthropos wine. Playsion wine will make you drunk if you drink enough, but you could drink gallons of Anthropos wine and nothing would happen. It puts joy in your heart, but that's all. You don't act crazy. You may slur your words, or stagger a bit, but there's absolutely no hangover."

Gerachti did not look joyful. Indeed it was impossible to judge from his masklike face whether he was feeling anything at all. Only the slight tremor of his hands and head revealed his fear. Just then he rose to his feet and left the room without a word, descending the steps into the stable. Alleophaz said, "I will make sure he is all right." He excused himself and followed Gerachti.

He returned five minutes later, saying, "He is all right for now. Once we have finished the meal, perhaps you could come with me, Belak, and we will try to get him to talk. I think I know what the trouble is."

They finished the meal in silence. It was a pity, because the meal was a glorious meal, and normally they would have eaten it as a celebration. What could have been a party turned out to be more like a funeral supper or a wake.

After Alleophaz and Belak left, Kurt said, "Let's sit round the fire." There was a huge open fireplace where logs crackled invitingly. Leather chairs and settees were arranged comfortably round it.

"What about the dishes?" Wesley asked, an anxious expression on his face.

"There's no place to wash them, and no place to store them once they're washed," Lisa said. "I've looked, and there's just nowhere."

So they sat down around the fireplace, and did not notice (for at least a couple of hours) that the supper table was instantly cleared of tablecloth, utensils and food. They simply vanished, leaving only a dark table of polished oak. (Later they puzzled over the fact that the children had been obliged to rub the horses down, but had not had to wash dishes. But for the present there were more immediate concerns.)

"That Gerachti is a pain in the neck," Wesley grumbled. "He seemed so arrogant at first—arrogant, but together, at least. It turns out that he's a neurotic wimp."

Lisa said, "Mum says arrogant people are often scared underneath. She talks about the armor of contempt that some people wear, and says they have spines of jelly which nobody ever sees. They're insecure, really."

"Well, Gerachti certainly is. He's a drip. I don't know how you kept your cool this afternoon, Kurt," said Wesley.

"He didn't bother me that much," Kurt said.

Wesley frowned. "You know, Dad's pretty arrogant. I wonder if *he's* scared underneath. What is there to be scared of? You know, if you think about it, Mom's always sort of soothing and managing him. What bothers me is that he's a bit like Gerachti."

"More than a bit. They're very alike," Lisa murmured softly.

"Oh, this is depressing talk," Wesley grumbled. "Let's talk about something else. Kurt, why don't you tell us about the way you led us through the forest. You did splendidly, I must say. How did you know which way to take?"

"It was the pillar of smoke," Kurt said.

"I could see nothing," replied Wesley.

Lisa laughed. "Are you serious, Kurt?" She frowned. "Yes, you are. You must be. I remember how sure you were when we were on the road by the river. But I couldn't see a thing!"

"Nor I," Wesley said. "Not a thing. What did it look like?"

"Well, it varied, and once or twice I lost sight of it altogether. Sometimes it was brilliant and clear, and at other times I could hardly see it—an' when it faded I had a feeling it was my fault—as though I wasn't seeing it properly."

"Your fault? How could it have been your fault?"

"I don't know. It just felt that way, as though I wasn't on the right wavelength or something. Then, late this afternoon, when the light began to fade, it slowly turned blue, like the lighted blue fog we were in earlier today with Gaal in that 'outside of time' place. I supposed that meant we were near shelter."

"Weren't you scared?" Lisa asked. "I mean, a column of smoke that you can't always see clearly, and that nobody else can see at all, is hardly a solid basis for leading someone through a notorious forest."

"Yeah, I was scared—at first, anyway. But once I started I was stuck with it. If it had disappeared I could never have found the way back."

"But how did you know it wasn't just your own imagination?" Wesley asked.

"I didn't!" Kurt almost shouted. "That was my biggest worry."

"You didn't? So why did you follow it?"

"Because there was only one way to find out whether it was real or not. And that was to act, to follow it."

"But the *risk*—"

"I know. I could have looked like a fraud or an idiot, and all of us could have gotten lost. But once I'd committed myself, there I was!"

"Whew! I admire your guts," Wesley said. "How come Lisa and I don't get wonderful experiences like that? What do you have that we don't? I'm green with envy."

Kurt laughed. "Mebbe your turn is coming."

"But the privilege, Kurt! It looked like a brilliant performance."

"It felt awful at first, anyway. I know I put on a brave front, but—I guess I can admit it now—I was terribly afraid. Mind you, I was excited as well. It's hard to describe. That's why I ignored Gerachti, though he might have been right, because I was so unsure. In any case, I had other things to worry about right then. And sometimes at those points the column would become clearer again."

There was a pause as the three found themselves staring at the flames in the fireplace. Lisa was beginning to get a little drowsy. Suddenly she remembered something, frowned and became excited.

"Wait a minute, Kurt. What about all those times when you would look at the trees, especially the large, older trees, and the outcroppings of rock? You would be puzzled for a moment, look at some huge chunk of rock and break into a smile. You would nod to yourself and go forward. We were all watching you, weren't we, Wes? Once or twice you even said, 'Yes, we're on the right track'!"

"Oh, yes! The rocks and the old trees! I don't know what I'd have done without them."

"You mean," Wesley asked him, "you mean that there were signs indicating which way to go? We looked but we had no idea what you were seeing. What was it?"

Kurt's face changed. "No-o-oh. No, it wasn't like that at all. They weren't pointing the way, at least not in the way you mean."

"So what was it you saw?"

Again a smile broke over Kurt's face. "It was incredible! You remember our last visit to Anthropos? Remember the two years we spent in Nephesh Palace after we got back from Mirmah's Kingdom of Ice? In the evenings when the women were weaving the tapestry Queen Suneidesis would sometimes read to us—"

"Yes—from that ancient book of the laws and history of Anthropos," Wesley said.

"That's it. Parts of it were deadly dull—"

"Oh, I don't know!" Lisa interrupted. "To me it was all terribly interesting—even the Wise Sayings!"

"I liked the history parts, the battles and so on, and all those weird visions," Wesley said.

"Well, yes, there were parts of it that I liked too," Kurt said, "but there was something about the whole book that got to me. I could tell that Gaal or the Changer or someone was behind the writing of it. It was ancient. If it was magic, it was *solid* magic, magic I could bet my life on. I knew it must be true! Even the boring parts were true—an' they would never change. They were fixed because they were true. I can't really put it into words." He shook his head, unable to explain the depth of his feelings.

"So what does that have to do with the rocks and the older trees?"

"Well, whenever I looked at an ancient rock outcropping or one of those big old trees, a sentence from the book would come back to me. I could sort of hear the queen reading it all over again."

"Sentences? What kind of sentences?"

"Well, one was 'Follow me.' Another was 'If you follow me I will never abandon you.' "

"I still don't quite understand," Lisa said. "Why would the rocks and trees do that?"

"It was because they were like the book. Old. Solid. Reliable. Unchangeable. Something I could be sure of. They reminded me of the Emperor himself. I had the feeling that they came from the same source as the book, that nothing would ever change those rocks and that the trees would stand forever—like *he* would. Then, as I thought about that same quality in the book, I would remember some sentence or other from it."

"I think I'm beginning to understand," Wesley said. "You'd be reminded of the book, and the sentences from the book would encourage you."

"And how! I'd already guessed the column of smoke was from Gaal. It was like he was saying, 'Trust me. I'm not going to fool you. I'm not going to leave you in the lurch!' "

"Oh, now I see," Lisa said.

"Once the sentence was 'I know the route you are taking, and when you have come through your test, you will be as tough as steel!' It was like he was speaking to me, telling me everything was O.K. I couldn't help smiling when that happened, so I kept on looking at the big trees and the old rocks to see their solidness. And every time I did there would be another sentence. Once it was a warning: 'I have shown you the right path. Do not turn aside to the right or to the left.' "

Then Wesley noticed that Alleophaz was standing and listening to their conversation, giving the impression that he had heard a great deal. Alleophaz said, "Belak begs you to excuse him. He is weary and has retired."

"How is Gerachti?" Wesley asked. He had been about to say, "How is that idiot Gerachti?" but thought better of the impulse.

Alleophaz sighed and sat down on one of the settees. "Not good. But he is sleeping now. I gave him a powder I carry with me, and he took it with water. But he was almost insane with terror."

"Why?" Lisa asked.

"You would have to know him to understand," Alleophaz said. "Gerachti's philosophy begins with the foundation of the universe. He maintains that the universe was formed by a supreme god, who made vegetation on our world, the animals and human beings. This god did it all miraculously, but for some reason has stopped doing miracles."

"Why?"

"Gerachti is not sure. All he knows is that he has stopped."

"Then what is he scared of?"

"Magic. You see, although he did not believe you at first, he believes now that you have tremendous, magical powers."

"But we don't!" Kurt said. "It's not us, it's Gaal—or the Changer—or someone."

"I know that, but Gerachti does not. He is almost crazy with fear of you, Kurt. He sees you as having the power of a major sorcerer. And he sees sorcery as evil. After all, you have created a spell that has produced a hut on the outside and a mansion on the inside."

"Oh, for crying out loud! I haven't produced this place! There's no way I could. I don't know a thing about magic."

"No. But you follow this Gaal person obediently, and you trust him. And it is because of that that these miraculous events take place."

"That's right—"

"Well, to Gerachti that is magic. And you control it. As far as he is concerned it can only be magic because his 'god' is no longer a performer of miracles. So all miracles have to be magic. And to Gerachti, magic is that 'deadly, potent evil'—an irrational force that will destroy humankind!"

"And he really is scared?" Lisa asked.

"Deathly afraid. After all, you must admit that this place is either a most wonderful miracle or else a supremely powerful piece of magic. If it is a miracle, then this god is still working. If it is magic, then the magician is deadly dangerous."

Kurt asked, "And which do *you* think it is?"

At the same instant, Wesley said, "It's not the miracle that impresses us—though, sure, it *does*—but the incredible kindness and thoughtfulness of Gaal. He's like that."

"Yes, Wesley, I am beginning to see that. And, yes, Kurt, I am much more inclined to see it as a miracle. But you are all going to have to tell me more. It seems you are not from this world. Or are you? Doors between worlds are not unknown. And you refer to names like 'Uncle John,' and a certain queen and an ancient book, and a 'Gaal' and a 'Changer.' Maybe you had better begin at the beginning and tell me all you know."

Wesley sighed. "Yes. I guess there's no point in keeping our plans secret now. To tell you the truth, we have none. Our assignment is to rescue a young king, but from what or whom we do not know. We were told that three men would hire us—and here we are with you and on our way to Bamah."

"Yes. But tell me about your previous visits."

They had planned an early night, but all thought of it had now drained out of their minds. So, interrupting each other constantly, they told him about Uncle John, their first two visits to Anthropos, and Mary and her attempt to pursue Uncle John and his new wife. They also described what they knew about Uncle John's two visits as a British schoolboy, one of the visits being at the dawn of Anthropos time.

"We are not even sure what period we've landed in," Wesley said. "This popping in and out of Anthropos history is confusing. Somehow I think we're in an earlier period than the last time we were here."

"I know little about Anthropos history," Alleophaz said, "but I am wondering about one thing." There were almost no logs left and the fire was beginning to burn low. A sleepy mood began to settle over them again.

Wesley roused himself. "And what is the one thing you are wondering, my lord?" he asked.

"I am wondering," replied Alleophaz, "whether the child who is going to change the world's history and the boy king you are to rescue are one and the same person."

Startled, Kurt sat up. "You know, I bet you're right, my lord. I bet that's why we've been brought together—to look for the same child." Then the glazed look returned to his eyes.

For several minutes they sat in silence. Finally Alleophaz said, "You all look as though the discussion should stop right there. I think it is time we all went to bed."

So to bed they went.

But Wesley could not sleep. Eventually, still wearing navy-blue pajamas, he put his shoes on and made his way through the stable onto the balcony of the hut. For a while he leaned against the balcony rail. It was a warm night, and the stars shone clear against the velvet blackness of the night sky. Wesley drew in a deep breath, and as he did so, became conscious of somebody else's breathing—the heavy breathing of someone sleeping. "Gerachti. It must be Gerachti," he murmured to himself. But where was he? Peering around in the dimness, he saw no one.

The sound seemed to be coming from his left, and from below the balcony. "He must have been scared. He's on the ground beside the hut," he muttered.

He stared down in the direction of the road and river, but all he could see was the trees that rose in front of the hut. "We could see between them when we arrived," he thought. "I guess it's too dark now."

His thoughts turned to what had robbed him of sleep. "I shouldn't be jealous of Kurt, but I am. I meant what I said after supper. He handled himself magnificently today. An' I'm proud of him—he was terrific. But how come he gets to see things an' I don't? Why not me, too?" He bit his lip angrily. "I can't sleep. It's because I'm mad, mad that he gets to do it, an' I don't. Is he better than me? Does Gaal have favorites?"

He changed his position slightly and started. A flickering orange-yellow light caught his eye. What was it? Where was it? Down below on the road? A fire? A *campfire*?

His thoughts went to the armed patrols. Was there a patrol camped below them? What should he do? Ought he to go down to investigate? But was there a way down the cliff? How could he find his way back?

Below him, near the foot of the cliff, a column of pale blue light appeared. Relief swept through his whole body and tears came to his eyes. "He's letting me see it too," he thought as gladness bubbled up in his head.

"I must waken Alleophaz," he murmured. He hurried inside, knocked on the door of the room where Alleophaz slept, and opened it. A lamp burned dimly beside the bed and Alleophaz sat up. "Hullo! Who is it?"

"It's me, Wesley. I think there is a camp of soldiers on the road below us. I thought I'd better let you know."

"Thank you. Perhaps we should get a closer look. But how would we get down there?"

Gladness stole over Wesley again. "I can see the column myself, now. It's pale blue light, and I'm sure it will guide us down."

Alleophaz leaped out of bed, wearing a long white nightshirt with lace ruffles at the neck and wrists. "I have a dark cloak that will cover this. And I see you are wearing something dark. Give me a moment to get my boots on."

In two minutes they were on the balcony again. "Ah, yes! I can see the fire—it *is* a fire, I am sure," Alleophaz said.

"And here's the column," Wesley said delightedly. "It's right here on the balcony, waiting to guide us down."

"It is? Then I am afraid you will have to lead us, just as your brother did today, for I can see nothing. It is difficult enough right here where there is a little starlight, but the darkness beyond will be impossible for me. I will put my hand on your shoulder so you can guide me. Hopefully, no one else will see the column either."

One behind the other, walking slowly and carefully, they made their way along a sloping path cut into the rock of the cliff face. The pathway was illuminated by the light from the blue column, in Wesley's eyes at least. To Alleophaz it was, he said, all blackness. Among the trees it was mostly downhill, though they crossed the stream again and ascended a little on the far side of it. Then the path led steeply down, so much so that they would stumble from time to time, having a difficult job not to go hurtling down. Wesley could not discern any trail, but the blue light never faltered, and they were never impeded by undergrowth.

Wesley's heart sang, sang so loudly that he almost burst into song himself. He was deliriously happy. He was playing a real part in the adventure, and he could see the column. He shivered with ecstatic exultation, wondering if the column was Gaal, and whether he should address it. But he decided it probably wasn't, and he shouldn't. In any case they were getting closer to the road, where the steepness of the slope eased.

Finally, the column stopped and disappeared, leaving them on a level place on top of a high bank. They looked down on a large and blazing fire on the far side of the road, where an open area stretched between the road and the river. Horses were tethered there, and they could hear the sound of music and men's voices singing. One soldier played a shepherd's flute, and another a stringed instrument not unlike a lute. The other thirty men were singing.

Then an officer appeared out of the shadows, bearing a partly opened roll of parchment that gleamed and flickered with reflected firelight. The singing died down as the men saw him.

Some of the men began to scramble to their feet. "At ease, men, you may remain seated," the officer said. "We have new orders from Bamah. It seems that his majesty the king has the same kind of problem that some of us have with our womenfolk—they do not do what we tell them to." There was a low rumble of embarrassed laughter. "But we men stick together, and we are the king's men, not the queen's. However, it is true that among the statutes of Anthropos is one that gives her majesty the queen the right to dispose of her own prisoners, independently of the king.

"It appears that the queen does not share the king's view as to the danger to the monarchy of the six people crossing Playsion at the moment on their way to Bamah. In attempt to thwart his majesty, the queen has charged her personal bodyguard with the task of capturing these six strangers to prevent his majesty from beheading them. If she succeeds, his majesty will have no authority to intervene. We are therefore charged to redouble our efforts to capture these invaders."

At that point his tone became more serious. "Men, I am well aware that the queen is popular, and that his majesty is not. The fact that his majesty is also descended from the royal house of Playsion is irrelevant. He is now King of Anthropos. You have sworn oaths of loyalty to him personally, and from his purse comes your pay. Any man found slack in his efforts to capture the invaders will be dealt with, and with the utmost severity."

There was a low sound of shuffling feet and adjusting positions.

"That is all for now, men. Lay out your bedrolls and get some sleep, for we have an early start. Geradach and Pelanti will replace the current sentries, and will keep the fire going during the first watch. Belarich and Vortic will stand the second watch. That is all men. Good night!"

"Good night, sir!"

Wesley was again aware of blue light around him. He turned and saw that the lighted column had begun to move back along the way they had come. They rose and resumed their way, but had not gone more than two paces before Alleophaz tripped and fell with a shout of pain. Wesley turned quickly. Over the dim and crouching silhouette of Alleophaz, black against the firelight, he could see that both the men and the officers had frozen. He heard the officer cry out, "Torches, men! Sergeant, take 'A' watch to the far side of the stream, and comb the hillside. I will lead 'B' watch on this side. Remember the reward—a hundred gold crowns for the capture of any one of the six!"

In the dark, Wesley whispered, "Can you get up?"

"I will try," Alleophaz answered very softly. He limped to his feet. "It is my ankle, but I can still hobble. Let us go!"

From the far side of the road they could hear the drum of running feet. The blue column was still moving slowly. It seemed in no hurry, but Wesley, so elated only minutes before, could think only of moving as fast as they could. Alleophaz hobbled behind him with gasps of pain, his hand gripping Wesley's shoulder tightly. They gained the trees again and began the slow ascent. "Remember, we are being guided," Alleophaz encouraged. "The soldiers have to both search for us and find their own way up this slope."

In spite of their slow pace, the sounds of the soldiers began to die behind them. They were still on a very easy slope, and continued with their slow progress for several minutes.

"I think we're going to make it. How d'you feel?" Wesley asked.

"There is much pain!" gasped Alleophaz. "If they get too close, you had better go on ahead."

Just then they heard a shout from the officer below, too near for comfort. They hobbled a few more paces, as Alleophaz gripped Wesley's shoulder with the grip of a man in uncontrollable agony.

"Oh, Gaal," Wes cried in frustration, "can't you *do* something?"

Suddenly Wesley saw that the column was moving back toward him, and then through or over him. He turned to see what was happening, and saw Alleophaz's pale and perspiring face, still twisted in agony but illuminated now by the blue light.

The hand fell from his shoulder as the older man sank to the ground. As Wesley watched, he saw his whole body begin to tremble and shake. The injured leg flayed out from beneath him and shook itself. A look of amazement replaced the look of agony on his face. Then Wesley realized that the light was no longer around him, but shone from inside Alleophaz, particularly from his injured leg. Then it went out, and a moment later there was a column of light ahead on the path again.

Alleophaz scrambled to his feet. His hand rested lightly again on Wesley's shoulder, and they proceeded on their way. "What happened to you?" Wesley asked.

"I do not know. My bad leg was shaking and kicking. Then the pain went and strength came back. It is—it is like a miracle!"

"Didn't you see the light? You were lit up like—like a candle from *inside* you."

"No. I saw nothing. There was just a wonderful feeling of warmth and strength and the strange trembling."

They ascended more steeply now, and had to stop talking to conserve their breath. They had lost two or three critical minutes, and the cries of men were louder now. Wesley glanced back and was dismayed to see the flames of several torches glittering and flickering through the trees. Yet still the blue column did not hurry them, seeming to be patient with their breathlessness. Wesley's thighs were hurting. He felt his strength draining away, and gasped, "You O.K.?" but there was no reply, for Alleophaz was panting too hard.

At that moment they reached the stream, and carefully made their way across it. "This is the sergeant's side," Wesley panted. He felt perspiration stinging his eyes and running down his back.

"They cannot have seen us yet," Alleophaz panted, "and they must proceed more slowly than we do, because they must search as they advance." They reached the rock face, and the blue column led them up the sloping ledge. The torches fell further back, and the sounds faded as they climbed the cliff.

But as they reached the top, they were stunned to see no cabin there. All they could see—and that only dimly—was the outline of a doorway. There was no balcony, no rail, no cabin. The blue column was beside the door frame. The outline of the sleeping Gerachti could barely be seen on the ground.

"Help me rouse him," Alleophaz cried. It was not easy, for the powder had had powerful effects. Somehow they got him, mumbling incoherently like a drunk, to his feet. The blankets of his bedroll fell round his feet, and Wesley scooped them up in his arms. Alleophaz, with the stumbling Gerachti leaning heavily on him, moved toward the door frame. Wesley followed him.

Suddenly there was a loud yell behind them, a yell of triumph. "They are here, men! They are here! I have them!" Turning, Wesley saw the sergeant coming over the top of the cliff, his face shining more with astonishment and exultation than with torchlight. Wesley could not imagine how he had arrived so quickly.

Alleophaz dragged the helpless Gerachti through the door frame and vanished. Wesley tripped over the end of the blankets he was carrying and dived after him.

Silence wrapped itself round them.

8
The Spirit in the Night

In the morning, once again the table had been laid for them and breakfast prepared by unseen hands. A bowl of hot cereal lay steaming in its center, and beside the bowl a large plate of crisp-crusted buns. There was also coffee, cream, butter, honey and marmalade. Wesley sighed with contentment.

"Where is Gerachti?" Alleophaz asked Belak.

"He is in a bad way, my lord. He is standing facing the door that leads outside. He neither moves nor speaks when I address him. He just stands, staring at the door in a sort of stupor. Shall I try to bring him here?"

"No, do not bother. He will not eat. We will just manage him the best we can." Alleophaz looked hard at Kurt. "Keep out of his way, Kurt. Try to ignore him. I do not think anything will happen—but watch out."

They sat down, and Wesley saw that Lisa was wearing jodhpurs. "I found them in the closet in my room last night," she said.

Alleophaz had been trying not to stare at her. "The women in our country wear garments of that sort," he said. "They are not quite like what you are wearing—but of much lighter material, and not tight round the calves, but loose."

"These are for riding," Lisa said. "I don't like riding side-saddle. I only had one lesson in it, an' that was years ago at a fancy girls' school in Switzerland when we lived there. So I never learned." She began to pour coffee. "There's no sugar. You'll have to use honey."

"We had quite a time last night," Wesley said.

"Oh, yes!" Alleophaz joined in. "We have not told them about it yet, have we? Wesley and I went down the road while the rest of you were asleep last night."

Between them they told the story of their adventure, and the animated conversation and questioning that followed drove the matter of Gerachti's strange behavior from their minds, holding their interest through cereal, buns, marmalade and coffee.

"An' when we stumbled through that door frame," said Wesley, "I suddenly realized the explanation of the 'bigger on the inside' phenomenon."

"How d'you mean?" Kurt asked.

"Well, you know how Uncle John describes the Gaal trees (by the way, I hope we get to see one) and how Chocma's cottage—and this place—turned out to be a palace *inside,* but only little on the *outside*?"

Kurt and Lisa nodded, while Belak and Alleophaz looked on with obvious interest. Wesley continued, "Well, I was too tired to think about it last night, but I've been doing a lot of thinking this morning. The first time we were in Anthropos we rode reindeer at one point, and we took refuge in a tower on a hill. There was an opening at the top of the tower, and a space. We sat round the rim of it—remember?"

Again, Kurt and Lisa nodded. Alleophaz stopped eating, and laid his knife and his bun on the plate, watching Wesley with his mouth half open.

"The hole we sat around was the hole 'where time is no more.' "

Again the two children nodded.

"I think," Wesley continued, "that when we all came through the doorway we passed out of time, and into another dimension, another sort of space, space where time no longer exists."

"You mean—that we touch the Eternal Now?" Alleophaz asked. "It is an interesting thought."

Wesley frowned. "Yes, I think I do. There's still a whole lot I don't understand. But it's as though when we are in Gaal's presence—an' I keep feeling we're in his presence here—we're no longer trapped in time, but sort of released from it. Space and time are somehow linked."

A stillness fell on the group, and for some time nobody spoke. Finally Lisa said, "That was a lovely breakfast. More coffee, anyone?"

But nobody wanted more. Slowly they all rose, and the children made their way into the stable, where Gerachti still stood facing the doorway. They pretended they did not notice him. Carefully the children loaded the mules and saddled the horses, taking care to cinch the straps for the saddles properly.

Wesley was very conscious of Gerachti's still and silent figure at the door, and wondered at Alleophaz's warning to Kurt over breakfast. "I hope Kurt's not in any danger," he thought. "I wonder what Alleophaz was thinking of when he said that."

Just then Alleophaz and Belak returned, wearing heavy capes and strange felt hats. Belak carried another cape and hat that Wesley supposed was for Gerachti. Then he noticed similar capes and hats hanging from hooks in their own horses' stalls. "Perhaps we are meant to put them on," he thought. Aloud he said, "Let us take the capes and hats. There was a red sky outside earlier on."

Belak was standing beside Gerachti, his face anxious and uncertain. "Here—I have a cape for you," he said, holding it out tentatively. "Here—put it on, Gerachti." Gerachti remained silent and still, his eyes on the door. Belak's short and tubby frame, his strange uncertainty, contrasted with the tense stillness of Gerachti's tall figure. Carefully he reached up on tiptoe and tried gently to place the cape around Gerachti's shoulders, but instantly and with a violent shrug Gerachti shook it off and it fell on the floor.

"Leave it," Alleophaz said. "Or carry it on your own horse. He may be glad of it later."

"He's more like an animal than a human being," Wesley thought to himself. Kurt and Lisa pretended to notice nothing amiss. They were leading two horses from the stalls, one of which was Gerachti's. Wesley pushed the door open and instantly Gerachti burst through it, knocking Wesley aside in his haste.

Wesley recovered his balance and slipped cautiously out through the door, wary of any soldiers waiting—but there was no sign of anyone but themselves.

He took several strides outside, then stood still.

"Red sky at night
Shepherd's delight;
Red sky in morning
Shepherd's warning.

"Now we know why we have capes. Mebbe we're gonna have a storm." Clouds threatened overhead, and the sky was sinister, glowering and intimidating.

Lisa led Gerachti's horse to him. She said nothing, and turned to go back into the stables, only to discover that there was nothing to see apart from the outline of a door frame, beyond which one could see the forest and the stream they had crossed the previous night. Yet, as she passed through the door frame, she was once again inside the stable.

Alleophaz and Belak emerged, passing through the door frame. A short distance away, just out of sight of the cabin, they found the remains of a campfire. A pile of ashes and blackened, half-burned logs lay heaped together. Alleophaz leaned over them and held out the palm of his hand. "They are still warm. I wonder where the soldiers are. They must have spent most of the night right here." He looked around again. "Perhaps we had best get moving."

A wind had begun to blow, and the tops of the trees were swaying.

As the children brought the last horse out, the door frame disappeared, leaving no trace of their night's lodging.

Gerachti had already mounted and was sitting erect, staring into space. He and his horse looked like an equestrian statue. The rest mounted—Wesley, Kurt and Lisa wearing the heavy capes and felt hats from the stalls. Only Gerachti was without either, and Belak had the cape in front of him on his saddle.

"The column of smoke is going across the stream—and back the way we came last night," Kurt said.

"Well, lead on then," Alleophaz responded. "I can see nothing. I imagine safety lies in following it, though I feel nervous, wondering where the soldiers are. Surely they have not given up."

"Well, sir, remember what the captain said, warning the soldiers not to go deeper than necessary into the forest," Wesley said.

Alleophaz said, "Hm! I had forgotten that. It is amazing they followed us as far as they did, or that they stayed here overnight. Perhaps they have decided that discretion is better than valor."

He followed Kurt, and Wesley was about to follow after Alleophaz, when Gerachti's horse pushed Wesley's horse aside. For the rest of the day, Gerachti kept as close as he could to Alleophaz. Lisa trailed Gerachti, with Wesley behind. Belak came last, urging the mules forward. Wesley smiled to himself. He, too, could still see the column of smoke and see it clearly, but he said nothing.

The sound of wind in the treetops became gusty, increasing steadily in intensity. Rain began to fall in large drops. As they passed the spring, Kurt followed the trail that led off to the right. They were still moving in the general direction of the Anthropos frontier and the city of Bamah.

All day long they continued much as they had the previous day, ascending and descending, twisting and turning, dismounting when they had to. They found no traces of the soldiers, and might as well have been alone in the world.

The storm grew progressively more violent about them. Lightning flashed and thunder crashed louder than the roaring wind, the sound amplified in the gullies they crossed from time to time. At first the trees afforded them some shelter from the rain, but soon it began to drip from the branches, and later to stream from them. They were glad of the capes, which grew heavier as the day wore on.

All were conscious of Gerachti, and they stole glances at him from time to time. Always he sat erect and dazed, rain streaming from his black hair and beard. He was soaked to the skin and shivering. Belak had made renewed efforts to get him to wear the cape and hat, but, coming out of his trance for a moment, Gerachti cursed, spat at Belak, and flung hat and cloak into the mud at his horse's feet. Wesley saw the gestures, but did not hear what was said for the howling of the wind and the groans of bending trees. "The man is mad," he said to himself.

At one point they descended to a bog and had to cross about a hundred yards where the larger clumps of grass and weed formed what looked like islands of safety in a wide lake of foul-smelling and treacherous mud. The blue-gray column of smoke stopped at each small island of safety, waiting until Kurt joined it there before it proceeded to the next safe clump. Kurt dismounted, leading his horse, retaining the reins and encouraging it to jump to the clump on which he then stood. It was obvious that the crossing was perilous, and that it would take time for them to cross in safety.

Once Kurt gained the third clump, Alleophaz dismounted and coaxed his horse onto the second. The horses themselves seemed afraid, their ears flattening and the whites of their eyes showing.

Gerachti, still mounted, shouted something to Alleophaz, pointing to the left as though he were indicating a safe route. Wesley, who was several yards back and behind Lisa, heard him shout, "No, Gerachti! This is the way! Come *this* way!"

With a wild cry, Gerachti turned his horse and began to climb the hill past Lisa. Then once again he turned and spurred his horse to a gallop, intending it to leap a considerable gap to a large clump of grass and weeds on the left. But at the edge of the bog the horse stalled, and its forelegs doubled under it. Gerachti was flung over its head, turning a slow somersault. His body twisted as he flew, and he landed face down in the mud, his head pointing toward his horse. Screaming and struggling in panic to lift his shoulders and chest from the mud, he freed both arms—but his legs were sucked down underneath him.

Wesley slid off his horse and ran to help. He snatched up a tree branch and extended it to Gerachti, who was just able to reach it. Pulling with all his strength, Wesley felt as if his back was breaking and that he would be dragged into the swamp himself. Belak was at his side and seized the branch also. For a moment Wesley was not certain what would happen. Then he felt Lisa's arms locked round his waist and pulling him. Inch by inch, their backs aching with the strain, they dragged Gerachti nearer the firm ground.

Alleophaz leaned out and seized Gerachti's left upper arm. The next moment they had him on firm ground, covered for the most part with foul-smelling mud and weeds.

For a moment he sat, gray-faced and white-lipped, trembling and coughing. Alleophaz checked Gerachti's horse, found it shaking but uninjured, and turned to Gerachti. "Are you all right?" he asked. Gerachti did not reply, but stood and turned to face Kurt, who was standing behind with the horses and mules. His whole body shook and his words were choked with emotion. "You tried to kill me!" he thundered. "You murdering sorcerer!"

"Get back with Belak behind the mules," Alleophaz said quietly to Kurt. "Wesley," he continued, "you saw the column last night. Can you see it now?"

"Why, yes," answered Wesley, surprised.

"I suggest you lead the rest of the way, then." To the rest he said, "I will keep Gerachti between Wesley and me. We must not stop here, or we will be done for. Let us move on, and hope we find shelter before darkness."

It took them more than an hour to cross the next hundred yards. To everyone's relief, Gerachti followed Alleophaz without incident. Kurt and Belak crossed twice, first with the mules (which was much

easier than Kurt had anticipated) and then with their own horses. Lisa was last to cross, and Belak helped her. "I'm not gonna get anywhere near that man Gerachti," she said.

Then, as though it had been kind to them and allowed them to cross in safety, the storm broke over their heads furiously once again. For two more hours they rode through it, drenched with rain, buffeted by wind, doggedly following Wesley as Wesley followed the column of smoke. After that the storm died down, and after another hour sunlight broke over them from a patch of blue sky.

Half an hour later Wesley swung round in his saddle, joy like the sunshine breaking across his face. He called past Gerachti to Alleophaz, "I knew it! It's a Gaal tree, an oak—the first oak I've seen here—an' the column has stopped beside it."

The sun still shone and the sky was now completely blue. But evening was almost upon them, and they had not eaten all day. They dismounted. The Gaal tree stood in a small meadow, deep in grass and with an abundance of wildflowers—buttercups, asters, two kinds of vetch, clover, bluebells and western wood lilies. A stream flowed past the Gaal tree, and the horses moved as one to drink. Gerachti, still dazed and silent, dismounted and sat beside the oak, a pathetic, mud-covered figure, clearly exhausted. Lisa, too, was pale, and weariness was etched in her face. She moved slowly and with effort. "I'm so *sore*," she said. Only Kurt and Belak seemed brisk and alive.

Alleophaz sat down next to Gerachti. "I will stay with him—for now, anyway," he said. "I have some medicine that may keep him from ague and fevers." Kurt joyfully approached the oak.

"Open in the name of Gaal!" he cried, and to everyone's wonder and joy a door in the trunk swung silently open. Kurt went inside it, only to emerge, laughing, a moment later. "There are no stables. But there are piles of towels and horse blankets. We can rub them all down and cover them with blankets."

Lisa slowly approached the Gaal tree, stopping to look at Gerachti. As she stared her expression changed, and fear and exhaustion gave place to compassion. "Poor man, he looks sick." She turned to Alleophaz and murmured, "If there's hot food, I'll bring it out to him. You may be able to persuade him to eat."

"Perhaps," Alleophaz said. "It is worth a try."

Lisa went inside the tree, emerging a few moments later with a jug and two mugs. She handed them to Alleophaz, saying, "It's soup of some kind—thick and delicious and hot. I found a hot tub of water in the room I chose, so I'm going to soak in it before supper."

When Alleophaz offered him the soup, Gerachti accepted it and ate mechanically. Wesley and Kurt busied themselves with the horses, and Belak elected to help them. It took them nearly an hour to finish, and by this time the sun had set. Alleophaz persuaded Gerachti to accept the medicine, wash in the stream, and put dry clothes on. Then Gerachti unrolled his bedroll in a needle-lined dry spot under a giant pine tree, and quickly fell asleep.

Alleophaz called, "Come on! It is time we stopped and went in for supper. I take your word for it, Kurt, that it is large enough inside."

"It is!" Kurt laughed.

Alleophaz held the jug up. "Anyone want soup? I did not have mine. It is still quite warm, and there is a clean mug here!"

"No, thanks," Wesley said. "I'll wait for supper."

Inside the tree they found a very large circular room. The windows opened on the meadow, and there was a stairway at one side leading to the bedrooms. Hot food lay steaming on the table, along with wine and fruit as they had enjoyed the previous night. After supper they sat round a fire of blazing logs again, contented and sleepy as they discussed the events of the day.

"How's Gerachti?" Wesley asked Alleophaz.

"He still does not speak," Alleophaz replied slowly, frowning. "He seems more willing to follow directions, though. He was exhausted, sleeping when I left him."

"Did you give him a powder again?"

"No, I gave him medicine to prevent fever, but he seemed too weary to need a sleeping powder."

"I do not think any of us need sleeping powders tonight, my lord," yawned Belak.

And since they all shared Belak's need to yawn, they left the fire with one accord, and made their way to bed.

Kurt woke abruptly in the night and rose to look through the window. Across the meadow and through the trees a brilliant blue light gleamed powerfully. His heart began to pound inside his chest, and he pulled on his boots and wrapped his not-quite-dry cloak around him. Creeping down the stairway, he crossed the circular room and whispered to the door, "Open in the name of Gaal."

Outside he could still see the silhouetted outline of the trees, black against the blue flickering light beyond them. For several minutes he stood in the open doorway, staring. There was a sudden and unexpected deep longing in his heart, and he struggled to find words to express it.

"Oh, Dad!" he said to the darkness. "Why aren't you like Gaal? Why are you never around? Why, when you are around, are you so ornery? Why can't you be—different? Why are you like Gerachti? Will you become like him in the future? I'm scared, Dad! I'm *scared!*"

He began to move toward the blue light. Slowly he crossed the meadow, climbing up the slope that led to the trees, drawn powerfully by the blue light. He never saw the shadow that rose beneath the pine tree to follow him.

Kurt emerged from the trees into a small meadow, where at the center a column of blue flame rose skyward. It was about fifteen yards in diameter and seemed to rise straight to the stars. The blue flames seemed both to be going up and coming down at the same time. He stared at them in wonder for several minutes, then slowly advanced toward them. When he was near enough to the column, he reached out and touched it. A thrill, like a vibration, ran from his fingers up his arm and enveloped his whole body.

"Oh—what is it?" he gasped. He reached out again, and again experienced the same sensation. Hardly knowing why he was doing so, he stepped forward and began to walk into the flames. Wave after wave of wonder swept over him, wonder that was not just emotional but physical as well. He was washed in liquid love, inside and outside, as though his body were not solid anymore and the blue flames were all through him, penetrating him, saturating him with love.

Somewhere near the center of the column he fell on his knees and flung his arms skyward. "Gaal! Gaal! Gaal! Is it you? Is it the Changer?"

He paused, then began to sob. Tears streamed down his face. "Changer! Changer! You are a Father—aren't you? I know it! I know it—and you are *my Father!*

"Who are you?" he cried again. "It feels like you—but you've never done this before! Oh, it *is* you, Changer, *Father!*"

He fell forward on his face, sobbing uncontrollably, and for half an hour the liquid love continued to pour through him. Finally he sat up again.

"It is you, isn't it?" he cried softly, then after a moment, "Oh, why can't it be like this always? Can I stay here—*always?*"

He had not seen the still figure of Gerachti ten yards in front of him, a naked sword gripped in his right fist. But soon spoken words began to penetrate his consciousness. "You need not go on sniveling, sorcerer! I am not moved by your pleading—which has gone on long enough!"

Kurt heard the words and recognized the voice. Lit by the blue light, he could see the face and form of Gerachti, as well as the sword blade. But neither the words nor the menacing attitude had any meaning. Liquid love flowed through him. Everything else seemed distant, irrelevant.

He did not know that all Gerachti could see was darkness and a weeping boy sitting ten yards from him in that darkness. "Your days are numbered, boy sorcerer, and your time has now come."

Gerachti stepped forward, raising the sword above his head, but as he neared the edge of the flaming column the sword was snatched out of his hand and flung into the outer darkness. A look of astonishment came over his face, and he was seized by an invisible antagonist. Wrestling, fighting, he was flung on the ground—struggling, grunting, panting, hitting out, rolling over, cursing, fighting for breath.

Kurt rose to his feet, still aware of light and love around and through him. *"Don't hurt him!"* he breathed. He could never afterward say how long the struggle continued—many hours?—but eventually Gerachti lay on his back, his arms pinned on either side by an invisible force as he sobbed and panted. "I did not know! I did not know! I did not know!" he repeated, and soon was weeping just as Kurt had wept earlier.

"I think I ought to go, Father!" Kurt said. He crept away, turning back many times to look at the column of light. Then he sighed, turned his back and headed for the oak. He fell deeply asleep the moment his head touched the pillow

9
A Sort
of Sanctuary

Five of the travelers were already eating breakfast when the outside door swung open and Gerachti entered through it. He grinned and said, "I just said what Kurt said yesterday: 'Open in the name of Gaal,' and here I am. It worked! Mind if I join you?'"

The five stopped eating and stared at him in astonishment. After a moment Alleophaz said, "Of course not. Sit here opposite Kurt, Gerachti, there is a place set for you right there "

Gerachti strode across the room, a smile on his face. He did not sit down, however, but stood behind his chair and said, "I think I owe you all an explanation, and an apology." He looked particularly at Kurt and said, "I cannot tell you how sorry I am, Kurt. I hope you will forgive me." Tears came to his eyes, and for a moment he had trouble speaking.

Kurt wanted to say, "Of course!" but the words never came. His throat went dry, and he could not make a sound. Everyone was very still.

Gerachti took a breath. "I tried to kill Kurt last night." Lisa gasped, but no one else made a sound or moved. Gerachti continued. "He came out of the tree sometime after midnight. He went up to the top of the meadow, through the trees and into a smaller meadow beyond. I followed and stood a few feet away with my sword ready."

For a moment a grim expression clouded his face. No one spoke. They were like stone statues.

"Kurt was trembling, crying. He talked, but his words made no sense to me. I thought he was pleading for his life. I now know I was quite mistaken about that. At any rate, losing patience, I raised my sword high above my head and stepped forward. I had every intention of swinging it down and cleaving his head in two.

"But as I tried to swing my sword arm down, a mighty force met me. The sword was snatched from my hand, and where it is now I have no idea. In terror I found myself wrestling against an assailant I could not see. He flung me to the ground, and though I struggled fiercely, he was determined to pin me there. I felt that my end was upon me, and I struggled with all my might for the longest time. But my strength gave out, and in the end I had nothing to fight with. I felt his weight pressing me down. His hands forced mine against the wet earth and his breath was hot in my face. Kurt was saying, 'Don't hurt him!' I suppose he was pleading mercy for me.

" 'Now,' he (whoever he was) said. 'Now I have you where I want you for a moment. All I want to do is to tell you that I love you.' "

"I never heard that!" Kurt said, half laughing, half crying. "I saw you wrestling and struggling with someone, but I never heard a thing! I was in the middle of blue light."

"Yes, Kurt, yes! The whole area was alight with blue—blue flames coming up from the earth through me and ascending into the skies, and blue flames descending over me from above. It was as though kindness and goodness and holiness were washing over me. I was weeping. I cried out again and again, 'I did not know. I did not know!' Then you left me, Kurt."

"I'm sorry, Mr. Gerachti I didn't know what to do. It seemed sort of—I dunno, well *holy*—like I'd no right to watch."

"Well, I am glad in a way that you did go. For when I think of what took place after you left—I would just as soon—not even talk about it now." His lips trembled.

Kurt reached across the table and laid his hand on Gerachti's wrist. "It's O.K.—I understand, if no one else does."

They stared at Gerachti, marveling at the vast and sudden change. There was no arrogance, no tendency to sneer, no bitterness. He was a different person.

"We understand to some extent, Gerachti," Alleophaz said. "We knew the terror that had gripped you. And we all wished you well."

Suddenly everyone was talking at once, as tension gave place to sudden and relieved joy. Lisa was saying, "Here, let me pour your coffee, Mr. Gerachti. Stop talking, everyone, and let him eat. The poor man must be starving."

But they didn't stop talking, and nobody minded the fact that it was all talking and no listening to what anyone else was saying. Somehow, Gerachti managed to eat a good breakfast, saying little himself, but grinning constantly.

Finally, Wesley succeeded in getting everyone's attention. "I have good news for you. I had a visit in my dreams last night from a spirit of light—Risano, he called himself. He gave us instructions for the next part of the journey. We are to sell the horses today and paddle upstream toward Bamah by canoe.

"He said we'd find another road on the far side of the river toward evening, and that almost at once we'd come upon a fairly large house with wrought iron gates. There will be a bell-pull, and we are to ring the bell."

"Are you sure?" Kurt asked.

"Absolutely. A man will come to the gate and ask who we are. We are to say, 'We are servants of the true and only King.' He will say, 'Who is this true and only King?' and we must reply, 'He is yet a child, he is yet a child!'

"At that he will open the gate and bid us enter. He deals in horses, and will purchase the animals for the price you originally paid, and he will give us lodging for the night. Then in the morning, we are to proceed by canoe to a waterfall, where we will hide until the queen's party arrests us."

"*Arrests* us?"

"Yes, of course. You remember, if we are her prisoners, the king will no longer have any claim on us."

Once breakfast was over, they packed the mules, saddled the horses, and mounted in high spirits.

Belak spoke earnestly to Gerachti, telling him how glad he was for what had happened. "I have missed being with you and talking with you," he said. "Oh, Gerachti! I am so glad!"

Gerachti was smiling, his eyes alight, and unaccustomed joy all over his dark face. "You are not nearly so glad as I!"

Then, looking up, he cried, "Now *I* can see the column of smoke! May I lead?"

Alleophaz looked over at Wesley. "Would that be all right?" he asked.

Wesley laughed, "Sure. Go ahead, Gerachti! That makes three of us—unless—" he looked inquiringly at Lisa, who shook her head. "Nope! Can't see a thing!" Her voice was tremulous, though cheerful, but her face seemed tight, as though it was an effort not to look disappointed. Alleophaz and Belak also shook their heads.

So they followed Gerachti up through the meadow and the trees to the small meadow beyond. Gerachti showed the rest where the events of the previous night had occurred, and pointed out where the tall grass had been flattened where he had wrestled. He found his sword and replaced it in the scabbard.

That day proceeded as the previous day had done, except that the birds sang, and at one point the valley echoed with the call of a bull moose. Once Gerachti ordered them to stillness with a motion of his hand. There was a doe in the trail facing them, and they gazed at it for several minutes. Gerachti talked to it gently. "You are a beautiful creature!" He was awed and delighted. "Yes, you are very beautiful.

Do you have a family?"

Alleophaz turned to Kurt and whispered, "I have never known him to be like this. It is worth our whole journey!"

Kurt whispered, "The doe doesn't speak. Are there no talking animals here now?"

"Just in Anthropos, perhaps," Lisa murmured.

Suddenly the doe flicked her white tail up and bounded in great flying leaps up the steep hillside through the trees on their left. Gerachti gave a great sigh, and they resumed their way. The column led them over a bridge and down the far bank of the river. They stopped in a meadow for a lunch that Lisa had prepared from the morning's buns and the previous night's turkey. The day had grown very warm, and the boys and men began to peel off their clothing. Wesley gazed in surprise at the tremendous arms and chest that Gerachti displayed.

"Wow! Does he ever look strong!" he remarked to Alleophaz.

"Yes," Alleophaz murmured. "He used to feel that manhood consisted in strength of arm and limb, and in skill with weapons. He devoted a lot of time to his physique. But I think that last night he began to discover what real manhood is all about. For the first time, he had to submit to a greater strength than his own."

That evening they reached the east Bamah Road. "I think I will go down to make sure the road is clear," Gerachti said. "I will be back soon." When he returned he was smiling. "The road is clear—and the house is only a hundred yards farther."

They found it as Gerachti had said and as Wesley's dream had foretold. Soon they were standing at a wrought iron gate on the right-hand side of the road. They could see a house in the background, and the river behind it, and a bell rope hanging from a hole in the stone gatepost. Wesley pulled it, and a bell above the gatepost clanged sonorously.

A man emerged from the house and came to the wrought iron gate. He stared at them through the grillwork, gripping the bars with his hands. "Who are you?" he asked.

As if they had rehearsed it, they replied as one, "We are the servants

119

of the true and only King!" (Belak stumbled over the words, missing "true and only"—but nobody noticed.)

The man's voice rang out again, "Who is this true and only King?" and again the small chorus was heard, "He is yet a child, he is yet a child."

Then they heard the sound of bolts sliding and the gates swung open. "Come in, and welcome." The man smiled broadly. "I am Sir Robert of Ashleigh."

His face was brown and his hair the color of carrots, long, curly and shining. He wore a white shirt with a wide, open collar and huge puffed sleeves gathered at the wrist. Tight black trousers and buckled shoes completed his costume.

He led them to the stable and called for servants to care for the horses. "I will buy them from you if I may. Just name your price. I understand you are to proceed by canoe from here. You are now, whether you know it or not, in Anthropos. You crossed the border just before you reached the road. How you came through the forest unscathed, I will never understand."

He first showed them where the two long canoes were moored, then led them to the house. Inside, he introduced them to his wife, Lady Dolores, and his two teenage children. There was a meal of roast pig in the large dining room, attended by a whole team of servants. They drank the same Anthropos wine as on the previous two nights, while their host drank mead. Then, after the table was cleared and the servants dismissed, they ate fruit and cheeses and drank more wine, listening to their host tell his story.

"Already I have told you that my name is *Sir* Robert of Ashleigh. Ashleigh is the house my ancestors built, the same house in which my servants have served your lordships, and within whose hospitable walls your lordships will be safe." At this he bowed, his carrot-colored hair falling about his face. He tossed it back as he straightened.

"He's a bit of an ass, but I like him," thought Kurt.

Wesley thought, "He talks like a real Anthroponian, but there's something odd about him. What is it that's wrong?"

"I was knighted by his majesty the king," Sir Robert continued. "Not the present king, who is no real king, but a corrupt and cowardly son of the House of Playsion—"

"My dear, it is unwise to speak so freely," his wife interrupted. "The walls have ears. The king could learn of your disloyalty."

"Madame, I care not! Let the king learn! I was the subject of his late father-in-law, the father of our present queen, and it is to her that I owe allegiance, not to this usurper to the Anthropos throne."

"My dear, he *is* the rightful king—"

"Never will my knee bow before him, nor will many like me in the realm of Anthropos. I bow before the Warrior Queen!"

His wife sighed. "She is a courageous lady. But she says herself that she prefers the prayer stool to the sword, and would gladly drop the sword if only his majesty would learn to wield it in defense of Anthropos."

"And that he never will," Sir Robert said. "And, as I was about to say, twenty years ago I was visited by a spirit of light—"

"Have some more fruit," said Lady Dolores, offering the silver bowl of fruit to Alleophaz.

Sir Robert's children glanced at each other, and the girl shrugged her shoulders. They rose as though a signal had been given. "May we be excused, Papa?" the oldest girl asked.

"I am sure our guests must be tired," Lady Dolores continued, as though unaware of the annoyance on her husband's face. "Perhaps you could tell them the rest of the story tomorrow?"

It was then that Wesley thought he saw a change flicker over Sir Robert's face, so that for a fraction of a second he seemed a different man—quieter, less pompous, no longer foolish and annoyed, but ruthless and calculating. He gave his wife a quick glance, and then was himself again, wearing a foolish smile. The change had passed in a flash, and so completely that Wesley wondered if he had imagined it.

"Of course, my dear." Sir Robert turned to his guests. "How thoughtless of me. The perils of the forest are well known, and for you even to have survived is much."

Alleophaz smiled. "You have been most considerate. But your good lady is right. We are weary. Would it seem discourteous if we all followed your children's excellent example?"

"Of course not." Sir Robert himself rose to his feet and the rest did the same. Soon they were in their rooms. Wesley and Kurt shared one room, while the rest were lodged in individual bedrooms in one wing of the manor house. The two boys sat on the edge of their beds, discussing the events of the day. Soon there was a knock on the door, and Wesley called, "Come in!" Alleophaz entered, followed by Gerachti, Belak and Lisa—all wearing their cloaks again. The boys stared, bewildered, but Wesley reached without thinking for his own cloak.

Alleophaz waited until they were seated, he and Gerachti on two chairs, Belak squatting on the floor, while Lisa perched herself on the end of Kurt's bed. For a moment or two no one spoke. Gerachti was smiling a little, looking at Alleophaz. "So, what is on your mind?" he asked.

Alleophaz drew in a breath. "I wanted to meet with you all because I fear that our host intends to betray us to the king's party. I cannot be sure of it, but there were one or two little things . . ." He paused, waiting for their reaction, which came quickly as several of them spoke almost simultaneously.

Gerachti's eyes were alive with interest. "So you *do* suspect him. Why?" he asked.

Kurt said, "Oh, it's not possible! He's a bit of an ass, I know, but he was so set against the king! What about all the things he said about the warrior queen?"

Belak looked bothered. "Oh, dear! This is awkward and embarrassing. Are you sure? His wife certainly would not be involved. Her allegiance to the queen is obvious."

"It was the obviousness of their loyalty that awakened my suspicions," Alleophaz said slowly. "They both, Sir Robert especially, seemed like unskilled actors overplaying their part, trying too hard to allay any suspicions we might have. Though, as you say, his wife could be loyal."

"If you are right, then his treachery might be recent," Gerachti said, frowning. "At any rate he knew the password, and passwords are changed frequently. Either he has been more skillful in deceit than you seem to believe, or else he has for some reason decided to betray us very recently. But the wife, now—I find it hard to suspect her. What else made you suspect the husband?"

"It was a little thing, and I cannot even now be completely sure. You remember when his wife interrupted the story he was about to tell? I cannot remember who said what, but he was annoyed at her attempt to turn the conversation. There was something odd about the way he looked at her."

"Yes—I saw it too," Wesley said. "It was almost as though he suddenly remembered something he had forgotten, or else he resented his wife's suggestion. But the whole thing happened so fast that I couldn't be sure. I thought I might be imagining it."

"No, Wesley, I do not think you were imagining anything."

There was another knock at their door, and the children froze. Belak drew in his breath rapidly. Gerachti, who was nearest the door, raised his eyebrows inquiringly, looking at Alleophaz. Alleophaz nodded.

Gerachti opened it, keeping his shoulder against it as he did so, but stepping back quickly when he saw who was there.

Lady Dolores entered. She smiled hesitantly. "You are all here! I thought this was Wesley's room—but it is just as well." She glanced from one of them to the other, making up her mind. The smile had died from her face, and she was frowning slightly. Finally she nodded. "I really came to find some way of letting you know that you are in danger. I have reason to believe that he who is now my husband is disloyal to the queen about whom he so freely boasts. Perhaps you should leave without ceremony and make good your escape. I do not know my husband's plans, but I fear that the house may already be surrounded by his majesty's soldiers."

Alleophaz said quietly, "We had suspected as much. But is your ladyship not running a grave risk in coming here telling us this?"

"My loyalty is to her majesty the queen. I spoke as I did tonight at supper in order to let my husband know that I did not suspect any treachery—"

"Yet you suspect him enough to tell us to flee . . ."

The lady's face hardened. "Sir Robert needs money and will get it from any convenient source. We have been married only a year. My former husband died, leaving me with the two children. His majesty the king granted Sir Robert's request to wed me, and for the sake of the children and our safety, I agreed." She paused for a moment and nobody spoke. Then Lady Dolores continued, "I must not stay. Never mind how my suspicions arose. You will not be safe in your beds tonight. You can leave by the window, but beware the king's men. This room faces the river, and ivy grows thick on this side of the house. If you follow the wall of the house carefully in *that* direction," she pointed toward Bamah, "you will come to the edge of the woods twenty yards beyond. The river and the road grow further apart at this point, and there is forest on this side of the road, between it and the river."

"Madam, we are most grateful. Yet I would beg one thing from you. Please seek at once to engage your husband in conversation."

"My lord?"

"If, as you suspect," said Alleophaz, "Sir Robert has betrayed us to the king's party, and if indeed the plan is to seize us tonight, then make some excuse for an urgent need to speak to him. I will follow you and eavesdrop. I shall, I suspect, be able to learn more from his response to you."

Lady Dolores smiled. "You think quickly and decisively, my lord. Very well. Follow me at a discreet distance. I will conduct you by way of a passage to the library. I suspect Sir Robert is there at the moment."

Alleophaz turned to Gerachti. "It is completely dark, and there should be no moon until almost dawn. I would like you, Gerachti, to go with Wesley and Belak to take the horses a little way into the forest and set them loose. Then take the panniers off the canoes. Put paddles on board and drag them into the trees. That way, if anything goes wrong and we have to flee on foot, they will look for us in the river. We will try to rendezvous at a safe distance from the house on the river bank toward Bamah. If we have not reached you by sunrise, *then go on without us.* Try to get to Bamah and to the queen, acquainting her with what has happened. Gerachti—you have in your possession copies of the trade proposals to his majesty the king. Make use of them as you have need. I will try to get a clearer notion of Sir Robert's plans while Kurt and Lisa remain here, but we will do our best to catch up with you."

He strode to the window and opened it, looking round carefully. "We are not on the ground floor, but the ivy has, as Lady Dolores points out, grown well. We should have no difficulty leaving by this route. It is unlikely that we will be observed climbing down." He turned to smile at them. "So be off with you. We shall follow as soon as we can."

Alleophaz bowed, moving toward the door to open it himself. "Lady Dolores, we may owe you our lives. Many, many thanks for running this risk. Please do not endanger yourself any further. And again, accept our most fervent thanks." He opened the door and followed Lady Dolores out. One by one, Gerachti, Wesley and Belak clambered through the window, and Kurt picked up his cloak from the bed and pulled it round his shoulders against the chill night air. Lisa shivered in her cloak and pulled it tighter. They both felt strangely excited and tense.

There was a moment of silence after everyone had gone.

"So now what?" Lisa asked.

"Just wait, I guess."

"I hate waiting. I just hate it." She made as though to bite her nails, then pulled her hand away from her mouth. "Y'know, there's something I can't understand."

"What?"

"Wesley said a spirit of light named Risano spoke to him in the dream. We did everything we were supposed to do, and yet here we are being betrayed. If it was a spirit of light, surely we would not have been led into a trap."

"You think Wes was deceived?"

"I just don't know. I'm scared. I don't like what's happening."

Kurt stared at a picture on the wall behind their bed. "It's a picture of a door, just an old door. Why do they have a picture of a door?"

"Kurt, I'm scared. I wish we could know for sure what's happening. This is awful."

"Yeah. I know." Kurt was moving toward the picture, a puzzled frown on his face.

"You're not listening, Kurt. I'm scared, I tell you."

Kurt stared at the picture intently. "I can't see it properly in this light. Just a second." He tried to lift the picture. "Good grief—it's heavy . . . *Oh, good grief!*"

The picture was pulled out of Kurt's hand. Slowly and silently a section of the wall behind the beds swung open like a door. Beyond the wall, a dark tunnel led down a flight of stairs. The children stared, momentarily speechless.

"Let's see where it goes and follow it!" Kurt said eventually.

"No. I want to stay here. Alleophaz is coming back."

Kurt hesitated. "I'll only go down a little ways—this could be another way to escape."

"No, Kurt! What would we do if Alleophaz came back and we weren't here? Besides, I—I don't want to be alone."

"Well, come with me then."

"Kurt, I really think—Oh!" Lisa stared into the dark stairway, her eyes alight with wonder. "Oh, Kurt—I can see it! It really is there!"

Kurt looked first into the tunnel, and then at his sister, a frown on his face. "You can see what?"

"The column of blue light. Look, right at the bottom of the stairway!"

Kurt laughed. "I can't even see the bottom of the stairway. Sounds like our roles are reversed!" He laughed again. "Lisa, I'm so glad you can see it! Even after all this time, I still had a feeling that you didn't believe me."

Lisa said nothing, but pushed past him into the opening and began to descend the stairway, her attitude transformed. A moment before she had been torn with fear, but now she was confident, even joyful.

Kurt followed her. "Hold on. The further we go the less I can see. It's getting darker as we go down. An' there's a lever in the wall here that must operate the opening from this side."

Kurt pulled the lever, and the section of wall began to close. Hastily he reversed the motion of the lever, and the opening remained as it was.

"Hurry, Kurt! The column's moving along the corridor. You still can't see it?"

"Not right now. But in the woods it was sometimes very clear, and at others not clear at all. That's when I started remembering the things the book said—y'know, that I could trust an' I wouldn't be let down."

Lisa paused, still watching the moving column of light. "I guess I owe you an apology, Kurt. At first I really thought you were out of your mind. Later I had to believe—after all, Wes and even Gerachti began to see it. An' at that stage I just felt envious—I didn't like being left out."

She resumed her downward course. The passage at the bottom went straight forward. After a minute or so, they began to feel drips of water from above, and the floor sounded distinctly wet. Five minutes later they became aware of fresher air, and, after pushing through leaves and branches, emerged by the river. For a few moments they stood and stared.

"We mustn't stay here—we gotta get back!" Lisa said. "Where's the column gone?"

"It's behind us in the bushes," Kurt said.

"I thought you couldn't see it!" Lisa replied, turning.

"It happened gradually. I still can't see it too clearly. Anyway, we'd better not delay."

Once back in the bedroom they noticed that the window was still open. Kurt pulled down on the picture and swung the passage door closed just as Alleophaz hurried through the other door.

"Give me a hand," Alleophaz said. "We must barricade the door. Apparently there is a passage leading from this very room to where the canoes are moored. Soldiers are being brought here by Sir Robert so as to prevent us from reaching them and escaping. Their real suspicion is that we have left on horseback—someone reported the missing horses already."

"We know how to get into the passage!" Kurt struggled to lift the picture. Again the section of the wall swung back.

"Wonderful! But let us barricade this door to increase our chances."

Excitement gave them strength, and they succeeded in wedging one of the beds between the door and another piece of heavy furniture, which itself backed against the outer wall. They listened for a second or two longer, but there were no sounds of anyone approaching. Then, throwing themselves down the stairway, they hurried to follow the column of blue light. "They'll suppose we left by the open window," Kurt thought, pulling the lever behind him.

"What is that light?" panted Alleophaz. "Is it . . . oh, I can actually see it! I am beginning to perceive as you do!"

They eased through the screen of shrubs hiding the exit and found themselves on the bank of the river among trees. They peered in both directions, hoping to see Gerachti, Belak and Wesley.

"There's the others." Kurt pointed upstream. "An' they've got a couple of animals with them—I think."

"Let us not rush. It could be the soldiers. I'll go. Hide in the bush if anything goes wrong," Alleophaz ordered.

But it was Wesley with the pack mules. "We've already unloaded the bedrolls and odd bits of supplies."

They turned the mules loose among the trees, slapped their rear ends and left them pushing their way in among the trees. Then, clambering into the canoes, the six travelers pushed off. Darkness

hemmed them in like a dense curtain, cutting them off from everything except a column of blue light. In near silence they dipped their
paddles into the water. Would they escape? The water was smooth and
the current slow, but they still had to paddle upstream. Would their
pursuers discover they were traveling by river?

Yet there was no other way to go. They were committed—committed to the darkness and to the mysterious column of light that led
them.

10

Shadows
in the Temple

Mary and the couple from Chereb approached Bamah and could see that the city was overshadowed by an oval mound. From the center of the mound a temple rose majestically, yet with sinister lines. Fearful in its immensity, dominating not only the palace but the whole city, the temple stared down on the city like an evil bird ready to swoop and strike.

They entered the eastern gate and proceeded along a wide tree-lined avenue, finding the palace at the edge of the great mound. At the palace they were detained in the guard house, waiting as word of their arrival was sent inside.

They did not have long to wait. Scarcely five minutes passed before an enormous young man, fully seven feet tall and weighing three hundred and fifty pounds, entered the room. His broad shoulders were emphasized by the puffed sleeves of his stiff blue velvet jerkin. Matching blue velvet trousers were tied above his white silk stockings, and black leather shoes completed his costume. Though his clothing was trimmed with lace, the total effect was of manly power and strength. The young man moved swiftly and with agility, taking the three visitors in with a quick penetrating glance, bowing low as he looked at them. Mary noticed his astonishingly thick eyebrows, projecting forward to match his thick black hair.

"My lord and ladies, I am Duke Dukraz," he said in a deep voice, his eyes continuing to examine each of them in turn. "Permit me to welcome you to Anthropos from your overseas estates, and to congratulate you on your recent marriage." He bowed again before continuing. "Unfortunately, her majesty the queen left the palace yesterday with an armed escort. We anticipate her return tomorrow evening. You are doubtless aware of the crisis that is developing here, and the regrettable necessity of your being confined to the guard house for the present."

Lord Nasa, also bowing, was quick to reply. "We are aware of some of the difficulties facing you. But it is strange to come here at her majesty's personal invitation, and yet to be treated as persons who are not above suspicion. I understand that her majesty left orders for chambers to be prepared for us in her own quarters. Has your royal highness inquired whether the chambers are ready?"

In no way intimidated by the duke, Lord Nasa raised his eyebrows a little. He stared back at the other man with a look that seemed friendly enough, but that expressed more pained surprise at their reception than pleasure. If the duke was taken aback by his response, he showed no sign of it. He continued to look Lord Nasa in the eye, staring from beneath his own projecting brows with a look that was not hostile, but cautious. He seemed to be weighing both their persons and his own words with care.

Mary stared from one to the other, wondering how the conversation would end. She also decided that dress made no difference. Whatever they wore, men were *men* here. In his own way, the man she had once thought of as a popinjay was as powerful as the duke, and seemed to hint at the possibility of the queen's displeasure.

The duke hesitated for a moment longer. "Please sit down," he said at length. Benches lined the walls of the guard house, and the four of them seated themselves. Again he looked slowly at each of them, seeming to make up his mind about something. "Perhaps I should ask you what you already know about the situation in the palace."

"A few things only," Lord Nasa said. "We know that his majesty is a member of the royal house of Playsion, while his queen is of the Anthroponian royal line. The queen has known us for a long time." Lord Nasa shrugged, then continued. "We also know that there are differences of religious belief between their majesties which have caused some tensions, and that some rumor of an infant future king has reached his majesty's ears. I presume that these facts have some bearing on your present difficulties."

"Where did you learn this information?"

"From her majesty."

A startled look crossed the face of the big man. Then, speaking slowly, half in question, he said, "You are not, of course, suggesting that her majesty was plotting against the king?"

Lord Nasa's eyes widened. "If I had the least suspicion of that, then obviously my lips would have been sealed. Remember, we are her guests. I would never have talked to you so freely about her majesty's preferences if I knew plots were afoot, or that her own loyalty was questioned. Her majesty may not care for her husband, and is clear about her loyalty to the Emperor, but she is not given to palace intrigue. So far as I am aware, she has no knowledge of a true claimant to the Anthroponian throne. I am sure her majesty will have said as much to the king. Her character is above reproach."

Smiling, the duke raised his thick black eyebrows a little. "You are better informed than I thought."

Lord Nasa also smiled, finding the duke's uncertainty amusing. After a moment he said, "You know, if his majesty had suspected the queen of disloyalty, then you would have been under orders to detain us. But you are not. Our arrival at a time of crisis seems to be the source of your uncertainty. Perhaps you could find out whether her majesty left instructions about our reception here."

The young duke rose, and the visitors did the same. If he was embarrassed by Lord Nasa's suggestion that he had been remiss, it did not show in his face. But there was a softening in his stance. "I will do as you suggest." Again he hesitated, looking hard at Lord Nasa. "I would appreciate a further opportunity of conversation with you, but for the present I will take my leave. If preparations have been made for your reception in the queen's chambers, then you will most certainly be conducted there." He bowed and left.

Before long, a tall and richly gowned older woman appeared, accompanied by two maids-in-waiting. "I am Princess Anne, cousin to her majesty, and her chief maid-in-waiting. Your journey must have been tiring. I trust you are well?"

There was a quietness and tranquility about her, an atmosphere of joy and warmth that drew them to her. "I am so sorry about her majesty's absence," she continued. "She had left instructions for your reception, but no one told the duke." Princess Anne smiled. "And the pigeon announcing your coming arrived, so that your apartments are ready—and waiting for you."

They followed her gladly, relieved to be freed from suspicion. Soon they stood in a pleasant suite of rooms overlooking the palace courtyard. A large sitting room separated a bedroom for Mary from the larger room for Lady Roelane and her husband.

Before she left them, Princess Anne made a request. "I will see that the panniers with your things are brought here, and that your animals are cared for. You are to have complete freedom in the palace, but Duke Dukraz has requested that your lordships remain here a little while, since he would appreciate the chance of talking further with you."

Then she looked at Mary, smiling. "You are free even now, my dear. But if you like, I can show you the palace. I could make sure the Captain of the Guard knows who you are, so that you can even come and go from the palace."

Mary did like. Freedom was important, and it occurred to her that a knowledge of the palace might later come in handy, especially if she were to wish to contact the sorcerers she was sure would be around. She smiled. "Thank you, your highness."

They walked together through the palace, which proved more complex the more she saw of it. Mary tried to secure in her mind the layout of the many corridors and rooms, for she knew she must find her way to the priests. But even she was a little confused. Princess Anne introduced her to a number of palace officials, including ladies-in-waiting (who fussed over her) and men with titles like Guardian of the Royal Wardrobes or Chancellor of the Exchequer (who ruffled her hair in an absent-minded and irritating way). Her sharp mind noted them all, sizing each one up carefully.

Eventually they crossed the palace courtyard, where she was introduced to Captain Integredad, the Captain of the Guard. He was a grizzled, bearded man with a twinkle in his eye. Mary stared at him, and wondered what manner of man he was. She had dismissed the Guardian of the Royal Wardrobes as a simpering idiot. She had glared at the Chancellor of the Exchequer, who scarcely looked at her. But about this man there was a quality, a quality shared by the long-vanished Uncle Alan, by Uncle John, by Lord Nasa, perhaps even by the big man with the gorgeous eyebrows whom they had been with so recently. All of them had the same feel about them. How could she put it into words? It was the way Gaal felt to her. Trust? Yes, that was it—they could be trusted. She sighed a deep sigh.

Then something else occurred to her. *She was not accustomed to trusting men.* Slowly the realization grew inside her, dawning on her like a revelation. It was not easy for her to trust women either, though she had begun to be drawn to, and to trust, Lady Roelane. It usually took a long time for her to trust anybody, and there were few people she trusted fully. As for men, they tended to arouse fear in her initially. Yet the twinkle in this man's eyes was the kind of twinkle that would never betray her. She remembered vaguely another pair of twinkling eyes—blue ones. Twinkling? Had they twinkled? If so, the twinkle had mocked her. No, they had not twinkled, they had just seemed amused.

"You are chilled, little lady," said the captain. "Come inside the guard house where it is warmer! Come and sit down."

They sat in a corner, angled toward each other.

"Oh—I'm O.K.," she said. "I was just thinking!" Vaguely she heard Princess Anne take her departure, entrusting her to Captain Integredad. But the thoughts that had passed through her mind had shaken her, so that for the moment she was scarcely aware of all that was happening.

"So. You were thinking. Thinking about what?" the captain asked.

"About someone's eyes. But I don't want to think about them. They scare me."

"Scary eyes? Well, I am sure I cannot blame you. When I was your age, the thought of staring eyes used to frighten me to death."

"Let's talk about something else."

"To be sure. What would you like to talk about?"

"About the temple."

"The temple?" The captain was clearly taken aback. "Ho, little lady, the temple is no place for you! Whatever would you want to know about the temple?" He paused a moment, peering at the temple through a window. "Though I must say it is an impressive piece of architecture, impressive in a veiled and sinister way."

Mary eyed him carefully. Ought she to trust him enough to tell him what her interest in the temple was? She stared hard at him, then made up her mind to risk his trust.

"I'm a witch, and I really want to meet some of the sorcerers in the temple. I think they could teach me more."

The captain said nothing for a moment or two. A look of sadness slowly took shape on his face. For a moment he seemed to have receded into some space where Mary could not reach him. Then he sighed, looking at her gravely. The twinkle had gone from his eyes. *"Lady Mary, never trust a sorcerer."*

"But I never have," she thought. "I just want to know what they know." Aloud she said, "Why not?"

For a moment Captain Integredad did not speak. Then he

shrugged. "I suppose for the most obvious reason of all—that sorcerers cannot be trusted. Look into their eyes, child. Usually they will stare back into your own eyes. They do not lack courage. The look in their eyes is too frank, *too* honest. But they are not being frank so much as watching you, trying to read you. Their lips smile but their eyes calculate. Look into their eyes and see whether sorcerers—any sorcerers at all—have trustworthy eyes. Trust neither witch nor sorcerer, Mary."

"But I want—I want to ask them questions. If they have secrets, I want to learn them."

"Oh, they will teach you! They want you as a follower, as a servant—or worse. But you will have to be cleverer than they are to wheedle their deepest secrets out of them. And they would demand a price, a very high price." Captain Integredad shook his head slowly from side to side.

"What d'you mean?"

"Mary, I would just as soon not discuss it right now. But it is a price you would not want to pay. And even if you paid it, there is no guarantee that they would keep their promises."

"But this is different! I'm a witch myself. I just want to learn. I really know what I'm doing."

"Do you, Lady Mary?"

"Of course I do!"

The captain stared at her. She was so small, yet she talked more like an adult than a little girl. "What is it you want?" he asked at last, with infinite kindness in his voice. "What would you gain by risking your life and your happiness by messing with very dangerous people?"

"I want power. I need plenty of magical power to get people to do whatever I want. With my Uncle John, for example. The woman I thought was my mother told me she wasn't my mother and sent me away. You can't trust people. I don't want to depend on people anymore. I used to like my Uncle John, but he's gone an' got himself married to an old lady, an' I don't know what will happen. In any case he and his old lady disappeared. I think they're somewhere in this world, and that's why I'm here. Oh, gosh, I . . ."

Captain Integredad's eyes looked hard at her. "Did you say, 'somewhere in *this* world'? What other world is there?"

Mary bit her lip. "I—I shouldn't have said that. I—oh, gosh!" For a moment her pose of assurance evaporated. Then, like the little girl she really was, she cautiously added, "You won't say anything, will you?"

"Mary, I have heard of other worlds. Are you serious when you say you have come from one?"

Mary, having lived for a while with Uncle John, still found it hard to lie, and struggled to know what to say. "Look, I shouldn't have said that. I'm sorry."

"But you said it."

Mary stared at the floor, avoiding the captain's eyes. For a minute or two she did not speak. Then, still looking at the floor, she said, "I don't mean any harm to anybody. It's not the first time I've been here. Though I think that last time it was—well, in a future time in Anthropos. I know it's confusing. But yes—I did come here from my own world—and by magic. But please don't tell anyone. I really only came to find my Uncle John. He's called the Sword Bearer."

The captain, a worried frown on his face, drew in a deep breath. Slowly he said, "The Sword Bearer is little more than a child himself. But it is true that he came from another world."

"I suppose he was, once—young, I mean."

The Captain of the Guard stared at her. Finally he said, "It is hard to know where my duty lies at times. There is one person I must tell, Mary, and that is her majesty the queen. My duty to her is clear—it is my duty to protect her. Therefore she, at least, must know."

Mary shrugged her shoulders. She was angry with herself for letting her origins slip out so easily. Captain Integredad's kindness had fooled her, precisely because it was genuine kindness. And he had been quick to follow the thread of her thoughts. Yet it could have been worse. She wasn't being detained, but she would have to find a way into the temple before the queen returned.

"Please—it'll be all right," she pleaded. "I know I'm only little, but I know what I'm doing."

"That is what my daughter once told me."

"Your daughter? But she wasn't a witch. I am."

"Well, like you, she thought she was. And she went to the temple secretly. I knew nothing about it till much too late."

"Oh? What happened?"

The Captain of the Guard turned his head away. Had his lip begun to tremble? Finally he turned to her and said, "They offered her as a sacrifice on the great altar outside the temple entrance. That was three years ago. Perhaps you can understand how I feel about the temple." Slowly he shook his head from side to side. "She is *dead*, Mary. She trusted them, and now she is dead. They are a vile and evil lot in there, and they can twist the king round their little fingers."

His gaze was steady, while Mary's mouth hung open and her throat was dry. "But surely," she began, then stopped. She had been about to say that such a thing could not be, but she was remembering the dreadful experience Lisa had told her about, so that her protests died on her lips. For Lisa had one day found herself on that same altar, the altar outside the temple. It had taken place in another time— *would* take place now in the distant future. She had been chained and manacled to the altar, Lisa had told her, and guarded by a strange being who was by turns a cat and a snake named Ebed Ruach. Mary's legs began to feel shaky.

"I—I think I'd like to go back," she said.

She was unexpectedly overwhelmed with a longing to be close to the safety of the Lady Roelane. Powerful people were also dangerous people. She wanted to hold and be held by the Lady Roelane, wanted the comfort of bodily contact with her, wanted her as a mother, whose comforting warmth could enfold her. "I—I really want to—to go back. Please take me back to the Lady Roelane."

In time she might recover her courage, but for the present she wanted comfort. She was still trembling when they found Lord Nasa and Lady Roelane. The captain smiled politely before leaving, but said nothing of what had taken place. However, immediately there was another knock on the door, and Duke Dukraz was admitted. Lady Roelane, perceiving Mary's distress, turned to him. "Your wish, highness, is doubtless to talk with my husband. Perhaps you will excuse the Lady Mary and myself." Swiftly she drew Mary into the bedroom and closed the door, so that only the faintest murmur of conversation came through it. Then she turned to Mary, who flung her arms around her waist, burying her head against her. Slowly the Lady Roelane began to stroke Mary's hair with a free hand. "Why, you are trembling more than ever."

Then wave after wave of stormy sobbing took control of Mary, and the older woman, still standing, began to sway from side to side, gently rocking the little girl as though she were soothing a frightened infant.

"Please be seated, your highness!" Lord Nasa said courteously. But his thoughts were on Mary. Was she weeping? He was sure he could hear her, but the heavy oaken door (padded on both sides with leather) made it difficult to tell what was happening. He turned his mind to his visitor, and became aware that he was being carefully scrutinized from beneath the heavy black eyebrows. He seated himself at the other end of the window seat, facing Duke Dukraz.

For several minutes there was silence.

Finally, drawing in a deep breath, Duke Dukraz said, "I am concerned about my sovereign, and have decided to take you into my confidence. The king has opted to follow the gods of Playsion, and this has me worried for two reasons."

Lord Nasa nodded but remained silent, waiting for the duke, who had been choosing his words with care, to continue. Eventually he said, "My first concern has to do with the priests. His majesty is willful and lacks discernment. I do not trust the priests, whether they be of Playsion or from Anthropos. Their sole aim seems to be to achieve political power. To them, I am sure, the institution of the crown means nothing, and they will stop at nothing to gain their objectives. If they cannot control his majesty, then they will not hesitate to eliminate him."

"You have expressed this to his majesty?"

"I have, but my protests are useless. His majesty is bewitched, and is entirely under their control."

"You mean—"

"I mean that they have pronounced some kind of spell over him. He has become a mouthpiece of some being that proclaims itself as 'Lord of Shadows.' He was weak at the best of times, but now his very thoughts are controlled by—by this spirit. He is like a man in a dream, a sort of channel for something greater and darker, voicing thoughts far more complex than his majesty could conceive. Whereas formerly I could guide his thinking, I am now utterly helpless before an intellect for which I am no match."

He sighed, placed his elbows on his knees and his head in his hands. The strong, self-possessed man seemed to have been replaced by a man with a great burden. After a moment he continued.

"It is not his majesty's intellect, but that of one of the great Lords of Shadows whom the sorcerers serve. They have created a monster, a man possessed by the gods, a man whose mind will eventually break down into insanity as it is crushed beneath the weight of the mind of a god. Indeed, I do not know whether his majesty still exists, or whether this lord of shadows merely is using an animated corpse. But this is only one of my worries. The second has me yet more deeply concerned."

Lord Nasa drew in a deep breath. "And your second worry?"

For several more minutes the duke lapsed into silence. Eventually he said, "Gods rule over countries and their peoples. Our priests have begun to worship the gods from Playsion—at my sovereign's orders— gods that do not belong in Anthropos. I am ignorant of such things, but I am dismayed to see us embark on a course which would arouse the wrath of any of the gods. Her majesty the queen worships the Emperor, who is not a human but a spirit being, a god, and according to reports from the early history of Anthropos a source of infinite power and goodness."

Lord Nasa nodded, and the duke continued.

"Battles are won and lost in the spirit realm, not here on the earth. That being the case, the priests may have done a foolish thing in following my king's orders and promoting the worship of the Lords of Shadows here. The gods decide issues of this sort, not men. Your Emperor sounds very powerful—but I have seen what these gods have done to his majesty, and I am nervous about meddling further."

Again, Lord Nasa nodded. "That is certainly true, and your assessment of the Emperor's power is correct. But, powerful or not, he holds his judgments back. He is patient, hoping Anthroponians will turn back to him from the gods of Playsion."

"What I want to ask you," the duke said eagerly, "is how may this Emperor, this god whom you serve, be appeased? Are there sacrifices that we may offer him? Will he respond to the surrender of human victims on altars of sacrifice? Or have we already gone too far? Is the matter already decided, our fate already sealed?"

"I am afraid I do not know whether—" Lord Nasa began, but the duke interrupted.

"Her majesty the queen speaks of prophecies of the total destruction of Bamah, of the sacrifice of a king, and of much more. It is precisely something of this sort that I fear. What are we to make of it all?" He seemed agitated, and had begun to rub his hands together as he continued. "Moreover, it is said that a king has been born here, a king who will stand for the Emperor and his ways. What do you know about this king? You referred earlier to the rumor of an infant, and declared that her majesty the queen was not inclined to palace intrigue. I believe you. But what do you know about the rumor, and how much substance might there be in it?"

Lord Nasa shrugged. "I have no knowledge of how much truth lies in the rumor. A king, they say, but where is he? Anthroponians have waited long for this king. I assure your highness that the matter seems altogether too insubstantial for me to credit. Frankly, prophecies mystify me."

The duke shook his head. "But there are certainly prophecies of the Emperor's terrible judgments. It is these I fear. Powerful as the

Lords of Shadows may be, they are no match for the Emperor. I feel in my bones that we are approaching a crisis."

"Her majesty has a far more comprehensive knowledge of the ancient records than I have myself," Lord Nasa replied. "What is more, she understands them—or seems to."

The duke sighed. "Then we must await her return. I suspect she knows more than she is willing to share with me. But I fear that if something is not done soon, his majesty's brain will give way, and we may have a madman on our hands. Even his voice has changed—it is his, yet not his. As for his eyes, at times they stare blankly, and at other times I know that another being looks at me through him. My spirit shudders when this happens, and a great fear steals over me."

Lord Nasa nodded. "You are suggesting, perhaps, that if his majesty's mind were to give way, the priests and sorcerers would seize power?"

"Precisely. Such an eventuality must be avoided at all costs."

"So why do you allow them to continue to influence the king?"

The duke rose to his feet, his face grim. "Because I am powerless to stop him from seeing them now. When this being that now occupies the king's body summons them, I must give way. It is not only his majesty but the crown itself that is threatened, and with it the very nature of rule. Already he is a pathetic puppet in the hands of Lords of the Dead and of the Shadows. Once the priests rule we will have the rule of Shadow itself—"

Lord Nasa also got to his feet. "And you fear your own gods?"

"I fear them greatly. They are vicious, cruel."

"Yet you worship them."

Duke Dukraz shook his head, beginning to pace up and down. "I never believed anything until recently, thinking priestcraft and sorcery nothing but ceremonial mummery. But I have witnessed the power that controls them—especially in his majesty himself—and I am afraid. If I were to worship any god, it would be the Emperor. However powerful and severe in his judgments, he appears to be the defender of the poor and the weak—and it is the duty of rulers to protect those they govern. The Emperor's vengeance against his faithless priests could be terrible, for at least he is a god of justice."

He continued to pace, frowning and biting his upper lip, his hands clenched behind his back. Then he paused and looked apologetically at Lord Nasa. "Forgive me, but I must leave you for the present. I am grateful for your listening ear. You have been a help."

Lord Nasa shook his head. "I fail to see in what way."

"You are an honest man, and it is always helpful to talk to one. There is little integrity in the court of his majesty."

He bowed and left the room. After he had gone, Lord Nasa continued to stand. Finally he sighed, shook his head and said, "He is right. I suppose we must await the queen's arrival. But the crisis may fall upon us before that."

11
Peril
at the
Waterfall

The canoers made rapid progress, though they had to paddle furiously against the slow current while watching for rocks jutting from the water. As the most proficient canoer, Lisa steered from the back of the smaller canoe and led them after the blue light ahead. Unaccustomed to canoe travel, and still fearing pursuit, Alleophaz and Belak gripped the sides of the canoe as Kurt and Wesley paddled hard. However, Gerachti (with Lisa in the smaller boat) scorned to show fear, though he sat as strained and stiff as the other two.

Darkness wrapped a heavy blanket around them all. A bizarre illusion seized their minds—it seemed to them that nothing existed but the column and themselves. River banks, trees and pursuers faded from their thoughts, leaving only the nightmare sense of peril behind. They could see nothing. Even rocks did not appear until the last moment, and Lisa could anticipate their approach only because of the column's movements. Then rocks would briefly emerge from oblivion, only to glide swiftly and smoothly behind.

Lisa's steering and paddling gradually became mechanical, though she never slackened pace. Soon she became dreamy, her arms moving automatically and effortlessly, the canoe simply sliding through the slick black waters.

"Where does this river arise?" Lisa asked drowsily at one point.

Gerachti replied, "Some maps call it the White Rure—white, I suppose, because of the rapids in its earlier course—others, the Alloway. According to the maps we consulted it springs from several sources in the mountains of northern Anthropos. What some people call the Black Rure, and others the River Nachash, joins it by turning a sharp corner some distance into Anthropos, where the White Rure joins the Black."

Slowly they grew used to their ride through the stillness of the night, the only sounds being those of the dipping paddles and the occasional gurgling of the water sweeping past. Lisa grew steadily more confident of the safety of following the blue column. There was no sign of pursuit, and as they continued, hour following hour, weariness began to steal into their limbs. The men soon joined them in their efforts, for there were enough paddles for everyone, and though canoeing was new to the older men, they imitated the children and were soon doing well.

Yet before too long they all had to force themselves to keep their eyes from closing and their heads from nodding. Finally, and with great relief, they saw the blue column of fire leave the river and lead them to a long, broad beach on the east bank.

Once they were on shore again the craving for sleep became too powerful to fight any longer. Alleophaz urged them to eat a little food, but they would have none of it. They wearily dragged the blankets of their bedrolls from the larger canoe and settled themselves as well as they could on the sandy beach. Sleep quickly overcame them, conquering even their fear of pursuit.

In the darkness they failed to see the wide track that came through the forest to the very place where they slept. Nor did they see further along the beach the dock of a ferry, and a rope connecting it to the far bank of the river. The place the blue column had chosen for them to sleep was apparently a place of extreme danger—yet it was the place to which the blue column had led them, and safety consisted in following it.

Eventually the gray dawn broke, and the outlines of tree-lined banks emerged from the blackness. Slowly light stole across the sky, and the sun climbed into a blue and cloudless sky. As the early morning hours passed, Lisa dreamed of a blinding light that she could not evade. In her dream she had been found by soldiers, who were shining a light in her face, a light so powerful that they themselves could not be seen. She woke, hot and sweaty, to find powerful sunlight pouring over her. "Oh, no!" she muttered. "It must be nearly noon!"

Unreasoning terror gripped her, and a bothered expression crossed her face. "Didn't I just dream something awful? What was it about?" she asked herself. But what was the dream? What *had* she dreamed? Strive as she might she could remember nothing of it. Her dream had evaporated, dissolved in the suddenness of her waking, so that she was left with terror but with no reason for it. She stared at the river and at the sunlight dancing dazzlingly on one section of it. Then as she rose to her feet she saw with a start the smoky column in mid-river, as if it were impatient for them to get moving. "Hey, everybody!" she found herself shouting. "Wake up! Wake up, everybody! The column is on the river!"

One by one they struggled into wakefulness, the two boys grumbling under their breath, and the men's mussed hair adding to an air of general stupidity.

"Hey! Wake up, everybody. We've got to get moving!" Lisa cried.

"Oh, can it, Lisa! Give us a chance to wake up," Kurt grumbled. "What's the hurry?"

Lisa did not know what the hurry was. Still gripped by the unexplained terror that woke her, she rapidly folded her blanket and threw it into the larger canoe. Then, as she turned from the canoe, she saw what the darkness had hidden from her the night before. At the far end of the beach a crude platform rested in the water. It was connected to a rope suspended above it, which linked in turn with a jetty at the far side of the river. "A ferry—it must connect the old road with the new!" she breathed. Though there was no sign of a ferryman, the sight of the ferry greatly increased her sense of urgency.

And then she saw the road of beaten earth leading back into the forest. "Look!" she cried. "A road and a ferry!" While they had slept they had been in the very place their enemies may have been aiming to reach!

Alleophaz sprang to his feet, followed by Gerachti and Belak. "This is no safe haven!" A note of alarm rang in Alleophaz's voice. "Into the boats! We can eat later. The sooner we are away from here, the better!"

They hurled their bedrolls into the canoes and began to launch them, just as Gerachti cried, "I hear hoofbeats!" A moment later a mounted group of armed men rounded a bend in the roadway, and their burst of yelling and shouting told the travelers they had been spotted.

Their enemies were upon them. For a frozen moment the party on the beach stared in shock at the sight of their pursuers. Then, aware only of a need to escape, they continued to push the canoes into the river.

Lisa's canoe was afloat first, though Gerachti clambered over the back end of it and nearly capsized it. The leading horseman broke onto the beach even as Alleophaz pushed the larger canoe afloat, scrambling over the stern as Gerachti had done.

The horseman, never hesitating, rode his horse into the water and raised his sword to strike. "Stop!" he yelled breathlessly. "In the name of the king, stop!"

Alleophaz swung round to meet him, a spare paddle in his hand. As the swordsman leaped at him, Alleophaz drove the butt of the paddle into the man's belly. Grunting and groaning, the soldier doubled, fell from his horse and dropped his sword into the water.

His head struck the stern of the canoe, rocking it wildly and almost overturning it. The boys dug their paddles deep into the water and pulled hard—and still rocking, they shot out into the river following Lisa. She pointed ahead to the column of smoke, waiting at a bend in the river two hundred yards away. Though at this point only Lisa could see it, they followed her lead without hesitation.

For several minutes nobody said a word, saving their breath as they paddled frantically away from the yells and shouts of their pursuers. Alleophaz turned his head to see what was happening and watched the fallen horseman being dragged by his comrades onto the beach. Then, as the distance increased, he saw the rest of the horsemen proceeded to load their horses, one man and one horse at a time, onto the platform to cross the river.

"They are not giving up," said Alleophaz. "They will follow that road to Bamah."

As the canoes rounded a bend in the river, the activity at the ferry was lost from view. For a long time afterward, still following the column, the travelers concentrated on putting as much distance between themselves and the ferry as possible. Their throats were dry, their arms and backs aching, and their lungs ready to burst. Blisters formed on their hands, though they did not feel them until later.

They saw no sign of the Bamah road—and though no one had eaten, there was no thought of food. But as one hour after another passed, their sense of danger lessened and they began to slacken their pace. Eventually the two canoes drew level with each other. Lisa suddenly called out in awe, "The column is headed for the shore—on the right! I guess it must know we're tired!" She turned to follow it.

"Where are you going?" Alleophaz called out to her.

"The column's headed for the shore."

"It might not be safe on this side," Wesley said, frowning, "though I can't see any road."

Alleophaz pointed to the right-hand bank further along the river. "There should be a large tributary joining the river soon, from the side we are heading for. And—look! There it is!"

A couple of hundred yards ahead of them they could make out a turbulence in the river where two currents met. They beached the canoes carefully in the shingle, only to discover they were on a narrow, tree-covered spit of land that separated the river they had journeyed on from another, smaller river which they could see through the trees.

"I wonder—" Kurt began.

"I suspect we are supposed to eat before we continue," Gerachti interrupted. "Anyway, it would do us no harm. We will soon lose our strength if we do not."

"The column has disappeared." Lisa's forehead wrinkled.

Belak said, "Well, we are not going to be able to move for the moment—that is, not if we are supposed to be following it."

They ate as quickly as possible and drank from the river. Wesley, ever the fusspot, worried a little. "The waters are clear enough, not that clearness means anything. Though come to think of it, I never heard of anyone getting sick from Anthropos water."

Lisa continued to frown. "I must keep a lookout for the column," she thought.

A few moments later she caught sight of it again, but this time it was moving along the narrow spit of land that separated them from the other river. "The column's over there now," she cried, pointing.

Belak said, "Oh—yes it is! I can see it too!"

"Do we drag the canoes across?" Kurt asked, puzzled.

Alleophaz said, "No—leave them here. This must be the end of our river journey. Besides, we have no time—I can see the column too, and it has not stopped moving."

So they snatched up their packs and abandoned the canoes, then stumbled in haste through the trees to the bank of the river on the other side. There they followed the column down an almost invisible path—narrow and overgrown, which they would never have discovered without the column's guidance. They followed it upriver, proceeding almost in the opposite direction to the one they had been traveling.

"Can anyone hear anything?" Wesley asked.

"What sort of thing?" Kurt returned.

"I can hear a deep sort of—well, like a waterfall."

Belak, in his squeaky voice, said, "I can hear it too."

They proceeded to an eastward bend in the river, the new sound growing clearer as they approached it. By now they were aware of a deep note like distant thunder. On rounding the bend they found themselves quickening their pace as a magnificent spectacle came slowly into view.

"Wow! Take a look at that!" Kurt said.

Over a two-hundred-foot bluff, the river plunged downward to greet them—a splendid cataract of crystal, tumbling through a rainbow-arched cloud of spray and mist. Vapor shrouded the foot of the falls where a pool glistened, emerging fern-fringed into the sunlight from beneath the mist. Ferns clambered on the sides of the falls between wet and shining rocks.

As they reached the pool they stood awestruck, waist-deep among ferns and bracken, deafened by the thunderous roar and marveling at what they saw above them. But soon their wonder turned to dismay.

"The column!" Lisa cried, her shrill voice penetrating the roar of the plunging cataract. "It's—it's way up there near the top of the falls!"

There was a shocked pause as their eyes focused on the column, hovering two-thirds of the way up the falls. Dismayed, they wondered how they could ever follow.

Gerachti broke the pause, yelling loudly to make sure he was heard. "It is possible. And if nobody minds, I will lead the way. The rocks will be slippery, so we will have to take great care! Alleophaz—forgive me for leading, but could you bring up the rear?"

Wesley gazed upward, dismayed. "However will we do it?" he muttered to himself. "Still, if Gerachti's game, I guess I'll try to follow. I hope Gaal—if that's who the column is—knows what he's doing!"

For a long time Gerachti frowned upward, working out the route of their ascent. He began the climb a little distance from the falling water, where the ascent was less than vertical. They formed a line,

Gerachti leading and picking his way carefully round the pool, pausing to look up from time to time. He was followed by Wesley, Lisa and Kurt, and behind them came Belak and Alleophaz. Soon they were tackling the wet and steep ascent, taking infinite care. Gerachti chose his way with caution, and stopped often to shout careful instructions.

They slipped frequently, scraping their shins, knees and elbows. Though they moved at a snail's pace they grew short of breath, and in spite of the coolness found beads of sweat running down their faces. Only the strong Gerachti was accustomed to using his fingers and arms so much, and the rest wasted much of their energy in inefficient movements.

At one point it was possible to pause, and they stood almost together, panting.

"The worst is over, I think," Gerachti shouted over the powerful roar of the water. "The remainder should be easier."

He was wrong. The worst section of all came immediately before they reached the column. Using his tremendous physique, Gerachti succeeded in reaching a sort of broad ledge over which the column hovered, ten or fifteen feet away and right next to the falling water. With incredible agility, he pulled himself onto the ledge by little more than his fingertips.

"I can't do that!" Wesley muttered to himself, dismayed. "I can't even reach the ledge!"

Gerachti grinned, then lay full length above Wesley and reached down to him. "Grab my wrists," he yelled, "and I will grab yours!"

Wesley seized the thick, dark and powerful wrists, and then Gerachti used his great strength to haul Wesley up. "Now, release my wrists—I will still hang on to you. Get a grip on the ledge and *pull!*"

The ledge was wet and slippery, but Wesley's fingers held firm. Once he was sure that Wesley's grip would hold, Gerachti shifted his own hold to Wesley's upper arms, and pulled. Wesley scrambled onto the ledge, exhausted, breathless and grateful. Then one by one, and in the same manner, Gerachti helped the rest to follow.

But when, having recovered their strength, they turned to look at the column of smoke, they had more reason to be dismayed. It hovered above the ledge on which they stood, right against the waterfall. Then it disappeared into the waterfall itself, only to reappear. Again it vanished into the wall of water, and came back. Then it disappeared a third time, and they waited in vain for its return.

A minute passed, then two. "It's gone!" Kurt's voice was edged with panic.

"I believe it is telling us it is safe to go forward!" Alleophaz called back.

"Safe?" Belak was shaking, partly from exhaustion, partly from fear, and they were all filled with deep uncertainty.

But not Alleophaz, who turned his untroubled face toward the falls. "Perhaps the time has come for me to lead the way," he yelled above the roar. Gently working his way past the others on the ledge, he stood beside the tumbling water, his body misted in spray. For a moment he hesitated. Then, as he moved forward they caught a glimpse of him framed against splaying water—and he was gone, and again they waited. Long seconds later he returned, treading very carefully on the rough but slippery stone. Rivulets of water streamed down his face and drained from his drenched robes.

"It is not at all bad!" he cried as he drew near them. "I expected a far greater weight of water, but there is very little falling just there!"

"Very *little?!*" This time the protest came from Kurt.

Alleophaz started to laugh, and controlled himself only with difficulty. "Take care how you place your feet," he yelled. "Test every step. The ledge is very slippery."

Grinning briefly at Wesley, he turned and disappeared. Wesley drew a tremulous breath and walked into the wall of water. He felt the shock of the icy water, and suddenly wondered if he had walked into a dream—for a few seconds he felt he was somewhere in the air above his body, looking down on himself, watching himself below with perfect calm.

Then, with equal suddenness, the water was gone and he was back inside himself, moving toward the smiling figure of Alleophaz. On his left was a gleaming, dazzling, sunlit wall of water, like a vast translucent window illuminating the high-ceilinged chamber around them. Though water splashed fiercely against the rocky ledge, behind the waterfall the roar was greatly subdued. They could talk rather than shout.

"Here is Lisa!" Alleophaz said. Wesley turned to see her emerge, gasping with the shock of the cold and dripping water. He grabbed her hands to steady her, and swung her closer to him. She was followed by Kurt. Then came Belak, who fell heavily onto his back, slipping slowly sideways with his lower half in the chamber and the rest of him lost to view. Wesley and Kurt grabbed his feet and pulled him through the wall of water.

Inside, and out of danger, Belak struggled to his feet just as Gerachti joined them. Suddenly they began to talk, and then laugh as they moved into a dry area of rock away from the falls. Even Belak, who had been badly scared by his narrow escape, joined in the laughter and talk. For a few minutes they seemed unaware of the fact that they were very cold.

Then a man's voice rang out. "You are under arrest!"

Emerging from a low tunnel the travelers had not even noticed, an older officer stood at the rear of the chamber, flanked by six soldiers with drawn swords.

12
Yearning for Terror

A good hour passed before Mary's sobs subsided. As she tried to get words out she said things like, "I'm s-so-oh-oh f-fri-fri-frightened," but mostly she just sobbed. Lady Roelane stood stroking her hair and rocking her. Later, Lady Roelane sat in a chair while Mary knelt on the floor and rested her head in the lady's lap.

Her torrential sobbing would die down for a brief period, then begin again, working itself to yet another peak, each crisis more subdued than the one before. Finally there was no sobbing left, only the strange spasms of breath that follow prolonged weeping.

Mary raised her head at last, and saw the mess her tears and running nose had made of the Lady Roelane's gown. Her tears began again as she sobbed. "Oh—l-l-look what I've done to your l-lovely dr-dr-ess!"

Lady Roelane rose to her feet, pulled several of her husband's handkerchiefs from one of the bags and passed most of them to Mary.

"Oh, it is a small matter. The dress was due to be washed in any case. Come sit with me in the window seat." And there they sat without speaking, the woman's arm round Mary and the girl's head resting against Lady Roelane's shoulder.

Mary's mind went back to that awful, awful night when her step-mother sent her away forever to the Friesens in Winnipeg—people she had never met before. At supper she had been in a foul mood, and had stormed out of the dining room in a rage. Then, in a strange adventure that she had never been able to explain, her bed had behaved in just the same way Lady Roelane had, cradling her and rocking her.

"An' then Gaal came striding across the snow," she said softly as the memory came to her. "It was ever so pretty. He lit everything up so that the crystals of snow flashed gorgeous colors—only I'm not really describing it properly—not like it really was."

If Lady Roelane (who could have had little idea what Mary was talking about) was confused, she gave no sign of it. She said nothing, but quietly and gently stroked the girl's hair with her free hand.

"He gave me the Sword of Geburah," Mary continued, "and told me to give to Wesley—he's not the real Sword Bearer, you know, my Uncle John's the real Sword Bearer." She sighed. "I hope we find him, even if that old lady's with him. An' then he—I mean Gaal, not Uncle John—Gaal gave me a poem to remember and messages to give the Friesens."

Again there was silence, and Lady Roelane's own thoughts began to wander. She could faintly hear the sound of the two men talking in the next room, and wondered what it was they were discussing. Why would the duke want to talk to her husband? Mary had been talking for some time when Lady Roelane began to listen once more.

". . . he's only trying to use you, y'know. It seems like kindness, but it's not really."

"Oh?" Lady Roelane, bothered by her inattention, was not sure what else to say

"Sure. He never actually gives you power. Not like the witch did. She was great. Mirmah, I mean. She gave me a ball and chain, an' I could go wherever I wanted with it."

Lady Roelane smiled. "That sounds like a rather strange idea—a ball and chain to go wherever you want!"

"Oh, no, not that kind of ball and chain. What she gave me was a tiny crystal ball, a sort of pendant. When I threw it into a fire it would swell up and show a scene inside it. Then I would walk into the scene."

"You mean she let you go anywhere you wanted?"

"Oh, she asked me to do one or two things for her—"

"But other times you were free to choose?"

"Well, no, not really."

"Then how do you know that this witch was doing not the very same thing you just accused someone else of doing—simply 'using' you?"

"Well, I could escape if I wanted to."

"Did you ever try?"

"Yes, I did. An' what's more, I almost didn't make it!"

"Then it sounds to me as though *escape* is the right word. The witch does not sound like such a wonderful person, after all."

"I know. Gaal said the same thing—or was it Queen Suneidesis? She said I didn't own the crystal ball, but it owned me. Hm!"

Then for several minutes she said no more. A look of contentment began to steal across her face, and her tears began to dry. When she spoke again, she frowned a little. "She told me that was exactly what the witch wanted to do—to own me and use me. It was a risk, an' it could've gone wrong. But—" she groped in her mind for a phrase— "but you know, *that's the way the cookie crumbles!*" The phrase sounded good, and she felt she had scored a point.

Lady Roelane drew in a deep breath. "Mary, a few minutes ago you were sobbing your heart out and telling me you were very frightened. But you have not yet told me what it was you were frightened about— did it have something to do with witchcraft? Just what were you and the captain talking about?"

"I told him about wanting to meet the sorcerers here, an' he told me his daughter was dead—offered as a sacrifice on the altar outside the temple three years ago."

"Oh, Mary!" A shocked and frightened shadow crossed Lady Roelane's face. "I can understand why you were frightened. I had heard that matters were not well in the temple. Do you know that the temple was originally built to worship the Changer-Emperor? I had no idea how far things had gone."

There was a long pause. Eventually she spoke again, but absently, almost as though she had forgotten Mary's presence. "You know, I should have realized. Bamah is to be destroyed, even the temple—the prophecies the queen has talked about make it plain. Mary, a little while ago you talked about someone using you. The way you said the word *use* made what you said sound evil—unclean, cruel, as though the person who used you, who made use of you, did not really care for you. As though he saw you more like a slave than a real servant. Or even worse than a slave—perhaps as a machine."

"Sure. That's exactly what he does. That's what everybody does. Him too."

"Who, Mary? You were not talking of Gaal, surely."

"I sure was!"

"Mary!"

"That's what he does! Don't let him fool you!"

Lady Roelane drew a deep breath in again. "Mary, something must have happened—you would not be talking like this without a cause. Tell me why you think Gaal 'uses' people."

"It would take a long time."

"We have all the time you need. We do not even have to finish talking today, so start telling me the whole story."

Mary sighed. For several minutes she said nothing, and then, just as Lady Roelane had done, she took a deep breath. "O.K. It's like this. I used to be ugly—even uglier than I am now."

"Mary, that is absurd. You are not ugly, and you must not say that you are. It is not true. You have the loveliest eyes, especially when they are not troubled. Sometimes they are extraordinarily beautiful."

"I'm fat. An' Lisa keeps bugging me about it."

"Lisa?"

"Lisa Friesen. I live at Uncle John's with the Friesens."

"Well, possibly you are heavier than you need to be, but that does not make you ugly."

"Only thin people are beautiful in our world."

"Then it is a world of great folly, not a world in which I would care to live. There must be a lot of needless suffering in it if you are despised because you are too heavy."

"You're thin!"

"But I hope I do not remain thin! I want to bear children. And after childbearing I will be buxom."

"Buxom?"

Lady Roelane laughed. "Fat—at any rate, fatter than I am now!"

Mary thought for a moment, then said, "Well, kids used to make fun of me, especially for my zits—pimples, y'know, an' the witch promised to make me beautiful."

"And did she?"

"Oh—did she *ever!*"

"Tell me about it."

Mary told how the witch had given her three horrid crystals to swallow that made her very beautiful. But as she admired herself in a mirror the witch had told her to stay away from, someone else appeared there who mocked her. Rather than seeing a reflection, it was more like looking through a window. It scared Mary deeply.

Lady Roelane thought, and then said, "I do not think it was a girl on the far side of the mirror, but some kind of spirit being, perhaps a shadow spirit."

Mary nodded. "I know. I just didn't want to say it."

"And do you mean that you trusted the witch after that?"

Mary shook her head. "All I wanted to do was to get away from her. You can't trust witches either." She paused, and the tone of her voice changed completely. "No—you can't trust anyone, not anyone! I trust you. You're nice, but, well, you're too *innocent,* too ready to trust people."

"You mean I trust Gaal."

"Yeah. See, I trusted him. But I don't trust anyone now. Not anyone. Gaal should have left me my Uncle John. I'll never trust him again."

"You will not trust witches and sorcerers?"

"Of course not. I trust ME, you know, like Julie Andrews sings in *The Sound of Music*, 'I have confidence in me!' "

Lady Roelane shook her head. She placed her hands on Mary's shoulders and looked into her eyes, still shaking her head. "I have never met a girl like you, Mary. Some older people, yes! But that someone who is little more than a child should talk as you do . . ."

"I've learned from real life," Mary said. "An' I'm smart. Everyone says I have a high I.Q. Well, I'm gonna use it to get what I want. An' nobody, not even you, is going to stop me."

"Mary, you amaze me! As for me, I may not be quite so innocent as you think. I have reasons for trusting Gaal, and the last person I would ever trust is myself. In this life you *have* to trust someone bigger and stronger than yourself, because if you serve Gaal—and even if you do not—the elemental spirits of the universe are far stronger than you. Believe me, Mary, the spirit world is powerful, far more powerful than any human being."

Mary said, "But if you can't trust either side, then you have no choice. Who else is there to trust but myself—*me*?"

Lady Roelane continued as if she had not heard. "Think of the mirror and the spirit behind it. How did it get there? Did you really think you could get away with keeping that false beauty?"

"Gaal wouldn't let me keep it anyway. He was jealous."

"Oh, Mary, it is not that way. Either you serve Gaal or you serve the Lords of Shadows. That is the only choice you have. You simply have to serve someone. Take your pick."

She raised her eyebrows. "I'll just have to take my chances." She shrugged, suppressing her terror.

Lady Roelane shook her head. "Mary, Mary—you do not know how lovely Gaal is."

"Sure I do. At least, I know how lovely he can seem. I sobbed my eyes out after seeing that thing behind the mirror. I was scared—just like when I came in here. An' then Gaal came. Oh, it was so lovely!"

Her thoughts seemed far away, and Lady Roelane continued to look at her, waiting for her to go on. "He took me somewhere," Mary resumed, "I dunno where it was, mebbe here in Anthropos. I was sitting at the foot of a tree at night an' he started to produce the northern lights. I've never seen them so clearly, only suddenly it wasn't just the northern lights anymore."

"What was it?"

"It was—spirits—dancing in the sky." She struggled for words. "Huge spirits leaping and turning somersaults in what he said was worship. Or was it me who saw it that way?"

"If he said so, then it was."

". . . an' it went on, and on, and on. Then dawn came, a dawn like no other dawn I'd ever seen. An' the sun rose. We walked together and the stones were leaping round his feet. I heard a tree weeping for joy, because he was there . . ."

Mary's face was alight for a moment before bitterness and sadness swept over her. "He said the same sort of things you are saying."

"Why can you not trust him, Mary?"

"Because he's not to be trusted."

"Why?"

"Because he doesn't give you power. An' I need power. You can get power out of the other side. Mind you it's risky, and you can't play safe. But I'll just have to take my chances." A noble sort of feeling was filling her, a feeling that she was someone lifting her head before a cruel universe. She was pitifully small, but bold and unafraid.

"Gaal gives power, Mary. He gives it to all his people."

"You have to do whatever he says to get power from him. He makes it *conditional.*" She felt proud of the word.

"No, Mary, he gives it as a free gift. You do not even have to be good—just forgiven."

Mary shook her head. "It may seem like that, but it's not."

"Mary, what would you do if you had lots and lots of power? What would you do with all that power?"

"I'd make sure nobody would boss me around. I'd do whatever I wanted."

"Bad things? Good things?"

"There's no difference?"

"I see. So just what would you do?"

Mary thought. "Well, I wouldn't mind bossing some people around!"

"Some people? How many?"

Mary giggled. "Mebbe I'd have a crack at ruling the universe!"

"Seriously?"

"Why not? It would be fun!"

"Do you think Gaal would allow that? He seems to think that he and the Emperor rule."

Mary's face changed. "Gaal again. Look, I wouldn't want to have anything to do with Gaal. I'd be in charge of my little area—I have a right to live life the way I want! Surely I can do that! I'll go my way an' he can go his!"

"And if he chose not to let you? Could you take him on, Mary?"

The bitterness flooded Mary again. "He's come to me twice since I've been here. He says horrible things about my real mother. He says he brought me here, an' that I didn't come by my own magic. He says he'll never let me go."

"And is the risk worth the terror you have experienced more than once already?"

A light began to flood the room, and both of them saw it. Mary leaped to her feet. "If this is him . . ."

The light continued to grow. A shape was becoming apparent inside it, and Mary's face flushed. "GO AWAY!" she shrieked. "Go away—an' NEVER COME BACK!"

Slowly the figure became less distinct. The light began to fade, and then disappeared altogether.

Silence filled the room, and Mary herself stood wordless for some time. When next she spoke, her tone revealed none of her feelings.

"Mebbe he'll not come back—ever again."

That night Mary dreamed the most vivid and lovely dream she had ever dreamed. At least it began as a lovely dream. *Lovely* would not have been the best word to describe it as it went on. She was on a sailing ship, like the vessel on which she had once sailed on the amazing voyage from Mirmah's kingdom back to the Playsion harbor of Chalash. But there was no crew now. Mary was alone on a ship that sailed across an inconceivably blue sea, one whose waters reflected the deep shades of the sky above her head. The ship sailed by magic, its sails billowing in an unfelt breeze, and left a wake of boiling white to fade into the sea behind. The sun warmed her, while a light breeze from ahead cooled her. Only the solitude gave her the faintest feeling that all was not perfect. It would have been nicer to have someone.

"The Friesen kids must be somewhere around. Surely King Kardia must be on board, or Tiqvah—or *somebody.* "

She made her way below decks, wandering down empty corridors, through vast unoccupied holds, into cabins where beds were perfectly made. But no, there was not a soul on board. The more she wandered, the lonelier she grew. And as she wandered, she knew that there was someone she specially wanted to find, but whom at the same time she feared to find. Yet on she searched, looking for the one she both desired and dreaded. While she wandered, she grew aware that the gentle swaying of the swells had increased considerably. Soon she was losing her balance, stumbling against the bulkheads. She fought her way up to the deck again and found the scene had changed.

Most of the sails had been furled by an invisible hand, and instead of running before a gentle breeze, the ship was now running into an ever more furious gale. Still driven by an unseen power, the ship was surging *into* the wind. Ahead of them, the sky was covered by a black cloud that seemed intent on destroying everything in its path. Mary bent her head, leaning into the wind that threatened to sweep her off her feet. It came in swirling gusts, so that one moment she was fighting her way into it, and the next was running forward to maintain her balance as it slackened.

In the dream her feelings deepened and intensified, engulfing her from the inside out. She spread her arms to the wind as though she were trying to hug it, crying aloud, "I never realized it till now. I love you, love you!" Tears streamed down her cheeks as she sobbed again and again, "I'm scared of you, and I thought I hated you, but I don't. I love you! Oh, I love you so much!"

She moved to the bow of the vessel, as far forward as she could get. The vast black bank of clouds rapidly approached the ship, and dark, mountainous waves rose ahead of them, ascending to a terrifying height. Mary's body shook, and her muscles turned to water. The first wave rose high above them and then crashed down on the deck—crushing her under its appalling weight, choking her as she tried to breathe, chilling her to the bone. The weight pressed her into the timbers of the deck, and swept her helplessly backward to smash against the mainmast.

Coughing and spluttering, bruised and bleeding, she struggled to her feet, only to see a second wave, vaster by far than the first, a veritable mountain of a wave, bearing down on them. Yet she spread her arms to welcome it. *How she loved that wave!* Greater than the chill of the icy wave was the great burning inside her, a burning she could no longer control, a burning that made her cry out, "Come to me! Come and destroy me if that's what it takes! I don't care anymore! I love you, love you! I didn't know it. You're all I want!" She knew now that Gaal was in the storm, in some mysterious way *was* the storm. And though the storm terrified her more than anything she had ever seen or experienced, her love for him as she now saw him—even as a storm—made her careless of death itself.

The mountain of water fell, smashing the ship and turning it to matchwood. There was no deck left beneath her, and her life was being pressed out by the water itself. She could not breathe against the blackness that shrouded her.

Then came a great stillness. "I guess I'm dead," she thought.

She woke at that moment to find herself back in her bed. In the faint gray of the dawn, she could perceive the outline of the guard house beyond the courtyard. She sat up, shivering a little in the cold, the emotion of the dream still churning inside her. She began to weep in quiet despair, with no sobs this time.

The dream needed no interpretation. "I didn't know I loved him," she said miserably. "The dream was dead on. 'Cos deep down I really do love him. I know now. I'd do anything for him, go anywhere. I was crazy to say he uses people. *But now it's too late. I told him to go and never come back.*"

She wrapped her arms round her knees, hugging them to herself. Finally, in quiet desperation, she sighed. "Well, I don't care. I'll go an' see the sorcerers today. There's nothing left now. Mebbe that's what I meant to do in the end."

13

Prisoners of the Crown

"You are under arrest, I say!" came the voice from the back of the chamber. "You are prisoners of the crown!"

Alleophaz separated himself from the group, standing between them and the soldiers. In a loud voice that carried a surprising weight of authority he said, "I and two of my companions are emissaries from his majesty King Kalastriel Bels of Glason. We bear letters from his majesty that are only for the eyes of the king and queen of Anthropos!"

The man with a colonel's badge remained where he was. "And the three children who are with you," he asked, "have they, by any chance, come across the stars by unknown paths from a distant world?"

Alleophaz frowned. "I did not ask to be insulted," he returned steadily. "As for the children, you are at liberty to question them yourself."

The colonel directed his attention to Wesley. "Tell me, young sir, did you come to this world from your own world?"

"Well, yes, as a matter of fact we did," Wesley answered.

Alleophaz swung round to face them, an astounded look on his face. Gerachti also looked very startled, as did Belak.

"And did you travel by miraculous power, using the hidden pathways among the stars?"

"So it would seem," admitted Wesley.

"And are there three more of you somewhere in Anthropos?" came a final question from the colonel.

"Yes—at least we suspect so. There's certainly another girl."

Gerachti laughed. "So that was why you did not tell us where you were from!"

The colonel continued. "Your lordships, my instructions are to take you all into protective custody. The forces of his majesty the king are determined to arrest you at the request of the priests, who tell a doubtful story of your menace to the state. The queen, who has her own sources of information, is most anxious to prevent this, and the most obvious way to do so is for her to arrest you. In this way, under the laws of Anthropos, even the king may not touch you."

Alleophaz nodded. "I see. But how may I be sure that you do in fact serve the queen? For all I know you could be arresting us at the orders of the king."

Wesley's limbs tingled. How could they be sure? They could hardly resist men with drawn swords—nor were they in a position to take flight, for there was no safe and rapid way down the rocks again. But Wesley remembered the guide that had gone before them, and a deep assurance stole over him. They had been led over this perilous route by the blue column, and whatever it seemed, this must be safety before them.

The colonel did not answer, but beckoned them onward into the tunnel The soldiers sheathed their swords, but Wesley noticed that they carried the torches in their left hands, and could readily use their sword arms if needed Three soldiers preceded them, their torches smoking in the tunnel. The three children and the three philosophers followed the colonel, and the remaining three soldiers brought up the rear. The corridor was wide, enabling them at times to walk three abreast, though two abreast was more comfortable.

Darkness opened up steadily before them. They walked for nearly an hour, looking in vain for light ahead. The walls on either side of them were damp, gleaming in torchlight wherever water flowed down them. There was a constant sound of dripping, and occasionally they slopped through shallow pools of water. Lurid, flickering shadows danced along the walls, bobbing and changing in shape over the uneven rocky sides.

Eventually Alleophaz began to murmur to Kurt. "So now I know why you said you were sworn to secrecy! I certainly would never have believed you had you told us you came from worlds afar!"

Kurt smiled to himself. "It would have been difficult to tell you where we were from." He pictured Hong Kong in his mind, the streets crowded with vehicular traffic, the underground and the train, Kai Tak airport and the endless parade of landing jets. "I suppose if we had been wearing the clothes from our world, you might have been more inclined to believe us."

"You were not dressed as you are now?"

"No. We were all wearing jeans."

"Jeans?"

Kurt laughed. "How do I explain jeans? People in our world tend more and more to dress in the same way. Jeans are pants for men or women. They're made of heavy cotton. They used to be just for laborers, but gradually they became high fashion. You can wear them to work or for leisure, though businessmen and religious people tend not to. When people relax you can hardly tell who's rich and who's poor. Well, you can—but not because they're wearing jeans. There's a different set of rules for that." He frowned, wondering how to explain brand-name products. Fortunately, he was saved the trouble.

"It looks as though we are coming to the end of the tunnel," Alleophaz said. Soon they halted where the tunnel ended in a flat surface of rock. Then, as the colonel reached forward and pressed a shallow area in it, a slab of rock that must have weighed many tons swung noiselessly outward. Immediately they covered their faces, shielding their eyes against the light that came from beyond the slab. For a whole hour they had been exposed only to torchlight, and now the mere daylight blinded them.

Still blinking their eyes painfully, they emerged from the end of a low and narrow passage into a small meadow among tall trees. Behind two tables a bivouac stood, and beyond the bivouac were tethered horses and more tents. A dozen soldiers sat at one of the tables, while food and dishes lay on an unoccupied table nearby.

A tall woman emerged from the great tent, followed by two maids. The travelers saw her, and their remaining fears about who had arrested them were relieved.

"Ah—there you are, Colonel Emoona!" the tall woman cried. "You found them! You have done well—and now we can proceed."

There was no mistaking her regal bearing in spite of the old and worn leather jerkin and the riding breeches she wore. Her hair was short and blond, her face narrow, with firm lips and widely spaced blue eyes, sparkling now with obvious delight.

She bade the soldiers sit, and turned to the rest of the group. "I am Queen Suneid of Anthropos. It is wonderful to see you! I came personally, because I fear greatly for your safety. Already I believe you understand the need for and the nature of your 'arrest,' but please be assured that you are to be treated as my guests. Come and sit down— there is food at the table. The afternoon is passing and we must soon hasten toward Bamah, for you are still in danger here, even under my protection."

They were presented to her one by one as they took their seats around the table. Quietly, Alleophaz pulled his sealed package from inside his clothing. Kneeling on one knee, he passed it to the queen, a smile twitching his lips.

"I deliver this to you," he said, "as a message from our sovereign to his majesty, King Tobah Khukah of Anthropos-Playsion. It proposes trade relations with Glason. Since you have 'arrested' us it is only fitting that you should 'capture' any documents in our possession."

The queen accepted it gravely. "I do not know how his majesty will react to this, for I fear he is no longer the person I married. But your safety with me is assured."

A magnificent repast lay before them, doubly welcome after their day of haste and evasion. There were pheasants, venison, meats of many kinds, fruit, wines and breads. While they ate, the queen inquired about their journey, and managed to draw from Alleophaz a clear account of the real nature of their visit. "It seems to me," she said, her blue eyes twinkling, "that you had a lot more in mind in coming here than trade. I sense a hunger in your hearts that has nothing to do with commerce between our two countries."

"We are philosophers, your majesty, and we hunger for truth."

"And you seek it here? Why?"

So Alleophaz told her of the vision he had experienced, and of the perilous two-year journey that brought them to Anthropos.

"And you have eluded the soldiers despatched to arrest you. Remarkable! The perils of the Playsion forest are very well known, for few people have ever ventured through it and come out alive. How did you do it?"

Between them the children explained about the strange column of smoke with inner blue fires, of the trees and rocks that reminded them of the old legends and sayings of the books of Anthropos history.

"Anthropos history? Now I know you have been here before," the queen observed quietly.

It took a little while for them to explain their visits to future times in Anthropos, and of their knowledge of the laws and customs of Anthropos. But the queen seemed to accept their experiences, saying that she had a copy of the original book, which seemed also to contain great power. They also began to tell her of Uncle John's adventures in the earliest days of Anthropos.

"Yes, yes, of course. The Sword Bearer. How often I have read about his adventures in the sacred books! But what occupies our attention most is the promised coming of the Emperor's Emissary who is to rule in Anthropos."

Her eyes burned with intense longing, and she spoke with a distant and wistful look which changed the whole appearance of her face. "I spend many hours seeking the Emperor's presence. During those times I have felt that the arrival is near. The young king of whom you speak may well be the one—but he will be a king in no earthly sense."

Returning to their present difficulties, she also explained the nature of the danger still facing them. "His majesty is most unlikely to give any orders that would affect my own right to dispose of my prisoners as I see fit. He is not the source of my fears, for the priests and sorcerers grow in power every day, and he is a puppet in their hands. More than that, the priests have begun to issue instructions in the king's name. This is where the danger may lie, for there are ambitious men in Anthropos who would not hesitate to make an alliance with the priests to overthrow his majesty."

They finished their meal quickly, and soon the tents were struck and packed on mules. The queen changed into a shirt of chain mail and a helmet, and buckled a short, two-edged sword to her side. The horses were saddled again, and the party descended through the trees to the trail that led to Bamah.

As they passed through a small meadow, Kurt noticed two trees on the far side. Hills rose in the distance between and beyond them, but a bluish light lit the trunks of the two trees.

He blinked, and the light was gone. Then the banter between Wesley and Lisa caught his attention, and the incident slipped from his mind.

There was no sign of the king's forces in the woods, and soon they reached the Anthropos Road. The queen, the colonel and Lisa (with whom the queen seemed to enjoy talking) led the way, while Kurt and Wesley followed immediately behind.

But as they turned a bend in the road they saw a large party of soldiers approaching them from the opposite direction. The queen said, "This is exactly what I had anticipated! Let us go to meet them."

"We already have plans laid, your majesty," said the colonel. "We may make short work of them, for our men are hardy and experienced—and there is much at stake here."

"Yes, very much," replied the queen. "And we are outnumbered, so let us remind them of the legalities first. They are hardly likely to rush at us without parley.

"I suspect their first goal will be to arrest us as traitors on charges trumped up by Shagah. We will not act until we see that this is indeed their intent. I also want to know who leads them, for if it should be the man I expect, then I fully intend to venture my person against him."

The colonel swung round to face her. "Your majesty must not even consider anything so rash! Much hangs on the preservation of your majesty's life."

"Quite so," she answered camly. "But think a moment, colonel. We are likely, however valiant and experienced our men, to be worsted by a mob the size of the one that approaches. See how their numbers seem to swell, even as they advance! Moreover, I want my liberty as well as my life. If they are able to confine me to my quarters, their objectives will be far easier to carry out."

"Your majesty, I have no wish to oppose you—"

"Then do not do so!"

"—but your majesty could lose her life!"

The queen reined her horse and turned to face the colonel. "Colonel Emoona, I know your faithfulness and your concern, but just now there are but two effective authorities in Anthropos, Shagah the Sorcerer, who leads the priests, and myself."

"Nevertheless, your majesty—"

"Permit me to finish, Colonel Emoona. Unless I am willing to lose my life, I may never be able to use it effectively! To risk life is to win life! You yourself taught me this, along with your lessons in swordsmanship!"

"Your majesty, your skill with a sword is very great—but great as it may be, your life will be in peril. I little thought that the day would come when those lessons—"

"I suspect it has come. Remember, I am your queen, and in this case I shall use my own judgment."

They rearranged their forces, placing the children and Belak behind them in the charge of two soldiers. Alleophaz and Gerachti accepted swords and moved up beside the queen and the colonel. By now they were within hailing distance of the advancing army.

Wesley strained his eyes to see better. The man heading the advancing force looked familiar. "It looks like Sir Robert! It is! Sir Robert Ashleigh!"

"The rat!" Kurt muttered.

On either side of the roadway where they met, a small open space spread out among the forest trees. Sir Robert approached steadily, drawing rein before the queen. Behind him were two sergeants at arms and a company of at least two hundred men. Sir Robert spoke softly, so that almost nobody except the queen heard him. "It is my painful duty to arrest your majesty."

But the queen's voice rang out loudly and clearly. "Arrest? Arrest your queen? How dare you, sir! On what charge, pray? And in whose name?"

Sir Robert still spoke quietly. "I suggest that your majesty not raise your voice. It is not part of my wish to embarrass or to humiliate your majesty. As for the charge, it is his majesty's—that of being a traitor to his majesty the king!"

"Then you must bear documents with his majesty's handwriting and bearing the royal seal. Present them to me!" she demanded loudly.

"The business of your arrest was too urgent for the preparation of documents. These will be produced in good time."

The queen drew her sword and held it above her head, addressing the ranks of the opposing soldiers. "Men of Anthropos! You may not be aware of Sir Ashleigh's purpose. He accuses me of treachery toward my husband, his majesty the king.

"The charges are false, foolish and utterly absurd. If there are any traitors here, you see them in the three who lead you. They have come not at the bidding of the king, but of Shagah the sorcerer. These men lie—they do not even bear documents. His majesty is well aware of what I am doing." Her voice dropped a bit before she continued. "I also note that there are none of your officers with you. Why is this? Do you realize what you are witnessing?"

A low murmur of surprise spread backward among the troops as those near the front spoke with those further back. Sir Robert, meanwhile, protested feebly, grappling with a situation he had not anticipated. Ignoring the men behind him, he attempted to interrupt the queen. The colonel moved ahead of the queen, drew his own sword and kept his eye on Sir Robert and the two sergeants.

The queen cried out again, her voice resonating over the men's heads. "Men who are loyal to Anthropos! The most treacherous man here present is the ambitious Sir Robert Ashleigh. It is he who wishes to replace my husband, the present king, and it is to him that a promise has been made by the Playsion priests. I call on your loyalty to the crown of Anthropos and to your reigning king. Do you wish a rule of priests? Or of Sir Robert?"

Uncertain silence answered her.

"As queen of Anthropos," she continued, "I therefore plead my right to a trial of arms, according to the ancient laws of Anthropos. It is my right to engage my accuser, Sir Robert, in individual combat with short sword, to make plain my innocence in the face of this false charge. I appeal to the Emperor and to Gaal. May the innocent be victorious and the guilty be damned!"

The silence was defeated by a growing cheer from the throats of the listening men on both sides. The king's soldiers crowded forward, and some climbed trees for a better view. The queen and Sir Robert Ashleigh in a duel to the death! Who would want to miss the event?

But among the queen's party feelings were different. She was loved and was risking her life. They cautiously completed the ragged circle in the clearing, but made sure that everyone stayed back to give the combatants room.

"By the Changer, I wish your majesty had chosen a different course!" the colonel muttered. "Whatever else you forget, remember the left feint, ma'am. And watch your guard."

"She is playing a skilled and desperate game—not against Sir Robert, but against this sorcerer, this Shagah," Alleophaz said.

"It is a dangerous game," Gerachti replied. "She could be dead thirty minutes from now."

Belak shuddered as Gerachti's words floated back. "It is a dangerous situation," he told the children.

"In chess you almost never put your queen in jeopardy," Wesley said, a worried frown on his face.

"Yes, but this is not chess," Lisa argued, "and Colonel Emoona seems to think she is good with her sword."

"But she could be killed!" Kurt protested. "Where would we all be then?"

"Huh!" Lisa said a little scornfully. "In *real* adventures, don't forget, the danger is also real."

A cloud dimmed the sunlight, and for a few moments the area was in shadow. The king's soldiers' initial enthusiasm seemed to die down almost as quickly as it had arisen, as an awareness that the queen's life was in jeopardy grew among the large group of men surrounding the field of combat.

Fear grew till they could smell it—fear of the danger to the queen, of Shagah and the priests, of the chaos that could follow, of the awesome danger the country stood in.

Only the queen seemed undaunted. She and Sir Robert dismounted as the sun came out again.

The queen held her head high and her sword ready, facing Sir Robert, whose face was pale and set, his red hair gleaming in the sun.

Each carrying a circular shield, they advanced. The queen called out, "Have you no chain mail, sir? And where is your helmet?"

"Your majesty is a woman," Sir Robert said tersely, "I am a man, and—"

"You will be less of a man when I split your head!" the queen retorted.

Some men sniggered, but one of the sergeants ran forward, pulling off his own shirt of mail and helmet. Sir Robert accepted them and put them on.

Then the distance dwindled between the two combatants, and they began to circle each other warily, each eyeing the other's moving sword.

Wesley's thoughts went back to his own actions in the long-ago (but yet to come) Battle of the Heights. He knew nothing of swordsmanship, and on that occasion his sword had seemed to know its own job and to act for him.

He was still blind to the finer points of the battle that now took place but was desperately anxious for the queen. He was too absorbed to notice the movements his own body made, as if it were fighting beside the queen. Lisa hid her face, but could not stop herself from peeking through her fingers. Kurt felt sick.

The fight stretched out into three distinct phases. The first phase was short, as each combatant carefully explored the skills of the other. They were fairly evenly matched. Those who knew anything about it knew that the queen's handling of her sword was superior, indeed flawless. But what Sir Robert lacked in finesse, he certainly made up in energy and determination.

Once they had gained a feel for each other's skills, they moved into a second phase—hard at it with parry, feint and thrust. Sweat gleamed on their faces in the sunlight, and their breath came in gasps. Sometimes the queen drove Sir Robert steadily back, both of their shadows rippling over the uneven ground, but then the reverse would follow.

Then Sir Robert fell, and the queen immediately stepped back to allow him to rise.

"*No,* your majesty, *go for him!*" the colonel yelled.

The crowd had been tense and silent, but more and more of the king's men began to shout in favor of the queen. She still seemed fresh, whereas Sir Robert's movements grew progressively slower and

clumsier. Nevertheless, the queen still could not gain a decisive advantage.

The third phase of the battle began by nearly ending it. The queen caught her foot in a rabbit hole at the edge of the road and fell heavily. Her shield arm flew out against the ground, leaving her vulnerable except for her sword. Sir Robert did not step back as the queen had done, but lunged eagerly at her with a roar of anger, his own sword pointed at her chest.

But the queen's sword flashed upward, and Sir Robert's sword arched through the air, turning end over end. He staggered back and fell on his side, then scrambled awkwardly to his feet to retrieve his sword.

"Oh, well done, your majesty! Beautifully done! You will get him now!" the colonel yelled.

The queen's eyes flashed as she rose, leaning heavily on her left foot. She clearly was no longer able to move easily, but now her superior swordplay was reaping dividends. And, strange as it may seem, the expression on her face began to change as the fight resumed. Her grim concentration was slowly replaced by a genuine smile, and she seemed to begin to enjoy what she was doing.

"She looks happy enough!" Kurt said, frowning. "D'you think she's faking it?"

Lisa said, "I don't know."

Wesley said nothing, though like Kurt he was frowning.

The queen's emerging smile contrasted with Sir Robert's growing look of desperation. He realized that her fall had made no difference, and his face bore the grimace of a man who looked upon his own death. Twice the queen cut through his guard and slashed his arm, while another thrust that he managed to deflect still sliced through his cheek. Blood ran both from his face and down through his mail shirt

His movements became frantic and unguarded, and after one wild swing he left himself exposed. The queen struck his sword arm hard, and they all felt the metal bite to the bone

178

His arm dropped uselessly to his side, and the queen lowered her sword. Again her voice rang out—breathless, but absolutely clear.

"I have no intention of killing you, Sir Robert. I prefer that you live and stand trial at my court for treason against the crown. Your master, Shagah, will not dare to interfere." She paused to recover her breath, then continued. "The Emperor and Gaal have stood by me! My innocence is revealed, and likewise your own treachery."

There was a roar from the soldiers on both sides—a cheer that owed as much to relief as to joy. Men shouted wordlessly, their fervor betraying the strength of the fear that had gripped them.

Colonel Emoona, ecstatic, bowed before the queen, his face red and his eyes sparkling. He rose to face her. "Your majesty, that was a magnificent display! I did not like you to attempt it, but it was wonderful to watch. You have greater skill and courage than ever I imparted to you."

The colonel turned to the troops and rapidly restored order, along with the help of his own officers. Sir Robert's sergeants had vanished, and a few other men were missing as well.

The soldiers brought the queen a cup of wine, and she gave them orders to tend Sir Robert's wounds and place him in chains. She also gave instructions for the protection of Sir Robert's wife and two children. "Send riders to their house. Tell them what has happened, and assure them that his treachery will not be counted against them."

She turned to Colonel Emoona. "We are almost in sight of Bamah," she said calmly. "Let us proceed to the city."

14
King Tobah Khukah

Captain Integredad stood by the palace gates with Mary at his side. The captain frowned as a tumult of shouting arose from below them in the city. "What is it?" Mary asked. "What's happening?"

The captain turned to two men beside him. "Go down there with haste. Bring me word at once of the meaning of this noise." Then to Mary he said, "Shagah dispatched a large number of the king's forces under the command of someone—some young upstart, I doubt not. I know not their purpose, but I suspect it was an attempt to capture her majesty. The noise bodes ill either way."

"Why? Why d'you say that?" Mary asked.

Captain Integredad sighed. "Mischief is afoot. I would that her majesty had eluded them and returned secretly with her prisoners. For this I prayed to Gaal and the Emperor. It is the tumult that worries me."

"But why?" Mary persisted.

"Why, child? Because it can mean only one of two things. Either the queen has been arrested at the order of Shagah, who presumes to give orders in the name of his majesty, or, what is less likely, the queen is returning in triumph, having wrested the army from whoever was leading it."

Mary frowned. "But if the queen won, how does that make matters worse?"

"Because Shagah's rage will then know no bounds." He sighed again and looked down at Mary. "Shagah. Everything that happens leads back to him. Which reminds me about you, little maid. I know how much I frightened you when I told you—"

Mary said, "Sure. It was pretty scary. I really cried after you took me back."

He looked down fondly at her, wishing he had another daughter. "So, little woman. You decided to leave them alone?"

Mary looked at the ground. Absent-mindedly, she made marks with the toe of her shoe in the dust of the road. Finally, and without looking at the captain, she said, "I love Gaal. I know that now. But he's left me, an' he'll never come back again."

It was now the captain's turn to ask why. "That makes no sense, little maid. The Gaal I know would not forsake one of his own."

"Yes, but I'm not one of his own, an' that's what I really know now. I tried to stop loving him when I joined the witches' club, but when I remembered, I just couldn't help loving him. I don't belong anymore, though. So I may as well go to see—who is this Shagah you talk about? Is he a sorcerer? Is he the boss of the priests? 'Cos if so, that's who I've gotta see."

"No, no, Lady Mary! If you love Gaal you cannot join his enemies! Call out to him! All of us disobey him at times—we all turn our backs on him. But from the ends of the earth he hears our cry. Cry to him, little maid, cry aloud to him!"

Mary shook her head, and when she replied her voice was almost inaudible. "I told him to go away, *and never to come back.* He heard me. I saw the light fade to nothing. He's gone, an' he's gone for good. I just know."

Then their attention switched to the streets below as the shouts from the city rose to a crescendo. Horsemen began to turn the distant corner of the avenue leading to the palace gates.

"I do believe it is the queen!" Captain Integredad said. "And the colonel beside her. Her majesty must have won the hearts of the king's army!" His voice dropped. "Yet no lasting good can come of it!"

Mary returned to their quarters as soon as the queen swept triumphantly through the gates. She had begun to tell Lord Nasa and Lady Roelane all about it, when there was a knock at the door. Princess Anne entered, followed by Alleophaz, Gerachti and Belak—and the Friesen children. Suddenly their sitting room, rather large for only three people, was pleasantly and comfortably filled. The hosts stood, and introductions and greetings became an excited, almost noisy affair. Soon they were talking and laughing animatedly together.

The children, however, were very aware of the restraint over the unexpected reunion. Wesley and Lisa both smiled and said, "Hi, Mary. How are you?"

A subdued Mary replied, "Fine. And you guys?"

Kurt, however, walked right up to her and seized both her hands. "Oh, Mary! It's so good to see you. Are you O.K.?"

But Mary's hands turned cold and sweaty, and her face was drawn. She avoided his eye, saying, "I'm O.K.," but couldn't fool Kurt.

She pulled her cold hands from his, but he put his hands on her shoulders and whispered so that she could hear him in spite of the noise of the general conversation, "No, Mary. You mustn't feel bad. You're still family, y'know. You're part of us."

Mary glanced up at him with a timid smile. "Thanks!" Then she looked down at her shoes again.

Princess Anne announced, "Her majesty has returned safely, and hopes to greet you personally in a little while. In the meantime she needs me, so I must pray to be excused." She left the room, and hosts and guests alike seated themselves. Mary sat on the floor against the window seat where Lord and Lady Nasa sat. The rest sat down wherever there were seats. Lisa sat on the arm of the chair Alleophaz occupied. Soon they were busy exchanging the stories of their many adventures. Mary alone remained silent, and the children cast occasional surreptitious glances in her direction. Suddenly, and rather abruptly, she asked to be excused, and left the room. Kurt made as if to follow her, but Lisa caught his eye, shook her head and mouthed, "Don't!"

They had hardly resumed the flow of conversation when there was a second knock at the door. Lord Nasa answered it and took from the hand of the page at the door a roll of parchment. He broke the seal and read it as he resumed his seat.

"It's from the king," he said. "We are all summoned to the throne room tomorrow morning at the hour of counsel. You children too."

The next morning Mary was missing.

Lady Roelane's face was pale and drawn as she told the others. "She never returned after she left so suddenly late yesterday afternoon. You remember, you were all there," she added, distraught and anxious. "I never slept. I searched the palace in vain last night. I also talked to the captain of the guard, who thought she might have been bound for the temple, and I would have gone there, but—"

"But I forbade it!" Lord Nasa interrupted with unaccustomed asperity. "I went myself, not that it did the slightest good. I found the place in darkness, and I only had a torch for illumination." He shook his head in anger. "No one responded to my shouts—the place was deserted. I did find an old priest sleeping on the floor, but he would tell me nothing, professing absolute ignorance of anyone of Mary's description. I lost myself several times in the corridors, and finally my torch went out. By the time I returned, day had broken."

They looked at each other helplessly, but realized they could do nothing. In silence, they left together for their audience with the king.

A palace official showed them into the throne room, a large and lofty rectangular room with a marble floor and fluted pillars. High on the rear wall facing them, an ornate red doorway opened onto a broad carpeted stairway. It descended to a raised dais, filling a third of the room. Two empty thrones of ebony occupied the dais, which was covered with beaten gold and strewn with silk cushions. On the sides of the thrones stood two smaller chairs—cushioned, but less ornate. On the floor below the dais, silken pillows had been scattered to provide seating.

"For whom are these other chairs?" Lord Nasa asked the official.

The man snorted. "The one on your right is for Duke Dukraz, Grand Marshal of the palace. The other one is for Shagah the Sorcerer, High Priest of Playsion and Supreme Marshal of the temple priests. Times have changed. Dukraz is no match for Shagah, who has his finger in every pie in Anthropos. He calls down the spirits of darkness, and they say he plays chess with Lord Lunacy, the Chief Lord of Shadows himself. Who knows what changes for the worse are coming in the kingdom!"

They seated themselves on the pillows and waited. Nobody said anything. Lord Nasa and Lady Roelane were obviously tense and very anxious, and a brooding sense of dread settled over everyone. Mary filled all of their minds, but the thought of what could happen was so appalling that comment died on their lips. Wesley, Lisa and Kurt struggled against a sense of doom.

Lisa's mind went back to the time she herself had spent in the temple. She remembered the mocking demonic voices, the terrible cold, the sense that she had crossed a line into evil that permitted no return. Where had Mary gone? Where was she now? "She's a fool—but oh, Mary, why, why?" Lisa thought. "What will happen to you?"

Kurt's mind was filled with the dread of seeing Shagah again. Would Shagah know him? To Kurt, Shagah was a vivid memory, but what was a memory for Kurt had not happened to Shagah yet. It belonged in the future of Anthropos, which the children had already visited. Could Shagah know the future? Would he know that it was through Kurt that he would eventually be destroyed, or that it was Kurt who would stand with Gaal on the wall of Nephesh? Would he know that Gaal would walk toward him on that wonderful day when Shagah and all the powers of darkness would be swallowed by the open mouth of the earth? He felt his heart pump in dread, dread of again seeing the sorcerer he remembered so vividly, and who had once manipulated him so shamelessly.

A door on their right opened, and they all jumped. But only priests came through it—a score or more, some waving censers. Their incense began to fill the room with subtle fumes, dark with heaviness and weight, and the smoke gave Kurt a headache. "I would like to know where they were last night," Lord Nasa muttered angrily. But they failed to notice Mary slipping into the room and taking a place at the back.

Then the door above the stairway opened and King Tobah Khukah arrived, resplendent in royal robes of gold and purple. He paused for a moment to survey the two groups gathered to receive him. Two pages appeared at his side, calling, "Kneel before his imperial majesty, King Tobah Khukah, Emperor of Playsion-Anthropos!" Lord Nasa and his party knelt down, unaware at first that the priests had failed to do so.

"Blithering idiot! Imperial popinjay! He's no emperor!" Wesley muttered to himself as he looked at the king.

The king began to descend the stairway and the pages fell into place behind him, picking up the long train of his robe. Immediately Queen Suneid followed, her head erect and her face strangely peaceful. A maid carried a smaller train of the velvet cape that hung from her shoulders. Wesley looked at the queen and wondered at her strong face, a face to which he could turn whenever he felt tension rising intolerably in him.

Duke Dukraz brought up the rear of the procession. Shagah, much to Kurt's relief, did not appear. The duke seated himself on the right-hand chair, leaving Shagah's seat vacant.

Then the children noticed Mary, but their curiosity had (for the time being) no outlet. Mary neither spoke nor raised her eyes. For all they knew she might have been in a trance, but she was simply weary, full of despair and shame.

The king and queen settled themselves on their thrones, and the pages and the maid stood behind them. Then the king spoke, and Wesley found his perceptions shattered. The man on the throne was no idiot. He (or whatever it was that spoke through him) seized immediate and total control of the room, even though he was merely issuing his welcome. "Please be seated, all of you." The king's deep voice filled the room. "A thousand welcomes to you!" He turned for a moment to look at the queen, his gesture one of apparent tenderness, then back again at those who were seated below him.

Even in those few words terrifying authority flowed from him— authority before which they all trembled, authority that hit them with almost a physical force. "Help—oh, help!" Lisa gasped. Lord Nasa remembered the duke's words "I am now utterly helpless before an intellect for which I am no match. It is not his majesty's intellect, but that of one of the great Lords of Shadows whom the sorcerers serve. They have created a monster, a man possessed by the gods . . ."

The more the king spoke, the more that sense of power and authority flowed over them and pressed them down. "My gracious and beloved consort and I give an especial welcome to Lord Alleophaz of Enophen, Glason, illustrious descendant of kings, and emissary from his majesty King Kalastriel Bels of Glason."

The smile he gave Alleophaz was warm on his lips but cold from his eyes. "Your two companions are likewise welcome, and the remarkable children who accompany you, emissaries themselves, as I understand, from worlds afar."

Kurt's mind, still on Shagah, went back to the night in the Tower of Geburah. "What a fool I was then!" he mused.

The king spoke again. "Let me come at once to the most important issue. Later, I would like to discuss with Lord Alleophaz the matter of trade with Glason. This we can do privately." The king nodded again at Alleophaz, still smiling. "However, I have invited some of the more senior priests to join us, since they are learned in all the ancient lore."

He rubbed his hands together, and his face exuded benign happiness and a sort of cool pleasure. "I am more than delighted to learn of the possible birth of a child who could change the history of Anthropos-Playsion."

Nobody moved or said anything, but waited to see how the king would continue. The censer-bearing priests began to circulate round the room below the dais.

The king said, "It is indeed wonderful news. Rumor has it that the child has already been born. Her majesty tells me that you, my lord"—at this point he directed his cool smile again at Alleophaz—"received a message from a High Lord of Shadows, saying that the child was born. Is this so?"

Alleophaz rose to his feet and bowed. "Whether from a Lord of Shadows I do not know, your majesty. I was seeking the source of all wisdom, and received a message in a vision. In that vision I learned of the birth of the child, and that we would be guided to him by three children, who would follow a column of smoke with blue fire at its heart."

"This sounds wonderful. A column of blue fire! What happened to it?"

"Your majesty, we do not know. We have seen nothing of it since we met her majesty the queen, who brought us here—as her prisoners."

"Ah, yes. That was unfortunate. Without understanding the issues clearly, we were all—and quite unnecessarily—alarmed. You must forgive us. Now that we understand the nature of the child's coming such precautions have ended."

He smiled gently, and with apparent fondness, at the queen. Yet Lisa could tell that his eyes were bright but cold. "I have explained to her majesty that your incarceration is quite unnecessary, and have suggested to her that you be released. We do see eye-to-eye on that issue, my dear?"

The queen looked him serenely and steadily in the eye. "Of course. As your majesty sees, they are my guests. I called them prisoners lest any misunderstanding should occur as to their status."

The duke said nothing, remaining motionless, his face inscrutable.

The king cleared his throat before continuing. "What would be helpful to us would be to know when the birth of this child occurred. We have traced the royal line in Anthropos, and there is no knowledge of any heir to the Anthropos throne. We might have difficulty establishing the paternity of the claimant."

The queen interrupted. "With your majesty's permission—you know that we have discussed the paternity of the child."

"True. And I found your views very stimulating. *Most* stimulating." He paused as if musing, and no one interrupted. Then he said, "It does raise the interesting concept that this Emperor-over-the-Sea might be emperor over all seas, in all worlds, and all universes. Marvelous!" He paused again, and the silence in the room could be felt. Wesley's heart hammered his ribs, as did Mary's—yet neither could have said why.

Eventually the king continued, still as though he were thinking aloud. "It is a pity no one has visited this emperor. I would be glad to render homage to him myself—but it is difficult to do so if I do not know where he dwells." He looked directly at Kurt. "Has any living person in your world visited or even seen him?"

Kurt struggled to his feet. He felt his throat closing and was filled with terror, though he knew that the Emperor *was* sovereign over all universes. All he could say was, "I—er—I don't know, your majesty. I don't think so." The pounding of his heart nearly robbed him of his power to breathe. A doubt entered his mind. Was the Emperor-over-the-Sea a real person?

The king smiled. "Oh, well! Perhaps we can establish who the child's father is some other way. Just so long as it is not just another peasant claimant to the throne!" He smiled brightly round at everybody with his cold eyes. ("Like a snake's eyes," Lisa said later.) Then he said, "Now, where were we? Ah, yes. The matter of when the child was born."

Alleophaz bowed once more. "Twenty-three moons have passed

since my vision, your majesty. Therefore twenty-three moons have passed since the child's birth. We set out to find him at once, but our journey has taken long and we were shipwrecked."

"And now that the column is gone—you are sure it really has gone?"

"None of us has seen it recently, your majesty."

For several moments the king was silent. "So the child has been alive for almost two years. This is indeed wonderful news! But where he was born remains a mystery. Now, my dear priests, I consulted you yesterday, asking you to find any prediction in the ancient lore which would tell us where to look for him."

One of the priests stepped forward. "Along with our chief, Shagah, we have done as your majesty requested, searching all the ancient records with care. We knew, of course, of the coming of the Glason emissaries, mistakenly perceiving their arrival as a threat to the king-dom." He hesitated, looking directly at Alleophaz. "I trust that our suspicions have not made your journey unnecessarily hazardous?"

Alleophaz bowed but said nothing. Inwardly he was utterly certain that neither the king nor the sorcerer-priests were to be trusted. But if diplomatic considerations were ensuring their safety just then—well and good.

Turning again toward the king, the priest said, "There are many references to the coming of a powerful emissary of the Emperor, but only one was found to the *place* of his coming. It points to Karsch, a hamlet a day's journey away, in the hills southeast of here."

"In Karsch, you say?"

"In Karsch, yes. The hamlet has quite a history."

"You can be sure that he is there?"

"At this point we are sure of very little, your majesty. All we know is that an ancient prophecy predicts that when the birth occurs, it will take place in Karsch. But who knows where the child—if he was born earlier—would be now? We have consulted both shades and the Shad-ows, but there is no response from them."

The other priests appeared to be ignoring the discussion, as those who carried incense proceeded ceaselessly round the room. The children found themselves getting drowsy from the influence of the incense, and Kurt's headache continued as a dull throb.

Alleophaz spoke again. "Your majesty, it is our purpose to find the child, for our lives are devoted to the pursuit of wisdom. We believe the child is the key to such an understanding, not only for Anthropos-Playsion, but for all the peoples of the world. We would go to Karsch and begin our search there, if this accords with your majesty's wishes."

The king looked long and hard at him. At last he said, "Very well. Search for the child, and leave no stone unturned until you find him. It is important that all of us accord him the honor such a child merits." A gleam came to his eyes. "I personally am most interested in him. I would be happy to have him here in the palace, or pay him my respects in his own home. An emissary of this emperor indeed! If the Emperor exists it would be a great honor to have such a being among us!"

The king nodded, then rose, and everyone rose with him. The interview ended as the king ascended the stairs and took his power with him.

15
The Ancestral Curse

Once the royal party left the throne room, the invited group did the same. In the corridor a buzz of murmured conversation broke out among them. "How much can the king and Shagah be trusted?" Lord Nasa asked.

"No further than they can be thrown," Gerachti replied. "Nor do they trust us, I suspect."

"They seemed to be certain that we would come back and report to them," Alleophaz mused thoughtfully, "yet we made them no promise to do so."

The Friesens and Mary were not listening but were talking among themselves. At least, the Friesens were talking. Mary still seemed withdrawn, her eyes downcast.

"The king gives me the shivers!" Lisa said.

Kurt replied, "I know. But I was glad Shagah wasn't there."

"Yeah," said Wesley. "You actually met him, didn't you?"

"Looks like Mary may be a lost cause," Lisa whispered, shrugging her shoulders.

Kurt disliked her casual dismissal of Mary and whispered, "Don't talk like that, Lisa! We can't let her stay in the clutches of Shagah. He would cheerfully have murdered both you and Wes—"

"Oh, *can* it, Kurt, I—"

"—not to mention Inkleth, whom he very nearly did murder. Remember the way Inkleth crawled to us over the grass? You may not like Mary, but you can't give her up to a murderous beast like Shagah."

"Kurt, you don't understand. Mary *wants* that sort of stuff," Lisa retorted.

"I know, I know—sure, Lisa, *but she has never met Shagah.* She doesn't know the danger she's in." Kurt's whisper was distressed. "I thought she was in a trance," he added.

Wesley shook his head. "I think something's happened we don't know about. To me she looked more like she was depressed, or—or despairing, more than anything else."

They had been walking as a group toward the queen's section of the palace, and the adults had continued their own conversation. The Friesens heard Alleophaz say to Lord Nasa, "No, our rooms are very adequate, indeed luxurious. But we must get together later—perhaps in your quarters, to discuss plans, I hope. In any case, we must become better acquainted."

Back in the drawing room of their apartment, Lord Nasa and Lady Roelane turned to Mary. For a moment they stared at her. Then Lady Roelane gathered her in her arms, saying, "Oh, Mary, I am *so* glad to see you are back. I grieved and feared for you last night. Where were you?"

Lord Nasa's voice was stern. "Yes, Mary. I sought you in the temple, but I found nothing. Were you there?"

Mary nodded miserably. She was thinking of all that happened during the night, and of what she had learned about herself. She tried to explain. "They hustled me right off to Shagah. There was this stairway—it was their magic. It is pretty powerful stuff. It's a stairway you can't quite see, but you have to see it to go up it. If you don't see it you don't even feel it. But if you do, it's solid for you an' you can go up it."

Mary's lips trembled, and a tear trickled slowly down one cheek. Lady Roelane released her, looking closely at her. The girl looked forlorn, and the two words she spoke came as a groaning echo from a deep, dark pit of despair, "Oh, oh!"

"What happened, Mary?"

"Nothing, really, well—nothing bad. I just went into these rooms, which became real if you could see them, an' Shagah was there. They left me with him, an' I'm afraid of him."

"So what did happen? What did he do?"

Mary shrugged. "Nothing, really. It was what he said—what he told me. He said that I came to them because I had to. I was under a powerful spell that came down my *real* mother's line."

"A spell? What do you mean? Are you talking about witchcraft again?"

A little of the old Mary came back for a moment. "You asked me to tell you what the matter was! I'm telling you. My great-great-great grandmother, according to Shagah, was a well-known and powerful witch. I never knew. An' she laid some kind of curse on our family, so that all the women were to be born as daughters of the Shadows. He said I couldn't escape being a witch."

Lord Nasa sat down, watching the two of them. Lady Roelane again stroked Mary's hair. "Yes, but Mary, you belong to Gaal now."

"I wish I did, but you know that's not true. An' you also saw what happened when the light came. I never should have said what I did. But the light faded. He went away—an' he *won't* come back. It feels awful."

Lady Roelane's voice was quiet. "Mary, it is not over yet."

Mary sighed. "Two nights ago I had dreams about Gaal. Y'know, I actually love him. I know it now. But it's too late. I'm still under this curse, and there's more to it I haven't told you."

"Take as much time as you need, and tell us," Lady Roelane said.

Mary drew in her breath. "Shagah told me about my own mother and dad. They weren't very nice. I don't remember anything about them. My mother was a witch, apparently, and she was also very brilliant, wrote a lot of books."

Lady Roelane was distressed by Mary's despair. "I'm so sorry, Mary. You must have felt awful."

"Well, she worked as a spiritist doing seances, an' she really could get in touch with the dead, not like a lot of them who were fakes. Apparently she was really good, an' she charged an awful lot."

She sighed, saying almost bitterly, "I guess I get my brains from her. Anyway, my father was a dead loss—and a major beast. Shagah told me he did things to me—things you don't do to babies."

Lord Nasa said, "And you believed him? How do you know he was not lying?"

"Oh, Lord Nasa! It all fits. Everything fits together now. Why would no one ever talk to me about my real mother? I only remember my stepmother—an' she was bad enough. I always thought she was my real mother. Oh, why does it have to be like this? I hate life an' I hate me!"

"Do not hate, Mary, at least not any more than you can help. You love Gaal." Mary was about to interrupt, but Lady Roelane continued. "Well, *he* loves *you* and so do *I*." She put her arms round Mary to comfort her. "I think I would like you for my own daughter."

Her words reminded Mary that she still had not found the person she had been seeking so long. "Oh, an' I still haven't found Uncle John. Oh, Lady Roelane, if only he hadn't disappeared! Where is he? I'd even put up with the old lady he married if I could find him. I'm sure I've come to the wrong time. Wherever can he be?"

Lady Roelane sat down and Mary sat beside her, enjoying their closeness. She cupped her chin, her elbows resting on her knees.

"What made you come back to us?" Lady Roelane asked.

"Well, I was frightened of Shagah, but he was called away," Mary answered. Expression dropped from her voice, and her words came dully. "He had wanted me to sleep there, but I'm glad he was called away 'cos I was scared—of him. After he left I was alone in those rooms all night. I think I fell asleep. He came back around dawn and told me I was to take part in the search for this young king with you guys, and report back to him afterward. He said I couldn't help but obey him."

Lord Nasa looked hard at her. "Mary, Shagah has no control over you. He just wants you to think he has."

"Mebbe so. But I am certain about this witch thing. First there was Mirmah, and then when I was mad at Uncle John I just *had* to join the witch club. I couldn't resist it. I was pulled, fascinated. An' I was good at it—or bad at it, as you guys would say. The power was real. I could actually feel it in me, an' I could do things with it. There has to be a reason for all this. An' I believe Shagah told me the truth."

She put her own arms around Lady Roelane's waist. "Roly—may I call you that?—it's just a pet name. But thank you for being so nice to me. I know I don't deserve it."

Lady Roclane laughed. "Call me whatever you like, dear. Though you are the strangest little girl I ever met, we have grown to love you. Goodness alone knows why."

Mary's thoughts were still back in the temple. "Y'know, Shagah can see into the future. He knows what's going to happen."

Lord Nasa looked eager. "Like what, Mary?"

"He says ol' King Kook will die suddenly—in the next month or so. Good riddance, I say."

"He actually said that?"

"Yes. An' he says that the queen has a great deal of power on her—he calls it *the* power, whatever that means—so he'll not tamper with her. Not yet, at any rate. He says she'll die naturally several years from now. An' if they can find out where this young king is, Shagah will rule."

"How will he rule?" Lord Nasa asked.

"He didn't actually say. I imagine he'll get rid of the young king. An' he talked to me all about the shadow side. He said they were all under the same head—spiritists, white witches, black witches, diviners, sorcerers, wizards, people who were into sacrificing their own kids, an' that lots of them didn't know what they were into."

Lady Roelane said, "That is true enough. Birds of a feather . . ."

"Most of them don't have much power," Mary continued, "an' some fake it. Most of the people into these things are what he called 'light-weights,' little more than conjurers, but a few have a great deal of real power."

Just then there was a knock at the door. Lord Nasa opened it and Princess Anne entered, announcing, "Her majesty, Queen Suneid!" The queen entered, followed by Alleophaz, Gerachti, Belak, the three Friesens, and finally Duke Dukraz.

Once they were all seated, the queen began. "You must forgive this intrusion. Let me say at once, children, that I welcome your presence here in Anthropos. I spend much time in fasting and solitude, and was aware of your arrival in the country."

"You were? All of us?" Kurt was filled with wonder.

"Yes, all of you," the queen replied. "And I believe all of you are servants of the High Emperor, with the possible exception of Mary."

The silence deepened as everyone looked at Mary. Lady Roelane's arms tightened round Mary's waist as the queen continued. "Though even about Mary, whose relationship with Shagah is unclear, I am content."

Wesley thought, "What an extraordinary person the queen is—like Joan of Arc!" But nobody spoke, and the queen continued.

"The issue of the young king for whom you search is one that is close to my heart. I know what the prophecies say, and I am sure the time has come for his appearance. In sharing my thoughts with you, however, I have to talk about my husband, his majesty the king."

She hesitated, then took a breath, choosing her words carefully. "Changes have occurred in him while I have been away. He is no longer the man I knew. I believe his personality is under the control of another being."

She glanced round at the duke. "Duke Dukraz shares my concern. Nevertheless, his majesty at this point seems to trust you people. What

Shagah thinks, I have no idea. Only rarely have we ever spoken." She paused for a moment and drew in another breath. "The question I pose is, Are you willing to face the dangerous situation here and do what you came for?"

Duke Dukraz said, "I doubt that either his majesty or Shagah will interfere with your search, until you have found the king. At that point you will face very real danger. They believe he is in Anthropos, but will wait for us to find him for them. They believe completely in your column of smoke and blue fire, for they know you are surrounded by powers that even Shagah cannot match. But sooner or later they will make their move."

"Yes," the queen murmured grimly. "And it might be better for us to preempt them."

"That is very interesting," Gerachti said. "How can you be so sure of their attitude?"

"Both because of the king's own words and because once you have experienced the supernatural, you soon learn you are in touch with both sides and you can perceive both. That is why we have to fight," the queen replied.

Gerachti nodded. "That is true. You know, even I am beginning to experience that."

"But as I understand it," Duke Dukraz frowned, "human beings always know only a limited amount, and those serving—or shall I say controlled by—the dark side are usually grossly deceived. Until very recently I was deceived myself."

He continued to frown for a moment, staring at the floor. Then he said, "I believe the real danger will follow your finding the king. You notice they only call him emissary, as though he were a lowly servant. They will send armies to secure the boy's death—but should you not return with the news they want, they will also summon the spirits of darkness."

"Do they have the power to do that?" Alleophaz asked.

The queen replied, "They certainly have. I have no doubt that Shagah, even now, is calling them down. He wants to use as many legions of goblins as he can lay his hands on and send them against you once you have found and identified this king-to-be.

"What is more, Colonel Emoona was arrested last night." She sighed, shaking her head. "He may already have been executed." There was a stunned pause before the queen smiled again. "Yet I never cease to be amazed at the Changer's ways. The spirits of darkness summon goblins, and the Emperor summons the beasts of the forest. I have been informed that you will have aid from the Koach."

"What are the Koach?"

Wesley said, "Oh, they're just like wolves—except that they talk like humans. Sorry—I didn't mean to interrupt, your majesty."

The queen laughed. "I take no offense." Then her expression changed. She shook her head, a solemn look on her face. "I ask you again. Are you willing to face great dangers to take this king to a place of safety?"

Belak asked, "But your majesty, where can safety be found for a child?"

The queen answered, "The place is hidden from me, but the strong powers with you will show you. The question is the danger. Are you all willing to face it?"

"With your majesty's permission." Alleophaz rose and bowed. "Our duty is quite clear. I, the two men with me and these children have received instructions from a higher source to find the young king. Our duty is to him even more than to Anthropos. What we do after paying him honor, I do not know. But the charge we have received comes from beyond the star-studded skies. So while we are delighted that his majesty seems willing for us to search the young king out, we obey higher orders."

The queen nodded. "It is well. I accept your pledge, for I have no reason to trust my husband's interest in the young king. We shall have to trust the Unseen Emperor, the Changer, for I fear the plans both of Shagah and his majesty bode ill for the child's life.

"However, you children must speak for yourself."

The three Friesens nodded, but Mary stared despairingly at the floor.

Alleophaz resumed his seat, and Kurt stood. He seemed a little flustered, but said, "Your majesty, when we saw Gaal—in this place of timelessness—he told us about the young king, but he would not tell us how we were to rescue him or what we were to rescue him from. And when we asked him, he said, as you just did, that we would know what to do when the time came."

The queen nodded. "Yes. That is how he is! He prefers us to trust him without knowing all that lies ahead."

Wesley also got to his feet and bowed. "Your majesty, you risked your life in combat, trusting the Emperor to save you. We want to do the same."

"Yes, your majesty, you were just super in the duel!" Lisa added, rising as well.

The queen smiled and thanked the two of them warmly.

Duke Dukraz turned to the rest of them and asked, "So what are your plans? Do you have any idea what you will do yet?"

"No details," Alleophaz replied. "We will pack our gear at once. Our horses, through her majesty's kindness, have been replaced and readied. We can set out for Karsch tomorrow at dawn, and at least begin our search there."

"And yours, my Lord Nasa and Lady Roelane?"

"With your majesty's permission," said Lord Nasa, "we would very much like to join the search party."

The queen laughed heartily, the laugh ringing bell-like to lighten their solemn discussion. "Of course. And you must forgive my merriment. I had anticipated and am delighted by your request. I have already ordered your animals prepared by dawn. You see, I knew what you would want to do!"

"Your majesty will remain here?"

"Yes, my lord duke. I want to see what happens."

"His majesty has urged me to go with the party," said the duke.

"He has?" The queen frowned. "Why, I wonder?"

"Does your majesty need me?"

"I would certainly feel better if you were here," she said. "The captain of the guard has a subordinate who could take over his duties. I will send the captain with the party."

Duke Dukraz looked thoughtful. "Hm! I wondered myself what the king—or whoever—had in mind. I believe I will stay." He turned to the others. "Nevertheless, I really do not believe you have anything to fear in the way of violence from his majesty's forces, certainly not until you have found and identified the king. And as we said, it will probably be worse than a human army that is unleashed—shades and goblins are more likely."

The queen rose to her feet. "The duke and I must leave you. For you have much to do before tomorrow."

As she turned to leave, she looked for a moment at Mary. But Mary, her head buried in Lady Roelane's lap, was sobbing bitterly again.

16

The World in the Woods

In the gray dawn they set out without breakfast, shivering in the early chill while loading the fresh food and supplies the queen had provided. As she had promised, the queen had assigned Captain Integredad to help them. All ten in the party were mounted, and four pack animals trailed behind.

Their night had been short, and now they were wooden, stupid and half-awake. Nobody felt much like talking, and even the crisp autumn air failed to stir them.

Very quickly they left Bamah behind and soon were among the trees, proceeding a little south of east along a cart track. The fall weather caused them to pull their cloaks around them more tightly, as gray fog made the surrounding trees eerie and ghostly. Humans, like the horses they rode, breathed out their own quota of mist into the morning's damp.

Kurt sidled his horse next to Mary's. She had not looked at any of the others, shielding herself by sticking close to Lord and Lady Nasa.

"Hi, Mary!"

"Hi."

He wondered how to start talking. Her distress had haunted his dreams and worried him into wakefulness before daylight. Now her very silence sealed his own lips.

He tried again. "Guess you've been having a rough time."

"Uh-huh."

"I—I'm probably not much use—but if there is anything I could do . . ."

She stole a glance at him. "You're nice." A few moments later, she sighed softly. "No, I guess there's nothing anyone can do. Roly—I mean Lady Roelane—tries to help, but it's no use."

"She seems a nice person. Lady Roelane, I mean."

"She is. She's great."

For several minutes they rode side by side without saying any more. Then slowly, Mary began to talk, first about the witches' club at school, and then about Uncle John's wedding, her resentment of the marriage, her dismay at the typhoon and her fears at finding the limousine empty. "It was awful, Kurt, and now—wherever can he be?"

Kurt shook his head. "Your guess is as good as mine."

Mary continued to unburden herself, telling of her arrival in Anthropos, of her desire (which she now called "crazy") to make Uncle John like her better than he liked "that old woman." She described their journey from the tower.

"Is that the same tower Uncle John described?" Kurt asked.

"It must be."

She told of her struggle not to let the couple influence her, her growing admiration of them, and her dreams about Gaal. Finally she described what Shagah had told her.

Kurt was shocked. "Oh, Mary—that's awful. I don't wonder you feel bad. But I'm sure you're wrong about Gaal. See, I joined the other side too. I didn't have ancestors who were into the kinds of things yours were, but I wanted to be a sorcerer. An' I chose Shagah's side."

He told her all about Inkleth and the events in the Tower of Geburah. Mary said, "Y'know, you told me that before. But I'd forgotten." She sighed. "It's no use, though. Gaal went away. The light faded and disappeared."

"It may look bad," Kurt said, "but I'll never forget the way he talked to me afterward. He sure was stern at first, but *man* was he ever kind in the end! He made you feel you were the only person in the world where he was concerned."

Mary sighed but said nothing more except, "Thanks, Kurt." Kurt looked at her and thought, "She's changed. She's more like she was in Anthropos last time."

The sun rose and began burning away the mist. The fog disappeared in a rosy glow, and before long patches of sunlight broke through the trees. Although the track wound onward in a confusing fashion, it headed roughly east, so that the sunlight was either behind them or on their left side for the most part. Then, as they entered a forest glade, Captain Integredad ordered a halt for breakfast.

"We might as well enjoy this weather while it lasts," he said. "For some reason the rains have not come yet this year. But we can expect them any day."

Breakfast consisted of cold meat, newly baked bread, butter, milk and Anthropos wine. As food and sun warmed them, they began to remove their cloaks. As they mounted their horses again, Kurt noticed the column of smoke waiting for them on the cart track. "The column!" He cried out, pointing. "Look, there it is! How many of us can see it?"

"It has come back!" Gerachti called out exultantly.

Alleophaz smiled broadly. "It is like greeting an old friend!"

Lord and Lady Nasa, Belak and the Friesens were all delighted to see it clearly. Captain Integredad stared in the direction they were pointing, a frown on his honest face. "I can see a bit of what looks like mist," he said slowly, "but it is not what you describe. I am not really sure I am looking at anything."

"Just keep watching it," Kurt said. "You have to learn to look properly, but it's a marvelous guide. I wonder if we'll be going to Karsch after all!"

For once the captain seemed a little nervous. "If the column is a guide from somewhere above, I would like one of you to ride beside me. It is as yet far from clear to me, and any orders from the High Emperor must be obeyed at once."

"I'll come with you," Lisa called eagerly.

Kurt moved his horse over to Mary's again. "Can you see it?" he asked her eagerly.

Mary shook her head. "Would you expect me to?" she asked bitterly. "I belong to the other side, don't forget."

Kurt shook his head. "I don't—can't—believe it," he said, "ancestral curse or no. All the things that happened to you last time we were in Anthropos would make no sense that way. Gaal doesn't give up. You don't *want* to belong to the dark side, do you?"

Mary shook her head. "Not any more. Honestly, Kurt, I'll never be able to explain why I joined the witches' club. I used to like it," she sighed. "Well, I thought I did. It must have been that curse that was on me. But I can't make Gaal accept me back, especially after I asked him to go away and never return."

Moments later they resumed riding. Captain Integredad and Lisa, who were leading, were soon deep in conversation. Knowing something of their origin, the captain began to ask Lisa about her previous visits. So Lisa described their journey through the television (it took a long time for her to explain TV to him) into an Anthropos jail and her rescue from the altar in the temple courtyard.

The captain sighed, remaining silent for several minutes. Then he began to tell her about his daughter. "It is not just witchcraft. It is the Lord of Shadows behind witchcraft, the spirits of gloom. Their sole aim seems to be to destroy, to ruin the lives of their victims. The sorcerer Shagah is really a fool, but I know he has enormous power— devilish power, power that I fear."

"Me too," Lisa muttered grimly.

"But he is only a pawn in the hands of the big players—those Lords of the Shade. And they themselves, I suspect, are no more than pawns between your Emperor's finger and thumb. When the dark spirits have finished with Shagah, they will kill him like an old and useless dog. But in the meantime they allow him to have power. You know, I would not be surprised if the spirits of darkness have something to do with this unnatural weather. Usually the rains would swamp us long before now."

Lisa was silent for some time, trying to envisage the worlds of shadow revealed by the captain's words. Eventually she said, "It must be awful."

"It is horrid. Three years ago my own daughter was murdered—murdered, I say—and on the same altar that you were chained to. The pigeon rescued you. Nobody rescued my daughter, and I knew nothing about it until a week past her death."

"Oh, how dreadful!"

"The vultures had her for food, and her bones were tossed onto the giant heap of bones they call 'sacred' and 'holy' because it is made up of sacrificial victims. You could have wound up there yourself."

Lisa shuddered. "Mary's into witchcraft. An' I've been mad with her about it. Surely we're deceived only if we *want* to be deceived. I keep saying that she's wrong, but mebbe I'm being too harsh."

"You were deceived yourself, were you not?" Integredad asked. "You have just finished telling me that you let Hocoino teach you to hate, and that you found part of you wanted to hate and enjoyed the idea of revenge."

Lisa blushed and fell silent for a little while. Finally she said, "I guess I'm the same as her in a way. Kurt doesn't actually say that, but I know he's mad at me because of how I feel."

"Mary has talked to me. I am very afraid for her. If something does not happen soon she may share the fate of my daughter."

They rode in silence for several minutes. The captain screwed up his eyes from time to time. "You know, it must be the column that I see. But tell me, is it turning aside?"

Lisa looked. "You're right—it has. I wonder why."

Just then it disappeared into the trees. As they gained the point where it had vanished, they saw a narrow path on their right and could dimly see the column moving ahead along it. Soon the whole party was following the pathway single file.

Gerachti's old fears began to arise. "This will lead nowhere," he muttered to Alleophaz, who laughed.

"I seem to remember you saying something like that when Kurt was in the lead," he said.

But the change in Gerachti was real. He laughed ruefully. "I guess old habits die hard, and I suppose I will never like half-hidden forest trails. But I now admit freely that the column has proved a reliable guide."

They entered a wide meadow, and when they were about halfway across it, the column simply dissolved into the air without a trace. "How strange!" Lady Roelane said. "So what do we do now?"

"We wait here until the Emperor sends his next messenger," her husband replied.

They had not long to wait. Alleophaz suddenly called out a warning. "Wolves!" he called. "Three of them! Over on our left by the trees—one large white, and two smaller gray ones."

"They're not wolves. They're the Koach," Wesley said. "The queen said we'd see them. They're *talking* wolves. The white one's just like Garfong. It must be an ancestor of his. If we stay still they may approach us. They're quite safe!"

The three philosophers from Glason stiffened but, having learned from previous experience, waited tensely to see what would happen. The wolves did exactly what Wesley had said. They did not lope or run, but walked like dogs walking toward their own masters. They halted ten yards from Captain Integredad.

The white-furred leader opened his mouth. At first it seemed to them all that they heard a howl, but it was no howl. It was the oldest language of all. Immediately, and without any awareness of what was happening, they began to hear the sounds in their own language. "You must be Captain Integredad. Welcome to the woods. We know all about the coming of the true 'once and future king.' We have been sent to lead you to the Prophet of the Woods, for the way is difficult and hard to follow. You will have to dismount from your animals and lead them, but we will stay with you." He turned, and the three Koach headed back in the direction from which they had come.

Captain Integredad stared at their retreat, shaking his head and saying, "By my sword and shield! This is the strangest matter I have yet encountered!"

They dismounted at the edge of the meadow where the Koach disappeared among the trees. There followed a long and bewildering journey which lasted an hour or more. They never saw a path as they proceeded downward, yet they had a sense that they were following a way that was invisible to them, that they were not merely pressing through trackless trees and undergrowth but were following a definite route

One or more of the Koach could always be seen. Once they crossed a marsh in the thickest, densest mist imaginable, treading on tufts of grass. A Koach guided the first of them from tuft to tuft, then each person in turn directed the one who followed. The horses seemed to be enchanted, showing absolutely no fear and stepping from one tuft to another with perfect ease. "I have never seen anything like this before," Alleophaz said. "It is certainly nothing like our experience in the Playsion woods."

After the mist-enshrouded marsh they climbed a steep slope through thick undergrowth, still traveling the real but invisible track. Finally, after struggling up the slope for more than half an hour, they emerged in a glade before a cave.

Sitting on a rock at the entrance of the cavern was an old, old man, thin and astonishingly wrinkled. His long white hair and beard flowed mingling almost to his feet, but what they noticed most about him were his eyes. They did not even observe their color, so vibrant were they with life—a laughing, glorious, powerful life that caught them up at once in the fun of it, so that they wanted to laugh along with him, or cry with tears of joy.

Yet the old man looked so fragile, so paper thin, almost transparent, that they wondered how he could sustain the power of that life without being blown away into nothing. This, clearly, was the Prophet of the Woods.

"I have heard the word *holy*," Alleophaz mused. "Is this what the word means?" But then he shook his head. "No, what he has is beyond mere power. He is *possessed* by *Another's* holiness!"

The three Koach stood before the ancient man. "We have brought them to you, O Prophet of the Woods!" they said. "Call for us when you need us again." With that they turned and vanished into the trees.

Rather than rising to his feet when he stood, the Prophet of the Woods seemed to float to them. It was as if his body were sustained by some unearthly power that held him gently and firmly, and in which he was utterly at rest. "Welcome, friends," he said in a voice with the musical depth of a pipe organ, "but look well at the table on my right." At one side of the cavern entrance a table had been prepared with twelve places. They glanced at it in wonderment. There was no food on it. But where could the old man get food for so many guests?

"Can you see the food I have prepared for you there?" he continued.

Embarrassed, some of them shook their heads, while others said simply, "No," or "We cannot!"

Mary said, "There isn't any food there!"

Alleophaz said, "Kind sir, I see nothing but fine silverware, including large silver platters and immense bowls. But of food and drink I see no sign."

The old man smiled and replied, "Yet the food is there. The Changer has already seen to that! It is good food and solid, but you fail to perceive it. My great-great-granddaughter, Shiyrah, will come in a moment and sing to you. She is herself a song, one that will quicken your faith and remove the scales from your unseeing eyes."

Then there emerged from the woods the most beautiful girl they had ever seen. She wore a simple gown of leaves, while her long black

hair tumbled over her shoulders and almost to her feet. Her eyes were violet and shone with kindness. And it was the kindness, rather than the beauty of her perfect, oval features, that they all remembered.

She lifted her bare arms and sang with a clear and pure voice. One by one they sat on the grass, as a strange weakness and trembling overcame them and tears were reawakened in some of their eyes. To each of them the song was different, but the end result of the music was the same—they knew they were loved. And when the song died into stillness, and the girl's arms fell to her side, the Prophet said, "Look now upon the table. Know that the change in what you see is not a change in the table, but a change in yourselves, and in your ability to see what is truly present."

They looked again, and cries of wonder broke from them. (But to tell what each cried would take a couple of pages, so what they said must go unrecorded.)

The girl laughed. "Come and taste it, then! My grandfather will sit at one end of the table and I at the other." (Lisa noticed that she left out the *great-great* part.)

"Yes, a hearty welcome to the Changer's table! Eat and be filled! Eat and be renewed!" the old prophet cried.

It was a meal like no other they had ever experienced. The food was more appetizing, the flavors were deeper and richer, so that a rare sense of completion and contentment possessed them all. They asked Shiyrah about her parents, and she said, "My parents and grandparents were put to death by the temple priests, and I escaped."

"That is terrible!" Lady Roelane said. "Why were they put to death?"

"Because they came of the stock of the Prophet of the Woods."

"The same fate met all my sons," the old prophet added. "But not until they had married and produced sons themselves. And now my sons and their wives have been taken too. And my grandchildren. Only my great-great-granddaughter remains." There was no trace of bitterness in his voice.

After a few moments, and in an awed voice, Gerachti said, "They must fear you very greatly!"

"Better for them if they fear him whom I serve!" the seer replied. "Our own lives are in no danger here. None who are not servants of the Most High can penetrate to this place.

"But our stay here will be short—even my own, now. I know also that I shall not remain alive until the young king returns from exile. My own death is not far off, but knowing *he* has arrived I can die content. This is why I have summoned you here, because of the part you will play in his deliverance."

The sun was now a little past its zenith, and a drowsiness too great to resist had fallen on all of them. "There is no need for you to hurry," Shiyrah said. "Lie on the grass and rest awhile. When you wake you will be ready to travel."

Deep slumber cradled them all that warm afternoon and through the evening and the night that followed. When they woke at dawn, they were astonished and refreshed, and ready for the task ahead of them.

17

Disguised by Surprise

Early morning sunlight woke Alleophaz. For several minutes he lay in a pleasant half sleep, conscious only that he was wonderfully relaxed and wanting to go on luxuriating a few moments longer. "Where am I?" he wondered dreamily. Slowly the events of the previous day reconstructed themselves.

"I lay down for a brief rest. Yet I must have slept for many hours," he mused. "Nor am I sorry. I wonder . . ."

He stretched lavishly and with a sense of total well-being. As he did so he became conscious not only of the blanket in which he had been wrapped, but of an unaccustomed roughness in the clothing he wore. He stared uncertainly at the coarseness of a peasant shirt that covered his body, but was startled into vivid awareness as he observed the color of his hands and wrists—the pale flesh tones of a man of Anthropos. He pulled back the sleeves to reveal pale arms.

"Gerachti!" he called. Gerachti, who lay next to him, stirred slowly and sat up. When he saw Alleophaz his eyes widened.

"Your face!" Gerachti cried.

"And yours," Alleophaz murmured in bewilderment.

Both bore the light skins of Anthroponians, and both wore peasant dress. For some minutes they stared at each other, then at their arms and feet, with cries of astonishment and fear. "What can have happened?"

Alleophaz drew in a long breath. "This is clearly the work of the prophet. He must have a serious purpose in mind. I cannot say I like what has happened, but we must wait and ask the reason."

Slowly the rest of the company stirred into wakefulness around them, many with cries of astonishment at their long sleep and at changes in their dress. All were robed in peasant dress, and Belak also carried the hue of an Anthroponian peasant.

"We've been asleep for ages! We'd better get moving!"

"Can you beat it! We've actually slept round the clock—I believe it's the next morning!"

"Look how we are dressed!"

"Is this a joke?"

"Oh! What has happened? Look! Look where the horses were tethered! There are asses there now!" And it was so.

Silently the prophet appeared among them. "These are your disguises. They are not permanent—especially the skin color changes of the Glasonites—but they are essential for the present. To travel to Karsch in silk and satin on noble beasts would be to let the world know what you were up to."

"I am proud of my skin color!" Gerachti cried hotly.

Gently the prophet said, "And so you should be! Its origin is divine. But just now it marks you too obviously as the king's enemy, and this disguise will protect you. But let us return to the table. You must break your long fast, and you must eat well."

The prophet was frowning as he said this. "Something evil is afoot. The rains should have come nearly two weeks ago. We depend on them for next year's crops. Yet there is no sign of them. I suspect some major scheme from the Lords of Darkness is afoot, but the Emperor has not revealed to me what it is."

"Yes, exactly!" Captain Integredad cried. "I said the same thing myself only yesterday."

The prophet smiled at him. "And I believe you were right. But now—breakfast!"

They turned to look at the table, and Kurt, always hungry, cried, "Wow! Look at the table!" He turned to the prophet. "You have already served us breakfast! Let's go for it!"

There was a pause. Events were overtaking the party at a bewildering pace. They had only just become aware of their disguises and of their very long sleep. Now they stared alternately at Kurt and at the table. Kurt seated himself, then turned round and looked back at the rest. "Come on! It's waiting for us! Why are you all staring like that?"

Lord Nasa hesitated. Then he said, "I do not see any food, Kurt."

It was Kurt's turn to look astonished. "But it's right in front of you!" Then light seemed to dawn on him. "I think I understand. I guess it's like the column of smoke. It's all here, but you can't see it yet. I can even smell the oatmeal porridge!" He smiled. "It makes my tummy rumble and my mouth water!"

All this time the prophet stood without a word, smiling.

"I can see something," Alleophaz murmured softly, "but it is not solid—I can see through it."

Then the prophet said, "Your eyes need to be opened again by knowing the unseen love of the Emperor for each of you. Then you will see—and smell!"

His granddaughter stood beside him. Once again she raised her arms, singing. Some of them still sat, tightly wrapped in their blankets. Others stood. Once again the song affected them profoundly, touching and awakening deep longings they never knew they had. The unseen love of the Emperor gripped and changed them. Their eyes were opened to see those very real things that had been hidden from them.

While they were all enjoying the breakfast, Mary said, "It reminds me of the movie *Hook,* when the Lost Boys were eating imaginary food that became real."

"Yeah—an' they had a food fight!" Kurt added, his mouth full of oatmeal.

"I hated that video," Wesley said, frowning.

"Why?"

"I dunno. Mebbe I was thinking of Dad. But I didn't even like the part about the food."

"Oh? Why not? I thought it was fun!"

"It was a bit gross," Lisa said.

Kurt was thoughtful. "I think I know why," he said after a moment. "I mean, I think I know why you may not have liked it."

"Why?"

"Well—can imagination make real food ex nihilo?"

"What's 'ex nihilo'?" Lisa asked.

"Latin for 'out of nothing,' " Mary answered before anyone else had a chance to.

"That's my point," Kurt said. "Nobody can do that with their imagination or anything else. Even Shagah can't. The Emperor alone can create things out of a vacuum. And no one has the right to try to play Emperor."

No one noticed the bemused look on Mary's face. She had stopped eating, excitement gripping her so that her eyes grew wide and staring. "That's *real power,*" she breathed softly. "Man, have I ever been wrong!" Several seconds elapsed before she began to eat again (and that was very unusual for Mary). She remained occupied with her own thoughts the rest of the time.

After breakfast, while they still sat round the table, the prophet told them where his plans came from. "The changes in your dress and skin tones and what plans I have to suggest all come from the Emperor-Where-Time-Is-No-More. Sometimes he refers to himself as The Unchanged and Unchanging Changer. He spoke to me in visions last night, assuring me that when you all woke, you would be dressed as you now are. If you were to proceed as you were yesterday, you would have been observed and your movements reported—and immediate danger would have come to the young king."

Captain Integredad frowned. "But I doubt that anyone was following us on the road."

"No, but there is danger. The king's spies are in every village, and they are paid well for any useful information. You will draw less suspicion if you travel by day in two separate parties. It is better—and this also comes from the Emperor—that you reach Karsch from different sides."

"I was taught to face danger head-on," Captain Integredad said.

"The time will come when you will have no other choice," the prophet returned. "But a wise strategist chooses the field where he has the greatest advantage. The Emperor has already chosen the site of your biggest battle—and in the meantime you will avoid the enemy."

As he spoke, a solemn feeling crept over the little company. They were involved in something larger than they had realized. Suddenly it seemed to them that the fate of a universe was involved in what they were doing.

Eventually Lord Nasa spoke. "So the Emperor himself is concerned about the little king!"

"The Emperor is more concerned about him than anyone."

"How are we to be divided?" asked Captain Integredad. "Her majesty made me responsible for *all* the members of our party."

"And rightly so," the prophet said. "Who could better care for them than the captain responsible for security within and without the palace gates? But you will have a difficult enough task."

"Will the children remain together?" Lady Roelane asked.

"No, your ladyship. The boys will accompany Alleophaz and Gerachti on a hunting and fishing expedition."

"Hm! I do not know how I will manage. It is years since I hunted, and I never did like fishing!" Gerachti protested.

"That is why Captain Integredad will accompany you. He is skilled in both. And remember, you are not hunting for sport—but to feed your supposed families. If you should be questioned, you will say you come from Piggul, a village none like to claim any acquaintance with. Its inhabitants are reputed never to wash. And, or so the story has it, they all smell like overripe cheese."

Alleophaz exploded into merry laughter. When he recovered, he said, "I begin to enjoy this adventure more and more! Does the smell come with the role, or are we supposed to grow smelly ourselves?"

"You have strange tastes, Lord Alleophaz!" Gerachti muttered grimly. But a moment later he began to smile. "I can see the affair is not without its humorous side, though," he added.

The prophet continued. "Lord Nasa and Lady Roelane will accompany the two girls and will be taken for peasant farmers. Talk little to people in the villages, so that their curiosity will not be aroused. Belak will pose as your man-servant."

"That sounds straightforward enough," Lord Nasa said, "though I am sorry to miss the hunting party!"

Lisa and Mary exchanged glances across the table. Mary looked uncertain, knowing Lisa did not approve of her. To Mary's relief, Lisa returned her mute appeal with a smile and a thumbs-up sign.

"What route do we take? And where will we find hunting equipment?" Captain Integredad asked.

"Everything has been prepared," the prophet answered. "First, the Koach will conduct Lord Nasa's party as far as the dirt road for Karsch. Then they will return and will stay with the hunting party for the rest of your journey. It will take both groups a day and a half to arrive where the young king is."

"What about the hunting?" Captain Integredad asked. "Will we be poaching—hunting in the king's forests?"

"No. The forests through which you pass will be the Emperor's provision for the common people. They are called folk forests."

Captain Integredad nodded. "Good—yet I have heard that certain lords contest their use, claiming them as their own."

The prophet smiled. "Should you encounter any such, have no fear. When you address them courteously with the words 'We come to the gift of the forest the Emperor gave to the common people,' something unusual will happen. Even though you utter the words courteously, a fear will enter their hearts, and they will move away. Remember the words, for they are words of power."

Wesley began to mutter the words to himself over and over. "We come to the gift of the forest the Emperor gave to the common people. We come to the gift . . ."

After breakfast, the party that was to go through Karsch left with the Koach. Mounted on donkeys, they waved good-bye to the rest and descended the hill in single file.

The prophet's great-great-granddaughter retired to the cave, while the remaining men and boys sat around the table. Alleophaz glanced around. "I imagine we have little or nothing to do now until the Koach return." Then, looking at the prophet, he made a statement which was also a question. "I suppose you have nothing to add to what you have already told us."

The prophet looked at them one by one before he replied. Finally he said, "What shall I tell you? The Unchanging Changer has not revealed to me the nature of the dangers that lie ahead of you. But it is certain that once you pass beyond the influence of this place, matters could change dramatically. As for the mysterious lack of rain, I am myself in the dark about it. Yet I feel it must have something to do with the coming events."

Nobody spoke, but every eye was on the prophet. Kurt had a question in his mind, but felt it might be a little impertinent. The silence continued until he could hold his question back no longer. "For instance, what *could* happen?"

The prophet smiled. "The stakes are high. You must realize that the real opposition does not come from human beings, but from diabolical spiritual beings of great power who know what hangs in the balance. This is why the lack of rainfall puzzles me."

"Hm!" Gerachti murmured. "We saw more than a bit of that in the palace. The priests were up to something, and we could feel the power of it. As for the king, he was there in body, but some other being had taken his personality over. It was gruesome." He shuddered.

218

Captain Integredad grunted. "There is collusion in the temple with unearthly powers. I am sure you are aware of it, prophet. My daughter—" The muscles around his jaw began to tighten.

"I know about your daughter," the prophet interrupted. "It was a vile and heinous evil. How could you do anything else except grieve terribly, shuddering and cringing at its loathsomeness? But we must have a care." He drew in a breath slowly. "Whatever happens, and however odious and mean the evils we face, we must not fight hate with hate. Hate—personified hate and pride—is the Enemy. Hate will destroy us if we let it penetrate our beings."

Their time in the strange little world in the woods had seemed almost a dream. They had been drawn into an environment free from danger, filled with a majestic all-pervasive peace, soothed with the wild and beautiful music pouring from the throat of the prophet's kin, and lulled into long and healing sleep—all but blotting out thoughts of the palace and the world of Bamah and the temple. But now that sense of peace and security drained away with their discussion.

Captain Integredad lowered his head, staring at the table. He made no reply, though his lips made a thin line.

Alleophaz frowned. "That is easy to say, sir prophet, but hard to practice. How can a man help hating? If *my* daughter had been murdered by ritual sacrifice—"

The captain looked round at them all. "I know that they—the priests and sorcerers themselves—are deceived. They are blind fools, victims deceived by greater powers. I told Lady Mary as much. But when I think of what they did—how can I do other than hate?" His eyes burned fiercely. "They tossed her bones on the 'sacred' pile that rises in a ghastly hillock below the temple. I do not even know which bones belong to my daughter. And so great is their power that I have to sneak there in the night to mourn over her resting place! How can I do anything but burn with loathing toward the men who could do such a thing to her? How could I not blaze inwardly, lusting to kill them all and put an end to the vile traffic?"

For a moment or two the prophet said nothing. Wesley felt his heart pounding as he stared at the table, feeling both indignation and acute embarrassment.

When the prophet spoke, his tone was gentle. "I, too, have been overwhelmed with the waves of hatred, waves that threatened to drown my soul. Remember that I have lost both children and grandchildren. Had it not been for the Emperor's love to me, I do not know where I would be now."

"With all respect, sir, however is it possible not to hate?" the captain asked. "Are you saying that no trace of it remains in you? Or that waves of hate have ceased to threaten you with drowning? How did you accomplish such a feat?"

The prophet shook his head. "I cannot say the waves never return. Occasionally they still arise. You ask me how I accomplished such a feat? I have accomplished nothing. I could never have conquered anything so powerful, so uncontrollable. But something happened to me, something cosmic in power and effect. Waves of love came, not my love but the love that the Emperor bears for me. They came sweeping over my horizon like an army. I was caught up in them. They did not batter me, but cradled me. I rested in them, letting myself sink into them and below their surface, warmed by their warmth, cooled by their coolness. I drank them in, grateful they could fill me, could penetrate to every part of my being. Waves of hate are no match for waves of the Emperor's love."

"I know what you are talking about," Gerachti breathed softly.

But the captain stared, completely unable to comprehend.

Shiyrah approached the group to stand beside the old man. "Sing to us, my dear," he said. "Sing of the love you know about. Do the rest of you not understand the love of the Emperor for us all?"

Softly, without moving, the girl began to sing deep notes. At first they were scarcely aware of her words, which seemed to differ for each one of them. At least they heard them differently. Before long it seemed to them that other voices were joining with her in harmonies that wooed and drew them. Rather than startling them, it seemed to them the most normal thing in the world that many voices should surround her, taking up the song. Yet the sense of wonder again brought tremors to their limbs and tears to their eyes. They themselves seemed to be musical instruments, resonating with the notes in their flesh and bones, becoming part of the music themselves.

Whereas previously the girl had raised her arms, now it was Kurt and Alleophaz who did so, drawn by a mysterious power, not knowing why they rose except that it was what they wanted to do. As the singing continued the melody rose higher, the harmonies sometimes rising with it, and at other times deepening. Sometimes the volume swelled almost unbearably, then it would fall almost into silence.

Captain Integredad rested his head on his folded arms on the table. From time to time he groaned, yet curiously his groaning blended with the music, like a deep note resonating with the rest. Time had ceased, or at least ceased to matter. Little by little his groaning gave place to sighing, and after a while he lifted his face, unashamed and perhaps unaware of the tears that flowed in an unending stream down his cheeks. His eyes were closed at first, but by and by they opened, and a look of wonder and astonishment caused his lips to part as he gazed above their heads, mouthing silent words. Kurt thought he was saying something like "waves of love!" Slowly he began to shake his head from side to side, and finally laid it once again across his arms. His shoulders shook, his sobs renewed themselves, and he shivered convulsively.

Some hours later the Koach returned, and the second party said their thanks and bade farewell to their host and hostess.

As the woods received them, Captain Integredad was still weeping. His shoulders still shook from time to time, driven by his soundless sobbing, yet most of the time his face bore a smile. At first nobody spoke, and even the Koach remained silent. Later they began to talk for the sake of talking, pretending to be unaware of the captain's strange behavior. In single file they plodded on while the captain wept. The others maintained their bright chatter, knowing that officers never wept, and so keeping up the pretence of not noticing.

Though he still led the party, Captain Integredad continued his episodes of weeping throughout the day. He made no communications other than pointing the way, and ate his meals alone, but did some hunting later in the day. He felled a very young buck, which he hung from a tree with a rope after Gerachti had helped him to skin it. They ate their evening meal in a clearing, and darkness fell before they finished.

That night they spread their blankets beneath the trees and let sleep take them quickly. Wesley, settled next to Captain Integredad, woke in the night. He saw the captain sitting, his blanket wrapped round him, silhouetted against the stars as though he were carved in stone and staring up at the star-spangled sky. After a while Wesley turned over and was soon soundly asleep.

18

Danger
in the Woods

The next morning the sun still shone warmly—too warmly. Nor was
there even the slightest sign of rain. Whatever the reason, next year's
harvest was threatened if matters did not soon change.

After they ate and cut up the buck and packed it in fresh leaves,
Captain Integredad began to talk. He seemed quiet, but cheerful, and
was smiling broadly.

He addressed himself first to the three Koach. "Welcome to our
company! I am afraid I failed to welcome you yesterday. You serve the
Changer as we do. Like ourselves, you are sometimes rewarded with
pain and at other times with pleasure. Thank you for guiding and
directing us. It is a great help."

The members of the party looked at one another, uncertain how
they should treat the captain's change of manner. Was he pretending
the past had not occurred? Should they ignore his weeping as well?

The white Koach leader, who had been lying on the grass, rose to his four feet.

As on the previous occasion there was the curious feeling that he had begun a howl, but their subsequent awareness was that he was speaking a language they all understood. "He speaks Glason!" Gerachti muttered in surprise. But the children, who had always thought Anthroponians spoke English, heard him in English. The Anthroponians, on the other hand, who were surprised that the children from other worlds spoke Anthroponian, heard the wolves speak in their own language.

"We are honored to play any part in the escape of the boy king," the Koach leader said. "I am Kai, son of Otok, son of Kan. My companions are Bukov and Katia."

There was a murmur of approval. The boys waved to them in greeting, and the men nodded and called, "Welcome!"

"What you must know," Kai continued, "is that while only three of us will travel with your party, a much larger number has been assigned to shadow your movements. They will remain concealed in the surrounding forest until we have need of them."

"You foresee trouble, Kai?" the captain asked.

"Yes. There could be trouble—serious trouble—from some of your own kind. Certain proud and foolish lords wrongly resent the presence of common people in parts of the forest they want to use. They are dangerous men—foolish, but very dangerous. Fortunately, they have a great and unreasoning fear of us, attributing to us mythical powers. Our very presence should send them fleeing." He lay on the ground, and again the captain expressed thanks on behalf of the company.

After a moment Captain Integredad continued his story, but now he addressed the company as a whole. "You may have guessed my weeping had to do with my daughter. If so, you were correct."

Men, boys and Koach listened carefully.

"My weeping was not sorrow. If it had to do with pain, it was pain caused by thorns of bitterness being removed, but mostly it was the weeping of indescribable relief. Ever since my daughter's murder three years past, hatred has gnawed at my bowels like a cancer. It was devouring me. What I really want to tell you is that pain and hatred are gone, and gone forever. I thought bitterness would consume me till the end of my days, but"—he shook his head—"I am filled with wonder and awe at what the Changer has done to me. Perhaps I will be tempted to welcome it again, as the prophet said. But for the present, I know where the answer lies."

Gerachti grinned at him. "You are not the only one. I found myself wrestling with him—I suppose it must have been this Emperor of whom you speak. I thought my last moment had come. Yet all he wanted to do was impart his love to me."

The sun seemed to be brighter than before, and yesterday's burdensome cloud of embarrassment began to lift from the company. They grew cheerful, but stayed wary, knowing that the most dangerous part of their mission lay ahead. It was not just that dangerous men could assail them, but that powerful spiritual forces from the Shadows would seek their destruction. They had not forgotten the ruthless authority possessing the king, or why it so feared the little king.

By and by they began to discuss the little king. "Do you know anything about him?" Wesley asked Captain Integredad.

The captain shook his head. "I know very little. I know that his evil majesty has been worried about the birth ever since he found out about it. The queen, on the other hand, had been expecting news of his birth with joy. It figures in the prophetic writings to which she devotes herself. He is to come as a great deliverer of the poor and the oppressed. But how or from whence we are to rescue him I do not know."

"So what are we supposed to do when we find him?" Kurt asked.

"What more can we do than bow and worship?" Alleophaz countered.

"He is in danger," Captain Integredad murmured. "You must be aware of that from the way the king reacted. I know that the queen is very concerned for his safety."

"When the king spoke to us at the meeting in the palace yesterday, it made me shudder," Gerachti said, frowning. "We Glasonites felt absolutely no trust in his words."

Alleophaz added, "You are right, captain. The child is in great danger, danger we now share with him. King Tobah hinted strongly that we should return and inform them of the young king's whereabouts. We have not the least intention of doing so."

"We were sent to rescue him," Wesley said. "That was why we were obliged to say nothing when we first met you."

"So just how will you do so?" Captain Integredad asked.

"I wish we knew. Gaal met with us in the place where there is no time and told us we would be informed when the right moment came," Wesley said.

"If only we knew now." Kurt frowned. "I don't like not knowing."

"I see no reason why we should wait for instructions from anyone," Captain Integredad said. "Can we not make plans ourselves? Is guidance from above meant to rule out our common sense and the talents we already have?"

"Of course not!" Wesley said earnestly. "But if Gaal told us he would give us more instructions, he will."

Smiling, Captain Integredad said, "Then, like Kurt, I wish he would hurry!"

They continued to ride through the forest following the Koach, not stopping till well after noon when they found a pleasant glade through which a wide, quiet stream ran. The stream ran close to the forest where they entered the glade. Its banks were six or seven yards wide, a narrow strip of land between the stream and the forest. But only that portion closest to the stream sprouted grass that was green. Moreover, the stream had dwindled to a trickle between deep and clear pools where trout swam. The grass beyond the stream was mostly brown, a further sign of the shortage of rain.

Kurt and Gerachti collected wood for a fire, while the rest opted to fish for the trout. Before long, the splash of trout rising to Captain Integredad's flies evoked shouts of excitement, and before long they had threaded a whole string of the hungry trout.

"Did you ever see anything like it?" Wesley asked in amazement. "You cast like a real expert!"

"Skill is not a requirement here," the captain replied. "They do not hesitate to bite anything that lands in the water."

Alleophaz laughed, but Wesley (a fairly competent fly fisher himself) suddenly found himself devoting his attention to a large and unexpectedly strong trout.

Kurt returned with his third load of firewood. As he began to make preparations for the fire with dried leaves and bracken, he noticed that the ears of the Koach were pricked. A moment later he saw them melt into the trees. He frowned. "Now what's happening?" he muttered.

Wesley landed his trout and had just unhooked it when they heard the sound of a horn winding. A moment later three foppishly dressed horsemen mounted on superb steeds burst from the forest on the far side of the glade. They raised a cloud of dust as they galloped to the bank of the stream immediately opposite the two fishermen. There they reined and stood staring at the three men and the two boys.

All activity ceased. Beneath the contemptuous gaze of the men on the opposite side of the stream, Wesley grew painfully conscious of their peasant clothes. His trout flapped vigorously on the bank, but no one noticed. The leader of the three directed his horse into the stream but failed to note the water's depth. He nearly unhorsed himself and was forced to make an extremely undignified retreat to the bank.

Gerachti turned his back to the men and sniggered audibly, but the only other sound was the flapping of Wesley's trout.

"It seems that you are amused," the leader said at length, his low voice trembling with quiet rage. His face was pale, and his breathing was the breathing of someone barely able to control himself. "Let me inform you that we have reserved this part of the forest for our own use. We advised the population near here, and you have disobeyed us."

Gerachti swung round to face them, his eyes blazing. He seemed about to speak, then changed his mind. Alleophaz was frowning a little, for the first time looking uncertain of himself. Both simultaneously had realized that they might give away the disguise of their peasant dress by speaking. Only the captain seemed unruffled. Firmly, but with perfect courtesy, he said. "This is an unwarrantable intrusion, my lords. This part of the forest is reserved for the subjects of his majesty."

The leading horseman was enraged. "Silence, *peasant!*" He spat the word like an obscenity. "As peasants you will speak only when I ask for an answer!" He paused for a moment, staring intently at them. "Where are you from?" he asked them after a moment.

"Your servants are from Piggul," the captain replied in a quiet voice and with a perfectly straight face.

"From *Piggul!*" Again, the words came from his lips like spittle. "I might have known." His contempt was beyond his powers of expression. His nostrils flared in agitation. "I have decided to be merciful. Leave your game and your fish where they are. You will get out of the woods immediately by the nearest route. And hurry! We shall need your donkeys, so leave them behind." All three horsemen fitted arrows into their bows and pointed them at the two boys and at Gerachti.

"I will give you ten seconds to disappear from my sight," he continued.

Again there was silence, and in the silence they were conscious that Wesley's trout still flapped desperately. All five stared back at the leading horseman, who began to count, "One . . . two . . three . ."

Then Wesley cleared his throat, and said, in a voice that was clear and strong and filled with power, *"We have come to the gift of the forest the Emperor gave to the common people."* Wesley himself was surprised by the sound of his voice echoing loudly across the glade. He had said the words of power the prophet had given them, but now he stood there with his heart beating anxiously.

The leading horseman's face reflected sudden horror. Trembling with fear, he dropped his bow and arrow. The other two turned in haste to make for the forest, struggling furiously to put their weapons away. Their confidence had evaporated, and their eyes were wide and staring.

Then Wesley again called, his words echoing the horsemen's instructions to themselves. He was not being arrogant, for the same authority that accompanied his first words stayed about him still. "Leave the forest at once and never, *not ever,* dare to return!"

The horsemen needed no urging—but a worse horror awaited them, as Kai and the Koach reinforcements streamed from the forest, loping rapidly to encircle the horsemen. The riders reined their horses, their momentum checked. Once the circle was complete, the Koach raised their heads and howled in terrifying chorus. The paralyzing sound drained all color from the men's faces and left their eyes wide and staring. The horses reared, one of them screaming. One man fell from his horse, only to scramble madly back in terror.

Wesley shuddered, while the others watched in appalled silence.

The howling stopped as suddenly as it had begun. Slowly the circle narrowed as the Koach, growling, approached the horsemen. The fur on their backs was raised high, and more frightening yet, they held their heads close to the ground and bared their teeth menacingly.

"We must stop them." Wesley was hoarse, the authority missing from his voice.

Kurt shouted to the three horsemen as loudly as he could. "We can call them off if you want! They will do what we tell them!"

The horsemen, still struggling to control their horses, seemed not to hear them. They struck their horses in desperation, attempting to break through the circle.

Kurt called out again, "Listen! They will do what we bid them! Do you want us to call them off?" One of the horsemen heard and turned, his face panic-stricken. He was nodding.

"Kai! Bukov! Katia!" Kurt shouted. "Stop—they've had enough!"

The Koach raised their voices in one last howl and immediately ceased their menacing approach. Then, as one, they turned and melted into the surrounding woods. The horsemen cautiously made their

way into the trees, steering well clear of the point where the Koach had vanished.

Wesley drew in a breath. "Wow! That was *something!*"

"I thank the Emperor that you remembered the words of power," Captain Integredad said. "I never thought of them."

"Nor did I!" Alleophaz said.

"I—I tried to memorize them," Wesley said. "They just came out when they were needed, I guess."

Captain Integredad spoke solemnly. "It is not men like that I fear most, but the dark powers we face. Make no mistake, gentlemen. The danger from those men was small. The danger ahead of us is great. And," he hesitated, "I still think it has something to do with the weather."

But the excitement of what had happened drove danger from their minds. Kurt said, "I thought we'd had it when Mr. Gerachti was trying not to laugh."

"I nearly gave the game away," Gerachti chuckled. "You see, I was furious when he started to address us as though we were peasants. Why it should have aroused my wrath I hardly know. My pride, I suppose. I was taught to believe pride was good, that it was necessary if we were in positions of authority to intimidate others. Pride helped, therefore it was good. I am less sure about that now."

For a moment nobody spoke. Then, as Wesley picked up his trout, Alleophaz said, "I think we owe Captain Integredad a vote of thanks too. Let us not forget that it was he who remembered that we all came from Piggul!"

Wesley laughed, turning to them all. "Did you all see their leader's face when he said that?"

Kurt resumed his work on the fire.

"What shall it be for supper?" Captain Integredad asked. "Trout or venison?"

Wesley, ever the worry-wart, suddenly looked uncertain. Rules were important to him. "Don't we have to keep everything? I mean, we're trying to pretend we're peasants hunting for our families."

"Even peasants have to eat!" Captain Integredad said, laughing. "There will be plenty left over!"

There is nothing like fresh trout cooked in the hot ashes of a wood fire, especially when you're hungry. Soon they were eating heartily, burning their fingers even as they relished the incomparable flavor. Trout and soft dry bread make a wonderful combination.

Then they rested a little and resumed their way through the forest.

Lord Nasa made his way along the corridor of the only inn in Karsch. The day had been hot and rainless, and the night was oppressive. He was thirsty and sought a drink from the pump in the courtyard, which lay behind the main room in the inn.

Their party had arrived just before midnight. After a hasty meal, Lady Roelane, Lisa, Mary and Belak had all fallen asleep. They still wore their peasant clothes, curled up on crude bunk beds lining the walls of their room. But Lord Nasa had been restless, tormented by nightmares he could not remember on waking. Now within the corridor, he saw that the door to the principal room of the inn was open. It was a large room serving as bar, lounge and dining room all rolled into one. A candle from inside the room sent a thin shaft of light into the corridor.

As he approached the door, he heard a pounding on the front door that led to the street. At that hour the front door was barred by a beam, resting in strong iron slots. From within the candlelit room a man muttered curses to himself. Lord Nasa stopped and listened. "Who or what could it be at this hour?" he wondered. "It must be two hours past midnight."

Then came the sound of a man's voice. Lord Nasa recognized it as the landlord's. "This is not an hour to open doors. Honest people are abed long since. And if you are travelers, we are already full. Who are you? What is it you want?"

From the darkness beyond the door came the sound of a man's voice. "Have no fear. I am alone and unarmed. I would have words with you, landlord—and will pay you well for your attention."

There was a long pause as the landlord weighed his choices. Finally he called, "Be good enough to wait a moment, please." There was a further sound of footsteps, as though he were moving about the room.

Lord Nasa thought, "There are windows from which he can scan the front of both wings of the inn." He tried to picture the scene outside. "There is also a full moon, so he will know if it is safe to open the door. If the man is really alone, as he claims, he may well admit him."

He was right. The bolts scraped back and the door creaked open. "Come in!" The landlord's voice sounded muffled as though he had poked his head through the door.

"Aha!" he continued. "I recognize you. You came to Karsch—let me see—two—no, *three* days ago."

"Four days ago."

"Hm! What can I do for you?"

"I see you have some new guests. Where did they come from?"

There was a long pause. Then, speaking slowly, the landlord replied, "You ask many questions. If you are a trader in silks, why are you so interested in our wretched guests?"

Lord Nasa moved a little closer to the door at the end of the corridor. "Aha!" he thought. "This must be one of the king's spies."

The stranger's voice was low, but the words were clear enough. "I will pay well. Perhaps it would be better if I were to lodge here."

The landlord ignored the hint. "And if the information fails to be what you sought?"

"I pay for the time you listen. There will be a bonus if the information is about the people I seek."

"I doubt they will be. They are ordinary enough."

"Nevertheless, I will pay you for your eyes and your ears."

Again there was a moment's silence before any response. "Tell me, sir, where are you from?" The landlord sounded suspicious.

"We hail from Bamah."

"Your accent is from Playsion. You could be of the king's party."

"I did not think we would fool you. Nor am I trying. But my wife and family are in Bamah now."

In the silence that followed Lord Nasa thought rapidly. "Hopefully our peasant dress will have served us well. We were alone as we ate, and we were careful about what we said. Nevertheless, it may not be safe to wait till morning to leave."

The landlord's voice continued. "Whom do you seek?"

"We are interested in every stranger passing through. But some of the people we look for are from distant lands and of noble birth. Rumor has it that children from other worlds are in their care. We would rather arrest and question innocent people than let dangerous people escape."

The landlord snorted. "There are no likely candidates here!"

"I have watched the comings and goings with great care. But a group arrived tonight, unless I am mistaken."

"So! You have been observing my latest guests also! Yes, indeed. They have taken the last chamber. Peasants from Piggul! No, there is no danger there!" He laughed. "I made sure they paid me in advance! And their money was good. *Piggul!*" He laughed again. "Tell me, *are you in the king's employ?*"

Pauses seemed to be a part of the conversation. Lord Nasa could imagine the two men staring at each other, weighing each other carefully. At last the visitor spoke again.

"Let us say that my master, whoever he may be, pays well for information to anyone who can be discreet—who can, in a word, guard the door of his lips. As for your Piggul visitors, watch them carefully. No one travels these days whom I will easily trust. Watch them as they eat their breakfast, and listen to every word they utter. I shall come here the moment the sun is risen."

"Why is your master so anxious to know the movement of strangers?"

"Let us just say that he has his reasons."

"Very well. But let me ask you, By what name do you choose to go here in Karsch?"

"You may call me Perfido."

Lord Nasa forgot his thirst. He turned quietly and made his way back to the others. He had learned enough, and knew that he would have much to do to if they were to creep away unobserved.

19
The Cave
in the Cleft

To facilitate their getaway, Lord Nasa quietly oiled the bolts and hinges of the front door. Silently, hardly daring to breathe, they crept outside. The moon had set, so it was dark as pitch when they emerged into the street.

The air felt and tasted fresh, and even a little damp. "Yet it is more than damp the land needs," Lord Nasa thought. "We will be in trouble unless the rains come soon." Yet he kept such worries to himself.

To the others he breathed softly, "Good. So far we have done well. It will look suspicious, I know. But the risk of being questioned more closely, even by the landlord, is great. It would be difficult not to give ourselves away."

They hastily packed the animals in the courtyard and eased out onto the road.

"Where now?" Lady Roelane breathed.

"Oh, oh! Just look!" Mary's hoarse whisper was full of excitement.

"Where?" Lisa asked.

"Aha! I see the column," Belak murmured quietly, "along the road, uphill. It looks so lovely! Now that we have not had it for several days it is exciting to be able to see it—especially now that I *can* see it."

"Oh, glory!" breathed Lord Nasa. "It is back!"

It was like, and yet different from, greeting an old friend. The blue glow kindled a warm glow somewhere deep inside them all. Filled with unexpected joy, they turned and made their way after it without speaking.

By the time their eyes became adjusted to the darkness, Karsch was far behind them and they felt it was safe to talk.

Lisa rode beside Mary. "So you can see it!"

In the darkness, Mary smiled. "I sure can."

"I think that means Gaal's forgiven you, Mary!"

"You really think so?"

"Sure! It's obvious! I'm sure he forgave you long ago."

Mary drew in a long breath. "I hope so. Oh, I do hope so!"

"Oh—and Mary?"

"Uh-huh?"

"I'm sorry I've—well, I've not been very kind. I mean over the past few months in Winnipeg."

Mary felt her cheeks burning and was grateful for the darkness. "It's O.K., Lisa."

"Well, I didn't realize all that was involved in your joining the witches' club at school. I've known for some time now that it was more than being peeved at Uncle John's wedding."

Mary drew in a breath. "Yeah, but—I know what you mean, an' I'm grateful. Y'know, even though my mother was a witch," she said, slowly and cautiously, "an' even though I could feel a pull to that sort of thing, it was my own fault. I chose it. I did what I wanted. But thanks."

For a few minutes Lisa did not speak. Then, choosing her words with obvious care, much in the same way that Mary had a few minutes before, she said, "Mary?"

"Uh-huh?"

Lisa lowered her voice. "You know what Captain Intcgredad said about the great Lord of the Shadows?"

"What?"

"Well, that these invisible powers are actually in control—in control of the king's mind, for example."

"Uh-hm."

"Well I gather you feel as though you can't quite get out of being on the Shadow's side."

Mary nodded. "I do, but . . ."

Taking her courage in both hands, Lisa said with a whispered rush, "I believe myself that Gaal has already accepted you. I'm sure he never was mad at you, but I know you are not sure. In any case, perhaps it's like you have to resign from one team when you join another, at least it's like that with some teams. Or it's like becoming a citizen of another country. It's different in Canada, but in the U.S. you're not supposed to have more than one passport unless you were born in another country."

Mary nodded but said nothing. She was listening intently.

"Well," continued Lisa, "couldn't you renounce your connection with the powers of the Shadows?"

"But how?" Mary whispered.

"By saying it out loud. By saying, 'I hereby declare I no longer belong to Lord Lunacy, the Lord of Shadows or any of the lords the priests worship.' "

Mary frowned and said, "I'm not sure. But I wonder if we could drift a little behind the others. I'm sure no one is listening to us, but I'd feel safer if we were a little ways ahead or behind. Then we won't need to whisper."

"It'd be easier ahead," Lisa said slowly. "We'll only have to pass Lord Nasa and Lady Roelane—an' they're quite a ways behind the column."

Without making their intentions obvious, the two girls gradually drew level with, then well ahead of, the couple absorbed in their own conversation.

After a few moments Mary said, "But I can't renounce my real parents. I don't even remember my mother, an' I don't know a thing about my father. I don't even know whether I've got brothers and sisters."

"I know. It's a shame, it really is. I'm so sorry, Mary. But *it's not them* you have to renounce. It's what they were mixed up with. You're saying you're not on the side they were on. Why don't you say the words out loud?"

Mary drew in a deep breath, then said, "My heart's beating so hard I feel it might pop out of my mouth any minute!"

Lisa groped for her hand. "Why, your hands are like ice!"

"I know. I'm real scared for some reason. I feel chicken—but I'm going to do it!"

"Mary! You're shaking like a leaf!"

"I feel like—like they're all round me!"

"They can't touch you, Mary. I won't let them!"

"Just hang on to me, Lisa."

"Sure!"

Again Mary breathed in deeply. Then she said loudly, her voice shaking and almost unrecognizable, "I'm sorry about what my mother did, and her mother before her. I choose a different lord. I hereby declare I no longer belong to any of the lords the priests worship." Then she said, "Oh, Gaal, Gaal! Where are you?"

"I'm sure he's here, Mary."

For a few moments there was silence. Then Mary said, "Yeah, I know." She sounded on the verge of tears.

Then they both noticed. The column of blue fire, still far ahead of them, grew taller and brighter for several moments. As it grew, the calm inside of Mary grew as well. Lisa laughed softly. Slowly, then, the column returned to its former size.

In the darkness, not able to express what she was really feeling, Mary hugged her cousin. Lisa responded in kind, her warmth and softness telling Mary that Lisa, too, had difficulty in putting deep feelings into words. "Now we know Gaal was here. And you've almost stopped shaking!"

Then Mary sighed. "I wish I knew where Uncle John and the old lady were—in what century, I mean. You've no idea how scary it was to find the limousine empty when we got to the hotel."

"I bet!" (Lisa's eager enthusiasm was another way of saying, "I'm with you. I really do understand about everything.")

"An' when I saw that Lord Nasa had the Sword of Geburah—"

"He does?"

"—I thought he'd know where to find him. But he obviously doesn't. He knows it belongs to the Sword Bearer, but that's all he knows."

"Hm!" Lisa was silent for a moment. Then she said, "They're real—like, neat. I like them."

Mary laughed. "Y'know, I told Kurt that when I traveled with them, I did my darnedest *not* to like them! But I gave up in the end." Slowly they let themselves drop back to join the others.

After some time Lord Nasa said, "The road seems to have narrowed. We are walking on grass half the time!" Yet still ahead of them the column of blue light drew them after itself. They proceeded for an hour or more as dawn slowly grayed the eastern sky. The outline of low hills grew clearer. Moorland surrounded them, and on either side they could see scattered copses of woodland. Then as the eastern sky grew rosy, they saw that something they had begun to suspect was true. They had drifted from the roadway and were following little more than a path. It was wide enough for two of them to ride abreast, but it was obviously not a road. Or if it was, it was a little-used road, for grass covered much of it.

The column of light was slowly being transformed into one of smoke, though they could still discern the glow of blue light within it. Quite suddenly it stopped and then disappeared.

"Whither now?" Belak asked.

"I have no idea," Lord Nasa answered, frowning. "There seems to be no side path."

A sinking feeling gripped Mary. "So what do we do?" she asked.

"I think we sit down and wait," Lady Roelane said, smiling. And that, though not without misgiving, is what they did.

Mary glanced at the others. "Belak!" she cried. "Your proper color is back!"

Belak grinned. "It happened last night. I saw myself in a mirror as I was leaving my room."

"You look better—like yourself, I mean."

"I am myself again—and quite happy about it, too."

When the hunting party reached the edge of the forest at sunset, they found themselves on the edge of moorland. Alleophaz kept touching his skin and saying, "It feels the same as it always has!"

"Nevertheless, it is back to its usual color. You are as handsome as ever!" Gerachti cried, laughing.

"I can see that *you* are. But I will believe it when I see myself in a mirror. The sight of that ghastly pink face in streams will haunt me forever!"

The Koach leader announced that the time had come for them to leave.

"But we have no idea how to find the king!" Captain Integredad complained. "He may be in Karsch, or he may not. In any case, the last thing we want to do is to draw attention to ourselves by making inquiries."

"Have no fear," Kai said. "The prophet assured me that you would have special guidance from this point." And with that they disappeared into the forest. The three men looked at one another in bewilderment, and the two boys looked from one to another of the men. Finally, Alleophaz laughed and said, "This is a strange adventure!"

Kurt frowned. "I wish we had the ancient book."

"What book was that?" Alleophaz asked.

Wesley answered, "He means the book of the ancient laws and customs of Anthropos, with the songs and prophecies and so on. It was a big old book, it was the book Kurt was talking about when—"

"—when I tried to explain how I followed the column, and why I

241

looked at the rocks and ancient trees," finished Kurt. "You were listening, Lord Alleophaz—in the cabin overlooking the road—remember?"

Alleophaz nodded.

"Queen Suneidesis used to read it to us," Kurt mused. "But I keep forgetting it hasn't happened yet."

Gerachti said, "I do not understand all these twists in time, but I do suspect it is time to make camp. I do not know what the captain thinks, but *I* think we should build a fire and have some food. Then if nothing turns up tonight, we can sleep here. I must say this business of not knowing our next move makes me nervous. I am used to having everything planned out ahead of time."

Captain Integredad agreed. "But I suppose you cannot always do that when you are dealing with supernatural beings."

Kurt said, "I think it's fun—though it *is* scary. We've gotten a bit used to it coming here to Anthropos."

Alleophaz smiled. "I am not sure I will ever get used to it at my age!"

"Nor I," Gerachti agreed.

They were up at daybreak the next morning, and as they ate breakfast, the sun rose. The weather was still clear and dry, and the night sky turned from dark blue to gray, then to ruddy gold in the east and a deepening blue in the west. The ground was baked and dry, and the grass was dying. There was no sign of rain.

During packing Kurt said, "I'm not sure, but I think I can see the column."

"Where?" several voices asked.

Kurt pointed. "Just to the right of that very tall cedar." One by one they straightened their backs, for most of them had been bending over equipment.

"You know, you might be right," Wesley agreed.

"I see absolutely nothing," Gerachti muttered.

"I—I am not sure," Alleophaz hesitantly declared. The captain stared but was silent. When he did speak he said, "What shall we do?"

"I see no point in moving if we are uncertain," Gerachti asserted.

"We could ask it to become *clearer,*" Kurt said, frowning.

"Ask *it?*" Captain Integredad seemed to be puzzling aloud. "How can you ask an *it?*"

There was a pause as they all continued to stare in the direction Kurt had first pointed. "You know," Alleophaz said at length, "some of us have long had the feeling that it is more than an it. It seems almost like a person, like a comforting friend."

Kurt called aloud, "If you can hear us, we'd—er—we'd like you to become clearer!"

They continued to stare. "I still see nothing—" Gerachti began, but he was interrupted by Wesley, who said, "Hold on! Hold on a minute! It is getting clearer."

"Aha!" Captain Integredad cried. "It is like last time! I just needed eyes to see! Yes, I can see it now."

Slowly the column of smoke grew clearer to them. Alleophaz asked musingly, "Is the change in the column—or in us?"

But nobody answered him, for a growing excitement began to fill them all. "This is fun!" Kurt declared.

"I can see it clearly now," Gerachti said. "And looking back, I wonder if I could not see it all along. I was just frightened of making a fool of myself. When will I learn?"

"But to realize it was there all along fills me with joy!" Alleophaz exulted. "I thought we had lost it. But it certainly seemed to go away. Whatever happened, it knew where we were, and now *it* has found *us!*"

It was a merry party that set out moments later, relief and new hope flooding their veins. "I wonder if we'll get there today?" Kurt pondered.

"Yeah, but what do we do when we find *him?*" Wesley puzzled.

"We'll cross that bridge when we come to it, Wes," Kurt replied.

The moorland was interesting. Soon they grew accustomed to the wiry tufts of grass beneath their feet and the copses strewn here and there. Frequently they encountered blazing gold gorse bushes, riotously mixed with brilliant, reddish-purple heather. The sky arched its blue canopy far above their heads, and the clear air tasted like wine and filled their limbs with vigor.

They had ridden for less than fifteen minutes before Captain Integredad said, "Hello! We are joining some sort of track!" They followed the grassy pathway up a rise, and saw the rest of their party sitting beside the track on the other side.

Lord Nasa spotted them, and they hallooed and ran down the short slope to greet them.

Later, the column led them beyond any but the barest sign of a trail. Yet still they trod on the same wiry grass on the rise and fall of moorland. Then they saw opening up before them a chasm, where the column dropped down a series of steps out of their sight. For a moment they paused, uncertain. Then, following one by one, they entered a steep valley in which a small stream flowed. But the column had disappeared. There was no sign of it.

"Wherever is it?"

"It's gone!" Kurt cried in distress. "What happened?"

Lisa said, "Surely we saw it come down here!"

Alleophaz murmured, "Something has gone wrong."

In the silence that followed, Lady Roelane said, "No. I am sure there has been no mistake. Look just a little above us on our right. I believe there is a cave of some sort in the rock."

They turned and saw a vertical opening where limestone rocks jutted from the hillside. A faint light seemed to come from deep within the narrow opening. A sheep was tethered near the entrance.

"Is this IT?"

"Is it a cave?"

They paused, staring. Alleophaz broke the silence. "Come. Perhaps someone is within. We must do what we came to do." Drawing a deep breath, he withdrew from one of his panniers a small, cloth-wrapped bundle. Gerachti did the same. They dismounted and loosed their beasts to feed.

The travelers approached the cave entrance and saw a heavy door standing open as if ready to receive them. Lord Nasa called, "Is anyone at home? We come to visit the child king."

A woman appeared at the cave mouth. She wore a brown, hooded cape over a simple white dress. Her widely spaced eyes appraised the visitors, showing fear. On her very youthful face they could also read signs of suffering gladly endured.

"My name is Mehta, and my husband is Ish," she said quietly. "Tell me of this child."

Alleophaz replied, "Three of us—we darker ones—are philosophers from Glason. Your servant dreamed of the coming of the child while we were still in Glason. We also dreamed of a meeting with three children from worlds afar, who now accompany us." He pointed to the Friesens. "It has taken us nearly two years to get here." He nodded toward the others. "Lord Nasa of Chereb and the Lady Roelane come to represent her majesty, the queen of Anthropos-Playsion, who knew of the young king's birth by the ancient prophecies. While his majesty the reigning king may wish the young king harm, our own wish is to render him our deepest homage."

"I, as you have heard, am Lord Nasa of Chereb, and very honored to be here. The young lady, Mary, came with my wife and me. She longs to pay homage to his little majesty. Captain Integredad is a loyal subject of the queen."

A man they assumed to be Ish joined Mehta, looking at the visitors over her shoulder. "Who are they, and what do they want?" he asked her. There was a muttered exchange between them.

The man pushed past her and stood in front of her. Like his wife, he surveyed the crowd before him carefully. For a few moments nobody spoke. Then the man said, "Apparently you have spoken courteously to my wife. But we have been warned in visions of the night about the Playsion king to whom her majesty is married. Do you intend to return to him?"

Alleophaz shook his head. "We are of one mind about this, for not one of us trusts the king. How matters at the palace will turn out is not clear. The priests, under their leader, Shagah, are becoming more powerful than the king."

Husband and wife glanced at each other. The man said, "You are sure you were not followed here?"

Lord Nasa said, "It seems unlikely. I know every visitor to Karsch is watched, but we left before any could question us."

Again Ish turned to Mehta, and they nodded at each other. Then the woman smiled at Alleophaz, saying, "Please enter our hiding place and greet our little one."

20
The King

Mehta led the way inside the cave. Before closing the heavy oak door, Ish waited until everyone had passed him on the way in. It closed with a resonating bang, which seemed to echo from somewhere deep inside the hill. They crowded along a narrow passage only to discover that it opened to form a large chamber where the air was fresh and dry. Smoke curled from a peat fire, drawn upward to escape somewhere far above them. The mother bent to touch the child before seating herself on a crude bench.

Mary, who had been frowning and glancing round, reached suddenly for Lady Roelane's hand, gripping it tightly. Her heart was beating hard, and a moment later she found why. She looked into the eyes of the two-year-old child. As she did so, her grip on Lady Roelane's hand tightened even more.

"Oh, no! No, it can't be! Oh, Roly—it's him, it's Gaal. *It's those same eyes!* Whatever shall I do? He's looking right at me."

Lady Roelane drew her to herself. "Do you not know he loves you?" she murmured.

Lisa said, rather breathily, "It really is Gaal! I just know it!"

Trembling had taken possession of Mary's body. She slowly sank to her knees, clutching Lady Roelane's hand now with both of her own and ignoring the roughness of the rocky surface that dug into her knees. Soon sobs began to shake her frame. She heard a child's voice saying, "She hurt, Mummy! She hurt-ing."

"Yes, Gaal."

"I pray fo' big girl, Mummy?"

"If you like."

The captain and the three Glasonites were already on their knees, their foreheads touching the ground. The rest remained standing, strangely awkward, awed, yet uncertain how to behave. Mary was unaware that the child had approached her.

"She *nice*, Mummy. She *nice!*"

At the sound of his voice, so close to her, Mary glanced up, but immediately withdrew her hands from Lady Roelane's and buried her face in them, while a further storm of sobs seized and shook her. It seemed to her that a myriad of bewildering yet strangely comforting thoughts and emotions swirled around her. She sobbed without knowing why, and without caring.

Did the little boy really know? Did he understand who she was, what she had done? How could he if he was only a child?

Then he was addressing her. A moment later she felt the gentle pressure of his hands on her head. "I like! Gaal like big girl. Don' cry—mustn't cry. Not no mo'." But Mary began again to sob, wailing helplessly with a wondrous sorrow too deep for words, wailing as though she were likely to go on doing so for the rest of her days.

Meanwhile Lisa, Wesley and Kurt stared wide-eyed at the small boy, who so effortlessly drew all eyes to him. Wesley's lips had parted, but no words came to them. He breathed deep sighs from time to time. Kurt whispered, "He's just like—just like any other child. But no. He's different—I mean—*something's* different."

Lisa shook her head. Her lips were trembling, but she managed to breathe out, "What did you ex—I mean, what did we expect him to be like?"

"That's what I mean," Kurt whispered. "I'd never thought about it. Yet it's—it's obvious, really. Except it's—*wonderful!*"

Gaal had left Mary and was touching the Glasonites one by one. "They nice too, Dad-dy! Why they kneel?"

The parents glanced at each other. Mehta drew in a breath. "People—er, people do that sometimes, Gaal. They—they feel the Emperor must be here."

"Emp'or *my daddy!* My *uzzer* daddy!" he said, smiling.

Then, "They black, Mummy. They black!"

"Not really *black*, Gaal, just dark brown."

"Dark b'own, Mummy?"

"That is right!"

Little Gaal thrust one of his feet forward. "I got new sandows!" the child said, pointing down at his sandaled feet and addressing everybody in general.

Lisa began to giggle, but she did so openly, realizing giggling was appropriate and looking all the while at the child.

"You like my sandows?" He pulled his one foot back and pointed to both feet.

Kurt opened his mouth, then closed it and swallowed. Finally he said, "They're *great*, Gaal! They're terrific! Don't you think so, Wes?"

Suddenly, it seemed all wrong to be standing in the presence of the child, and the three children and Lord Nasa and Lady Roelane sank to their knees before him.

Wes said, "He's my King!"

"And mine!"

"He sure is!"

A strange stillness had fallen on the group. Awe had become a Presence they could feel, charging the cave with an impenetrable quiet.

The Glasonites offered their packages.

The mother said, "See, Gaal, these kind men have brought presents for you!"

"P'esents? Fo' me, Mummy?"

"What do you say, Gaal?"

"What they bring, Mummy?"

"We will look at them later, Gaal. So, what do you say to the men?"

"They good men!"

For what seemed a great while they stayed like that. There was no need of words or any movement. The child was content, now resting against his mother's robe. Moments slipped by one after another, but nothing disturbed the stillness. Time had ceased, and rush and hurry were no more. Every face registered untroubled calm. Mary's wailing had been stilled. She was half sitting, looking now at the child, marveling at what had happened, at what was still happening and seemed unlikely ever to end. She looked as though she would be content for it to continue forever.

Rudely shattering the stillness, a sudden hammering at the oak door echoed harshly through the cave, awakening strident echoes from its depths. A muffled shout reached their ears. "Open! Open, I say, in the name of his majesty, King Tobah Khukah!"

Hastily they scrambled to their feet, looking in uncertain fear at one another. What now? Had they been followed? Too late for speculation. But where could they go? Into the depths of the cave? How long before the door burst open? And how long before they were found?

Pounding and the shouts continued as men hurled themselves against the door to break it open. Several of the company cried out, for the very floor suddenly became wildly unstable. Waves were passing through what had a moment ago been solid rock. There was a rushing and roaring sound, and above it the ringing laugh of a delighted child.

The rushing turbulence ceased as suddenly as it had begun. Had you been watching everyone (say, on a television screen) you might have been puzzled by the still calm and quiet that prevailed immediately again. Were they stunned by events their minds refused to

251

cope with? Or had a vast blanket of quiet settled on them all? All movement had ceased again, as though they all were willing to accept the most dramatic events placidly. The momentary fears that had registered on their faces seconds before, to which they would have clung if they had been able, had left no trace. Kurt was the sole exception. He cried, "Wherever are we?"

He might well ask. The rocky ground where they stood was much more uneven than that of the cave. They were in a sort of hollow surrounded by rocky mounds about twice the height of their heads. Above the nearest of these rose a sheer cliff wall stretching far above them, so that they craned their necks in a futile attempt to see the top.

They were not under an open sky, even though unimaginably vast spaces were about them. Any ceiling that might arch overhead was far too distant to be seen, the space stretching above them into infinitely distant shadow. A dim, reddish flicker—not unlike firelight—could be seen, but they could not perceive its source. In addition, a strange blue light pervaded their immediate surroundings.

Mary found the tiny hand of a child inside her own. She glanced calmly down to see that it was Gaal's hand she was holding. She smiled and softly said, "Oh, it's you!" For some time she looked down at him, a serene smile on her face.

He looked back at her, grinning merrily, not at all serene. "I like! I like dis!" Apparently he was talking about their adventure. Once again the little king broke into peal upon peal of laughter.

" 'I-sa-no!" he cried gleefully. *"You* did it, 'Isano! *You* did it!" He released Mary's hand to run to the tall creature—the source of the soft blue light—standing now a few yards away. If Mary, Lord Nasa and Lady Roelane recognized him, they gave no sign of surprise. The three philosophers sank to the ground in awe.

"No, no, no!" the spirit of light cried, laughing as merrily as Gaal had laughed a moment before. "Bow down to the child, by all means, but not to me, your fellow creature and fellow servant. I may look impressive, especially when I shine, but my status is not too different from your own! In fact, yours has even greater honor!"

They stared at him, immobile. Alleophaz murmured something softly, but nobody heard him. He closed his eyes drowsily.

"Where are we?" Kurt addressed his question to Risano. Only Gaal, Risano and, strangely, Kurt were immune from the strange stillness that affected the rest.

"Where are we? In the cave still! You are exactly where you were a moment ago, before the king's soldiers pounded on the door—and, incidentally, there were nearly thirty of them."

"Oh, come off it!" Kurt called. He was uncertain whether he ought to take such liberties with the laughing giant of a creature before him, but he sensed that his words would be taken in good part. "What about that cliff above us?" he continued. "Where was *that* a few seconds ago?"

"Oh, *that!*" Risano said, his eyes twinkling merrily. "I will give you three guesses, young man!"

"Guesses? As for the cliff—why, it's a cliff—isn't it? What else could it be?"

"I agree that it certainly looks like a cliff. At least it does so from our present vantage point. But suppose I were to give you a hint, and tell you that the cliff you think you are looking at is made of leather."

"You're fooling me!"

"Not at all!"

By now Kurt's eyes were on the sheer vertical rise that frowned grimly down at them, awing them by its majestic size.

Wesley said, "How could it be of leather? Where would one find that much leather in the whole universe?"

Risano's smile never wavered. "It does seem a lot, does it not? But again, everything depends on your exact vantage point."

No one spoke. They seemed to have no urgent need to know where they were. Placid faces, apparently undisturbed by any concerns, the danger that seconds before had shattered their peace seemed no longer to have power to disturb.

"But *leather!*" Kurt persisted.

Risano laughed again, a deep and rolling laughter that, spilling from him, caused others to smile. But their smiles were "Mona Lisa" smiles, serene and gentle.

Once his laughter settled, Risano said, "Imagine that you are a microbe examining the side of someone's leather boot. Not the whole boot, mind you, but just the edge of the sole. You would not be able to see the soft part of the leather surrounding the foot. It would be much too distant from the little microbe. All the microbe would be able to see would be the edge of the sole. In fact, even the edge of the sole would stretch above it like a cliff, very much as the edge of the sole of the officer's boot stretches above you now!"

"You mean—"

"I mean that is what you are looking at. I had to make you invisible somehow, so I reduced you to the size of microbes. It was just as effective as any other way. In a moment the officer will tread on you all. But have no fear. A boot of that size is far too big to get into the spaces where you stand. In any case, such are the indentations on the under surface of the sole, that they would arch like vast bridges over your heads."

Risano talked as though what he said was reasonable—ordinary and unremarkable, even—like an explanation of why you wear warm clothes in winter, or cooler ones in summer. His tone of voice suggested that, of course, to be invisible, to be as small as a microbe, was nothing out of the ordinary. The stamping of cosmic-sized boots was an everyday affair. And to observe everyone but Kurt, you would say they had not woken up. They appeared alive yet tranquil, serenely alive, so to speak. Indifferent to danger. Profoundly at leisure.

The rest were roused from their trance by the distant rumble of thunder far above them. "What's the thunder?" Lisa eventually asked.

"Thunder? Oh, yes! It is the soldiers. They are talking, and it *does* sound like distant thunder down here. They are wondering where you are, and are concluding you must have gone deeper into the system of caverns. They saw all your donkeys outside (where their horses are now tethered), and the officer has concluded they should explore in search of you. However, they are wondering how safe it will be. They believe you are armed and dangerous. They fear a trap!"

Mary nodded, smiling, as though fearful, suspicious troops were something she encountered frequently. She looked at Gaal, who still held the crouching Risano's hand, looking up at him. Softly, Risano addressed him. "Thus will my Lord destroy death and darkness, by being small and weak. You, my Lord, will entitle yourself to every crown that exists, and do so by your very weakness."

Mary shook her head slowly. Wonderingly, yet softly, she asked, "Small? Weak? How can you destroy great power by weakness? After all, we're facing not just the priests, but the spiritual forces with them. All by smallness and weakness?"

The strange calm began gradually to wear off them.

"It seems curious, does it not, Mary?" said Risano. "The greatest power of all overcomes by a display of weakness; it wins by letting itself apparently be defeated."

Mary drew in a long breath. "It makes no sense."

"How are we overcoming King Tobah Khukah's power right now, Mary? Are we fighting it? Are we at the moment bigger and stronger—more impressive, more fearsome than our foes?"

"Oh!" Mary began to giggle. Gaal was watching her closely.

"He who has real power does not concern himself with whether he *appears* to have power or not. Infinite power can afford to appear defeated and undignified. What matters is how the war ends. Darkness is easily fooled by those who understand it. Self-conceit destroys itself if you give it a chance."

Mary looked thoughtful. After a moment she said, "Yes, *but Gaal is going to die when he grows up!*"

"Exactly. He will fool his enemies by his apparent weakness. But tell me something, something your Uncle John has already described to you. Did he win, or did he lose the battle with the dragon-bull-serpent?"

"Uncle John said he won." She shook her head and continued. "Uncle John saw Gaal pull the horns from the black bull. But even so, Gaal died!"

"Yes. At that point he began his greatest conflict—with the might of Death itself. And in his struggle with Death, are you saying he lost? Did Death defeat him—or did he defeat Death?"

Mary frowned, then looked surprised. "You know, I'd forgotten. No—I didn't realize he was fighting Death. You mean even in his death he was fighting? Obviously he won."

"He won by what somebody once called 'a deeper kind of law, a law that stood at the core of creation.' It is the law of love, the law of purity and self giving. In the end it always wins over hate."

"That's why he'll never die!" Mary spoke wonderingly.

"Nor will you!"

"I won't?"

"Oh, you will *look* as though you are dead. You will pass through death, all right. But that is just it. You will pass through—and come out the other end with a body that defies time, one like Gaal himself will have!"

A low murmur seemed to pass through the group. Suddenly a menacing shadow closed over their heads. Immediately they looked up. The precipice that had dominated the scene a moment previously had disappeared. Instead, they found a roof over their heads, a high, rough roof, looking for all the world like an arch of black rock. It was a boot.

The distant thunder seemed to rise to a crescendo.

"The captain is urging the rest of them to get moving," interpreted Risano. "He claims knowledge that you are unarmed, that you can be taken easily."

Alleophaz, who looked as though he was still under the spell of the remarkable peace, sounded mildly puzzled. "But however did the officer find out where we were—I mean, where we *are*?" he asked.

The dark ceiling lifted as suddenly as it had descended while from the dim and distant regions above, the rolling of gentle thunder continued. Lord Nasa asked the same question that Alleophaz had asked. "Yes, I am quite sure that even if suspicions were awakened in the inn at Karsch, word could never have reached Bamah soon enough to mobilize any troops."

Risano said, "The troops were already in the area. The captain who leads them was once one of the temple priests. He is in touch with the dark powers himself. They knew you were here, and also knew you would not return to Bamah. Therefore they hastened to come to destroy you. But I have for the moment shrouded you in secrecy. The dark powers do not know everything."

"They were going to destroy us? We are under the protection of the Glason Crown!" Gerachti raised his eyebrows. "Surely they would never dare!"

Risano laughed. "The Glason king knows nothing about your present whereabouts. You could have suffered another shipwreck for all he knows. Besides, would he embark on a costly, overseas war over the deaths of three of his citizens? And remember, the children from distant worlds do not enjoy even the small protection of a Glason king. As for Lord and Lady Nasa of Chereb, their deaths would become known as a tragic *mistake*. Gerachti, you are protected by powers far greater than those of your king!"

He paused and then laughed again. "Oh, but we are better protected than by any earthly kings or queens of any age!" He looked down at Gaal. "It is this little one that his Emperor-Father has sent us and the pigeon you have sometimes seen who will protect you. Who do you think sent *me*?"

Lady Roelane asked, "So what will happen?"

"Right now, the troops are leaving this part of the cave to penetrate its endless passages and depths. This will take some time, for the system of caves and tunnels is extensive. It may take them as much as a day and a half to assure themselves you are not in the cave at all. Meanwhile, the dark powers will be focusing too much on your *possible* whereabouts to pay attention to your *real* whereabouts. Therefore, you will soon have a chance to escape from the cave."

"And then what?" Lord Alleophaz asked.

"Then you will try to conduct the young king and his parents to safety."

"But to safety where?" Wesley asked. "After all, we've still had no instructions. I wouldn't have a clue as to where safety could be found."

Risano smiled. "One thing at a time. Your first task concerns the temple. In any case, I doubt you will get to safety without an encounter with the legions of darkness. The Emperor will not hide your presence from the dark powers forever."

Kurt grinned at Risano. "You wouldn't happen to *be* the column yourself, would you?"

Risano returned the grin. "In one sense, yes. But in another sense, no!"

Kurt frowned. "What kind of an answer is that?" he demanded.

"Well? Are you all ready?" was the spirit's only answer.

"Ready for what?" Kurt asked.

"To leave the cave and enter the next phase of your adventure."

"You mean right now?"

Risano nodded. "There are soldiers at the door of the cave, guarding it, and two or three inside it. They were left in case you returned from some hiding place they were not aware of. Do not be afraid. When they see me, I doubt they will remember anything else."

There came a sense of vertigo as their bodies resumed normal size. But once restored and again in a normal-sized cave, Risano himself became a blazing and dazzling sunlike vision of greatness, pouring forth a torrent of light. They caught a glimpse of soldiers, their faces bleached white in the shocking light, falling unconscious on the floor of the cave. Risano did not wait, but strode to the door. The watchers inside the cave dimly perceived shocked faces and the instant collapse of the guard outside the cave.

"They will be like that for several hours longer," Risano said as he reentered the cave and the blazing light faded. "The other soldiers, seeking you in the depths of the cave, will be long in returning, for they have lost their way in the darkness. And beyond that I will find means to keep them here until you are well away."

He paused, and they stared at him. "I have another little surprise for you." They waited expectantly. "Time does strange things when you are in another dimension. It is now dawn of the day following the day you entered. It is, so to speak, *tomorrow,* now."

There was another pause. Events had happened too rapidly for them to adjust. Finally, Captain Integredad asked the obvious question, "So what now, my lord? We shall be delighted to get well away—but where to? Where are we going?"

Risano held the door open. "You will soon find out. You will find out as the adventure opens before you."

21
The Return of the Queen

Once outside the cave they saw more guards—like statues of slain warriors, still as death in their unconsciousness. Clearly it would be many hours before they came to. Time seemed now to be on their side. It was also barely light with the dawn of the following day.

In the early morning light they glanced down at a series of pools— all that was left of the small stream below them. Some of the soldiers' horses drank there. Other horses, along with their own mules, scrabbled for food in the dry grass on the banks of the stream, while some browsed the moors above. The horses were still saddled, their panniers still attached.

Kurt, prompted by some obscure instinct, scrambled back over the edge of the valley and onto the moor. A few seconds later he returned, shouting loudly, his voice echoing across the valley. "Hey, guys, it's here! It's actually happening! It's begun!"

"What d'you mean? What's begun?"

"The adventure! You know, the one Risano said would 'open before us'! *The queen's coming!* And thousands of her soldiers with her!"

The captain climbed up and gazed across the moor. *"Thousands* of soldiers, my lord Kurt?" he murmured, grinning, "There may be a hundred or so. Perhaps not even so many!"

Immediately there was a hurried scramble over the ridge above them. Forty or fifty yards from the edge of the valley they saw a large company nearing, and at their head, the queen, the old prophet and Duke Dukraz. In their excitement they waved, and many of the soldiers waved back, shouting. All were on horseback, and a few, they noticed, rode two to one horse.

The sun's first rays lit up random patches of grass and chased away the lingering mists. Everyone sensed they were taking part in a grand occasion, that protocol would have to be observed. Captain Integredad's party restrained themselves respectfully, waiting for the queen to speak. As she drew rein, she hailed them. "How delighted I am to see you all, and to see you looking so well!"

The men bowed, and the boys, remembering their manners, also bowed, while the women and girls curtsied. The queen and Duke Dukraz and many of the soldiers dismounted. The duke immediately turned to assist the prophet down from his horse.

Captain Integredad, a look of worry on his face, said, "A thousand welcomes, your majesty! But your sudden appearance now causes us to suppose some ill may have occasioned your leaving Bamah—"

"And you are correct, my good captain. I have come for your help. I will ask the prophet to tell you all that has taken place." But the queen was looking beyond them. "Who are those persons I see with you?"

Ish and Mehta had remained shyly in the background with Gaal.

Captain Integredad said, "Your majesty, they are the parents of the child, of the young king. Ish, the father, is carrying the child. The mother's name is Mehta."

"The young king himself! So you found him! I might have known. Her name is Mehta, you say?"

"Yes. Such is her name, your majesty."

The queen smiled warmly at Mehta. "Greetings, Mehta! Did you know that the ancient book—the Archives—speaks of you, predicting your arrival? But it does not tell us your name. It only says that you were to bear the child. And you, sir," she added, looking at Ish, "must have faced serious doubts about your wife. Yet Anthropos history has many records of a pigeon that has repeatedly led the way for Gaal's people."

The children looked at one another, nodding.

"It is not really a pigeon," the queen continued, "but a Sacred Spirit. What you see in the child"—she paused, glancing at the child with profound emotion visible on her face—"that very precious child, is the result of a miracle that the same Sacred Spirit performed in Mehta's body, creating a child both of the Emperor's lineage and of the royal lineage of Anthropos, the line descending from the original Regenskinder."

A mantle of awe continued to settle about her as she gazed at Gaal. As it deepened, her manner began moment by moment to change. By turns her face expressed fear and amazed wonder. "Long have I awaited this day," she murmured to herself.

Carefully she dismounted, walking past the horses to stand facing the little king. Behind her Duke Dukraz and the prophet knelt. One by one, by common consent, the rest of both parties followed their example, so that the whole company dismounted and knelt. All conversation ceased. The queen was already kneeling before the child. Ish lowered the little boy to the grass. He stared at the queen, at the large crowd of worshipers, a puzzled look on his face.

"Emp'or here, Mummy? Emp'or here? They wors'ip again?"

"I think so, Gaal."

"He my daddy too."

"Yes, child."

He stared at the queen for a moment, then began to move toward her. Mehta made a move as though to prevent him, then, hardly knowing what to do, arrested the movement. Her hands flew toward her face, partly covering her mouth. "Oh, no—oh, dear! What now?" she breathed softly.

Gaal stood in front of the queen, who stared back, still awestruck. He said, "Emp'or my Abba!" then went right to her, reaching as far as his little arms were capable round her waist as she knelt, and leaning his head against her. The queen's face crumpled as she gathered him to her. It looked for a moment as though she would lose control. But after a moment she won out over her feelings, except that tears flowed freely down her cheeks, and the look on her face became one of mingled joy and wonder. She remained like this for a minute or so, then, rising to her feet, she took the child's hand and looked directly at Mehta. "You are a remarkable woman. I am amazed at the faith in the Emperor you had to be willing for this to happen. You are an example to all women everywhere—not only of great faith, but of supreme courage—the hardest courage of all, the courage to obey when you knew the consequences."

Ish and Mehta had come to stand before the queen, and it was now their turn to kneel—to their queen. The queen turned to look at Ish. "And you, sir, are almost as remarkable. Did you know what you were doing?"

"Yes, ma'am. I was of a mind to hide her somewhere quiet. I care for her. But a spirit of light came in a dream and told me what had happened to her."

The queen shook her head pensively, her eyes alight with joy. "It is amazing, is not it? The ancient book told me it would happen, and a messenger from the Emperor told me it would be soon. It is a great marvel."

Gaal repeated, "Emp'or my daddy! An' he"—pointing to Ish—"my daddy too."

The queen smiled down at him and bit her lip, having another momentary struggle with her feelings. She handed Gaal to his mother and turned to the rest of the kneelers, saying, "I believe you can all feel free to stand now. The little king is going to be the kind of sovereign who appreciates bowed and willing hearts that are eager to obey him more than ceremony."

Glowing, she continued, "In earthly kingdoms, many people who bow the knee have stiff necks and rebellious wills. This king is going to be different. Sometimes we will find ourselves kneeling to him, and will be able to do nothing to prevent it. But for the moment . . ."

One by one they rose, and a more relaxed atmosphere began to prevail. Lisa said, "Have you noticed the feeling that's come over everyone?"

"Feelings have their place," Wesley said. "D'you remember in Mirmah's kingdom as King Kardia was sailing beneath the ice? He described how Gaal came walking across the water. He said he felt awe when he saw him, you remember—Gaal came on board the ship."

Kurt added, "I won't ever forget the feeling when I knew he had forgiven me on our first trip. I'd messed up good that time."

Mary said, "Feelings—yeah! It's the amazing feeling that—that everything's O.K.—when that was the last thing you expected!"

The queen turned to Captain Integredad. "You had asked what brought us here. As I said, it is for the prophet to explain."

The prophet smiled at them all and for a moment said nothing. Again they were overwhelmed by the strange combination of fragility and power that seemed to rest on him. Lisa whispered something to Mary, pointing to Shiyrah, whom she had noticed on horseback next to a young officer.

Then the prophet began to speak. "I learned from a vision in the night that her majesty was in grave danger, and I knew her work in Anthropos was not finished. The Emperor himself transported my granddaughter and myself to the queen's bedroom in the palace. I woke her, warning her that she must leave at once. There were plans to execute her for treason at dawn the next day. There would be no trial."

The queen spoke gravely. "Most of the soldiers in the army had proved fickle—lured by promises of wealth and promotion made by Shagah and the priests. I had thought that perhaps, after my triumph in the duel with the villainous Sir Robert Ashleigh, things might have turned out differently." She sighed and shrugged her shoulders. "But it was not to be. I realized also that my husband—that is, his actual person—was dead. His body had been borrowed—taken over, but all that once was King Tobah Khukah, all his inner being had been destroyed from inside his body, which was now possessed by the strange and powerful being you already know about.

"Whoever that being was and is, he had murdered my husband and was merely making use of his bodily parts. The person who had held my loyalty was no more. The Lord of Shadows—for I suspect it was he—was energizing, *animating* his bodily parts, and it was he who had ordered my execution, not the weak king who had been my husband."

She smiled, raising her eyebrows a little. "So, here I am! And with the pick of the army! I may have few men, but they are the very best!"

The captain nodded. "Your majesty, I have been looking at them. You could not have had a better bunch even if you had picked them! But your majesty's wishes and plans—what are they?"

"Now that the child is in our care, my wishes are that together we return to Bamah with the men who accompany me. We are going to destroy the temple!"

"With only a couple of hundred men, your majesty? These men are superb, but our enemy's army is measured in hundreds of thousands," Captain Integredad replied.

"Quite so. But surprise, as you well know, is everything in battle. It will be on our side. We had already ordered the men you now see with me to stand by for emergency movements."

The prophet explained, "If we can succeed in burning the temple, it will be a serious, though temporary, setback to the power of the temple priests and of spirits of the shadows. The burning of the temple will cast both the spirits themselves and the main army into confusion, for the temple is the center of power for both. They could, and will, build another temple. But that would take them many years. Both men and spirits know our task force is small. But very soon they will be surprised at our daring!"

Lord Nasa was frowning. "How can our movements remain secret?

The spirits can see our every move! Why, already we have been surprised—in the cave—by a number of soldiers in the charge of a priest!"

"That is where the prophet has been so helpful," the queen interjected. "He tells me he cannot shield us from human beings. What he can do *and has now done* is to shield us totally from the eyes of the spirits of the shadows—and therefore also the priests—making us utterly invisible to them, veiled by a cloak of secrecy. And this man," she turned to one of the horsemen, "bears a copy of the book of the histories and prophecies of our nation. It has remarkable power."

"I know!" Lisa cried. "An awesome light comes out of it—at least it did out of the real one—and *WOW!* Does it *ever* affect the other side!"

At this point the queen turned to look directly at Captain Integredad. She withdrew her sword from its scabbard. "Now, Captain. I have only one or two junior officers with me. They need the command of someone of experience. You are one of the reasons I have crossed the woods and the moors. Kneel before me, Integredad!"

The captain knelt with bowed head, and the queen placed the sword on his shoulders. "I hereby appoint you head of the task force. Rise, Colonel Sir Verdadera Integredad!"

The former captain rose. For a moment he looked stunned, his face flushed and his mouth slightly open. Her majesty had vaulted him past his majority to a senior rank. Then, recollecting himself, he bowed. "Your majesty does me great honor. I will do all I can to live up to it as I serve you."

Throughout this time the men and officers had been dismounting and sitting on the dry and wiry grass. But at this they struggled to their feet and gave loud cheers, for the former captain was very popular. The sun still shone fully and a soft breeze blew over them all. No sign of expected rain clouds could be seen.

The queen smiled and looked up to catch the eyes of the Friesens and Mary. "I came for the child and for Sir Verdadera Integredad, but equally importantly I came for you. No one in Anthropos has information about the secret tunnel leading from the temple to the river bank. I have reason to hope that one or all of you may be able to help."

The prophet said, "At least, the old stories tell us that there is such a tunnel. But I know neither its location nor how it may be entered. All my inquiries to the Emperor have been unavailing. He tells me nothing about it. But someone here must know."

"I do!" Lisa cried. "I left the temple by that route. The pigeon showed me a rose on a huge pillar in the temple, and a door in it opened when you pressed it. You went down ever so many steps—real deep down, and there was a tunnel—"

"Did the tunnel emerge by the river?"

"Yes. I had to command the rock to open in the name of Gaal. It just swung open when I did. It was real wide—wide enough to let six men on horseback pass at the same time."

"And you could find it again from the river bank?"

A sudden doubt occurred to Lisa. Could she find it again? "I—well, I hope so. There was this magical dead tree. At least I understood it was magical. But—" Lisa looked unhappy as another doubt occurred to her. "I think the pillar—I mean the pillar inside the temple—was made of stone, not wood. And I gather that the present temple is made of wood."

The prophet smiled. "Aha! The stone pillar is the same, though. It was built soon after time began, when there was yet no temple—none knows how or when—and it now supports the whole building. The rest of the structure is wooden. But you say that the tree was a *magical* tree. That would indicate that the powers of darkness know about the tunnel."

"Yes. There were branches of the tunnel that were evil."

"Hm! Magical trees come and go. I have reason to know that spirits of darkness do not have access to the tunnel now. That could mean your tree may have been withdrawn. When present, it is a mark for the shadow spirits. They know they cannot open the door, but they can have access to it in other ways."

Lisa was filled with sudden doubt. Were they depending on her for the queen's plan? What if she were not able to find the place on the river bank! "I—I hope I'll be able to find it. Gosh—I didn't realize the whole expedition might depend on me. I sure hope the tree will be there this time."

Colonel Integredad was issuing orders to the young officers and soldiers. Soon these had descended into the valley to secure the horses that the enemy soldiers had brought (eventually they were able to seat everyone on horseback) and to drive the mules some distance across the moor. The valley below and the moor above became a scene of activity. Both boys joined in the fun of what was happening, making themselves useful.

While the preparations for the return journey continued, Shiyrah came to greet Lisa and Mary. "You can have little idea of the relief it is to see you safe," she said, embracing them both.

"Oh—there were one or two tense moments, but it hasn't been that bad!" Lisa protested.

"You little know!" Shiyrah returned. "We were concerned about you every moment. But—all thanks to the Emperor!—you are still safe."

They sat on the grass together. "What d'you think will happen when we get to Bamah?" Mary asked.

Shiyrah looked at her and smiled. "Well, my . . . er, my grandfather—he is my great-great, you know, but it is too much trouble to say—thinks we will get into the temple by the passage Lisa knows about. There is lots of the priests' anointing oil inside, and he knows where it is, and has already been instructing one of the sergeants to spread it around to the greatest advantage. He feels sure the place will go up in flames very easily. The wood is very dry, he says. But I am so worried about him."

"You are? Why?" Lisa asked.

"I do not know how his spirit stays in his body. He is really very, very frail. I try to take care of him, but he is determined to see this expedition through. It is exhausting him, though he will never give up—until he drops dead. I wish he could go on forever, but that is just not possible."

Both girls felt uncertain of themselves, yet flattered and grateful that the older girl was confiding her feelings to them. Lisa wondered whether she ever had anyone to talk to, and whether there was any relationship with the young officer she had seen her with. Mary frowned. "I know the prophet looks *flimsy,* as though the wind would blow him away, but the *power* that comes from him . . ."

"Everyone says the same. But he is mortal. He has to die sometime. After all, few people live to his age. I dread to face it, but I feel his time is not very far off."

"I—I hope you're wrong," Lisa said thoughtfully. She looked at Shiyrah admiringly. "I wish I could sing like you. It's not just your voice, but the effect of your singing on us. It must be lovely to be able to do that."

"Yes and no!" There was a faraway look in Shiyrah's eyes.

"I'll have to get you to sing over us all again," said Lisa. "I wish so much didn't depend on me. It's awful. I'm scared now that I may not be able to find the entrance to the passage. Or, that if I do find it, it will not open if I command it to in Gaal's name."

After a moment Mary said, "Sure you'll find it! An' of course it'll open." But as Mary looked at Shiyrah, she saw her thoughts must still be on the old prophet. "You're worried, aren't you?" she asked gently.

Shiyrah nodded and sighed. "I am so used to having him. What will I do when he dies?"

Just then the same young officer whom Lisa had noticed approached the three girls and bowed to them.

Shiyrah looked up at him and smiled. "These are my friends from other worlds, Mary and Lisa, and this young gentleman is Kosti, who made sure I did not get into mischief during the journey here."

The officer looked startled. "Did you say the young ladies *came from other worlds?*" he asked.

"Yes. There are doors between worlds and times, you know."

"There are? I certainly did not know. But since meeting the prophet, I am learning that there are many things I do not know!"

He grinned and sat down with them. "It is an honor to meet you. And—I hope I am not intruding?"

"Of course not!" Shiyrah was quick to say. "You have been getting the horses ready?"

"Yes. I think there will be enough for everybody, so that we will not have some horses carrying two men. We should be able to set out reasonably soon. Then the long journey begins."

"How long will it take us?" Lisa asked.

"I'm not sure. But we will have to avoid settlements and travel by night a lot. I suppose the prophet will serve as our guide. He seems to be able to see in the dark, and to find a route through the wildest country. What is more, we will have to go to Ashleigh, where we are to leave King Gaal and his parents. Since the autumn rains have not come yet, and the autumn weather seems as though it will hold for a while, we may manage it." He grinned. "Everyone is complaining about the weather. But I am all for it. It is an ill wind—"

A series of bugle notes startled them all, pealing out across the moors like the call of a giant rooster. "Oh, dear," the young officer said. "That means for everyone to hurry up. I must report to the colonel." He glanced at Lisa and Mary. There was a wonder in his eyes. "I will have to come back to learn more about your world and time another day. Good-bye for the present." He looked at Shiyrah almost tenderly. "Until we meet again."

Soon after that they set out. Colonel Integredad had given the soldiers and their officers precise instructions for their deployment should they encounter enemy forces. But to travel, they rode as a three-abreast column, Gaal and his parents, the queen and the prophet in the center. Over the moors they trotted, past the copses and over the dry, wiry grass with never a pause. In much less time than the boys and men had taken to reach the cave from the woods, they were now approaching the forest again.

"We're here!" Kurt exulted. "We've made it!"

He spoke too soon. Suddenly a bugle sounded. From the woods

where they had been hidden, nearly two hundred men on horseback came charging out to meet them. Their movements had again been discovered, and they were under attack—by a well-armed force twice their own number!

22
Under the Cloak of Secrecy

In less time than it takes to blink, Colonel Integredad nodded to his bugler, who sounded the deploy. Immediately, and from both sides of the column, two wings formed, flanking the colonel on either side so that he led from the center. The maneuver was expertly executed. At the same time a dozen horsemen surrounded Gaal and his parents, the Lady Roelane and the girls. The queen had already made it clear that she would choose to fight, so Duke Dukraz rode on one side of the colonel, the queen on the other. The boys found swords strapped beside their saddles and (perhaps rather foolishly) insisted in taking part. Yet Lord Nasa hastily exchanged swords with Wesley, giving him the jeweled Sword of Geburah.

"Here! Use it!" he cried, thrusting the sword into his hand and snatching Wesley's own sword before he could draw it. "And tell that idiot Kurt to get back with the women!"

Unfortunately, "that idiot" was already galloping furiously after the colonel's advancing troops. The gap between the two groups of men was lessening. The queen's forces were heavily outnumbered, yet they had certain advantages. They were the better and more experienced fighters, with superior leadership. And the ground favored them, for they rode downhill to meet the foe.

As the two small armies met, the clash could be heard a mile away. It was a sound of swords against shields, of rearing and whinnying horses, and of yelling men. Poor Kurt was unhorsed as soon as he got into the fray. He lay winded on the ground, seeing flailing and tramping hooves, none of which (by some miracle) trampled him. His ankle caught in the stirrup, and his horse accidentally saved him by dragging him clear of the fray, battering and bruising him in the process.

After being driven back initially, the superior numbers of their enemies pushed the queen's forces back uphill, as though their greater mass was what mattered. Then for a long time, it seemed that anybody might gain the upper hand. In the end, superior skill, superior experience and strength won out. The warrior queen and the duke dispatched men one after another to oblivion, spreading fear with their successes.

Colonel Integredad himself was attacked by the captain of the opposing force—a Playsion officer specially trained in priestcraft and witchcraft who had placed a curse on the colonel's right arm. However, he had failed to take into account that the colonel was left-handed. Even so the colonel's shield arm hung helpless at his side, so that he had to use his sword arm to protect as well as attack. The enemy officer was badly shaken by his mistake, but what dismayed him more was the flashing sword that seemed to weave its own magical spells from the colonel's left arm.

A moment later the colonel's sword plunged into his heart. As the colonel withdrew his sword, his opponent's body slumped forward in death—and in death the shallow spell was broken. The colonel raised his shield arm triumphantly and turned to put it to use once again.

What had seemed like an easy victory for the rebels had become a rout for the company. Their little army was exhausted. They had slain two hundred and sixty horsemen, yet had lost fewer than thirty, with others bearing minor injuries. Gaal's family and the women of the company were safe. Belak had been put in charge of the men surrounding them and had assumed command with unexpected aplomb, impressing even the horsemen warriors.

Wearily, Colonel Sir Verdadera Integredad saw to it that the wounded were cared for and ordered the burial of the very many dead in a mass grave. Yearnings to the Emperor were offered. Then they made their way into a nearby glade where, sheltered by the forest, the prophet provided them the Emperor's table.

As with great weariness they tried to eat, Shiyrah sang to them. So absorbed were they with the music that they ate and drank with no thought for what they were doing, caught up as they were in the Emperor's great love for them. She sang on, and one by one as they were satisfied, they rested their heads on the table as though they were drunk, as in one sense they were. She sang away the damage to Kurt's ankle. They all woke a little stiff, but greatly renewed, once night had fallen. The moon greeted them, and after that they traveled by her light.

The journey to Bamah took extra time because of the little king, yet all of them knew the king was worth everything.

Shiyrah rode next to the prophet with her lieutenant friend, though at times they were forced to ride single file. Lord Nasa had found himself riding behind them and beside the queen. "Your majesty, I gather we travel under a cloak of secrecy at the moment."

The queen smiled and nodded. "Yes. But secrecy from the spirits of the shadows, not from human beings. I am sorry we cannot have it both ways." She shrugged her shoulders. "But if I am to choose, I would prefer the shadow spirits to be blinded, for their blindness affects the priests."

"Hm! Well, yes, I suppose so. I understand the reason, yet it is a topsy-turvy way of planning war strategy—that is, if we go by the way war is usually conducted. In war you think of swords, not spirits. Yet somehow I trust the prophet."

They rode in silence for a while before the queen spoke again. "We grow used to thinking of human enemies as the ones that matter most. Spears, shields, arrows and swords could rapidly end the life of the little one we are charged with conducting safely. Yet I notice that the more primitive my subjects are, the more conscious they seem to be about the existence of spiritual beings, good *or* bad. Sometimes I think the least-educated know more about things that matter most, more than those of us who think ourselves well-taught. I am therefore grateful for this 'cloak of secrecy' you refer to."

"This—to me—topsy-turvy idea takes a bit of getting used to. I doubt I ever will," Lord Nasa replied.

"Quite so. Of course, what we call the cloak of secrecy will not last forever. The Emperor sometimes allows the enemy to know these things, just to let us—and them—see that he still reigns."

Lord Nasa grinned and raised one eyebrow. "And in the meantime we will have to watch out for the king's forces. That, I suppose, is why we travel by night."

"Exactly. But even at night we must be alert. We must assume every person throughout the realm to be a potential traitor," the queen added grimly. "We will pay dearly for any carelessness. But at least we can worry less about the priests for the time being, for the dark spirits will not be giving them much information."

They continued for a little while in silence. Suddenly the queen drew rein. "Listen! Can you hear anything?" she asked.

Lord Nasa listened. "I am not sure, your majesty. What am I listening for?"

"It is very faint—a sort of high-pitched shrieking."

They had stopped at a small meadow, which the prophet and the colonel were already crossing. Lord Nasa drew in a breath and listened. After a moment he nodded. "So the Qadar are after us—the famous scourges of the night skies!"

"Yes. I am sure that they will hunt by day or by night until King Gaal is safely out of the country—indeed, out of this continent!" the queen continued. "But night is their usual time. And we are about to cross a meadow, and the sky above our heads is quite clear of clouds." Having expressed herself in this way, the queen urged her horse forward. The rest of the company followed.

Lord Nasa frowned, and Lisa called out, "I hear the Qadar! Shouldn't we . . ." She left the sentence unfinished. Moonlight revealed fear in the faces of many of the soldiers.

The prophet called to all who had been following. "Stand in the open!" he cried. "I want you to see for yourselves that we need not delay for any of the assaults of the dark powers. Our movements, as I told you, are hidden from them for the time being. The assaults will not occur. *The Qadar above us right now are about to attack something else, not us!*"

"I see them!" Lisa cried. "There! Against the moon! It's like last time!" She pointed to the big orange harvest moon that lay low, just above the trees beyond the clearing.

Slowly the company gathered in the open meadow. Soon they could see about half a score of small specks against the fall moon. Some of the horses were restless, wide-eyed, and began to rear in spite of their riders' efforts to control them.

One of the specks grew larger and seemed to be hurtling down to attack them.

"My stars!" Wesley murmured. "The wretched thing's seen us! Didn't the prophet say—"

"Have no fear!" the prophet called. "The Emperor makes no mistakes!"

One of the soldiers muttered, "The old man is gone mad!"

Necks craned skyward. The swooping Qadar could no longer be seen without the moon as a background, so they strained their eyes to see where it was. But soon every member of the company could see that not just one, but all of the Qadar were hurtling, apparently toward them, from the skies. They themselves seemed to be the object of the attack.

"Stay where you are! Do not take shelter!" the prophet called.

Steadily the bearers of deadly peril swooped nearer. The blood-curdling shrieks they vented unnerved some of the soldiers, in spite of the prophet's assurances. A few horsemen had more difficulty than ever in controlling their rearing horses.

"It's not working! What if there isn't any protection?" Lisa murmured. "I don't care what the prophet says. *It's my life!*" She saw once again a vivid picture of the terrible night on which she had ridden with the wounded Princess Suneidesis, fleeing the Qadar across darkened skies. It reawakened her past terror. Quite suddenly she rode her horse to the shelter of the nearest tree. Several of the soldiers followed her.

The prophet was pointing skyward and explaining, "They are not diving toward us! I do not know what they are attacking, but woe betide whoever or whatever it is."

By now it was easier to see that the swooping Qadar were not hurtling toward the company, but at something in the forest a little ahead of them. A moment later they had disappeared. The riders who had taken refuge slowly returned, looking sheepish. Lisa knew her face was red, for she could feel the flush. She hoped the moonlight would be merciful to her. "I thought of that awful time when Theophilus had been so stupid," she told Mary. "Princess Suneidesis was unconscious. Man, was I scared! Anyway, now I've demonstrated how stupid I am, and made an ass of myself."

The prophet smiled to himself. In future the company would be more likely to realize that their protection was real.

Mary, more than Lisa, seemed to have recovered from all her old fears. Since the meeting with the little king, her manner had changed radically. She had even learned how to help others in their fears. "What did you tell me was the full name of that 'equine angel' Theophilus?"

In spite of her embarrassment Lisa smiled. Already the party had resumed their journey. Once they were inside the trees, Lisa began to giggle. "Theophilus Gorgonzola Roquefort de Limburger V," she spluttered. Then, a little self-consciously she said, "I'm probably giggly after being so scared. You know, Theophilus hardly smelled at all, even when he was sweaty, and never of strong cheese."

They had not been in the trees for long before the shrieking of the Qadar could be heard overhead again. "Seems weird not to be crouching under a tree when you hear the Qadar overhead," Kurt said to his brother.

"You're right," Wesley replied. "An' I can't blame Lisa for her panic, either."

Kurt grinned. "I remember her crashing through the stained glass windows of Chocma's palace to escape the Qadar. Man, she almost didn't make it! Both she and the princess were pretty far gone."

"Think we'll have a chance of seeing what they were after?"

"The prophet didn't say. I guess it depends on where this path goes."

As matters turned out, the site of the Qadar attack did lie on their route. Fifteen minutes later, as they descended into a valley whose bed formed a channel for a half-dried stream, the prophet pulled on his reins and stopped. "The Qadar have been here." He urged his horse forward, and they followed him into an incredible scene of carnage.

A circular area that extended about three hundred yards on either side of the stream had evidently been very recently stripped of every tree so that it was illuminated by moonlight. Uprooted trees lay everywhere in disordered confusion. Boughs of trees had been torn from the trunks, as though indiscriminate rage had been unleashed. But among the boughs and the uprooted trees were dismembered human limbs and heads. Horses had been torn apart piecemeal. Chilled with the horror before their eyes, the company was gripped with silence and stillness. Even the warfare-hardened soldiers seemed shaken.

"Oh, how horrible! *Horrible!* I'm—gonna—*barf!*" Lisa murmured weakly.

Mary said, "We see this sort of thing on the news programs daily at home. But like this, it—in your own experience—it gets to you far more."

Wesley and Kurt reined their horses before the crater of an uprooted tree. Gradually their eyes grew used to the play of light and shadow. Everywhere they looked, the destructive rage and fury of the Qadar attack was evident. The entire company was sickened and stunned. "Man, oh, man! Look what we just missed!" Kurt murmured.

The prophet's words broke over them all. "Listen to me. The men of this group of warriors had been sent to do to you exactly what the Qadar have done to them. You have already experienced the ferocity of the fighters. Look well at the horror you now see. It was intended for you. It represents the wrath of the Emperor, who controls the errors the shadow lords and spirits cannot anticipate." He paused before continuing. "I did not realize the group had penetrated so close to us. It is an elite unit, designed to kill and dismember opposing armies. They did not realize they were as close to us as they were."

"Hm!" the colonel added as he dismounted to make his way among the carnage. "The woods seem to be full of army units. This is now the third we have encountered on our return—the group in the cave, the two hundred or so that attacked us, and now these."

Their words brought home to everyone the grim nature of the tasks before them. Every eye was turned to the prophet, except those of Colonel Integredad, who was now busying himself searching for identification signs on the enemy soldiers. At that moment he straightened his back and turned to the prophet. "You are right, as usual. This unit has been formed from Playsion troops. But how is it that the Qadar did not realize whom they were attacking?"

The prophet smiled grimly. "Even forces loyal to Gaal are inclined to murder one another in their blind fury." He sounded uncharacteristically cynical, but he continued. "As for the Qadar, they are trained to respond to movement. They were looking for us—but our movements, as you saw, are hidden from them. They saw the movements of this group and . . ." His voice trailed away as he waved at the chaos and destruction about them.

Though some of their horses drank from the bloody waters of the stream, they spent as little time as possible at it. "We cannot stop to bury the remains, much as I would like to do so, but must press on if we are to accomplish the first part of our mission," the colonel said, "unless you, sir, feel we should."

The prophet shook his head. "These are horrifying times. If you notice, carrion crows are already circling overhead, waiting for our departure. The book her majesty committed to one of your soldiers describes scenes in which scavenger birds gorge themselves on rebel remains. It is a sign of the Emperor's judgment on them."

They continued for nearly two days before anything else happened. As dawn began to pale the sky to gray they camped, rising in the late afternoon to eat and to prepare the next day's journey. Then, toward dawn of the second day, the prophet called a halt and addressed them.

"We seem to be approaching large numbers of goblins that will move across our path. I can sense their nearness. We may well collide with them if we do not take care. They can neither hear us nor feel us, though if they should collide with us or our horses I am not sure how they will react. However, let me assure you that they will neither hear nor sense any movement we make."

Almost at once they encountered the edge of the goblin multitude. There was little or no undergrowth in the trees at that point, so they could see some distance ahead. Everyone could see myriads of goblins in the moonlight, sweeping through the woods that lay in their path. The company stood still, and the goblins passed through only their forward positions.

The prophet understood goblin speech, and for some time he listened. His wrinkled face grew longer as he did so. "Never have I known such numbers before!" he said slowly. "The earth has spewed up these foul hordes from the depths at its core. In the fires of deepest earth they thrive, whereas water destroys them."

The queen waited, watching him closely. Slowly he shook his head, and for a few moments said nothing more. Eventually he began to speak. "I understand, now, why the rains have been withheld for so long. *Rain is their ruin!* It dissolves them, unmasking their very beings and personalities so that they exist no longer, spawned as they are by darkness! Yet why are they here?"

After a few moments the queen spoke. "You were listening to their speech. What are they saying?" she asked.

"They are under orders from the Lord of Shadows, and are themselves to submerge the region around Bamah by the weight of their numbers. Some will pack the area around the temple, and a few, I imagine, will be inside it. Your majesty's hope that we would surprise the spirits of the dark regions is now no more. It appears they are expecting us."

"Then it is doubly important that we find the passage that leads to the temple."

"We shall find it. Of that I am sure."

Lisa heard what they said, and the words hit her like a weight falling down on her shoulders. *Everything now seemed to depend on her.* What if she could not find the entrance again? What if the order "in the name of Gaal," the password, would not work when you said it from outside the entrance? Perhaps it was meant only to work from the *inside* of the passage! In that case they would be no further ahead, and the whole enterprise would fail.

The leading horsemen were kept busy as they tried to keep any goblins from colliding with their horses. The goblins came in all sizes, most of them smaller than human beings, their heads large and bulbous. Many had animal-like forms and exuded a great stench.

The whole company was kept busy directing their horses, which snorted and reacted nervously. They did not altogether succeed in avoiding collisions, and numbers of these occurred.

"Oh, shoot!" Lisa muttered. "I thought *that* one would pass beneath my horse, but it caught its head on the horse's belly. The next one's banged into it—an' now they're fighting with each other."

A number of fights broke out as the goblins blamed one another for the collisions. In the end the company decided there was little chance of their being discovered, and rather enjoyed the confusion. But the horde of goblins took almost an hour to pass by, and none knew how long they had been swarming through the trees before they reached them.

Colonel Integredad joined the queen and the prophet when they again moved forward. "Your majesty, I am debating the matter of the route of our retreat from the temple. My present thought is to return by the way we came—that is, by the tunnel."

The queen turned her head to the prophet. "Perhaps you have some thoughts, sir prophet."

"I know that whatever happens, your majesty must escape and survive. Even if you have to go overseas and form a government in exile, it is important for the sake of the Emperor's plans, and for the survival of the royal line, that you escape."

"I could not agree more heartily," the colonel interjected. "For my part, I would prefer that your majesty not even venture within the temple."

The queen smiled. "I am determined to see that wretched place destroyed. And who can say, in a venture of this kind, where the safest place for me would be. For my part, I prefer to be surrounded by the most valiant fighters. In this kind of undertaking there is nowhere free from risk!"

"Then why does your majesty not consider taking refuge in Ashleigh, the home of Lady Dolores of Ashleigh, where the young king and his parents will stay?"

"There is no place of perfect safety. I still debate in my mind the wisdom of leaving the little king there. As far as I know, all the servants are loyal. But if even one of them is not, then all our work is in vain. As it is, one unguarded word or action, and Ashleigh would be swarming with the king's soldiers."

The prophet sighed. New lines of weariness showed in his much-wrinkled face. His eyes were deep-sunk and fatigued. "I wish I had all knowledge, but I do not. No. There will be no absolute safety for any of us now. We are committed to our plans, which are right, but beyond the little king himself, no one's survival can now be guaranteed."

23

Against
the Temple

The company reached Ashleigh as darkness fell. They left the young king, his parents, Shiyrah and Lady Roelane there before proceeding to attack the temple. The queen, Lisa and Mary were to be part of the task force—Lisa, since she was essential to its success, and Mary, because she insisted on accompanying Lisa.

Lady Roelane worried about Mary, and said to the colonel, "She is a child! You will be exposing her to very great danger!"

He replied, "Yes, but Risano visited me during the day as I slept. He will be present at the battle, but invisible, and will protect all four children from harm. He told me to arm the girls. It is the Emperor's idea, apparently, that they gain confidence in combat. I will see to it that both girls are armed with short swords and scabbards."

When they forded the Rure they were haunted by the cries of the Qadar, but never once did they have the least suspicion that their own movements were spotted by them. They settled in a forest clearing, where they rested and ate their meal as the sun rose. They were to make the attempt on the temple that night.

The prophet addressed them while they ate. "The word of the Emperor came to me as we traveled. The king's army has set out to travel south, believing you are hiding somewhere near Karsch. Word has reached them of the way you have dealt with the three units dispatched to find you, and the army chiefs are alarmed at your power."

Colonel Integredad's eyes, weary with the responsibility of their safety, lit up with joy. "Wonderful!" he cried.

"Wonderful indeed. However, your movements were spotted by a peasant, who will tell them soon enough that you seem to be on your way to Bamah."

"Which means the army will return—perhaps soon," the queen said quietly.

"Possibly so, your majesty," the colonel said. "But clearly the army will not have arrived by tomorrow night. We shall strike first!"

"You will still have the goblins to cope with," the prophet added, "but you will defeat them."

"That's terrific!" Kurt enthused.

Wesley, his eyes shining, said, "Yeah. Though we may meet the goblins, and will have the Qadar to deal with! Our cover will be over then."

The moon rode high in the heavens as Colonel Integredad, well ahead of his troops, approached the Bamah bridge with care. He knew their watches from long experience, and knew that they drank strong Bamah wine from a barrel by the guard house. He also knew the officer in the guard house who, like the sentries on watch, drank more than his share.

Integredad had planned well but was still anxious. Had the bright young subaltern he had sent ahead succeeded in drugging the sentries' wine? Or had he been caught and killed? Expertly he reconnoitered, watching carefully, trying to spot the sentries. His mood lifted as he made them out, slumped over tables at each end of the bridge. The subaltern had done his job well—and the next change of watch was four hours away.

At that moment the subaltern himself quietly joined him. Standing full in the moonlight and grinning, he asked, "Satisfied, sir? I have bound and gagged them!"

"I am more than satisfied! You have done an excellent job, Grimeldo!"

The task force soon joined them, and the colonel signaled for the troops to follow him across the bridge. Then, making sure that Lisa was at his side, he ordered the troops to keep well under the high bank of the Rure as they made their way north, lest they be spotted from the city. They noted the low level of the Rure, where dried and cracked mud spoke of the drought.

After they rounded a bend in the river, the colonel, the queen, Lisa and Mary (who wanted to stay with Lisa) moved away from the bank to find the forked tree—if it still was there. But they discovered a difficulty—the banks were covered with an abundance of brambles, pouring their thorns in cascades over them.

Lisa's heart beat suffocatingly. The banks looked very different. "It's got to be around here somewhere, but I can see no forked tree. It used to be clear. Everything was bare then." Her voice was hoarse and shaky.

The queen looked at her sharply and seized her hands. "Why, you are trembling, child! And your hands are cold!" She began to rub Lisa's hands with her own. "This is hard for her, Colonel!"

Colonel Integredad nodded. "But essential, your majesty."

"You say it was a spot not unlike this?" the queen asked.

Lisa nodded. "But there's no forked tree. The opening was under a bare forked tree—a sort of skeleton."

"Look again at the city walls," the colonel said kindly. "Do not hurry. We still have a fair amount of time. You could try saying—whatever it is you say—all along the bank."

Lisa did not know whether the words would work.

"Why not say them here?" he asked.

In a rather faint voice, Mary said, "Open in the name of Gaal!"

There was a pause. Nothing happened. Lisa knew the soldiers would be looking at her. "Try again, dear, only louder."

Lisa took a deep breath. This time she almost shouted the words. But there was no response. Hopelessness began to numb her inside, and her mind seemed to be wrapped in fog. Her eyes glazed, and she began to feel unreal. She followed the colonel and the queen further north as though she were dreaming. She tried the command a second, then a third time, but with no success.

A fourth time when the queen asked her she shook her head. "It is not going to work," she said tearfully. "I—I must have offended Gaal or something."

The queen pulled her to herself and held her. A moment later she said, "Somehow I do not think so. Perhaps the shadows and their spirits are having a crack at you. Anyway, try just once again—and let it ring out!"

Again Lisa drew in a big breath. At the top of her lungs she yelled, "Open in the name of Gaal!"

This time it was different. Even as she shouted, Lisa felt something happening inside and around her. She gasped, "It—it was *real* that time! Something happened, I *know* it did!"

Yet, as far as they could see, nothing had. Yet all Lisa's uncertainty seemed to have lifted off her like mist. "I know we can't see anything," she said, frowning a little, "But something *just must* have happened—this time it was *real!*"

"There it is! Look a bit further up river!" Colonel Integredad cried. "I saw a wide gap open up in the bank! It is good you yelled, because it is about a hundred yards further on."

They hurried their way up the river then, scrambling up the bank and hacking at brambles with their swords. But swing as they might with their sharp blades, they could make no dent in the brambles.

The queen nodded to herself. "I suspected as much. This is witch-craft. The brambles are not real. The Lord of Shadows does not know

286

for certain that the entrance comes out by the river—they are much more suspicious of the palace. But they determined that if it should happen to be here, we would not find it."

"I might have a solution," said Lord Nasa of Chereb.

"Oh?"

"I entrusted the Sword of Geburah to Wesley, and I suspect he could easily cut through the thorns. Like the Sword Bearer, he comes from a world afar. Try your luck on them, Wesley!"

Wesley took the sword, and as Lord Nasa had suspected, he hardly needed to use force, slicing his way toward the tunnel as easily and effortlessly as if he merely were letting his body fall into a pool. The brambles shrank bank, dissolving themselves as he advanced so that a wide swath soon appeared between the tunnel and the river bank.

They led their horses up the bank, then mounted them and trotted into the opening. Once inside, Lisa called "Close, close in the name of Gaal!"

Colonel Integredad grinned hugely. "Excellent!" he cried. "And as far as I can tell, not a soul knows we are here!"

"Further in, there's a chasm with a log crossing it," Kurt said. "Uncle John told us about it—and Lisa, you crossed it, didn't you? It's a bit scary."

Lisa nodded. Now that her trial was over, she glowed with joy and relief. They left the horses in charge of three or four of the soldiers on the river side of the canyon.

From that point they proceeded on foot to the chasm. Lisa remembered how long and narrow the log was that bridged the canyon. She was delighted and surprised to find that the span was now wide enough for three soldiers to walk abreast. Why this was so she did not know, but thanked the Emperor just the same.

Sooner than they realized, they reached the entrance to the temple. It was part of the ornate carvings on the stone pillar. Lisa knew from Uncle John's stories that though the wall of the pillar was very thick, you could press the carving of the rose and a door to the temple would open. She pressed the rose. To her relief, the door swung wide, and the entire task force poured into the dimness of the temple. The column door swung back into place with a hollow boom.

For a moment they stood still, taking stock of their surroundings. Moonlight flooded through high windows, revealing pillared and empty temple spaces. The temple had no proper entrance. The far end was simply a huge arched opening. It framed a moonlit altar on a mound, creating the illusion that the altar was actually in the temple entrance. It was in fact a hundred yards further into the open.

And there they saw dense masses of goblins crowding the mound. "The ones we encountered," said the prophet. "You will fight them— and by all means hate them, for they are the essence of Shadows. But do not hate the king's soldiers, for they are merely deceived."

The colonel glanced at the queen, raising his eyebrows. "With your majesty's permission?"

"Proceed with your plans, Colonel. If you have no objection, I will stay beside you and, if it should prove necessary, fight at your side. In the meantime, please give your orders."

"Very well, men. You all know your assigned tasks. Carry on!"

Unnoticed by the distant goblins, some of the soldiers seized barrels of sacred anointing oils for the incense lamps and began systematically spraying the walls and temple furniture—pouring it in abundance at the base of the walls and the many wooden pillars.

Meanwhile, Duke Dukraz, Lieutenant Kosti and Lord Nasa, along with a platoon of soldiers, established a guard around the pillar to secure their line of retreat. From the pillar, ranks of soldiers extended behind the colonel, the queen and the children as they hurried to the entrance.

And there the goblins spotted them, and their plan of attack crumbled. The goblins rushed en masse to the temple, filling the area with astonishing rapidity and numbers.

It was like being caught in a panicking football crowd, as those in front were pushed forward by those behind. At first the goblins seemed leaderless and showed no inclination to fight, but the colonel's party struggled merely to hold their ground against the crush.

Goblins got in the way of the men preparing the fire, and members of the task force began to lose sight of one another. The ranks holding the line forward of the pillar were disintegrated, broken up by the sheer weight and pressure of goblin numbers. Within less than a minute after the colonel gained the open archway, the goblins were packed densely both inside the temple and outside it.

The prophet called loudly from beside the pillar, his voice ringing and echoing through the temple. "Do not ignite the fire! *Your line of retreat has been cut off!*"

It was true. The line planned to hold for the retreat was in total disarray, so densely had the goblins filled the temple. The soldiers quickly withdrew their torches.

The colonel looked back, wondering whether he should return to remarshal the troops, but upon seeing the solid press of goblin bodies he decided to stay put and protect the queen and the children. He paused to take stock, silently cursing himself for not anticipating what could happen. The tide of goblins behind them grew stronger and began pressing them in the direction of the altar.

Again the prophet's voice rang out. "Remember, fire does not harm them. Only hail and water dissolve them into oblivion. You need your retreat, or you will be cut off!"

Colonel Integredad raised his voice. "Lieutenant Kosti! Call your men together! Have your bugler call the retreat when you are ready!"

From deep inside the temple came the cry. "It will take time, sir! We are in confusion and disarray! I will sound the assemble and extend our line to meet your own!"

Cut off from the rest, the colonel's party was a small island of soldiers and leaders in a dense sea of goblins. With pressure all round them it was even difficult to remain on their feet. The colonel ordered them to form a square and to keep their shields together.

"Kurt! Get the girls behind us. Men—form the flanks! Girls—stick with your backs to her majesty, Wesley and myself. You two—Breen and Chasio—stand between the girls and watch out for them. Do not separate or be driven from us!"

Kurt nodded, and they struggled into position. Facing the goblins on four sides, they drew their swords. The goblins fell back a pace but also drew swords, and soon the group was engaged in bitter hand-to-hand combat.

What had begun as fairly easy incendiary activity extended itself endlessly. Leaderless or not, there was now no want of goblins, and the company dared not let their sword arms drop even for a moment. Their breath came hard and sweat poured from them. The ground became a mass of green slime, reeking of dead goblin as the slaughter continued.

The queen fought with skill and determination. Wesley found once again that the Sword of Geburah was a law to itself, and he sliced at goblins with a dexterity that he had never learned. Colonel Integredad saw his sword strokes out of the corner of his eye and murmured, "He is far better than I thought!" Again and again members of the little group would slip and fall, to rise with the slime of disintegrating goblin on them. But they had long since ceased to care. They were too hard-pressed to worry about appearances.

Deep inside the temple, Duke Dukraz and Lieutenant Kosti decided to divide their efforts. The prophet sat at the foot of the stone column, his arms upraised. He seemed to be weakening himself, and yet an invisible power was pouring from him in waves. His face was gray, sweat trickling down it, and exhaustion was written over his visage.

"If anyone saves us it will be he," the lieutenant said. "But can he last?"

Duke Dukraz nodded, suggesting, "Why do you not protect him till his power takes effect? I will force my bulk through this mass and drag back the separated soldiers. If you can regroup them here, we might stand a chance!"

The duke's height enabled him to see clearly the groups of men who had been scattered by the force of the goblin bodies. He forced his way forward, picked up a man in each arm and dragged them through the press to where the old and increasingly haggard prophet sat. It was exhausting work, but he seemed tireless. The ranks of recovered soldiers grew, and they prepared to fight their way through to the colonel.

But all was not well with the colonel's party. Do what they might, they were out in the open and being driven toward the altar. The goblins were still outflanking them, pressing into the temple on both sides.

It was then that the colonel saw behind the altar what he had dreaded to see. "Your majesty! The first army units have arrived! They cannot yet press through the goblins, but they are here in force."

The colonel also saw the figure of a determined King Tobah Khuk-ah pushing his way powerfully through the goblins, sword in hand. "The king is coming for us," the queen said. She took a deep breath. "Colonel, I once thought I could kill that body of his. It is all that is left of him—a body without a soul. But seeing his body as he used to be, I know I cannot kill *IT!*"

"Then I will slay it for you!" the colonel promised grimly.

Three soldiers lay dead, and others were wounded. For the first time, Wesley's sword point dropped. "I never thought we would end like this! Oh, Gaal, what have you brought us to? I guess this is the end." The Sword of Geburah pulled his arm up with a jerk, and he was at it again, whether he wanted to be or not.

In their hotel room in Hong Kong, Jane Friesen called to her husband in the bathroom. "Darling, this wall television thing's begun again, and the children are there!"

"Nonsense, darling. It's your imagination again. You know the hotel simply does not have wall-size TV."

"Imagination, is it? This time you come and look for yourself."

"I'll be there in a minute."

"It's a regular battle scene. There's a woman in armor like Joan of Arc! They're fighting in some sort of building. And there's a symmetrical structure—sort of Mayan. What *can* the children be up to? There's been absolutely no time for any rehearsals."

When Fred Friesen entered the room, he stopped and stared at the strangely illuminated scene on the wall, and watched for several minutes in silence. Then he turned to the telephone and dialed a number. "Housekeeping? Please send someone up to suite 1C immediately."

A moment later there was a knock on the door. Fred opened it to admit an official who said, "I am the supervisor for the luxury suites. How may we serve you, sir?"

"This wall television—or whatever it is," Fred pointed at the wall, and the man stared.

"Is there something wrong with the wall, sir?"

"Well, don't you see?"

"See what, sir?"

"Don't you see the wall-size television with a scene of fighting? You people told me there was no such thing in the hotel. If I'm paying for this . . ."

A hint of anxiety appeared in the man's face. He glanced at Jane. "Is he . . . ? I see a blank wall, ma'am. Is your husband . . . ?" He left the sentenced uncompleted.

Jane smiled reassuringly, taking the man by the arm and moving toward the door. "It will be all right. I'm sorry he called you." She smiled again, winking and saying, "He gets like this occasionally—takes a drop too much. I can take care of things."

The man looked anxiously at Fred. "Thank you, ma'am. But you're sure you don't need—"

"No. We'll be fine. You may go now. I'm so sorry we troubled you."

The supervisor left, closing the door behind him.

Lord Nasa joined the little group that was fighting so hard and told them what was happening around the column. "It will take some time for the defense to be organized."

He took his place beside them and fought on. Wesley stared at the scene before him, horrified. Their retreat was cut off, and their hopes against the goblins looked faint. His sword continued its expert play, but his face was drawn with weariness. He murmured, "We've had it," and repeated the phrase a second time with finality. Inevitable death

stared them in the face. Shaking his head slowly, he said, "I didn't know such numbers were possible. I never thought—I never imagined . . ." The sentence died on his lips.

"There's an absolute *sea* of them!" Kurt agreed breathlessly, his voice an echo of Wesley's. "And there's that awful thing—the king's body controlled by that powerful spirit of darkness."

But when he spoke next, Wesley's dreary voice produced a paradoxical reaction. "Well—let's die like men!"

He sounded like a ham actor playing a Shakespearean tragedy. His voice was mournful, so funereally resigned that it touched an electric button in Kurt. To the surprise of everyone, he first began to snigger, then, unable to do anything else, burst into peals of laughter. Wesley's remark lifted darkness and despair from him, awakening a reckless resolve. And Kurt's laughter in turn began to put heart into the rest of the defenders. Fear began to disperse, even as the goblins advanced, and a joyous abandon seized them.

"Let them come!" Kurt cried. "Let them all come! We'll show them."

Wesley glanced quickly at his brother, amazed at the change in him. Then came a further change. He continued to laugh even as a battle frenzy fell on him—the sort of frenzy you read about in ancient Celtic tales. And the column of blue fire materialized over his head, resting on him. They told him about it afterward, though he himself never saw it. In fact, his memories of the whole incident were very vague. He only knew that rage—a laughing rage—took possession of him.

He gripped his sword with a cold fury. Screaming cheerful defiance at the approaching army and the whole goblin horde, he began what could only be called a frenzied dance. He found himself hating the evil behind the goblin horde, the menacing shadow itself. To the goblins he slaughtered, his dance was a dance of death. They flung themselves at him but could not touch him. With every sweeping slice of his sword he killed, dispatching scores of goblins and an occasional venturesome soldier. He converted fighting into a wild ballet—leaping over their heads, somersaulting in a weird and deadly frolic of unmitigated slaughter. On and on the dance continued as he whirled in an exotic gambol of ominous beauty.

Lord Nasa glanced at the blue column above him and grinned. "Risano's frenzy is on him. The dance is not Kurt's, but Risano's."

Armed with lances, swords and daggers, the goblins slashed at whatever they could see. Wesley was forced to let the sword have its way again, but his heart was not in what he was doing. Every eye was now on the horrid king, who was rushing closer as though the goblin mass pushed them into his arms.

The unnatural creature in the dead king's body aimed, they thought, at seizing and killing the queen. But it found itself confronted by a determined Colonel Integredad, who engaged it with vigor and skill. With parry and thrust, clashes and clangs, with yells and gasps, their duel was joined. But the colonel soon found his sword strokes were inferior to those of the creature he faced.

Yet he was not entirely outclassed. Swords flashed in rhythmical strokes. In spite of the creature's skill, it seemed that with every sword stroke more wounds were inflicted on the body it inhabited. Yet wounds made no difference to it. The body was able to fight with no sign of weakening. Even a thrust clean through its heart had not the slightest effect. The colonel was dismayed, for the body never bled. *He was not fighting the king, but an unnaturally animated corpse.*

Dismayed, he fought on, his eyes widening. Then, quite suddenly, foam spumed from between his lips in a shriek of disgust—and the same frenzy of battle fell on him that had fallen on Kurt. Swiftly his sword strokes began to outclass those of his rival, eluding his opponent's sword and shield alike. A moment later he severed the body's right arm—its sword arm—and with a second unbelievably swift blow its left arm. The left arm fell to the ground, its shield still strapped to it.

When the body finally fell backward, a Qadarlike creature erupted from the king's corpse. The colonel was knocked to the ground as the beast shot into the sky with a terrible shriek, like an angry rock hurled from a catapult. A chorus of Qadar shrieks answered from far above, and by the early dawn light the fighters glimpsed the dark creatures circling high in the heavens.

Then from deep within the temple the prophet vented a powerful but inarticulate cry of triumph. And at his cry a wide avenue opened up between the pillar of passage and the queen's party. Goblins were mercilessly pressed to the sides and crushed into liquid against the walls of the temple. Power held the remainder back, allowing no more to enter the temple.

The trumpeter sounded the retreat, and the colonel called to the queen and the rest of the soldiers, "Now is the time to RUN! Wesley and I will cover you and will fight on!"

The queen, the girls and three of the soldiers turned and ran. "The rest of you form a line! We will let them push us back gradually while the temple is set on fire."

The death of "the king creature" had disheartened the attackers, and their opposition began to falter. Then rain began to pour, and the ferocity of their onslaught steadily diminished.

"Has the fire been started?" the colonel asked.

"No, but I could order it myself, sir!" cried a soldier behind him.

"Then do so, and as soon as the flames have got a grip, sound the retreat again—and we will run for it!"

Distressed, Lieutenant Kosti stared at the dying prophet. "There are tears in your eyes," the prophet whispered.

Huskily the lieutenant replied, "You must not die. Do not leave us!"

"I have lived to see the burning of this temple. Another temple may succeed it, but that is the Emperor's affair. I have seen enough to take my departure. My mission is finished."

He feebly turned his head to watch the flames rising from all parts of the temple. Almost as though they were alive, flames leaped six or eight feet from the oil-soaked wood. Little points of crackling yellow flame burst from between widening cracks that opened in pillars, paneling and side columns. Flames ran along the floor, beginning to leap up the central pillars and lick their way greedily up the temple walls. The prophet took it all in, the flickering firelight reflected in his eyes. He nodded, smiling. "It is enough," he murmured. "This temple will go. And the dark spirits will know that however long their reign may be, their doom is now sealed. That knowledge with its bitter rage is their true destiny. Sooner or later, darkness enchains its own!"

He gripped Kosti's arms with the last of his strength. "Swear to me that you will leave my body here to burn with the temple," he demanded, piercing the younger man with the power of his gaze.

"Oh, no, sir! How could you ask me such a thing?"

"Listen to me! For this moment I have stayed alive all these years! In a few years the real king will return, and by his death he will tear the horns from the head of the bull. Therefore let my body be consumed by the very flames that announce their coming doom to the enemy." The old man gasped for breath. "There is something else I would ask of you. I know that what you long for will come to pass. You will marry Shiyrah. Swear to me now that you will care for and protect her as long as you both shall live."

A trembling sigh escaped Lieutenant Kosti's lips. After a moment he said, "I swear. I swear to abide by both things you ask of me." He longed to say more, to speak of his awe and love of the prophet, whom he had so recently come to know. But even as he looked back into his eyes, he saw that the stare had become fixed in death. Quietly he laid the body down on the floor of the temple.

He looked up and saw the queen standing near him, not far from the open door in the column. She nodded her head. "I know it is hard for you, but he is right. He must have what he has asked. You will have enough to do comforting that remarkable granddaughter of his." Then she left him.

Lieutenant Kosti glanced around to confirm that the fire had a firm grip on the entire temple, and took his place by the door. The colonel, Wesley, Kurt and one or two soldiers ran toward the column. Kosti was illuminated by the flickering flames, while Lisa stood in shadow just inside the column.

"Pick up the prophet, Kosti!" the colonel ordered.

"Sir, he made me swear to leave him here. It was his dying wish.

The queen is a witness to it!"

Colonel Integredad stared for a moment, then shrugged. "We had better get moving."

Lisa, ignoring the flames, waited as the rest ran by her. Then the lieutenant helped her to enter herself, and they let the door slam behind them.

Lisa followed Lieutenant Kosti down the steps.

24

Over the River and Through the Woods

Lisa stared at the blue-lit interior of the column. "Blue light: true light," she murmured to herself. "The shadow spirits fear this light. They never came into it last time, they just wanted to lure me into the other light—*their* light."

"We had better hurry," Lieutenant Kosti said, and they hastened down the stairs together.

"That was awful," Lisa said to Kosti. "The prophet, I mean. I'm—real sad—about his death, but for you it's much worse. And for Shiyrah . . ." She left the sentence unfinished.

The lieutenant panted, "Yes. I do not know how to break it to her."

They continued their descent without speaking. They could hear, echoing hollowly, the voices of those who hurried ahead of them. Mary was trying to keep up with the queen. "Just before we fled into the temple, I heard the Qadar high up in the sky, your majesty," she panted.

"Yes. I heard them too."

"But they didn't attack us."

"No." She sighed and said, "I had the rather silly notion that the *thing* using my husband's body had only me in mind. That might have been true. But as the evil within him left the body, I realized the spirits of darkness were only incidentally after me. It was the little king they really wanted."

"Oh! So, your majesty, you're saying that may be why the rest of the Qadar didn't bother attacking."

"That is right. Somehow they sensed he was not with us. Little King Gaal was their real goal."

Mary was quiet for a moment. "I'm so sorry, your majesty!"

"You mean about my husband?"

"Uh-huh."

The queen sighed and said, "We might as well slow down. Nobody will pursue us, so there is no desperate hurry after all." Once they had slowed to a walk she said, "My husband's death was less of a shock than you might think, Mary. It was more like a relief. I realize now that I have been grieving him for a long time."

After some time, the queen continued. "And you must not mind me talking to you, Mary. It is a relief to have someone to talk to." She looked down at Mary, giving her a wintry smile. "I can tell, too, that like me, you have changed. Mary, I now see evil less as fearful or terrifying and more as ugly, foul and disgusting. When I think of the selfish contempt the Lord of Shadows has for the Regenskind, I have no words disdainful enough to describe him or his cohorts."

Mary understood thoroughly. She had memories of her own. Very soon they arrived at a jam created by the difficulty of the chasm-crossing. From behind the crowd, Colonel Integredad called, "We need not hurry!"

The queen also called out, "Every person in Bamah will be staring at the fire, and the army and priests will be devoting all their energies to unsuccessfully trying to put it out. So take your time crossing!"

Once they had crossed, the colonel addressed them again. "In a moment you will mount your horses and will leave this place. As her majesty has pointed out, this is the ideal time to do so. I doubt that there will be any pursuit. I know how the priests think. The temple has supernatural power that they use. Every soldier and every civilian they can lay their hands on will be forced to try to put the fire out. And everyone who is not fighting fire will be staring at it! But we must remember what our real goal is. In any case, they do not know where to look for us.

"What is our goal? *It is to make sure that the little king gets safely out of Anthropos-Playsion!* And to that goal we must give all our energies—and our very lives, if necessary"

He paused a moment to let the words sink in, and then continued. "That, and that alone, is what our aim has been all along. The burning of the temple will serve to destroy the enemy's power center, but it will not destroy the enemy, only distract him for the moment. You have all done a superb job. Every one of you has played your part splendidly. We might now get away freely, but you must not count on it!"

He commended groups of them, mentioning some by name, especially Lisa. He described his admiration of Wesley's swordplay and his amazement at Kurt's battle frenzy. Then his face became serious and his tone solemn.

"But we must be under no illusions. We have not destroyed the powers of darkness, only shaken them. Sooner or later they will be onto us—and it could be sooner rather than later. We must get the little king out of the country before that time. How this is to be achieved is uncertain at the moment, but . . ."

As he spoke those words Kurt's memory flashed back to the time they had been "arrested" by the queen. He saw again the small meadow in which he had observed two trees. He also saw vividly the picture beyond the trees, hills of a country he did not recognize. He remembered what it was that had gripped him about what he had seen, a bluish light illuminating the tree trunks, *as though they constituted a gateway to a country beyond Anthropos-Playsion!* He remembered Lisa and her constant admonition "Blue light is true light."

Immediately he called out, "I know how we do it! I know how he is to leave the country!"

Quickly he described what he had seen in the meadow. The colonel frowned uncertainly, but the queen cried, "And I could take us there. I know just the spot you speak of." She glanced at the colonel. "You have doubts?"

"I do not know, your majesty. I am not a man of vision, but of action. However, we have experienced the children's visionary tendencies and their results. Certainly we must go there. However, we must lose no more time now."

Lisa opened the stone door for them, and as they emerged they saw the rain had ceased. Dawn had broken in the east, but the pale sunlight was washed out by the billowing sheets of flame ascending majestically and leisurely into the sky.

"Just look at that!" Wesley said to Kurt. "Did you ever see anything like it!"

Kurt's only response was, "Wow!" For a moment he stared with widening eyes.

"With your majesty's permission?" said the colonel.

"Proceed, Colonel."

"I believe we can dispense with caution, ma'am. Even if the sentries should see us, they are hardly likely to attract the attention of their superiors at the moment."

"Very well."

"Mount your horses, men! We must be on our way to pick up the little king!"

The company thundered across the bridge, emptied by the sentries lured away by the fire.

Still galloping hard, the weary troops arrived at Ashleigh late that afternoon. The Lady Dolores of Ashleigh ran outside to meet them, and they exchanged greetings and news.

"You have come for the little king." Lady Dolores curtsied to the queen and then to the colonel.

"Yes. But we need rest and food badly," the colonel replied. "We have neither eaten nor slept since yesterday morning."

"Take the horses round to the back where they are less likely to be seen," she said, "and I will open the rear entrance and meet you there."

As they were being conducted into the rear of the house, the queen said to Lady Ashleigh, "We may need to make a sudden getaway."

"Your majesty could use the secret passage," Lady Ashleigh replied. "Kurt discovered it last time he was here. I knew it existed, but my husband would never tell me where it was to be found. It goes from the room where I have put little King Gaal and his parents as far as the woods by the river bank. I will see to it that there are enough canoes there for the whole company."

The queen's eyes sparkled. "I know this country like the palm of my hand. Kurt has spoken to us of a meadow on this side of the Rure. If I am not mistaken, there is a path that comes out on the east bank of the river leading to that meadow. From this meadow there is one of the Emperor's doorways—a doorway to another country."

"What should I tell the young king and his parents?"

"Warn them to sleep with their clothes on, ready to depart at a moment's notice."

"Do they know anything about the secret passage?"

"No, your majesty. But I will inform them and give them torches."

Lady Dolores curtsied, then ran inside the house to make sure the servants opened the rear entrance. A meal was prepared for the company, and after that they found places to sleep—some on couches and chairs, some on the floor, and others (the lucky ones) in the bedrooms.

But at midnight a sentry roused the colonel. "What is it?" Integredad asked.

"There are a couple of men on the lawn some distance from the house," came the answer. "I do not know what they are doing, but they have lit a fire and are spouting gibberish and drawing circles in the air."

"Could be priests. Stupid of them not to be more careful—perhaps they do not know we are here. Are you armed?"

"Sword, bow and arrow, sir."

"You have your trumpet with you?"

The sentry nodded. The colonel said, "I will come with you."

They crept from the house, making a wide circle to a spot from which they could both see and hear the men. They lay in the darkness not more than five yards away and watched in silence. Two figures in silhouette threw powder onto the fire, so that it flared up with strange green colors. Then they began to circle round it and to chant, and their faces were illuminated beyond the fire as they ringed it.

"They are indeed priests, and this is a standard ritual for calling on boarwartz," the colonel whispered. "But they are also casting a spell on the household. We must kill both before the spell is complete—or we will never get away."

The sentry smiled. "One arrow each?" At this distance it was impossible for the worst of archers to miss—and he was far from the worst of archers. The colonel returned the smile and nodded.

The sentry waited until the priests had their backs to him, then stood and drew his bow. An arrow sped through the flickering darkness and pierced the first priest's chest. As his body slumped to the ground, the second man hesitated before fleeing. But the bow spoke again, and a second arrow pierced him before he had taken two steps.

The colonel turned the bodies of the two priests over, then nodded to himself. "Both dead," he said with grim satisfaction.

"Did they know our company was here?" the sentry asked.

The colonel shrugged. "I do not know. Their incantation was all priestly garble—set against the house, regardless of who might be here."

"So will the boarwartz come, sir?"

Again the colonel shrugged. "Since we cannot be sure, we should not stay. Sound the alarm now—I will go to the house and round everybody up."

At once the trumpet sound pierced the stillness of the night. Colonel Integredad ran to the house. His first thought was the safety of the little king and that of the queen. His second thought was the ferocity and size of the giant, deformed goblins known as boarwartz—dreaded throughout the forest but rarely seen.

Every member of Lady Dolores's household fled with the company, including the servants and her own children. They all emerged from the house via the secret tunnel and began climbing into the long canoes—just in time. As the last canoe left the shore they looked back to see the lawns crowded with hideous goblin shadows. There was a cry of alarm, "*Boarwartz!*"

The queen called out to reassure them. "Have no fear! They can only watch us from the bank now, for they are deadly afraid of the river. Remember, they dissolve in water!"

"Nevertheless," the colonel muttered, "I have a horrible feeling of danger. To get away this cleanly seems unnatural. We are not free yet!"

"Do not despair yet," Gerachti called to him. "The hard part is over now!"

The colonel shrugged his shoulders. "I wish I could agree, but I do not," he said. "I know the enemy!"

More than one of them seemed to share his conviction. Kurt said, "Something's going to happen. I can feel it in my bones."

"Has the prophet's mantle fallen on you?" Wesley grinned. "Come on! You're singing my tune for once, and I seem to be singing yours."

"You can laugh, Wes. But I feel just as I did when we were climbing up to Lion Rock. And something happened that time, only this is even more scary."

"Really? No kidding!"

"But something *good* happened then," Lisa said.

Shiyrah had said almost nothing since her great-great-grandfather's death. Sitting behind Lieutenant Kosti at the front end of the children's canoe, she turned and said, "Kurt is right. Goodness and evil seem to be coming to a climactic clash. I am not sure of this, but I think it will be over rather quickly."

"For better, or worse?" Wesley asked, a worried look clouding his face.

"I wish I could say," Shiyrah replied. "I have a feeling we are going to have to fight hard."

"Does the queen have the book from which the light shines?" Lisa asked.

Shiyrah nodded. "Yes—and it is well that she has."

Nobody had enjoyed as much sleep as they would have liked, but the urgency of their mission fueled their paddling for many hours. From the lead canoe (bearing Gaal and his parents) the queen constantly watched the east bank, straining to identify the point at which the path to the meadow emerged. As dawn broke she called, "Pull over to the right—I believe this is the spot."

She was right. And of goblins there was no sign.

"So far, so good," murmured Alleophaz, looking worried.

"Surely you are not troubled?" Gerachti asked him.

"I cannot believe the priests would give up this easily."

"They are defeated and they know it!" Gerachti said contemptuously.

"I wish I could be sure."

Leaving the boats, they crossed the old Bamah road on the east side of the river and followed the winding path through the forest. They came at last to the meadow, which was shaped like a slightly squashed circle. On the right side, close to where they had entered, they could see the two trees Kurt had described.

"It's just like I said—all lit up!" Kurt called in triumph. "You can even see the blue light on the trunks!"

They could all see the hilly landscape between the trees, shining like a vision in the morning twilight.

"It's like a revelation from another world!" Mary said.

"No, no!" Gerachti called. "It is not another world—it is Glason. I would recognize that group of hills from any angle. I was born near there!"

Hastily they bade farewell to Ish and Mehta, awed at what was about to take place. "Hasten!" the colonel called. "I have a dread that the most perilous moment has arrived. We could lose everything if we make any false moves now."

Quickly he began to dispose his forces. A line of soldiers ran to form a shield as Mehta, Ish (carrying little Gaal) and the queen hurried toward the trees, with Shiyrah and Lieutenant Kosti behind.

"Go with them—and hurry!" Colonel Integredad called to Alleophaz, Gerachti, Belak and all the Ashleigh household. "We will come if we can. For now—oh-oh! Here they come—*boarwartz!*"

By now the large crowd was halfway to the two trees. At the colonel's shout they glanced back and then began to run in earnest.

From their left boarwartz poured from the forest to pursue them on all fours. They came as bestial creatures, looking like ancient aurochs, but with enormous heads that bore a central horn, and boar tusks that gleamed in the early morning light. Certainly they inspired terror in the group. Yet almost immediately from the forest on their right, from either side of the two trees, Koach also burst in large numbers. They moved with incredible speed, howling, snarling and surrounding individual boarwartz just as they reached the men and women making for the Glason vision.

"They're after Gaal!" Mary called.

"Look! The queen's slashing at them with her sword!"

Faintly, they heard the queen call, "Keep moving! The Koach will protect us. Keep your swords handy!"

Lisa cried, "Oh, go, go, GO! Look! They're almost there!"

Then, so quickly that they could scarcely take it in, the whole group seemed to be standing on the brink of something. They heard Alleophaz calling out to them, his voice echoing loudly across the glade, "Children from worlds afar! Come and visit us in Glason!"

Then, all except the queen and some of the soldiers disappeared. Only the picture of the Glason hills remained. The queen had not left, and some of the soldiers stuck to her side.

Fred and Jane Friesen stood and stared at the "TV wall," where a new scene appeared silently like the first. Bizarre creatures from a world of fantasy flung themselves at their children and other characters they did not know. Their children and Mary all swung their swords desperately, looking weary and pale with sweat streaming down their gaunt and hopeless faces. Then as sound grew to accompany the action, they could hear the din of battle. Fred's stunned face paled till his skin was paper white. His wife stared horrified at the scene, which was growing more three-dimensional every moment.

Jane said nervously, "They're not acting, Fred. I *know* our kids, and they can't act as well as that. Whatever this is, it's real. I feel faint." She stared in silence before asking, "Fred, d'you think they're in real danger?"

Fred stared, trembling a little. "I—I'm not sure. They might be."

"Oh, Fred, what can we do?"

There was no reply. She turned, and to her dismay she found they were no longer in the hotel. All around was the scene of the battle, and they were near their own children. She reached out for her husband and clung to him. "Fred?"

"We're having a nightmare. But this isn't a nightmare—this is reality."

"Can they *see* us?"

"I don't believe so. Lisa just looked right through me."

They saw with dismay the growing number of the wounded and the dead, and smelled the stench of fallen boarwartz. Fred made a feeble effort to seize his daughter. What he intended to do with her was not clear, but in any case his arms were insubstantial, ghostlike, and had no effect.

They leaned against each other, shaken and shivering. Jane turned to hide her face on her husband's shoulder, but could not keep from watching.

The children's efforts flagged with the weariness of the short night and the struggle with the inexhaustible masses of boarwartz. The

Koach helped enormously by worrying at the huge goblins and distracting them. Wesley, who still swung the Sword of Geburah like an exhausted expert, struggled on simply because the sword gave his arm no choice.

Meanwhile, inch by inch, they were being forced in the direction of the bluelit opening. Lord Nasa and his lady still faced the boarwartz with Kurt and the two girls, while Wesley defended their rear.

Then they heard the terrible shrieks of the Qadar, and before they knew what was happening the swooping shadows were diving on them. The queen, ready for this moment, dropped her sword and picked up the great volume of the history and prophecies of Anthropos and opened it. Immediately they were all blinded by dazzling light that filled the meadow and the surrounding forest. At the same instant, a flash of lightning and a crash of thunder shook them all.

Fred and Jane could feel rain falling and the sting of hail on their shoulders. Then the whole battle faded from around them, and once again they faced the blank wall of the hotel suite.

They were soaked from the rain, and water streamed from their clothes onto the carpet. At their feet lay a chunk of hail the size of a tennis ball. Fred picked it up.

"Is it real?" his wife asked.

"It's certainly cold. I think I'll put it in the refrigerator."

"You mean to keep it?"

He sighed and long sigh. "I know what we saw was real, but I want some evidence tomorrow of where we've been."

His wife said, "I know how you feel. I'm not even sure you're real yourself at the moment." She moved toward him, took his hands and placed them round her waist. "Do *I* feel real to you?"

He smiled and stroked her wet hair. "You feel more than slightly damp, and yet reassuringly familiar. I can smell your perfume. I suspect all we've been through is real, though I don't understand any of it. But what is going to happen to the children? Will they return?"

"They'll return all right, if all those stories they told us are true."

They sat together on the settee, and for a long time neither of them said a word. Eventually Fred drew in a deep breath and spoke again. "I'm not used to eating humble pie, but I have a feeling that I shall need to develop an appetite for it very soon now. And we might as well take hot showers and change."

Rain drenched the company and hail pelted their shoulders, disheartening them at first until they saw the effect on the boarwartz. The goblin monsters began dissolving rapidly, and those who could still run disappeared into the forest. The Qadar had disappeared totally. The Koach stood suddenly foeless and began wagging their tails and sniffing among themselves.

Wearily, the humans made their way across to where the queen was standing. Too exhausted to do more than bid one another farewell, they merely nodded when the colonel said, "The Emperor never fails. I should have been more confident."

The queen addressed the children. "And he used you young people. He brought you here from worlds afar. Had you not been led to us through the forest in such a remarkable fashion we would not have known quite how to proceed. Had Lisa not been able to find and to open the secret passage, our plans for the temple could not have been carried out."

"But your majesty used the book!" Mary said.

The queen smiled and nodded. "And you, Mary, now know with certainty which side you are on!"

Mary blushed and nodded. With unaccustomed awkwardness she said, "But all of you have been awfully kind—your majesty and the colonel especially."

The queen nodded. "We must not delay, but go to our kind hosts in Glason to commence our government in exile."

With many other expressions of gratitude and farewell, the soldiers, the colonel and her majesty, half turning and waving, disappeared in twos and threes. Then the picture of Glason faded, and they were able to see the normal bushes and trees behind the two huge oak trees.

"So now what?" Wesley asked, puzzled.

"I don't know," Lisa replied.

Just then the tall figure of Risano appeared beside them. He smiled down upon them. "I have an apology to make to you all, especially to Mary."

Mary looked sharply at him, but said nothing. The others looked surprised.

"I had no intention of deceiving you, but knew that if Mary were to get on with Lady Roelane, I would have to make Lady Roelane much younger than she actually is. So I persuaded her husband and her—against their better judgment—to go along with my wishes. You can see the result."

"You're changing!" Mary said suddenly, addressing Lady Roelane. "Roly—what's happening to you?"

Lady Roelane smiled. "I am not sure. I would need a mirror—but I think my husband and I must be reverting to form!"

" *'Reverting to form'*?" Kurt almost shouted. "What form?"

"They're both getting older," Mary said quietly. "I'm beginning to clue in." Suddenly she flung herself with a sob at Lady Roelane. "Oh, I didn't know, I didn't know, I didn't know!" she repeated between her sobs. Then, "Oh, I'm so glad! I don't want to leave you—not *ever!*"

She untangled herself and looked up into the older woman's face. "Then you're not—Lady Roelane—at least—you're also—Mrs.—er— *McNab!*"

The former Lady Roelane smiled and pulled Mary to herself again. "I'd rather you called me Aunt Eleanor, dear. And I'm not going to leave you. Not ever."

"I don't care!" Mary cried. "I don't care how old you are! You're *you,* an' I know you now. You're not changing, you're the same as you've always been. I know you now. Oh, what a fool I was!"

The other children's mouths hung open. "It's Uncle John," Wesley breathed as he stared at Lord Nasa of Chereb. Slowly the former Lord Nasa and his wife were becoming a middle-aged couple.

"Let's just say I have been back to Anthropos many times," said

John, "but I haven't told you about them all. I am the Sword Bearer, but I am also known here as Lord Nasa of Chereb. I may tell you the full story some other time."

Risano interrupted them, smiling. "It is time for you to resume your normal clothing."

Instantly they did. Cries of surprise erupted, and Wesley and Lisa burst into laughter. Uncle John was still wearing his gray top hat and morning suit, and Aunt Eleanor wore her wedding dress. Wesley handed him the Sword of Geburah with its scabbard. "You'd better take this. It looks better with a morning suit than with jeans."

Kurt gazed at him, shaking his head slowly. "So that's how come you had the Sword of Geburah! I never even wondered about it."

Lisa joined Mary and Aunt Eleanor in a triad of hugging, saying, "Of all things! I would never have guessed, you were such a perfect lady—oh, drat! I've put my big foot in it now!"

Aunt Eleanor laughed. "Well, I do try!"

Risano said, "Now—look again at the gateway!"

They turned to look, and instead of bushes they saw buildings in the street of a modern city. "Darling—it's Canton Road!" Aunt Eleanor cried.

"You can get through the store to the hotel," Mary added.

Then, without even stopping to bid Risano farewell, almost as though they were in a dream, they began to walk toward the two oak trees.

25

A Helping of Humble Pie

The Friesen parents were sitting glumly in the small lounge of their luxury suite when there came a knock at the door behind them.

"You answer it, darling," Fred said.

Jane opened the door. "Oh! Oh, my! Fred—I feel faint!"

Uncle Fred leaped to his feet in time to see a man wearing a top hat, a morning suit and bearing a sword at his left side seize Jane by an elbow and steer her to a chair. The top hat fell from his head as he did so. Fred stood rooted to the spot as Eleanor entered, arrayed in a white wedding dress, with Mary clinging to her. Behind them, his own children entered the room.

The room rotated slowly round him as he sat down. Aunt Eleanor, a ministering angel in white, sat beside him. "I'm so sorry, Fred. We should have known what a shock it would be. We were just anxious to tell you we were all right."

After a minute he gained his breath. "We saw it all," he said slowly, as his wife nodded confirmation. "At least we saw a battle scene, in which you were fighting with horrible creatures, and we realized it wasn't play-acting, or just television, but horrible reality. I—I guess I owe my children an apology. You too, John and Eleanor. And Mary more than anybody."

"Oh, Uncle Fred," Mary cried, "if anybody owes apologies, I do. I behaved so badly at lunch that day, ages ago when—"

"It was this lunch time, dear," said Jane, who seemed to be recovering from her shock. "You left just a few hours ago for Shah Tin."

"You mean, it's still—how do I say it—*today?*"

"It's the time thing again," Wesley said wonderingly.

"Of course," Lisa and Kurt echoed.

"You mean you *saw* the battle, Dad?" Kurt grinned.

"Yes—and for a little while we were actually there. But you didn't seem able to see us," their mother told them.

Her husband rose to his feet slowly, pausing to make sure he was no longer dizzy, and went to the kitchen. He returned with a frozen hailstone. You can imagine the excitement that followed, the expressions of wonder, the cries of, "You mean, you actually—" "But I don't understand—" and "O-o-oh, I *see!*"

Wesley said, "Dad."

"Yes, Wesley?"

"Does this mean it's—I just want to be sure—but does this mean it's O.K. now to talk about Anthropos?"

His father sighed. "I've been a little stupid. Well, more than a little. It's taken a lot to change me, but—to answer your question—yes, of course it's all right."

Tired or not, they sat around for a long time. Jane ordered coffee and sandwiches from room service, and they continued talking well into the night.

Once, when the conversation began to lag, Kurt said, "I wonder what will happen to the queen. Uncle John, you probably know. After all, you and Aunt Eleanor were there after that."

For a moment John McNab said nothing. Everyone was looking at him. When he spoke again his tones were mysterious. "She grew old over the years it took to form an Anthropos-Playsion government in exile. It's even possible you may see her again."

"And the duke and Captain Integredad?"

John nodded. "You just may see all three of them—the queen, the colonel and the duke. So you'll have to find out what happens for yourselves." And nothing they could say or do would get another word on the subject from him.

Fred shook his head. "This Gaal business is solemn stuff."

"Solemn, but filled with joy and glory," Uncle John said.

"Will we return?" Lisa asked. "Alleophaz was hoping we might get to visit Glason."

"Over my dead body!" her father protested.

John laughed. "She belongs to Gaal now," he said. "We may none of us ever go to Anthropos again. In any case, Lisa really doesn't get to decide things like that herself. She can rebel against Gaal, of course—"

Fred McNab groaned. "This is terrible. It's all so new!" He shook his head again, sighing. "I'm not exactly relishing the taste of humble pie—it must be an acquired taste."

Will any of them return? I don't know. Like them, we'll have to wait and see. But if they do, I'll let you know.

Appendix
How I Came to Write the Archives of Anthropos

I have five children, all of them now grown. When they were small I used to read to them the children's books that had once meant so much to me. One favorite, I remember, was *Wind in the Willows*, and there were so many others. Among them was C. S. Lewis's Narnia series. At that time Lewis was pioneering a new genre in children's stories reflecting the author's own experience of God in allegorical form.

I had quickly found that when a parent reads to his or her children, the attraction children have to television is overcome. I only had to ask them, "Do you want me to read to you?" to have them jump up immediately, forgetting TV.

One day I realized the children, even the youngest of them, were reading far beyond what I was reading to them, and I told them they were too old to be read to. At that point something happened which in retrospect seems to have provided another generation of children with reading pleasure. My own children ganged up on me and came with the request that since I wrote books for adults, I could write them for children too. (Of course their assumption was incorrect!) "We won't bug you anymore," they said, "if only you'll write a book for us. But it has to be *just like Narnia!*"

So, intrigued, I decided I'd have a crack at it. I conceived the possibility of getting through the television (ours was old-fashioned by modern standards). I wrote, and then read them my opening chapter of what eventually turned into *The Tower of Geburah*. They asked, "What happens next?"

Unfortunately, I had no idea. Then began a hand-to-mouth experience, a learning-by-doing. For instance, I had never thought of a plot, but had plunged right in. Clearly there had to be a plot, and I had to invent one. But I quickly found that my plot would not work. My characters (based, very approximately, on three of my own children) were stronger than the plot, and insisted on having their own way. In addition, I had to keep two plots going together, the inner plot of what was to happen in Anthropos, and the outer plot of real life. And since the inner plot was itself allegorical, it had to correspond, at least as far as I could make it, to real truth.

I am not saying I succeeded in what I was attempting, for I am very conscious of the lack of quality in what I wrote. I think I got better as time went on, but I still have to rely heavily on editorial suggestions. In any case I never succeeded in approaching Lewis's superb writing.

At some point I told either Andy Le Peau or Jim Sire of InterVarsity Press that I was writing a story for my children, and they asked to see it. Since IVP had not then published children's books, I hardly expected them to take a professional interest in what I was doing. In any case I had severe doubts about the story's worth. One can hope, but as with all the books I have ever written, there are moments of feeling, "This is the greatest thing I have ever done! People will be wild about this book!" And those despairing moments of "I give up! This is *hopeless,* absolutely hopeless. I don't have what it takes anymore!"

IVP, however, seemed to like *The Tower of Geburah,* and it was published. People said (quite accurately), "He's just trying to copy Lewis." I was. This was what my children wanted. That is, I was trying to copy Lewis at first, but I soon ceased to. Copying gets you nowhere. You have to make any genre your own for it to work.

But Andy, at least, was not content. "Where did the tower in *The Tower of Geburah* come from?" he asked. "Obviously it must have some kind of history." I began to worry. Andy was right. I had just invented the building. The tower had come "out of the blue" as I had needed it. It had seemed convenient. What a poor job I had done! I felt resentful. Was I condemned to worry about details of that sort? When you write a series of stories, you have to keep more details in mind, something I am very poor at, and therefore I am liable to make multiple errors. I wished Andy had never raised the question, or other questions he asked. Perhaps I should not have presumed to write fiction of any kind. I wasn't cut out for it.

But the questions continued to haunt me, bringing into existence, eventually, the Archives of Anthropos. As one book followed another, I felt more and more the pull of what had been controlling my thinking all along. All our thinking is based on the mythologies of our culture. My "mythology" was no mythology. Scripture was that for me. My heroes lived their lives from Genesis to Revelation. They filled my thoughts. Other stories were evaluated by Scripture's stories.

Gaal (Hebrew for "shepherd") had been the Christ-figure in the Anthropos books all along. Thus his death (in *Gaal the Conqueror*), and in *Quest for the King* his birth, became increasingly important. If Anthropos is about humankind, then the incarnation, death and resurrection of Jesus the Messiah must become central.

As the series developed, I also chose to draw an increasing contrast between the prophet and the sorcerer (as seen especially in *The Sword Bearer*). To me there is a vast difference between the two. I know that the power of the Holy Spirit is a reality, but charismatics and noncharismatics alike sometimes use that power, whether in preaching the gospel or in healing the sick, to glorify themselves rather than God and to demonstrate their own power. To me, that constitutes the essence of witchcraft.

The Iron Sceptre continued the time line (both in Anthropos and the "real" world) begun in *Tower*. But in *The Sword Bearer* I began to take on many of the vexing questions about the prior history of Anthropos that Andy had set before me. *Gaal the Conqueror* then became a sort of sequel to *The Sword Bearer*.

Thus the books in the series came to be written out of "chronological" order. To help readers, IVP has begun to number the books properly. So if you wish to read them in the least confusing arrangement, follow the sequence listed on the back cover.

As you can tell from having read *Quest for the King*, this fifth book in the series introduces a significant departure from the other books. While it does follow *Gaal the Conqueror* chronologically in regard to the "real" world, it does not in regard to Anthropos. The children, Uncle John and Aunt Eleanor now find themselves in a period of Anthropos's history that falls between books 1 and 2, that is, between *The Sword Bearer* and *Gaal the Conqueror*. This twist in the two time lines may provide you some mindbending delights, but I also seek to show in this way a God who is beyond the constraints of time in achieving his will.

I do not know whether there will be another children's book, though I do have a final one in mind. If it is ever written, it will continue the theme of prophet-sorcerer that has characterized the books so far. But I have many more adult Christian books in my head that I want to get on paper. Besides, I travel and preach. And who knows what each day may bring to any one of us?

Jesus once said, "As long as it is day, we must do the work of him who sent me. Night is coming, when no one can work." I have had two heart attacks fairly close together. Survival is no longer my prime goal in life. Trying to do whatever my Master wants is. But, who knows? I really would like to have a crack at another children's book.